THE PRINCE'S
TEXAS BRIDE

BY
LEANNE BANKS

AND

THE RELUCTANT
PRINCESS

BY
RAYE MORGAN

MILLS
BOON

Dear Reader,

You may remember Prince Stefan Devereaux from *Royal Holiday Baby*. Well, the truth is Stefan is a strong man who can, on occasion, be a pain in the patootie. I took one look at him and knew what he really needed was a strong woman who didn't give a flying fig about his title. Eve Jackson is just that woman. When Stefan hires Eve to get his royal stables in order, he has no idea how quickly Eve will get under his skin straight to his soul. When his life takes a screeching unexpected turn, Eve encourages him to be his best self. You'll see. Stefan learns that having Eve in his life is not optional, it's mandatory. But can he convince a woman who insists she's not princess material that she is the queen of his heart?

Enjoy this story!

xo,

Leanne Banks

THE PRINCE'S
TEXAS BRIDE

BY
LEANNE BANKS

First published in Great Britain 2012
by Mills & Boon, an imprint of Harlequin (UK) Limited,
Eton House, 18-24 Paradise Road, Richmond, Surrey TW9 1SR

© Leanne Banks 2011

ISBN: 978 0 263 89400 4

23-0112

Harlequin (UK) policy is to use papers that are natural, renewable and recyclable products and made from wood grown in sustainable forests. The logging and manufacturing processes conform to the legal environmental regulations of the country of origin.

Printed and bound in Spain
by Blackprint CPI, Barcelona

Leanne Banks is a *New York Times* and *USA TODAY* bestselling author who is surprised every time she realizes how many books she has written. Leanne loves chocolate, the beach and new adventures. To name a few, Leanne has ridden on an elephant, stood on an ostrich egg (no, it didn't break), gone parasailing and indoor skydiving. Leanne loves writing romance because she believes in the power and magic of love. She lives in Virginia with her family and four-and-a-half-pound Pomeranian named Bijou. Visit her website at www.leannebanks.com.

This book is dedicated to Doris and Bud Banks.
Thank you for all your love and support and for
teaching us the game chicken scratch!

Prologue

The full moon wasn't offering any answers.

Eve Jackson sat in the small palace courtyard and drank in the scent of blooming flowers and ocean air as she debated the most recent offer she'd received from the official representative of the Royal House of Devereaux. She still wasn't sure she could possibly fit in as the chief stable master for the royal horses. She was from Texas, for Pete's sake, and had never traveled out of the States before this week. She'd been raised to say "yes, ma'am" and "no, sir," but the idea of performing a curtsy made her laugh every time she even thought of it.

The lure of the job, however, was too tempting for words. Her current job as a regional manager for a major hotel chain bored her so much that there were days she was tempted to poke herself in the eye with a pencil. Training horses was her first love, but when Eve had received the opportunity to go to college, she'd chosen a practical, marketable degree. Her parents had been so poor that she'd been sent off to her Aunt Hildie for most of her teen years.

Training this stable of horses was her dream job and she'd been offered a startling amount of money to do it. But she wondered if she could be happy here in a place and culture so far removed from rural Texas. And there was another concern. She felt a shift of air against her skin and her nerve endings prickled in awareness. She wasn't alone. Glancing around, she saw Prince Stefan Devereaux, tall with his chiseled features unsoftened by the moonlight, watching her from just a few feet away.

Crap, she thought, trying to remember what the proper protocol was for greeting the ruler of Chantaine. She stood because she figured she wasn't supposed to remain seated. *Crap,* she thought again. Was *he* supposed to speak first? It seemed rude to just stare back at him.

"Hi, Your Highness," she said. "How's it going?"

His lips twitched and he moved toward her. "Fine, thank you, Ms. Jackson. I hope you're enjoying your visit to my country."

"It's beautiful," she said. "Though much smaller than Texas. Not that there's anything wrong with that," she rushed to say, in case he thought she was insulting his country.

"Yes, it is, to both of your observations. My representative told me he presented you with the latest offer, but you haven't given him an answer," Stefan said. "The terms are generous. Why haven't you accepted?"

Demanding and direct, she thought, but she supposed he had the right. This was the third offer his representative had made to her, and the palace was paying for her trip to Chantaine. Eve had met Prince Stefan Devereaux of Chantaine on two other occasions. Both times, he'd surprised her. From his sister Tina, Eve had gotten the impression that he was a pompous prig. He was. For some reason, she'd also expected him to be prissy and ignorant. He was neither.

"Are you uneasy about living so far from your home?" he asked and paused a half beat. "I was under the impression you were more adventurous than that."

She lifted her chin at the subtle challenge in his tone. "It's a big move. I have to make sure it's the right one."

"You don't have children or a husband. You're young and free. What's holding you back?" he asked. "Or is there another concern?" He studied her for a moment. "If there is, you must tell me. If you're not going to accept the offer, we need to know. I must fill this position. My horses deserve consistent care."

"Your country is beautiful. I want to work with your horses," she said and decided to blurt it out. "I'm just not sure about this royal thing. I'm not big on the curtsy and I'm likely to mess up how to address you and others."

"No need to curtsy unless it's a public situation. I can have one of the advisers prompt you if necessary. When you and I are alone, you may call me Stefan. In public, it's Your Highness. It's quite simple," he said dismissively. "What else?"

"I'm not sure about the chain of command. Who is my boss? Your aide or you?"

"I am," he said. "I may deliver instructions through an assistant, but you answer to me. If you have any questions or concerns, you may approach me directly if I'm available. Anything else?" he asked, a faint thread of impatience sliding into his voice.

"Just one thing," she said, meeting his gaze but preparing herself for a big, fat turndown. "If you choose to fire me, I want six months' pay and my airfare back to the States."

His Royal Highness blinked. "Why would you request such a thing?"

"What happened to your last stable master?"

"He was fired because he wasn't doing his job properly," Stefan said.

"And the one before?" she asked.

"He was fired for negligence." Stefan narrowed his eyes. "Are you suggesting I'm a difficult employer?"

"I'm suggesting that when prized horses, powerful men and women grow accustomed to getting their way they can become...temperamental."

Stefan met her gaze and his lips twitched once again. "I don't recall ever being compared to a prized horse, but I'll choose to take it as a compliment. I'll meet your conditions if you'll meet mine. You must move to Chantaine within two weeks."

Chapter One

Day two of palace orientation and Eve's eyes were glazing over.

"Wait for His Royal Highness to address you first. Wait for His Royal Highness to extend his hand first. If you are wearing gloves when greeting His Royal Highness, you need not remove them first. Women need not wear hats before 6:30 p.m.," the elderly male adviser droned on. "Call the prince by Your Royal Highness on first meeting. Thereafter, if the conversation continues, refer to him as 'sir.' Stand whenever a royal enters the room. Never turn one's back on a royal.…"

"Oh, Jonathan, give the poor girl a break," a young woman said from behind Eve.

Eve whipped her head around, spotting Princess Bridget, whom she'd met during her previous visit to Chantaine. She remembered the underlying, not-quite-buried impatience she'd sensed when she'd met Princess Bridget, a young woman close to her age.

Eve immediately rose and attempted an awkward curtsy.

Princess Bridget waved the gesture aside and tossed her head of brown, wavy hair. "Please don't. Will you join me for lunch? I need a royal break," she said. "We can discuss American reality shows."

"Your Highness," Eve said, *trying* to follow the rules she'd just been given.

"Stop, stop," Bridget said, taking Eve's hand and pulling her away. "And if you dare call me ma'am, I'll scream the palace walls down. Please call me Bridget. I'm counting on you to forget everything you've learned today so that you and I can become great friends. Thank God we have an American around now. You're just what we need."

Eve felt a combination of relief at getting away from the interminable orientation session and anxiety at Princess Bridget's plans for her. "I don't really watch a lot of reality TV."

"Well, I'm sure we'll come up with something. You know, ever since Tina got pregnant and left Chantaine, I have to do most of the public appearances." Bridget stopped and met Eve's gaze. "I'm not well suited for this. Tina was born and bred for this job. It drives me crazy."

"What specifically about the job drives you crazy?" Eve asked.

Bridget paused, blinking. Her eyebrows knitted in a frown. "I haven't thought about that. I've just been so resentful to be thrust into this right when I was enjoying my time in Italy."

Eve nodded. "I hated my last job, but it paid very well.

After working in that position, I realized that being able to do something that was my passion every day was a gift, if not a luxury."

Bridget paused again. "How profound. And I was hoping you would be a rebel."

Eve chuckled. "I am a rebel. I just try to be smart about it."

"Hmm," Bridget said. "Maybe I can learn from you. I think we should have champagne for lunch to celebrate your arrival. Dom Pérignon. If Stefan finds out, he'll be livid. I do so love to make him livid."

"No champagne for me. I don't want to start my second day on the job making my boss livid."

Bridget gave a pout and sighed. "You have a point. It wouldn't do for him to fire you right off the bat. Chardonnay?"

"And water, please," Eve said, thinking she definitely needed to remain sober around these Devereaux.

Bridget led her to a small table on a balcony that overlooked the east end of the palace grounds. Floral gardens were surrounded by lush, green grounds with trees that transitioned to rocky cliffs and sandy beaches. The ocean was a mouthwatering shade of azure.

"Beautiful view," Eve said, shaking her head in wonder. "Stunning."

Bridget stared out the window and nodded. "Yes, it is, but it can be a bit confining being surrounded by all that water. No easy way out," she said, then shrugged. "Can't change that at the moment." A staff member approached the table with a pitcher of water and filled two glasses. "Thank you, Claire. Could you also bring us a nice bottle of Chardonnay? Is lemon-roasted chicken and a green salad okay with you?" she asked Eve.

"That would be great, thanks," Eve said, swallowing

a secret laugh over the fact that she'd probably be eating peanut butter and jelly on the run if she were at the Logan Ranch.

Bridget met her gaze. "What are your interests? Besides horses, of course," she said. "Do you like to shop? Do you like music? Art?"

"Yes to music and art. I'm more fickle when it comes to shopping. With my new position here, I imagine I'll be busy enough in the beginning that I'll be getting most of my music fix from my iPod. What about you? Are there times of the year that are busier than others?"

"It seems as if it's always busy since Tina left, but I'm dragging my other sister and brother to participate in the royal appearances more often. I keep nagging Stefan for a vacation, but I think he's afraid once he lets me off the island, I'll never return," she said with a laugh.

"I apologize for my lack of knowledge, but does Chantaine have museums?"

"Two," Bridget said, not hiding her disapproval. "I've tried to talk Stefan into expanding, but he insists that both parliament and the citizens would balk when so many of our people are struggling economically."

Eve nodded, her mind wandering the way it often seemed to do whenever someone presented her with a problem. "It might go over with everyone better if you could make it a children's museum," she mused, and took a sip of her water.

Bridget stared at her for a moment. "That's a brilliant idea. If you're this brilliant about everything, it's no wonder Stefan was so intent on hiring you. You're right about starting out with a heavy workload, though," she said sympathetically. "I just remembered there's a parade in three weeks. The royal horses are featured, ridden by several top leaders and advisers."

Eve swallowed her water the wrong way and choked. "Three weeks?" she echoed.

Bridget nodded in commiseration. "Yes, and I can't help but believe that the horses are a little green." She shuddered delicately. "I hate the image of Count Christo being thrown. He's eighty-two years old. Sweet man, a little daft. He always insists on bringing a whip with him when he rides in the parade."

Eve felt her heart sink to her feet. "A whip?" she said, appalled, then sucked in a breath of air. "A *whip,*" she said again, her voice rising.

Bridget shot Eve a cautious glance. "He hasn't ever actually used it."

"But he carries it," Eve said, distressed. She'd learned the uselessness of whips a long time ago.

"He's an old man," Bridget whispered. "It gives him a false feeling of control."

Eve took another deep breath and clenched her fists in her lap. More than anything, she wanted to run to the stables and begin her work with the horses. More than ever the rest of this palace protocol and orientation seemed like horse crap. She didn't want to waste one more second. Glancing at Bridget, she saw that dashing away from the princess wouldn't be possible. She clenched her fists again then released them, resolving that she would head for the stables as soon as the meal was done.

Hours later, after Eve had skipped the afternoon orientation session, she worked with a third of the many palace horses. This one was a gentle palomino mare that, like the others, hadn't been ridden often enough. She pushed down her anger that the horses hadn't been exercised. Yet, at the same time, she knew Stefan had been stalling. For her.

A smidge of guilt mixed in with her anger.

The scent of horseflesh reached her on a cellular level as she reined in the palomino. The horse submitted to her, but Eve felt the mare's urge to run. She would need to ride most of the horses once a day, if not twice during the next weeks. And the whip—God help her. How was she going to get the whip away from Count Christo?

Eve returned the mare to her stall and walked to the separate building that housed the stallion. Black was Arabian and quite the handful. She would work with him first thing in the morning, she decided as she leaned against the wall opposite his stall where he paced restlessly. The good news was that he wasn't beating down the walls of the barn.

She felt more than heard footsteps approaching and, even before she turned, her nerve endings went on alert. Turning, she saw Stefan's strong, tall form. Emanating a restless energy and power that reminded her of the stallion, he wore black riding pants and a half-buttoned shirt. His gaze was intent. "I'm the only one who rides Black," he said.

Eve refused to be intimidated. This was her job now. She would own it. "How often do you ride him?"

"Two or three times a week," he said. "Hard."

"He needs a minimum of five times per week," she told him. "Look at how restless he is."

"That's because he's a stallion," Stefan said. "Are you questioning my treatment of the horse?"

"Of course," she said. "That's why you hired me."

His mouth lifted in a half grin. "We'll do Black my way."

"For a week," she said. "If he's still restless, he'll be ridden more often, and I'll be the one riding him."

Stefan chuckled. "You?" He shook his head. "He's too much for you to handle. He was too much for the previous two men to handle."

"We'll see," she said, confident she could handle Black. She was not nearly as confident about Stefan. She watched him as he approached the stallion. The horse seemed to immediately calm. Stefan placed a bridle and saddle on the horse. He led him out of the stall, mounted him and galloped into the distance.

Chill bumps rose on her arms at the sight of man and horse flying into the moonlight. There was a mystic connection between the two of them that she couldn't deny. She felt a rush of excitement and tried to temper it with resolve. Stefan was a powerful man, but he had distractions. He wouldn't be able to ride the stallion every day. He had other demands. It wouldn't take long before she would step in as a substitute to help Black release some of his energy. Less than a week, she suspected, and she would be ready.…

Exactly one week later, Stefan stared into the empty stall of his prized stallion and felt a stab of alarm. *Where is Black? Has someone let him out? Escaped?* He walked into the stall and stared at the walls. *What had—*

Realization hit him and his alarm shifted to anger. Eve had taken Black for a ride. She'd told Stefan her plans, but since he'd stated that he would be the only one to ride the stallion, he'd dismissed her statements. He'd assumed she would follow his orders. Frustration rushed through him as he glanced at his watch. He'd left his office later than usual for his ride this evening, but she still shouldn't have defied his orders.

He paced from one end of the barn to the other, his temper rising with each step. Hearing the sound of hoofbeats outside, he immediately strode to the barn door. He watched in shock as Eve swung off the stallion and led him around the corral for a cooldown. Black loped alongside her as docile as a lamb. He heard her voice, low and somehow seductive, as if she were making small talk with the stallion.

As she turned around, Black glanced upward. The horse must have caught his scent. His ears prickled and he gave a soft whinney before pulling away from Eve and trotting toward him. Stefan felt a measure of satisfaction that Black had left her behind so easily.

"There you go," Stefan said to the horse, rubbing Black's sleek throat. "I've missed you, too."

Eve, her hair escaping the long braid that hung down her back, stepped toward Black and Stefan. Her hands rested on her hips, her lips were firm and unsmiling.

"You were told not to ride him," Stefan said, deliberately keeping his voice mild as he patted the horse.

"And I told you that he needs to be ridden more frequently. If you don't do it, then I will," she said. "You've only shown up twice this week. He's been so restless it's a wonder he didn't kick down the walls of his stall."

"It seems you don't understand. What I say goes about Black," he said, turning toward her.

She met his gaze. "But you still expect me to be in charge of his health, well-being, diet, etc...."

"Yes," he said, relieved the impertinent woman was beginning to understand.

She nodded. "Okay. I quit," she said and turned to walk away.

Stefan stared at her in shock, again. "Bloody hell," he muttered under his breath. "You can't quit."

She glanced over her shoulder at him. "Sure I can. You and I agreed that you would let me be in charge of running the stables. That includes Black. If you're going to interfere with me performing my job—"

"Interfere," he repeated, nearly speechless at her lack of respect. "As your employer, it's my right to agree or disagree with how you conduct your duties. Particularly in regards to Black—"

"Not if your plan isn't in the best interest of the horse," she interrupted, surprising him yet again. With the exception of his siblings, very few people interrupted him. "And as far as Black is concerned, you're not rational about him. Your insistence that you be the only one to ride him is ridiculous. You're a busy man, leader of a country for Pete's sake. You have obligations and responsibilities that are more important than making sure your favorite horse is getting enough exercise."

"I don't need you to inform me about my position. I *make* time to ride Black. It's as much for me as it is for him," he said, revealing more than he'd intended.

She stared at him for a long moment. "So is this about your ego, or about how going for a midnight ride saves you from the craziness of your position?" she asked softly.

He felt as if she'd stabbed him. What right did she have to judge him? His rides with Black were the only time he felt truly free.

"I'm not trying to step on your toes or prevent you from the pleasure of riding Black. I'm just being realistic. He's a prize of an animal, smart, powerful and fast," she said, glancing toward the horse. "But he's full of energy and if he isn't exercised more frequently he's going to be miserable. I don't think you want that."

He clenched his teeth then sucked in a quick breath. "How did you do it? No one has been able to ride him except for me."

She lifted her lips in a smile that made his gut twist. "That's my secret," she said. "I'm a horse whisperer," she said in a self-mocking tone. "That's why you hired me."

"For the others," he said.

"Hmm," she said with a nod of understanding. "Looks like you have a decision to make. Let me know by morning, and I'll take the first flight back to Texas."

He caught her wrist as she turned around and she glanced at him in surprise. "You're not getting out of the job that easily," he said. "Ride Black, but do so at your own risk. I'll let you know which nights I'll ride him."

Her gaze searched his face. "So you do have a reasonable bone or two in your body," she said.

His lips curved in amusement despite the fact that he was still irritated with her. "Of course I do. I'm forced to be reasonable day in and day out with government leaders and advisers."

"Which is why you really need those rides with Black," she said.

Her perceptiveness was both a bother and a relief. There weren't many, if any, people who Stefan allowed close, and he'd been told by more than a few that he was difficult to read. The truth was that his passions always felt as if they were just beneath the surface, ready to burst through, so he felt he had to exert enormous self-control.

Gazing down at her, he saw a combination of

compassion and challenge in her dark eyes. Her lips were pursed as if she were trying not to smile. His hand still encircled her wrist and the skin there felt soft in contrast to her spine of steel. What an odd mix of a woman, he thought. He wondered what she was like in bed. He wondered what she would do if he kissed her. A hot visual of her naked beneath him whipped through his mind.

His immediate surge of desire took him by surprise. Eve wasn't his type. She was argumentative. She had zero understanding of palace affairs. For God's sake, she worked in a barn. In that flash of an instant, he glimpsed a shot of awareness that deepened her already dark eyes. In the next second, he saw the same surprise he'd felt.

Taking a breath, she stepped back and pulled her hand from his. "If you can let me know by 8:00 p.m. on the nights you'll be riding him, that would help me," she said.

"Waiting till that late will tie up most of your evenings," he said.

"I don't have anything else on my calendar. You see, I have to get ready for this parade my boss neglected to tell me about," she said in a confiding tone.

"That's why I required you to come to Chantaine within two weeks," Stefan said, mildly amused.

"It would have been nice of you to let me know ahead of time," she said.

"I'm not that nice," he said. "Would it have made a difference?"

"I guess not," she said. "I just wouldn't have sat through any of those orientation sessions," she said.

"I was told you skipped the afternoon session," Stefan said.

"That's true," she said. "As soon as Princess Bridget

told me there was going to be a parade with some kook waving a whip, I was outta there."

"Count Christo is eccentric, but I wouldn't call him a kook," Stefan said.

"You don't have to," Eve said. "And I'll tell you now, he won't be carrying a whip when he's riding one of your horses."

"Eve," Stefan said. "The count is an important and revered member of Chantaine society."

"He won't even miss that whip, I promise," she said.

"Eve," he said again.

She waved her hand in dismissal. "That's a week and a half away. No worries Your Highlyness," she said with a sparkle in her eye.

"Highlyness?" he echoed.

"That's what my aunt Hildie calls Tina every now and then."

The tidbit amused him. "I bet Tina loved that."

"Oh, you have no idea," she said and gave a pretty little salute with her right hand. "I should hit the sack, Your Highlyness. I rise early these days. Sweet dreams."

The next day as Eve was grabbing a sandwich at her office in the stables, she mulled over the possibility of providing Black with a companion. The stallion led such a solitary life he might be more content with a gelding as a friend, or perhaps a goat.

"There you are," Bridget, wearing a dress and heels, said from the doorway. She walked inside the small office without invitation, wagging her finger in disapproval. "You've been invisible during the last week. I was certain you'd flown back to Texas until I overheard one of the staff discussing how early you leave your quarters in the morning and how late you return at night. You're going to exhaust yourself before you've even been here a month, and Tina will have all our heads. This must stop."

Despite Bridget's propensity for exaggeration, Eve felt a little less alone by her presence. She'd been so busy with the horses that she hadn't had time to think about anything else except late at night before she fell asleep. She would die before she admitted it, but she was a little homesick.

"I'm fine," Eve insisted and set down her sandwich. "I just needed to jump in with both feet with the parade coming around the corner."

"Well, it's simply not acceptable," Bridget said. "I'm sure you haven't even taken off one day since you arrived. Therefore, you shall go shopping with me this afternoon," she said in full princess mode.

Eve shook her head. "It's sweet of you to ask, and I'm honored, but I can't. It would just put me behind. I have to start scheduling appointments with the riders so everything will go smoothly during the parade."

Bridget wrinkled her brow in confusion. "We've never had appointments before. We just show up on parade day, mount the horse and ride."

"How did that work out?" Eve asked, already knowing the answer.

"Fine with me. There have been a few little problems. One of the mares bucked her rider and took off through the crowd. One of the geldings stopped halfway through and refused to go any farther."

"And what about that year when one of the horses reared up and a half dozen of them went to the beach? Not just to the beach," Eve said. "But in the water."

Bridget winced. "Oh, yes. I couldn't really blame

them. It was a very hot day and the master of ceremonies was long-winded, which meant we had to wait forever to get started. I guess you're right. Good luck getting some of the old guys to agree to the appointments, though."

"Thank you," Eve said in a long-suffering voice.

Bridget sighed. "Well, if you won't go shopping with me, then you must join us for dinner tonight. It's family night. Stefan requires us to have dinner together every week since Jacques is on break from college. He'll be there as well as Phillipa."

Eve immediately began to shake her head. "I'm not family. I wouldn't want to intrude," she said, also confident that she would feel totally out of place at a table full of royals.

"No intrusion," Bridget said. "Besides, you're like family because of your association with Tina."

"Oh, no, thank you, but—"

"I won't take no for an answer. You must eat. You may as well eat with us. The food will be better than that sandwich," she said, waving her hand in disgust at Eve's lunch. "If you don't come, then I'll have to tell Tina, and she'll fuss at Stefan and me. Trust me, it will get messy."

Eve sighed, realizing it would be easier to give in to Bridget's invitation and beg off early. She could pretend to be a fly on the wall and resolved to keep her mouth shut. "If you insist," she said.

"I do," Bridget said, smiling broadly. "We'll dine at seven on the third floor. It's a bit smaller and more intimate. I'm delighted you'll join us. Ta-ta," she said and turned to leave.

"Bridget," Eve said before the woman vanished. Geez, that woman could move like the wind despite the fact that she was wearing high heels. "What should I wear?"

Bridget glanced over her shoulder. "Oh, it's not formal. Just a dress will do."

Eve had brought only a few dresses with her since she figured she would be spending most of her time with the horses. Her choices were black, brown and black. She decided on black and pulled her hair out of her braid. For her corporate job back in the States, she'd always dressed in a conservative, businesslike manner, with careful attention to grooming.

Looking in the mirror made her wince. She'd been so focused on getting the horses ready for the parade that she'd done the bare minimum in the grooming department. Her fingernails were all broken down to the quick, her hair was out of control, her lips were chapped and smudges of violet rimmed her brown eyes.

"Thank goodness for concealer," she muttered under her breath, then got to work. Nerves danced in her belly and she chastised herself. She shouldn't be nervous. Although she'd never shared a meal with a roomful of royals, she knew which fork to use and when. Her aunt Hildie had made sure she knew her manners. Eve felt a jab of homesickness take her by surprise, then pushed it down. It wasn't as if she were being sent away from her parents when she'd become a teenager. She'd made this choice of her own volition. She was here for her dream job.

The prospect of interacting with Stefan on a semisocial level still made her uncomfortable. She was at ease dealing with him over matters concerning the horses, but beyond that, she found the man unsettling. After hearing his sister Tina talk about how overbearing he was, she'd been certain she'd find him a selfish chauvinist. But she was beginning to see that he was far more complex than she'd first thought. He had a lot on his shoulders and he didn't shift one bit under his responsibilities. To her, it appeared that he was trying to bring the siblings together for the sake of Chantaine, and the independent-minded Devereaux weren't making it easy.

Eve finished getting dressed and walked from the staff quarters to the palace. A guard allowed her entrance, and she climbed the marble steps to the third floor and wandered down the long hallway to an open doorway from where she heard voices—Bridget's in particular.

Eve peeked around the corner and caught her first glimpse of the lavish dining room. With a different table, the room could have easily held twenty people. Instead, a round table dressed in a crisp white cloth and set with crystal glasses, sterling silver and bone china sat in the center of the room.

The elegance and luxury of the room reminded her of the differences between her background and that of the Devereaux family. Her parents had moved frequently to stay a step ahead of the debt collectors, which meant she'd never stayed in one school very long. A flood of memories washed over her of walking into school, wearing clothes with holes in them, suffering the stares of her classmates and feeling completely out of place.

Her stomach knotted. What was she doing here? She took a deep breath and told herself this was a different time, a different situation. The siblings distracted her from her panic.

Bridget, Phillipa and Jacques stood beside the table.

"The goal for this evening's meal is to get Stefan to

cut me some slack," Bridget said. "I need a vacation in Italy. Phillipa, you can cover for me for just a couple weeks—"

Phillipa shook her head. "You know I'm in the middle of my dissertation. I can't take off for two weeks."

Bridget sighed. "Maybe we could cut down some of the appearances." She glanced at Jacques, who bore a striking resemblance to Stefan. "And you could help."

Jacques looked appalled. "Me? I'm playing in a soccer match in Spain this weekend."

"Well, I can't keep doing all this on my own. Lord knows how Tina managed it," Bridget said.

Eve strongly considered turning around and leaving at that point, but Jacques glanced up and looked at her as if she were a lifeline. "Please do come in. Eve Jackson?"

"Yes, Your Highness," she said. "I'm surprised you remember since we met so briefly last month."

Jacques's lips lifted in a flirtatious grin. "Please call me Jacques, and I make a habit of never forgetting the name of a beautiful woman."

Eve couldn't resist smiling in return. She could tell Jacques was on the road to be a class-one heartbreaker. "Thank you, Jacques. I appreciate the flattery, especially since I haven't spent much time outside the barn since I arrived."

"I'm determined to change that," Bridget said. "Just because your position requires you to work with the horses doesn't mean you're married to them. Tomorrow you can join me for a day at the beach."

Eve shook her head. "No beach for me until after the parade."

Bridget scowled. "Tina is going to—" She broke off as Stefan walked into the room. "Welcome, Stefan. I persuaded Eve to join us tonight. She's been cooped up in the barn far too long. I'm sure you don't mind."

Eve blinked at that last remark, feeling a stab of chagrin. She'd assumed Stefan had already been informed and approved of her presence at the meal.

Stefan looked at her, his gaze falling over her from head to toe and back up again. "Of course not. I'm glad you thought of it, Bridget," he said, his gaze not straying from Eve's. "Our pleasure, Eve."

"Thank you, Your High—" she started, but stopped when he sliced his hand through the air.

"Stefan, please. Shall we sit?"

As if on cue, three staff members immediately entered the room.

"I chose Chateaubriand for the menu tonight," Bridget said. "I asked the chef to choose everything else…well, aside from the chocolate mousse torte. Do you like chocolate, Eve?"

Still self-conscious, Eve fidgeted with her hands in her lap. "*Like* is an understatement. I've been known to make dessert the main course when it's chocolate."

Bridget laughed in approval. "Well, you won't want to skip any of the courses tonight. Our newest chef is fabulous."

"Here, here," Jacques said. "Much improved over food at the university."

Eve lifted her water glass and took a swallow. "Newest," she echoed. "How new is he?"

Bridget glanced at Stefan. "Three months, would you say? The employment director had to replace the former chef."

Hiding a grin of amusement behind her glass, Eve took another sip and met Stefan's gaze. "Is that so?"

He raised a dark eyebrow as if he knew exactly what

she was thinking. "The employment director made that decision. I had nothing to do with it."

"Oh, I know why he was dismissed," Phillipa said. "He was coming to work later and later due to a drinking problem. The employment director set him up with a special rehabilitation program."

Stefan lifted his glass of wine, his lips twitching in amusement before he took a sip. "Eve seems to be under the misguided impression that I fire so many staff members we may as well have a revolving door for them."

All four Devereaux stared at her with questions in their eyes. Eve coughed as her water went down the wrong way.

"What on earth made you think that?" Phillipa asked. "Stefan delegates almost all of the hiring to the employment director."

"I never said that. I—" The gleam in his eyes told her he was enjoying her discomfort far too much. Eve frowned at Stefan, rising to the challenge. She was a Texan, for Pete's sake, and she refused to be intimidated. "How many horse managers have you gone through? How long did my predecessor last before you bumped him off?"

Shocked silence followed, and Eve lifted her chin even as she felt herself being stared down by everyone in the room.

Stefan's bark of laughter broke the silence and the tension. "To Americans," he said and lifted his glass. "You don't take crap from anyone."

Stefan's siblings gaped at her in surprise. Bridget recovered first, lifting her glass in salute. "We can learn by her example."

Stefan lifted his hand in disagreement. "There's a

difference between defending oneself and constantly quarreling."

"But, Stefan—"

"Enough, Bridget," he said and turned to Phillipa. "How are your studies progressing?"

Stefan held her attention with how he conducted himself. He exhibited a magnetism that combined power, intelligence and complete masculinity. She'd never met a man who possessed such a combination. She was accustomed to sly cowboys and corporate managers with egos bigger than their paychecks.

She studied his hands as he cut his beef and lifted his glass of wine to his lips. His fingers were long, and she remembered feeling the faintest bit of a callous in his palms when he'd shaken her hand. She'd liked that about him.

Now, as she watched him talking to his siblings, she liked the way he focused on them instead of himself. She wondered if he kept his concerns and worries from his siblings. She wondered if he'd protected them a bit too much.

"If everything works out, I may do an exchange course in Italy this summer. Florence," Jacques said with a half grin. "My advisers say I'm spending enough time on soccer and they want me to be well-rounded."

"Florence," Bridget muttered and gave a low, barely audible growl. She cleared her throat. "Speaking of art, Eve and I were talking just a couple of weeks ago about the idea of building a children's art museum in Chantaine."

Eve cringed at being dragged into Bridget's power struggle with Stefan.

"Bridget, you know the agreement about our family dinners," Stefan said with a sigh. "No discussion about financial proposals or arguments about politics. This is a time for us to be family."

"Well, it's hard for me to be family when all I do is work, work, work," she said. "Have you noticed that you haven't asked me anything about my personal life? Why?" she demanded. "Because I have no personal life. If I can't have a personal life, then I'd like to have a sense of satisfaction. Even Eve said being happy in your job is making sure you have a passion for what you're doing."

Eve felt Stefan's hard glare. She felt stuck in the middle of a place she absolutely didn't want to be. Lifting her glass of wine, she took a sip and latched onto the first thing that came to her mind. "Anyone here know how to play the game Chicken Scratch?"

Chapter Two

With the exception of Stefan, it had been like taking candy from a baby. Stefan had actually won the third game. Eve spread out her hands to collect the dominos. "Well, this has been fun, but I need to visit the barn one more time tonight."

"No," Jacques said. "I was just getting used to it."

"Me, too," Bridget said. "I almost won the second game."

"Afraid you'll lose again?" Stefan challenged.

Her stomach did a crazy tumble at the expression on his face. "Not at all," she said. "I really do need to visit the barn again. If you liked the game, I'll leave my dominoes here so you can practice."

"Please do," Phillipa murmured. "We need it."

Eve smiled at the brainy princess determined to master the game. "If we play again, I bet all of you will beat the pants off of me."

"I'd like to see that," Jacques said with a devilish look in his eyes.

"Jacques," Stefan said with a frown. "Ms. Jackson is our guest while at dinner. She deserves our respect."

"Exactly," Eve agreed. "Your elders always deserve your respect."

Jacques laughed. "If you're my elder…"

"Jacques," Stefan said again, this time a touch of amusement slid into his tone as he gave a barely perceptible shake of his head.

"Thank you all again for everything. Joining you for dinner was an—honor," she said and smiled. "Good night and sweet dreams," she said, turning to leave.

"Sweet dreams?" Phillipa echoed.

"It's an expression," Eve said. "I'm wishing you sweet dreams."

"That's lovely," Bridget said. "Sweet dreams to you, too."

"Thank you," Eve said and felt Stefan studying her. She felt a quiver of something strange in her belly and pushed it aside. "Your Highnesses," she said and walked away.

The family dinner had gone much better than usual due to Eve's presence, Stefan thought as he paced his quarters. She'd amused him by the way she'd pushed back when he'd teased her. The sound of her Texas drawl slid over his nerve endings like a smooth brandy. Her little game had distracted his family from the usual squabbles and griping, and allowed them to enjoy their time together. He would make sure she was included again.

Glancing at the clock, he thought about his early meeting with dignitaries from Russia in the morning.

It would serve him well to go to sleep, but he was too restless. Lately, he'd been even more restless than usual. Bumping up his exercise routine hadn't helped. The advisers had been pressing him more than ever on a matter that he'd avoided like the plague. But he knew they were right. He couldn't delay this part of his duty forever. He glanced out the French doors of his balcony and watched the clouds slide over the moon. Inhaling, he caught the scent of impending rain. The atmosphere felt moody. Like him, he thought with wry chagrin.

An impulse shot through him and he considered it for thirty seconds. As ruler, he'd learned early on he would have to be selective about giving in to impulses. This one would help him sleep and quiet his spirit. He changed his clothes and called his personal guard, Georg. "I'm going to ride Black."

"Yes, Your Highness. Would you like me to arrange for the horse to be saddled before you get to the barn?"

"Not necessary. I'll do it," Stefan said.

"Enjoy your ride, sir," the security guard said.

"Thank you," Stefan said and headed for the barn.

He heard her talking with Black before he looked inside the horse's stall. Black nodded as Eve talked as if he understood exactly what she was saying. "So, how do you like the idea of a goat?" she asked. "I have a feeling you would do better with a pet than another horse."

"A goat?" Stefan echoed and watched Eve whirl around in surprise. She adjusted her black Stetson. "Black would stomp the poor animal to smithereens."

"Maybe not," she disagreed, stroking the stallion in question. "By nature, horses aren't solitary animals. He's so restless. I think a pet might help him calm down."

Stefan stroked his chin. "I'll think about it," he said

and wryly wished a pet goat would solve his own restlessness. "Did you ride him this evening?"

She shook her head. "No. I just visited him because
I had a feeling you might want a ride tonight."

He appreciated her perception. "Family night can be
an obstacle course, but I think it's necessary."

"I agree with you. Were you and your sisters and
brother ever close?"

"That's a good question," he said as he entered the
stall. Black immediately approached him, and Stefan
felt a rush of pleasure at the way the horse responded
to his presence. "We had different assignments, different nannies, even different advisers. Tina and I shared
some similar training. I think that's why we're so close.
Then Fredericka had her substance abuse issues and it
became a priority to make sure that none of the other
Devereaux went down that same road. If anyone was
the glue between us all, it was Tina. When she left, it
was a terrible blow."

"Bet you're still bummed about it," Eve said, resting
her hand on her hip as she studied him.

"Bummed, but mostly resigned. I'm glad she's agreed
to visits," he said, feeling a pang of missing his sister.

Her lips twitched. "And now you get to deal with
Bridget," she said. "My aunt would say that should be
a character-building experience for both of you."

"Is this the same aunt who addressed Tina as 'Your
Highlyness'?"

"The one and only Hildie," Eve said with soft smile.
"She's the best."

"And you miss her," he said, reading the combination
of affection tempered with sadness on her face.

Eve glanced away then lifted her chin. "Probably
more than I expected, but I'm too busy to spend much

time feeling homesick. Speaking of time, I shouldn't keep you from your ride. Your boy is ready for you," she said, nodding toward the stallion.

He realized he'd just been dismissed and he wasn't sure he liked it. A surge of strange feelings rumbled through him. Sympathy for Eve…curiosity…something else he couldn't name. "Would you like to join me?"

Eve blinked in surprise. "Join you?" she echoed in disbelief.

"You can bring one of the geldings. It will be a short ride tonight since the weather is threatening," he said. "If you think you're up to it," he added, deliberately challenging her.

"I'm up to it," she retorted immediately. "I'll get Gus and meet you out back."

Moments later, she joined him and Black. "Where are we going?" she asked, leaning forward to give Gus a reassuring stroke on his neck.

"The beach," Stefan said and, even in the darkness, he saw her face light up.

"I haven't ridden there yet," she said. "I've stuck to the trails on the palace grounds."

"You won't after you've ridden on the beach," he said, urging Black into a fast trot. Leaving the confines of the stable yards behind, he led Eve on a winding path through dense woods. In the past, his security had wanted to ride with him and he'd always felt it was the worst kind of intrusion. He'd known forever that his life would never be totally his, but Stefan just wanted a few moments to breathe and escape. He'd never invited anyone with him on his night rides, but tonight he'd sensed the same combination of claustrophobia and loneliness in Eve that he often felt himself. Hers came from adjusting to living on an island and homesickness. A ride on the beach might offer her the same temporary cure it did him. He pulled his horse to a stop as they entered a clearing that offered a view of the beach below.

"It's beautiful," she said in a low, but awed voice.

"Yes, it is," he agreed. "I wanted to warn you that the slope's a little steep down this hill. Black could find his way down this hill blind, but Gus may need some extra time."

"No problem. I wouldn't do it any other way," she said.

Just as Stefan had said, Black made it down the hill in no time. As soon as Black hit level ground with the beach mere yards away, Stefan could feel the stallion pulling on the reins. He knew what was coming. "Patience," he said as the horse pranced. "She'll be here in just a moment or two."

Hearing the sound of Gus's hooves behind him, he turned, expecting the gelding to stop. Instead, Eve urged the horse into a fast trot and rode right past him. "See ya!" she called with a laugh, and Gus took off.

Black gave a snort of protest as Stefan watched in surprise. Seemingly one with the horse, she rode better than any woman and most men he'd met. Exhilaration raced through him. With her hair flying behind her and her compact body huddled closely against Gus, she was pure pleasure to watch. Black pulled against the reins, and Stefan allowed him to run. It wouldn't take long to catch them.

A moment later, Black pulled alongside Eve and Gus. Eve glanced over at Stefan and her breathless laughter drifted over him with the ocean breeze. The sound of her exultation made him smile. The night was dark; a storm was on the way, but he suddenly felt as if the sun had come out from behind a cloud.

Black increased his speed and Gus struggled to keep up. "Go ahead," she called with a wave. "It's your time. Take it."

Stefan gave Black the reins and the stallion sped down the beach. He felt the rush of adrenaline punch through him. His heart raced, and he felt free. The speed and wind blew the clutter from his mind. This never got old. For Stefan, this was what got him through his worst days. Black loved this run, too. If given the chance, the horse would run around the entire island, but Stefan had made a deal with security. Another fifty yards and then he would turn back. He reined in the horse. At the turn, Black slowed even more, sensing that turning around was the beginning of the end of the ride.

In the near distance, Stefan saw Eve riding Gus at the edge of the ocean. Surprising him again, she slid off the horse, kicked off her boots and rolled up her jeans. He rode closer as she waded into the water. "Careful," he called. "The bottom drops off sharply. You don't want to get—"

She took a step and sank in up to her chest, holding on to her hat. She let out a squeal that sent a shot of alarm through him. He swung off of Black, ready to pull her from the water. But then he heard her laughter. The sound reminded him of happy bells. As she trudged out of the ocean, she tugged at her wet shirt, pulling it away from her stomach, still giggling.

"You're drenched," he said. "I tried to warn you."

She waved her hand and lifted her gaze to meet his. Even in the dark of the night, he could see her eyes glint with amusement. "It's just water. I couldn't resist. I haven't left the barn long enough to visit the ocean since I've been here. It was just too tempting and I knew Gus wouldn't go anywhere without me."

Her lack of concern over the dunking was refreshing. Every other woman he knew would have been embarrassed and disgruntled. "I never intended for you to chain yourself to the barn. You're entitled to take some time for yourself."

"Not until after the parade," she said. "I don't want these babies misbehaving when they're on my clock." She put her foot in the stirrup and began to lift herself, then stepped back on the ground, shaking her head as she pulled up her jeans. "A little heavier than usual," she murmured.

"A good soak will do that," he said in a wry tone.

"To be perfectly honest, if my boss weren't with me, I'd ditch the jeans until I got back to the barn," she said and lifted herself again.

When she wobbled, Stefan gave her an extra boost on her backside. "Don't let my presence deter you from your—comfort."

Eve glanced down at him and for an instant he felt the scorching heat of sensual assessment in her gaze. She shook her head as if she were trying to clear it. "You surprise me, Your Highness. I didn't know you were capable of flirting with your stable maid," she drawled.

"You're far more than a stable maid," he said and then mounted Black. The way she'd emphasized the difference between his position and hers irritated him. This ride represented a time out for him. He wanted no reminders of his position. Determined to hold on to the last few moments of the ride, the sea air, the breeze, the darkness, he kept the stallion moving at a trot instead of a canter. Still it was no time before he and Eve arrived at the barn. She took care of Gus while he cared for

Black. The stallion still seemed a bit restless as Stefan stepped from the stall.

He felt Eve move to his side. "He acts like he needs another ride," Eve murmured.

Stefan glanced down at her, noticing the way she rubbed her arms. The shirt was still dark from her stroll in the ocean, and he suspected her jeans were very uncomfortable. He swore under his breath. "You're still wet and I can tell you're chilled. You need to get back to your room immediately."

She wrinkled her brow in surprise and shrugged. "I'm fine. Like I said, it's just water. I'm seriously considering a goat for Black. I think—"

"Enough about Black tonight. Go to your quarters and dry off," Stefan said and, when she didn't move, the next words automatically came out of his mouth, "I command it."

Her eyes widened like saucers. "You *command* it?" she echoed in disbelief.

Stefan bit back an oath. He'd known from the beginning that Eve wouldn't respond well to orders. He rarely pulled rank. Why in hell did she bring out the urge entirely too often? He bloody well couldn't back down now. "I do."

She blinked. "I'm not sure I like that."

"It's not that difficult to understand. You insist that my horses behave correctly because they are on your clock. In a way, you are on my clock," he said. "I won't have you getting pneumonia on my watch."

"Are you comparing me to a horse?"

"No," he said. "Besides the fact that Tina would kill me if anything happened to you, I wouldn't be able to stand it myself."

"But I'm not your responsibility," she argued.

"You are in my country. Therefore, you are my responsibility."

She stared at him for a long moment and shivered. His gaze lowered to her damp shirt stretched taut over her breasts, her nipples forming a tempting outline. He felt an immediate visceral response. Instinct urged him to rub her arms with his hands, to pull her against his body and make her warm. He clenched his hands into fists. Denial had been drilled into him since the day he was born, even more so when he'd come to understand the playboy image of his father and grandfather. When he'd come of age, many people had expected that he would follow in his father's footsteps.

Stefan had wanted more. He wanted the opportunity to change and improve his country. For that, he had to be taken seriously. He'd kept his affairs scrupulously private. His duty and the sins of his father had forced him to hold his libido in check. Right now, though, for the first time in a long time, he fought the urge to pull the mouthy American Eve Jackson into his arms and make love to her against any flat surface available.

He reined in his surprising need. "I'll walk you to your quarters," he said.

"Oh, that's so not necessary. I walk to my quarters by myself every night," she said.

"You're not dripping wet every night," he said, extending his hand, determined to maintain control. "Come, now."

Eve rolled her eyes, but placed her cool hand in his. "Sheesh, did anyone ever tell you that you take this Highlyness thing a bit far?"

"No one except my sisters," he said as he led the way to the staff quarters. He rarely walked this path. Now that he saw it, he decided it needed a few more lights. "How late do you usually stay at the stables?"

She shrugged. "It depends. I usually grab a sandwich for dinner and head back around nine or ten."

"I'm not sure it's best for you to be walking back to the staff quarters unescorted every night," he said.

"Oh, give me a break. I've spent my life going anywhere I need to go unescorted. Besides, I'll bet you didn't tell your previous stable master that he shouldn't be walking around the grounds unescorted."

"Trust me, he didn't look at all like you. Plus, he never felt the necessity to work full-time let alone overtime. I prefer you leave the stables before dark for the next couple of nights. I'll get motion lights installed."

"We'll see," she muttered.

He gave a double take. "We'll see?" he echoed. "I just gave you a very reasonable order."

She sighed. "Do you really think you have criminals wandering around the palace grounds?"

"I'll admit it's not likely, and the security here is as good as it gets without causing claustrophobia, but nothing is perfect. I will be more comfortable if you avoid walking alone at night until there's more lighting."

"So this is about your comfort and not mine?" she said.

Damn, the woman was difficult, he thought. "Perhaps. You need to remember that you're not just an employee. Because of your relationship with Tina, you're also a friend of the family. We protect our friends." He noticed her fighting a shiver and swore under his breath and rubbed her arms. "I shouldn't be keeping you out in the cool air. Go inside and get warm."

Her gaze met his for a moment and he saw a shot of liquid heat flash through her eyes. He saw the possibility of passion and felt it deep in his gut. She took a quick breath and her lips parted, drawing his attention. He wondered how that argumentative mouth would feel beneath his. He wondered how she would respond.

For once, Stefan had finally met a woman who didn't give a damn about his title or position. She had no interest in pacifying him and would argue with him at the drop of a hat, yet he sensed that a part of her wanted him. Tempted, more so than he'd felt in a long time, he wondered if Eve could handle an affair with him. He suspected she met his requirement of being discreet. How messy would it be once their affair ended? Because they all ended.

She closed her eyes as if she were trying to shut down her emotions. That annoyed him. He wanted her open to him. He wanted to see the desire in her eyes again.

Taking another breath, she opened her eyes and took a step away from him. "Thanks for the night ride," she said in a husky voice that brushed over his nerve endings. "Good night."

He watched her jog inside the back door to the staff quarters and felt a surprising urge to go after her. He snuffed it out, of course. Even though Eve aroused more than his curiosity, he couldn't rush into anything. There was too much at stake to be impulsive. There always had been and there always would be.

At ten o'clock the next morning, Eve was returning one of the horses to the stall when she heard Bridget's voice.

"Bonjour, Mademoiselle Jackson," she called. "I am your rescuer and have come to help you escape your drudgery for a while."

Eve sighed, although she couldn't deny she was

amused. Bridget would do anything to get out of palace duties. She closed the door to Gus's stall. "Bridget, that's very sweet of you, but—"

"No refusals allowed," Bridget said. "You and I have received orders from on high."

Eve turned to face the princess and blinked at the sight. It was clear what the plans for the outing were from Bridget's beach cover-up, gigantic sunglasses, a large-brim, black straw hat and designer beach bag.

"Orders from on high?" Eve echoed.

Bridget nodded. "Stefan has spoken. He says you need a day off, and I've been assigned to take you to the beach." She lifted her finger. "Don't you dare fight me on this. It wasn't my idea, but it's my first opportunity to have a little fun in what must be a century. If I have to attend another charity tea, I'll scream. Besides, Stefan is right. You must take a break. Forgive me for being blunt, but you're looking a bit, well, haggard."

Eve hardly knew how to respond to Bridget's mouthful of drama. She'd already shot down Eve's objections before she'd had a chance to voice them. "I have difficulty believing the palace protests other members of the staff working too hard."

Bridget gave a *tsk*-ing sound. "Eve, other members of the staff take every possible break. Besides, you're not just staff. Tina gave you to us. The rules are different. Oh, for goodness' sake, I'm suggesting a day at the beach. Not the guillotine. Your reluctance is insulting. Do you dislike me so much?"

Eve laughed in exasperation. "I don't dislike you. I just need to stay on top of my duties. The parade is days away—"

"And everything is going to go brilliantly. In the meantime, the sun is shining and the beach is calling."

She clapped her hands lightly. "Come, come. You do have a swimsuit, don't you?

"Yes, but—"

"No buts," Bridget said.

"You Devereaux drive a hard bargain," Eve said.

"Oh, good," Bridget said. "I smell the sweet scent of surrender. Don't worry about sunscreen. I have plenty. Move along."

Within forty-five minutes, Eve and Bridget were reclining in lounge chairs on a semi-private beach where, magically it seemed, servers appeared to deliver refreshing beverages and snacks.

"Are you sure you don't want more than water?" Bridget asked.

"For now," Eve said, closing her eyes and enjoying the feeling of sunshine and gentle ocean breeze over her skin. "You and Stefan were right. I needed this."

"Of course I was right," Bridget said, neatly eliminating Stefan from the equation. "The staff has prepared lunch. We can eat in an hour or two. They'll also be putting up umbrellas soon. It has occurred to me that you've been too busy to make new friends in Chantaine since you arrived. In the same vein, you haven't had the opportunity to meet any men. While I'll confess that the selection is much better in Europe than here," Bridget said in a dry voice, "I could introduce you to someone who could amuse you. You and I could visit one of our nightclubs."

"Not my thing," Eve said, keeping her eyes closed.

"Why ever not? What do you do for fun?"

"I enjoy riding and taking care of horses. I enjoy the beach. I like to read. I like to play card games and Chicken Scratch—"

"Oh, well, I can agree with Chicken Scratch. We are

all determined to have you return for family dinner night and another round of it," Bridget said.

"Great," Eve said wryly. "I can't wait to have the entire Devereaux dynasty gang up on me."

Bridget laughed. "It's your fault. You started it."

"I thought this was supposed to help me relax," Eve muttered, but focused on the sound of the ocean waves. She cautioned herself not to get used to it, but this was bliss. She drifted off....

"Is she getting too much sun?"

The voice, which seemed to affect her on a cellular level, awakened her with no warning and she sat up, disoriented. "What?"

The tall, strong body of Prince Stefan towered over her, casting a long shadow. Eve covered her eyes at the bright sunlight.

"Not at all. She applied sunscreen, and the staff put up an umbrella to shield her. Poor thing must be dead tired. She's been asleep for the last half hour. Stefan, you're working her too hard," Bridget said.

"It's not me," he said. "She insists on working from before dawn to after dusk. The American way."

Eve drew in a mind-clearing breath and tried to dismiss the effect Stefan had on her. She noticed he was dressed in a dark suit and the contrast with the white sand distracted her. She wondered how he would look wearing just a swim suit. Or less. "I'm awake now. You can talk *to* me instead of *about* me."

Bridget giggled. "I tried to talk Eve into going to a nightclub with me, but she wasn't interested. You should wave your imperial wand, Stefan. That was the only way I was able to persuade her to join me at the beach. I'm sure Tina would want to make sure we're introducing her to new friends, including new male friends."

"Perhaps Eve isn't interested in the kind of men she would meet at a club," Stefan said.

"Won't know till she tries," Bridget said in an airy voice. "However, I would be more than willing to escort her to Italy. I have the perfect club selected for tonight, thought—"

"I couldn't be less interested in a club tonight," Eve said. "The little trip to this perfect beach has relaxed me so much it scares me. Even though I'm being a slug today, I'm certain I'll sleep like a log tonight. I think it's the sea air."

"Good to hear it," Stefan said with a nod. "The family is having an early dinner with Jacques since he will be returning this weekend. We want you to join us."

Eve slid a sideways glance at Bridget, who looked as innocent as possible in her black bikini and straw hat with a martini in her hand. "I'm sure you would prefer to keep the night to just your family. I don't want to interfere."

"We insist," Stefan said, using the royal *we*.

"This is about Chicken Scratch, isn't it?" Eve said glumly.

"My siblings are compelled to hold a rematch," Stefan said.

"Okay, okay," Eve said. "But only two games."

"That leaves no opportunity for a tiebreaker," Bridget said.

"Exactly," Eve said.

Stefan met Eve's gaze and shot her a grin that mixed challenge and sensuality. The combination sent a ripple down her spine. "I look forward to the evening," he said and walked away.

Eve sank back against her lounge and groaned. "I thought you intended this to be relaxing."

"It is," Bridget said cheerfully as she lifted her martini glass.

"How can I relax knowing I'm attending a family dinner at the palace where all of you want to rip me to shreds?" Eve asked.

"The dinner will be delicious," Bridget said. "We only want to best you at Chicken Scratch. It's a matter of honor."

"Good luck," Eve said. She was from Texas, and a Texan fought till the bloody end.

"Would you like a drink?"

"Not until we're finished with the game," Eve said.

Chapter Three

After consuming a gourmet meal, Eve and the Deveraux clan engaged in a death match of Chicken Scratch. They cajoled her into playing more than two games and each of them won once, but Eve won most overall, much to the siblings' dismay. Stefan had been forced to leave early to take a call.

Jacques bared his teeth playfully. "You're in our targets now even more than ever. Don't get used to winning."

"I'll try not to," Eve drawled, "but since most of my experience is with winning…" She gave a mock shrug.

Phillipa giggled. "She pummeled us even after all our practice."

Eve smiled. "You have to remember that I've been playing this game practically since the cradle."

"That's okay," Bridget said, putting her nose in the

air. "We're just getting started. We *will* conquer Chicken Scratch *and* you."

"Well, you'll have to do it without me for a while since I'm returning to university," Jacques said.

Bridget rose and gave her brother a big hug around his neck, which seemed to surprise him. "I'll miss you. Just be careful with the girls. You know how Stefan is about living down the Deveraux playboy image."

"I'm careful, but I'll never lock myself away from the women the way Stefan does."

"Yes, well, that may be part of the reason he's always in a bad mood. I may put together a plan to change things in that area," Bridget said, her eyes glinting with a diabolical gleam.

Eve almost felt sorry for Stefan. "Time for me to go. Thank you again for the wonderful dinner and company. Good luck at university, Jacques."

"Thank you," Jacques said, rising. "I'll look forward to a rematch when I return on break."

"My pleasure, Your Highness," she said, then looked at Bridget and Phillipa. "Sweet dreams."

"And to you," Phillipa said, smiling.

Eve left the palace and headed for the staff quarters, when she overheard a muttered string of oaths followed by a succession of what she suspected were more expletives in a language she didn't understand coming from behind a tall hedge. What she did understand was that Stefan was the one voicing the litany. For a millisecond, she considered continuing down her path away from him, but some part of her wouldn't allow it.

Turning around, she took in a breath of the night air filled with the scent of flowers, and then peeked through a large hedge. Stefan stood with his back to her, hands on hips, still hissing in frustration. "I hope it's not the landscaping that has you so upset," she said. "If that's true, then your groundskeepers better grab a canoe and get off the island."

Silence followed, then a heavy sigh. He turned toward her voice and his gaze found her immediately. "Join me," he said. "If you dare."

For a moment, she wondered if she really did dare. Then she shook off the silly thought. Sure he was a prince, but he was still just a man. She walked through the maze of hedging to step inside the small courtyard. "Needed some fresh air, eh?" she asked. "What's got you so pissed off this time?"

"This time," he said, lifting a dark brow of disapproval. "The way you say that suggests I'm pissed off most of the time."

"If the shoe fits," she said. "You stayed upset with Tina for a long time."

"She abandoned ship with zero notice," he pointed out.

"True, but pregnancy trumps charity teas," she countered. "And when are you not frustrated with Bridget?"

"Tell me the truth," he said, dipping his head close to hers. "Would you want her for your employee?"

He made an excellent point, but she didn't want to contribute to the strife-ridden relationship between the two of them. "I don't think Bridget is the reason you were swearing at the shrubbery a few moments ago."

He held her gaze for a long moment and sighed. "That's correct," he said, then turned away, shoving his hands into his pockets.

"Just curious," she said. "What language were you using?"

"Italian, French and Greek," he said with a shrug.

"Must be something big to require swearing in four languages," she said.

He stood with his back to her for a long moment and she wondered if it might be best if she left. She didn't appear to be helping.

"For some time, I've been trying to recruit a new medical specialist for Chantaine's health care. Our current chief of health and medicine is retiring soon and we need to bring in a younger M.D. for this position. I'd all but sealed the deal when the doctor of choice announced he'd chosen another position."

Surprise rushed through her. "Wow, you have your finger in a lot of pies. I didn't know you were involved in health care. I figured someone else was in charge of that."

"There have been other people in charge of Chantaine's health care, but I'm taking a more active role than my predecessors. It's not acceptable to me to coast when my family has received such an enormous benefit from our birthright. It's time for us to give in return. Some in the government welcome my input and some do not."

The passion in his voice emanated throughout the space they shared. "I don't know what the position of ruling prince entails, but I had thought it was more about decorum than governing."

"I've been extensively educated in matters of government, world economics, health care policy and infrastructure design. I'm not going to let all that go to waste by sitting on a yacht in the Aegean Sea and showing up for photo ops every couple of months."

"Okay," she said warily. It was obvious this was a touchy subject. "I wasn't suggesting you spend your life on yacht, although it may not be a bad idea for a vacation every now and then. You seem pretty wound up. Maybe you *should* take a little vacation."

He met her gaze and his lips twitched. "How many vacations have you taken?"

"I wasn't born into your world. My family was very poor," she said. "I worked as a matter of survival, through high school, then paid for most of my own college education. As soon as I finished, I worked that job until I came here. There's been no time for vacation."

"But even if there were, I suspect you wouldn't take it. You had to be forced to spend a day at the beach today. You and I are alike. We don't want to take a break until the job is done."

"Yes, but your job will never be done," she said. "If you don't pace yourself, you're going to burn out everyone around you, including yourself."

"You sound almost as if you care," he said.

His response took her off guard. "Maybe I shouldn't, but I guess I do," she said, surprised at how much she was beginning to care for the whole Devereaux family, including Stefan. Unnerved, she decided to leave. "Well, since I don't think I'm helping you get to your royal Zen state, I'll head to my room—"

He reached out to wrap his hand around her wrist. "Au contraire, you underestimate yourself."

Her heart jumped at the sensation of his thumb skimming the underside of her wrist. "I have enormous confidence," she said more breathlessly than she'd intended, "that I have very little effect on you except to irritate you."

His eyes darkened with a hint of challenge that made her a little nervous. "Again," he said, tugging her closer. "You underestimate yourself. You make me curious."

He lifted one of his fingers to her lips, and she felt a

buzzing sensation that started at her mouth and seemed to travel down every nerve ending in her body. "No need to be curious," she said, wondering why her lungs weren't functioning properly. "I'm boring."

He gave a low laugh and shook his head. "No chance. I think you may be a little curious about me."

She opened her mouth to protest, but the lie stuck in her throat. The truth was she found Stefan much more fascinating than she'd expected. He leaned closer and closer, and she held her breath in a mix of expectation and—strangely—fear. She would have to figure out the latter. Why on earth should she be afraid of—

His mouth took hers and every thought except him left her. His lips felt smooth and sensual. There was a reason she should hold back, but she couldn't quite muster it from her cloudy mind. His tongue teased the seam of her lips and she instinctively opened, wanting more. Something inside her cut loose and she arched against him, craving the sensation of his hard chest against her breasts.

She lifted her hands, sinking her fingers into the hair at the nape of his neck. It was surprisingly soft while the rest of him was oh, so hard. In an instant, the tenor of the kiss changed from exploring to hot and aching. She felt his hand slide to the back of her hips, pulling her against him intimately.

Her heart hammered in her chest, her blood roared through her veins like wildfire. She felt an indelible connection that seemed to go deeper than her cells. Crazy, some part of her said, but it was faint compared to the desire, need or whatever it was that filled her to bursting.

He gave a low groan that vibrated deliciously through her. The need inside her grew exponentially.

"I must have you," he muttered against her mouth. He swore. "I want you here, now," he said and took her mouth in another, more passionate, less controlled kiss.

She craved more of his passion, less of his control. Some part of her trusted him like she'd never trusted any other man.

Groaning again, he pulled his mouth from hers and tucked her head beneath his chin. The sound of their breaths mingled with a bird calling in the distance. Eve's mind spun like a water spout. Even though she knew she would drown, she didn't want it to stop.

"I'll figure this out," he said in a low voice. "We'll have an arrangement. We can meet in secret. I'll call you and give you a key to—"

"Arrangement," she echoed, her mind starting to function again. "Secret?" She looked up at him. "What are you talking about?"

"Surely, you don't expect a public relationship with me."

She blinked, not sure what she'd expected.

He gently squeezed her shoulders. "Eve, neither you nor I want to carry out an affair in public."

Affair. It just sounded dirty. Icky.

"Do you really want the press investigating every bit of your past? Every bit of your family's past? Do you want to endure the speculation of being a prospective princess of Chantaine?"

"Princess?" she finally was able to say. "I have never, nor will I ever be, a princess in any sense of the word."

"Exactly," he said and chuckled. Then he turned serious and laced his fingers through hers. "Does that mean you and I should deprive ourselves?"

His touch almost short-circuited her brain function. She frowned as she tried to concentrate. She closed her eyes and tried to think. His scent slid past her self-defenses. She frowned. "I don't know about this. I'm going to have to think about it."

Silence followed. "Excuse me. You're going to have to think about it?"

Eve opened her eyes and nodded. "Yes. You're not just my boss, you're a prince, for Pete's sake. This could turn into one big, hot mess."

"You're refusing my suggestion because I'm a prince?" he said more than asked, and he didn't sound particularly pleased.

She shrugged. "Well, yes. It's not as if a relationship between you and me could go anywhere. Obviously, you agree it's a dead-end adventure. And if you fell in love with me, it would be terribly messy."

He stared at her in amazement. "If I fell in love with you?"

She nodded. "It has happened before."

"I suppose it didn't occur to you that you could fall in love with me," he said in a lethally sexy voice.

She swallowed over a knot of denial. "It's not likely," she said.

He tilted his head to one side. "Why is that, *chérie?*"

Her nerve endings were still leap-frogging over themselves, but she refused to give in to the situation. "Because I've never fallen in love before. Why on earth would I start with you?"

He blinked as if he hadn't heard her correctly.

"Well, other than the fact that you're sexy, intelligent and probably loaded," she said and felt as if she were digging herself deeper into a hole. She didn't like the quicksand sensation at all. Eve preferred staying in control and that was what she would do right now. "I think we should just forget this ever happened."

He laughed, which infuriated her. "Do you think you can do that? Do you think it will be that easy?"

"We're both adults," she said, pushing aside her doubts. "I've had to exercise mind over matter many times during my life. I'm sure you have, too. There," she said, extending her hand. "Let's shake on it."

He took her hand, but instead of shaking it, he shook his head. Then he lifted her hand and turned it so her wrist was open and vulnerable. He pressed his mouth against her skin, and she felt her pulse jump. "Sorry, Eve, I don't make promises I don't intend to keep."

Eve successfully avoided Stefan for the next three days. She told herself that if she created some distance between herself and the kiss that had somehow turned into an *event,* then she would gain the proper perspective, which was that it had been just a kiss and the reason she'd experienced all those feelings was because she'd been tired. Most important, she felt more in control when she wasn't around Stefan.

The day before the parade, she was checking off the items on her countdown list. She couldn't deny a bit of nerves in anticipation of the event, but was satisfied she'd done as much preparation as possible during the time she'd been in Chantaine. She'd touched base with all the riders except for Count Christo. The man had completely ignored her calls. He was the one who liked to wield a whip, and she was determined to find a way to extract it from him before he mounted one of her darlings.

She picked up the phone to call the groomer, when

she heard a knock on her door. Glancing up, she found Phillipa in the doorway. "Well, hello, Your Highness. What brings you here?"

Plastering a smile on her face, Phillipa laced her fingers together, then unlaced them. "Please call me Phillipa. This is just a little visit. I know the big day is tomorrow and I wanted to see how you're doing."

Eve noticed that the bookish princess shifted from one foot to the other. "Is something wrong?"

"Oh, what could be wrong?" Phillipa asked, walking into the small office. "Have you been here all day? Did you go out for lunch?"

Confused, Eve wondered what was behind Phillipa's discomfort. "We've been grooming today, so I've been here since 6:00 a.m. I ate a sandwich at my desk for lunch. Are you sure there's nothing bothering you? Are *you* concerned about the parade tomorrow?"

Phillipa waved her hand dismissively. "Oh, no. People don't focus on me. I know how to keep a low profile."

"Okay," Eve said, still confused by the visit. "Is there something I can do for you?"

Phillipa shrugged and smiled again a bit too brightly. "Not a thing. Stefan and Bridget both have events today, so they asked me to stop in and visit you."

"That was nice," Eve said, torn between the royals' compassion and her desire for them to have complete confidence in her. "I've hammered out all the details."

Phillipa clasped her hands together. "What are your plans for the rest of the day?"

"Double check my to-do list for tomorrow, give the beauties a little extra attention, then hit the sack," she said. "Why?"

"Just curious. I can have chef deliver a light dinner to your quarters," she said.

"Not necessary. I won't be eating much anyway."

"Oh, I insist," Phillipa said. "All of us are very pleased with the job you're doing. We're very happy that you're here in Chantaine."

"Thank you," she said, wishing she could feel more pleased, but something just didn't ring right about this situation. Although Phillipa had been warm and friendly to Eve, she'd never visited her in the stables. Eve had been told the youngest princess was working a grueling schedule to complete her advanced degree as quickly as possible.

"You're welcome. I look forward to seeing you tomorrow," Phillipa said and turned away.

Eve frowned for a moment. Something was going on, but she wasn't sure what it was. She groaned in frustration. Maybe she was just being paranoid.

After a restless night, Eve arose when it was dark and dressed in a formal riding outfit. She much preferred to stay in the background but had been told that the press might ask her a few questions. After eating a protein bar and drinking a cup of coffee, she went to the stables and supervised the rest of the grooming. The parade was scheduled for two o'clock and would depart from the Palace Square.

One of her missions was to separate Count Christo from his famed whip. The elderly man strutted around his assigned horse. Eve had assigned the man Pilar, a lovely older mare. "She's beautiful, isn't she?" Eve said to the count. "Pardon me, I'm Eve Jackson, the royal stable master. I've heard of you. Aren't you the famous Count Christo?"

The count lifted his shoulders and chin in a show of pride. "Yes, I am, and yes, this is a lovely mare. Are you sure she'll be able to keep up with me? I'm quite the horseman, you know," he said, pulling out his whip and tapping it against his hand.

Eve's stomach dipped at the sight of the whip. "Pilar has one of the best pedigrees in the prince's stable. She has spirit and she responds well to a gentle lead. I'm sure you've encountered that kind of mount before."

"Of course," he said, still tapping his hand with the whip.

"Would you mind if I looked at your whip? I've never seen one quite like that before," she said.

"It's been passed down through generations of my family. Napoleon gave it to one of my great-uncles," he said as he handed it to her.

"It looks as if it's barely been used at all," she said, sliding her fingers over the leather.

"Oh, of course not," the count said. "It's mostly for show. A true horseman only uses a whip in the direst circumstance."

A sliver of relief slid through her and she smiled. "You're a wise man."

"You were worried I would whip the horse," he mused, surprising her with his perception.

"It's my job to be protective of them and anyone who rides them," she said.

His lips lifted in a half smile. "Don't worry. The whip shall remain sheathed."

She sighed and dipped her head. "Thank you very much, Count Christo."

"My pleasure," the count said. "It's nice to see the prince's new stable master so conscientious. A refreshing change."

"Thank you again," she said, this time unable to resist

a smile, then left to check on the other riders and horses. She came upon Bridget on one of the geldings.

"Everything okay?" Eve asked, automatically checking the security of the saddle and stirrups.

"Peachy, as you Yanks would say," Bridget said. "The good news is that Stefan found a way to take care of those pesky protesters."

Eve blinked. "Protesters?" she echoed in confusion.

Bridget grimaced. "Oh, no. Stefan's assistant didn't call you? We thought he would be the best one to explain the problem."

"What problem?" Eve demanded, her mind whirling at all the problems protesters could cause. What if they decided to throw rocks at the riders or horses? She shuddered at the thought.

"There was an article in the newspaper yesterday. Stefan and I were busy, so we sent Phillipa around to check on you until Stefan's assistant got in touch with you. I can't believe he didn't do that," Bridget said with a frown. "I assure you Stefan will be furious. But he's fixed it. The royal guard will march alongside the parade to protect us."

Eve frowned. This was supposed to be a joyous occasion. A celebration of Chantaine's beautiful horses. "Why the protest?" she asked.

Bridget sighed. "The citizens think Stefan is spending too much money on the horses…and his new horse master. To them, the horses don't earn their keep."

"Well, that would be easily fixed," Eve said.

"How?" Bridget asked.

"Put Black out to stud. The payment for his sperm could feed a third-world country. Sounds like it's time to spread it around," she said.

Bridget snickered. "Can't wait to see you convince Stefan of that."

Furious that he hadn't discussed this with her, she balled her fists, but hid them behind her back. "No time like the present. Later, Your Highness."

Eve searched the crowd for His Highness and immediately spotted him. He stood tall and confident, resplendent in his dress riding clothes next to Black. She marched toward him.

"Your Royal Highness," she said and bent her knees. As a curtsy, it sucked big-time, but it was better than nothing.

"Ms. Jackson. Good to see you. All the horses are in good form," he said.

She moved closer. "I just hope they *remain* in good form. The *protest* I never heard about could cause problems."

"I've taken care of it," he said.

"I should have been informed. It will look ridiculous to have an army of soldiers escorting the horses. This is supposed to a celebration of pride in the heritage of the royal stables of Chantaine."

"Unfortunately, not all the citizens see it that way," he said.

"There's an easy solution to the money problem," she said.

"What's that?" he asked, glancing around the crowd.

"Release Black's seed," she said.

His head whipped around as he focused on her. "Pardon me?"

"You know what I'm saying. You need to let Black provide stud service. You'll make tons of money."

"I've been waiting—"

"For what? The perfect filly?" she asked.

His eyebrows knitted in disapproval. "Who are you to tell me when I should send my stallion out for stud?"

"I am the royal stable master. You hired me for this very purpose," she said, lifting her chin.

A trumpet sounded. "We'll discuss this later."

"Darn right, we will," she said. "And you better cut the number of guards for this party in half or you're going to look like you're headed into war."

Chapter Four

Eve walked the route of the parade next to the horses. Actually, she ran, trotted, skipped and walked, dividing her attention between the horses and potential protesters. At one turn in the street, she heard hecklers and searched the crowd. Within seconds, the palace guard swarmed like bees. She wished she could talk to them and tell them the value of the prized horses that represented their country, but she knew it wasn't her place.

Pushing aside the effects of the heat of the afternoon, she returned to the last of the parade where Stefan rode astride Black. At every turn, the crowd screamed and clapped in delight. Understandably so. Both Stefan and Black were prime specimens. The spectators threw flowers at them, and she was relieved to see Black take it all in stride.

Suddenly from the corner of her eye, she saw a child streak out of the crowd toward Stefan and Black.

Instinctively, she chased after the boy child. She barely caught him in her arms.

"Prince Stefan," the child wailed. "I want to ride with Prince Stefan."

"Sorry, sweetie," she said as the child struggled in her arms. "I don't want you to get caught in the horse's legs. I don't want you to get hurt."

She felt Stefan's glance at her and looked up at him. Her gaze met his, and the connection between them zinged again. He glanced at the boy and lifted his hand, waving her to bring the child to him.

"Are you sure?" she called, surprised yet not.

He nodded and she carried the little boy to him. One of the guards stepped forward to help lift the boy into the saddle in front of Stefan. The crowd roared with delight. "Find his parents to meet me at the end of the route."

Eve searched the crowd and immediately spotted the astonished, beaming parents of the boy. The young couple were already walking down the street. The father carried a sleeping infant in an infant carrier on his back.

Eve caught up with them. "Hello, I'm Eve Jackson, the royal horse master. Is that your son taking a ride with Prince Stefan?"

The woman gave a huge nod, clearly still stunned. "My son, Ricardo, he is so active. He got away from both my husband and me. Thank you for catching him. I can't believe he is riding with Prince Stefan."

Eve couldn't help smiling at the joy on the couples' faces. "His Royal Highness asked that I make sure you meet your son at the end of the parade. We don't want your son to be frightened."

"Frightened," the father echoed. "I can only wish. The boy shows no fear."

"I understand," she said sympathetically. "Mr.—?"

"Benito," he said. "Raul and Gina Benito, thank you for your kindness."

"My pleasure," she said and gestured for a guard to escort the young couple through the throng of observers. She ran ahead to make sure her assistants were taking care of the horses and riders properly. She knew there would be hundreds of photographs taken by the press of all the horses and riders.

The next hour passed in a flurry of activity as the horses were released from their royal duties and guided back to the barns.

"Ms. Jackson," a man called from a few feet away. "Welcome to Chantaine. Your first royal parade is a huge success."

"Thank you. I'm thrilled for the citizens of Chantaine to get the opportunity to see the beautiful horses that represent their country," she said and motioned to one of her assistants to take two more of the horses back to the stable.

"Oh, but they are not Chantaine's horses. Everyone knows Prince Stefan has a weakness for fine horseflesh. These are Prince Stefan's horses."

"Number one, I wouldn't call it a weakness. Number two, these horses do represent Chantaine just as your beautiful beaches and the palace and palace grounds do."

The man lifted his eyebrow. "Easy for you to say. You make a much better salary than most of the citizens of Chantaine. The prince's horses aren't remotely self-sustaining."

"It wouldn't be hard for them to be self-sustaining," she couldn't keep from saying in defense of the stable.

"What do you mean?"

"Black. He's worth a fortune as a sire," she said, then feared she'd revealed too much. He didn't look like a member of the press and she didn't see a camera. "I need to go. I was taught to earn my keep," she added meaningfully, and then walked away.

Much later that evening after she'd showered and put on her pj's, her cell phone sounded, signaling a text message. She glanced up from the book she was reading and glanced at her phone. Meet me in the lower courtyard in thirty minutes. SD

Eve was torn between irritation and curiosity. The man was way too accustomed to giving orders. In other circumstances, she would have laughed and said forget it. But this was Stefan and the situation was totally different. Plus she was dying of curiosity.

She jumped out of bed and changed into a pair of jeans and a white button-down shirt. With her hair still damp from the shower she'd taken earlier, she just decided to let it air-dry. After a few moments of feeling antsy, she gave in to her restlessness and decided to take the long way to the lower courtyard. She stopped by a bush of blue flowers that reminded her of Texas bluebells and felt a twist of homesickness. Back home, she'd stayed busy with her job, working with the horses on the ranch where her aunt worked and volunteering. Staying busy kept her from thinking too much about how much she missed her brother since he'd left all those years ago. It also kept her from getting involved in a serious relationship. From a young age, Eve had been determined to steer her own ship, and she'd never met a man with whom she'd willingly share the wheel.

She heard the snap of a twig, but before she could turn around she heard his voice.

"Congratulations, Eve. Well done."

Pleasure welled up inside her and she turned around to find Stefan, his shirt partly unbuttoned, his hair mussed and carrying a bottle of champagne and two glasses. Surprised by his gesture, she felt a secret rush of delight. "Congratulations to you, too. The crowd loved it when you gave Ricardo a ride on Black. Champagne?"

He shrugged. "You worked hard. I thought you deserved to celebrate."

"You could have just sent the bottle to my apartment, couldn't you?" she asked, unable to resist the chance to tease him.

He shot her a look with a glint of the devil in his eyes. "Okay, *I* deserve to celebrate, too. Come on," he said and walked toward the lower courtyard. They entered the area surrounded by tall hedges and he gestured toward the stone bench. "Hold these, please," he said and handed her the glasses.

"Wow," she said.

"What?" he asked as he released the cork without spilling a drop. He tilted the liquid into the two glasses.

"You said *please*. I don't hear that word from you all that often," she said and offered him a glass.

"Are you always this charming when someone tries to thank you?"

"You knew what you were getting when you hired me," she said and lifted her glass in salute. "Congratulations on choosing such spectacular horses for your stable and for giving a little boy and his parents the story of their lives."

"Congratulations for pulling it all together," he said and clicked his glass against hers.

They both took a sip of the champagne. "I must confess I was worried about the combination of the protestors and your royal cavalry."

He smothered a chuckle. "Royal *guard*."

"Close enough," she said and took another sip. "Have you been busy with interviews with the press?"

"And a cocktail party with the riders. I told my assistant to make sure you were invited."

She shook her head. "I thought it would be better for me to make sure the real stars were taken care of after the show."

"Of course," he said. "Next time, remember you have staff for that."

"No one refuses the prince?" she said. "Except for his family."

"Are you saying you don't want to attend a party at the palace as a guest?"

She opened her mouth, then closed it. "It's a little out of my everyday routine," she confessed.

"I can't believe you would be intimidated. I haven't seen anything else intimidate you," he said.

"When I was eight years old, my brother told me to never let them see me sweat."

"That's pretty young for that kind of instruction. What was the occasion?" he asked.

Another move due to her parents' inability to keep jobs and pay bills. Another new school when she'd wondered how long they would stay in this place. How long until people found out her father drank away most of his paycheck? "One of those times in elementary school when the kids teased or bullied. It happens to most kids at one time or another."

He looked at her for a long moment and frowned. "I don't like the idea of that."

"What?" she asked, his intent gaze making her stomach slip and slide.

"The idea of someone bullying you."

Something in the way he looked at her made her feel as if she were taking a free fall with no net. She tried to shake it off, but wasn't completely successful. She wasn't accustomed to someone being protective of her. "It didn't happen often," she drawled.

He chuckled. "I bet it didn't," he said and chucked her chin with his index finger. "Do you see him often? Your brother?"

His question slid under her radar, right through her ribs. She rarely mentioned her brother because his absence from her life was still painful to her. "Eli left a long time ago. He had to go. It was the only way." She took a quick breath and shook her head, hating the fact that Stefan had found her vulnerable spot. "Can we talk about something else?"

He paused a half beat, then nodded. "Of course. We're here to celebrate," he said with his most charming smile and clicked his glass against hers again.

She took a quick sip but spilled the champagne on the front of her shirt as she pulled the glass away. Frustration prickled through her. "This is why I don't drink very often," she muttered, futilely pulling at her shirt.

"I can see where it would be distracting during a date," Stefan said.

Glancing up, she saw his gaze fixed on her breasts. She looked down and was mortified by the outline of her nipples against the shirt. "Oh, great. This is embarrassing," she said and crossed her arms over her breasts. "See why I'm not big on formal parties? Even a private celebration in the seclusion of a faraway courtyard is not safe."

Stefan took her glass and tossed it onto the soft bed of grass along with his, then took her chin in his fingers. "Trust me, Eve. If a man chooses to be with you in a courtyard, he's not thinking of safety," he said and lowered his mouth to hers.

Her heart stuttered in her chest. In another lifetime, she wondered if she could have turned him away. She'd turned so many others away. But she sensed that Stefan was strong enough. Man enough. She paused a heartbeat, then opened her mouth, opened herself to him.

Something between them clicked and snapped at the same time. If she believed in that kind of thing, she would have said it was electrical. But Eve didn't believe. At least, she never had before.

He deepened the kiss, sliding his tongue past her lips, tasting and testing her. She slid her hands upward to his strong shoulders, wanting to absorb his strength and power into her. The kiss turned deeply passionate, almost carnal, making her cling to him.

He murmured something delicious against her lips, and suddenly she felt the night air against her back as he unbuttoned the bottom of her shirt. His hand on the bare skin of her waist stopped her breath. Seconds later, one of his hands slid upward to her breast, and she pushed against it, resenting the barriers of her shirt and bra. She wanted to feel his skin.

Part of her was shocked at the force of her desire, but another part of her knew she'd been waiting for this—for him—for years. She felt as if she were riding a tsunami of sensation and refused to fight it. She tugged at his shirt, he pulled at hers, and buttons flung loose. Seconds later, he unfastened her bra and her breasts sprang free. He immediately covered one of her breasts with his hand.

Her nipple was hard and sensitized to his touch. He swore under his breath as he toyed with her nipple at the same time as he French-kissed her. She drank in the spicy, masculine scent of him and felt as if the world was turning sideways.

Stefan clasped his hand beneath her hips and lifted her upward. At the same time, he lowered his head to take her nipple into his mouth, she felt his hardness pressed against her.

Dizzy with want, she slumped against him.

Stefan groaned, lifting his head and pulling her tightly against him. "We need to be together," he whispered. "I want you in my bed."

A shiver of the need he expressed raced through her. "How? Where?"

He gave a rough sound of frustration. "If it were up to me, it would be here and now. But I want privacy for the both of us."

She sighed and tried to gather her wits. Was this what she really wanted? Was he what he really wanted? Eve was only certain of one thing. She couldn't *miss* him. Stefan affected her in a way no man ever had, and she craved the ultimate closeness with him. She wanted him so much it scared her, but she wasn't going to let her fear keep her from him.

"Then when?" she finally asked and met his gaze.

His dark eyes met hers, and she saw the strained passion there. The strength of it reassured her rather than frightened her. "You make it difficult for me not to take you now, *chérie*. Tomorrow night," he said. "I'll make arrangements for you to come to my suite. I'll work it out tomorrow."

A ripple of anticipation and nerves raced through her. "It may not be wise—"

He covered her lips with his fingers. "It's beyond choice. We both feel it."

She nodded, savoring the heat of his body. "Okay," she said, then whispered, "But this is totally against all my rules."

He chuckled and lifted her hand to his lips. "Mine, too, Eve. Mine, too. Now, before I give into my darker urges, I'd better walk you back to your quarters."

"What about the champagne and the glasses?" she asked.

"Don't worry. I'll send a member of my security to collect them," he said and took her hand. "Let's go."

The next morning, she awakened a little later than usual. Stefan had insisted she take a day of vacation. So she slept until 9:00 a.m. This was the first morning she'd woken up not feeling like she was going to hyperventilate. Not that she would admit that to a soul.

Stretching her arms, she yawned, then smiled, pleased that the parade had gone off without a hitch. She'd passed her first test. Thank goodness. A sliver of anxiety rippled through her at the thought of Stefan's plans for tonight. Had she lost her mind? He was not only her boss, he was a prince.

He was also a man, she told herself. A man she wanted and who wanted her. Taking a deep breath, she slid out of her bed and stepped onto the carpet. Her toes appreciated the soft cushion for her first steps of the day. She realized she'd hit the ground running so much she hadn't noticed the small comfort.

Stretching again, she walked to the tiny kitchenette and started her coffee. She peeked inside her mostly bare refrigerator and pulled out cream for her coffee, marmalade for her toast and orange juice. She popped bread in the toaster and wandered toward the door of her quarters to pick up the paper. She'd made double sure she would receive the daily paper. After the incident with the protestors, she'd decided she needed to stay informed even though the Chantaine newspaper read like an odd combination of a scandal sheet and traditional news.

The front page was filled with photographs of the parade, featuring the royal family and government officials on horseback. The largest photo showed Stefan riding with the young boy on Black. Her heart twisted at the image of him. Lord help her, the man was so handsome. She noticed the way his hand curled around the boy, holding him securely. The boy smiled broadly while Stefan's mouth lifted in a ghost of a smile.

Fascinating man, she thought. For a moment she wondered what Stefan would be like if he weren't a prince. She closed her eyes, trying to imagine him as a Texan. He would be a Renaissance man, she decided, with a huge empire. Obscenely successful, she thought. Nothing less would be acceptable. His woman would be... She frowned in concentration. Blonde, beautiful, but brainy. The perfect accessory on his arm.

Nothing like me.

She frowned again, feeling a stab of displeasure and immediately pushing it aside. She shook her head at herself. This was what happened when she had time on her hands. Her mind traveled down all kinds of crazy paths. She rattled the paper and refocused, scanning the rest of the front page. A headline at the bottom of the page grabbed her attention. Royal Stable Master Reports Prince's Horse Is Worth Billions for Sperm.

Billions! She'd never said billions. Who was reporting this? She hadn't talked to anyone…except the man at the end of the parade. Her stomach sank in realization. Even though she'd cut the conversation short, she'd obviously said more than she should.

Less than a moment later, her cell phone rang. She darted through the living area to her bedside table where she'd left it and immediately glanced at the caller ID. Her stomach sank even further. The palace office was calling.

"Hello. Eve Jackson," she said and began to pace.

"Ms. Jackson, this is Louis calling for Franz Cyncad. We have a public relations concern. Your presence is required in the Palace Office."

Great, she thought. Franz was right up there at the top of the food chain. "I can be there in twenty minutes."

"Mr. Cyncad is finalizing the appropriate strategy. He will meet with you after lunch at fourteen hundred."

Eve bit back an oath. Not only did she know she would be disciplined or perhaps even fired, now she had to *wait* to hear about it. "I'll be there."

"Very well. Goodbye," he said and disconnected the call.

Adrenaline pumping through her, Eve immediately went into survivor mode. With her upbringing, it was second nature. She wondered if she should go ahead and make a call to her former boss. She'd made sure to leave on good terms. She might not be able to get her exact position, but the company had been pleased with her work. Or she could start contracting for several horse ranchers. Stefan would pay her severance.

Her heart was hammering and her stomach was

twisting as she glanced out her window at the cobble-stone drive, the lush green trees and pink flowers. She felt a deep sense of regret twist through her. For the first time in weeks, she was acutely aware of the fact that she didn't want to leave. She loved the horses, and her feelings for Stefan...were overwhelming. Until now, she'd been totally absorbed with the parade and inter-mittent bouts of homesickness she'd pushed aside. Eve had learned at a very young age that denial was an im-portant tool of survival.

But this wasn't her childhood, and she wasn't going to be chased out of her home due to bankruptcy. So maybe she shouldn't jump off the first available cliff. She took a deep breath and slowly released it.

If she was going to be fired, how did she want to spend her remaining hours on Chantaine?

Stefan? Impossible. Tonight, the night they would have made love, was never going to happen.

She swallowed over a hard lump in her throat. Push-ing that option aside, she made her plans. The horses, then the beach.

Eve took a micro-shower, French-braided her hair, then visited the royal beauties in the barn and petted and cooed over them. Her heart twisted at the way they all seemed to know her. Even Black indulged her for a few moments before he stamped away.

She stood for a long moment, inhaling the scent of fresh hay and clean horses, branding it into her memory. Then she grabbed a taxi for the beach and made the driver promise to return to fetch her at twelve forty-five. Eve spread her towel on the sand, stripped down to her bikini and sat down on the beach.

She stared at the waves. Whitecaps topped azure water as the tide crashed into shore. The surf was a little rough. She would test it in a few moments, she decided. For the moment, she would focus on the sensation of sun shining on her and the way the ocean looked as if diamonds flickered on top of it.

Inhaling the unique scent of Chantaine, she tried to find a way to preserve the vanilla beachy smell in her mind, the memory of that evening ride with Stefan. All that would never happen between them flashed through her mind. Eve couldn't stand it. She picked up her towel and scrambled up the sandy hill to the road to hail a taxi.

An hour later, Eve sat in Franz Cyncad's office trying to look cool as she resisted the urge to drum her fingers on her black pants–clad leg. Franz was frowning. Not a good sign. He glanced up at her from behind his desk and his gold-rimmed glasses. "You spoke to Marco LaChalle yesterday during the parade," he finally said.

"I didn't meet anyone named Marco. I was focused on the horses and our surprise child rider. A man approached me toward the end of the parade. I barely spoke to him."

Franz pulled off his glasses. "You told him Black could earn billions in stud fees."

"I told him Black could earn a fortune in stud fees," she corrected, still determined to remain calm.

"He apparently interpreted a fortune as a billion," Franz said.

"That was his interpretation, not mine," she said, now barely resisting the urge to fidget. Was she going to survive this or not? Based on Franz's dour expression, she suspected not.

"Unfortunately, we must deal with Mr. LaChalle's report. We need you to recant your position."

It took a full moment for Franz's comment to sink in. "I can't do that. It would be an outright lie," she said at the same time Stefan walked through the door. "Black *is* worth a fortune in stud fees."

"He's not ready," Stefan said.

"Your Highness," Franz said and stood.

Suddenly, Eve remembered she was supposed to do the curtsy thing. "Yes, Your Highness," she said and stood. "But I disagree. As a professional," she added. "It's appropriate to have a specialist assess a stallion for stud purposes at the age of four. Black is over four. His pedigree is phenomenal. He has the potential to produce amazing foals."

Stefan shot her a cool glance. "You are not the appropriate person to assess when Black should breed."

She nodded in agreement. "True. I'm only the stable master you hired to train and advise you on your horses. So, whatever."

Stefan blinked. "Whatever?"

"American version of do what you want. I've done what I can do," she said.

His eyes narrowed. "What would you suggest, Ms. Jackson?"

Oooh, she thought. The Ms. Jackson wasn't a good sign. "I suggest you get Black assessed by the veterinarian, then get moving with providing his sperm, at a cost, to superior mares. Spreading his sperm is part of his purpose. I'm sure Black would agree with my assessment," she said wryly.

Stefan lifted an eyebrow and paused. "Put out a press release saying the palace is having Black assessed for stud service. Be prepared for a deluge of calls. Keep records. We'll return calls later," he said.

Silence followed. "Will Ms. Jackson be remaining on as stable master? Or will she be moving on?" Franz asked.

"Ms. Jackson remains," Stefan said and turned and left the room.

Eve stared after him, stunned and uncertain.

Franz glowered at her. "God help us. More records. More return calls. Would it have been so hard to recant your position?"

"Sorry," she said. "But yes."

Franz sighed again. "Double the workload," he muttered.

"It will ultimately be double the money. Black will earn his way and make your job easier. Just give it a little time."

"We don't have a lot of time, Ms. Jackson," Franz said. "Chantaine's economy is in the loo. Our people are suffering."

"I'm sorry to hear that, Mr. Cyncad, but the world economy is struggling. Everyone is suffering. We're all going to need to get creative to find a way to get Chantaine on the high road. I'm on your side."

"Hmm," Franz said, putting his glasses his face and returning his attention to the laptop in front of him.

Eve waited a long moment. "Do you need anything else, Mr. Cyncad?"

"Not now, Ms. Jackson. I shall contact you if I need to. You may proceed with your plans for the day."

Eve paused, still confused. "Thank you," she said. "Have a good day."

Franz gave a short nod, and Eve left the man's office,

still unsure of her status. She hadn't been fired. Still, what about her relationship with Stefan? Would she be meeting him tonight? Or not?

Chapter Five

After her meeting with Franz and Stefan, Eve felt at loose ends. She checked on the horses, but it was a day off for them, too. After the weeks of preparation, the royal horses seemed determined to laze their day away. She did busywork in the barns and returned to her room, but she didn't know what to do with herself.

In the back of her mind, she wondered if Stefan still wanted to be with her, but based on his curt appearance this afternoon, she couldn't imagine her phone ringing. Her cell rang, catching her off guard. Her stomach clenched. Was it Stefan? She glanced at the caller ID and felt a stab of disappointment. It was Bridget.

"Hello," Eve said. "How are you?"

"Bored and irritated. I was supposed to go to dinner tonight with a friend, but she bailed because she's not feeling well. You must come with me," she said, sounding autocratic, then changed her tone. *"Pleeeeeeeeeease."*

Eve laughed despite herself. "Sorry, Bridget, but I don't think I would be very good company tonight."

"Oh, why not? The parade was a huge success. I took a quick glance at the photographs in the newspaper. You should be flying high," she said.

"You obviously didn't read the entire front page. There's been some controversy about breeding Black, and I was called to the woodshed by Franz Cyncad."

"Woodshed?" Bridget echoed. "What woodshed?"

"It's a figure of speech. The woodshed is where you're taken for punishment, a spanking."

Bridget gasped. "Franz struck you? Does Stefan know? This is totally unaccepta—"

"No, no, no," Eve said. "Franz didn't spank me. He's just very unhappy with me."

"Oh, well, Franz is always unhappy. It's in his job description. If you had a meeting with Franz, it's all the more reason you should come out to dinner with me. Put on a dress and I'll have my driver pick you up in an hour."

"Bridget—"

"I'm not taking no for an answer," the princess insisted. "Oh, for goodness' sake, this is getting insulting. Am I such horrid company that you won't join me even when you have nothing else to do?"

Eve sighed, still full of conflicting emotions. "Okay, okay. Thank you for inviting me."

"That's the spirit," Bridget said. "Ta-ta for now."

Although she would far prefer a barbecue place where she could wear jeans and a T-shirt, she couldn't fight the urge to *get out*. She took another quick shower and pulled on a black halter dress. Instead of putting up her hair, she blow-dried and fluffed it. Since she had time, she applied a little makeup, mascara, a little bronzer, lip gloss...

Her cell phone rang. She glanced at it, hoping desperately that it was Stefan. But it wasn't. She picked it up. "Hello. Eve Jackson," she said.

"This is Raoul, Princess Bridget's chauffeur," the man said.

Her heart twisting in disappointment, she took a deep breath. "Thank you. I'll be right down." Grabbing a sweater, she took the stairs down to the limo.

Raoul stepped outside. "Ms. Jackson?" he said as he opened the door to the backseat.

"Thank you," she said and climbed into the limo.

"Welcome," Bridget said, smiling as she held two glasses of champagne, one in each hand. "Girls' night."

Eve remembered last night and the champagne she'd shared with Stefan. She slid into the seat and closed her mind to the memory. She accepted the glass extended to her and clicked hers to Bridget's. "Girls' night," she agreed, determined to forget her rotten meeting with Franz Cyncad and the fact that Stefan was clearly displeased with her.

They went to a restaurant in a swanky section of the capital of Chantaine. Eve felt self-conscious at first because they were seated in the center of the restaurant, but Bridget chatted constantly, distracting her. The princess was clearly happy to be away from the palace.

"Do you want to get married?" Eve asked, after Bridget had stared at a hot guy who passed by them.

Bridget shrugged. "Not too early," she said. "There's danger in marrying too young, and I'm determined to avoid it. No kids until I'm thirty years old. I want to have some fun. What about you?"

"I haven't thought much about marriage. I've always thought I would take care of myself. Safer, that way," she said.

"Hmm," Bridget said. "I could find a man who would take care of me. I just don't want to give up what little freedom I have in exchange for that."

"Same here," Eve said and lifted her water glass in salute to Bridget. She'd switched to water awhile back.

"I'm not ready for the night to end," Bridget said. "I know of a club close by."

"I'm not sure that's a good idea," Eve said.

Bridget pouted. "Why not?"

"I'm not much on clubs," Eve said.

Bridget shook her head. "It will be a good change for you. We'll just stay for a few minutes."

"I'm not sure—"

"Oh, for goodness' sake," Bridget said. "It's just one night and trust me, our clubs are nothing compared to Rome or Milan."

"Never been to clubs in Rome or Milan. Don't really need to go," Eve muttered, but felt as if she were being swept forward by a force of nature. Tonight she would ride it. Tomorrow she would return to her boring self.

Forty-five minutes later, she found herself sitting at the bar while Bridget danced with a friend of a friend of a friend on a crowded dance floor. Her bodyguard, Rodney, stood nearby, shifting from one foot to the other, clearly as uncomfortable with the scene as she was. Because Eve was bored out of her mind, she decided to torture herself and checked her cell for messages. So far, there'd been none. She shouldn't be surprised, she supposed.

She glanced at the phone and saw one missed call

from Stefan. Her heart jumped, skipping several beats. Suddenly a text appeared. Where are you?

With Bridget, she texted back.

Why? Never mind.

Eve frowned. What did that mean? She shook her head. This was insane. She'd never gone crazy for any other man. Why should she start now? Stuffing her phone into her purse, she was determined not to give him another thought. At least, not tonight.

The woman was going to drive him insane, Stefan thought as his chauffeur and two of his security detail drove closer to the bar where his sister and Eve were apparently enjoying Chantaine's nightlife. He ground his teeth at the thought of it.

"I'm sure Rodney's had enough of this unplanned excursion," Stefan said. He'd seen this coming with Bridget. He'd just hoped she grown more mature about accepting her duties and security protocol. "If Princess Bridget protests, escort Ms. Jackson to my limousine."

"If she goes calmly, sir?" Georg asked.

"In that unlikely event," Stefan said drily, "Ms. Jackson can ride with the princess."

Four minutes and forty-five seconds later, his sister burst through the door with the assistance of two security men, screaming at the top of her lungs. Eve walked behind them. "You can't do this. It's my night off. I can do what I want. I could have ditched Rodney, but I didn't. Just wait until I get my hands on Stefan. Just wait—"

Stefan watched as Eve put her hand on Bridget's arm as if she were trying to calm her. Bridget pulled back her arm and continued to scream. His sister would likely be embarrassed tomorrow.

"Open the door and offer Ms. Jackson a ride in peace," Stefan said to his top bodyguard, Franco.

"Yes, sir."

Stefan could tell Eve needed some extra explanation in order to leave his wailing sister with her bodyguard. She slid into the seat across from Stefan and he made a mental note to thank his sister when she decided she was speaking to him again. Eve usually wore jeans, but tonight she wore a dress that revealed her long, shapely legs.

"Your Highness, your sister's gonna be ticked off with you for a long time," Eve drawled.

"She'll get over it when I let her take a vacation to Italy soon," he said. "It's unfortunate that you had to witness her—" He wanted to choose his words carefully.

"Hissy fit?" Eve said. "She's on a short leash and doesn't like it."

"There's good reason for it," he said. "I insist on her safety."

She frowned and studied him. "Have there been threats?"

"Threats? Rarely. Risks, always. It's part of the job," he said. "Does that frighten you?"

She crossed her arms over her chest. "I don't like the idea of any of you being hurt."

"Neither do I," Stefan said. "That's why I have only the best security and that is why Bridget and you shouldn't have been in that club tonight. Bridget knows she's supposed to submit her schedule to security before she goes anywhere. She's in a high-profile position now. She can't take the same kinds of risks she could before. Plus, she put you at risk."

Eve's eyes widened in surprise. "Me? The only risk I was facing was boredom at that club."

"I intend to keep it that way," he said and paused. "Why didn't you wait for me? Did you get cold feet?"

She lifted a dark eyebrow. "Based on our lovely conversation during my meeting with Franz, I didn't know what to expect."

"That was about your slip to the press," he said, dismissing the concern. "You are still my employee. Can you compartmentalize or not?"

She met his gaze for a long moment. "I don't know. I know I was raised to say please and thank you and I prefer being treated the same way, even by royalty. I respond better to an invitation than an order."

Stefan realized he would need to take a step back and frustration nicked at him. He wanted Eve in his bed. He couldn't totally explain it, but something about the woman made him keep turning toward her. It was almost as if she had some sort of magnetic pull on him, which was rubbish.

He supposed he could tell his chauffer to return to the staff quarters at the palace and he and Eve could go their separate ways, but Stefan wasn't willing to give up his time with Eve even if she wouldn't be spending the night in his bed as he'd planned. He pressed a button to talk to the driver. "Send security ahead to my Aunt Zoe's house at Gerando Beach. I'll give her a call to see if she minds me dropping in." He turned to Eve. "Would you like to go to the beach tonight?"

"I don't have a suit with me," she said, but her eyes lit with interest.

"No need for one. We'll be on a balcony of a private home listening to live music and watching the surf. Interested?"

She paused a half beat, then smiled and he felt as if

the sun had come out from behind a cloud. "Yes, that sounds nice."

Aunt Zoe was in Switzerland, but she'd left instructions with her staff that her house was always available to the royal family. After Stefan's security finished securing the seaside home, Eve and Stefan walked inside. The two-story foyer featured large windows, an unusual chandelier of crystal and copper, and a double staircase.

"It's beautiful," she said.

"Yes," Stefan agreed and extended his hand to her. "But upstairs is better." He led the way upstairs and down a hallway to a den with a swirling paddle fan overhead, white cushy-looking furniture, a bar and kitchen.

"Aunt Zoe designed it all. It's a hobby for her. She also has homes in Switzerland, Bellagio and Manhattan," he said.

"Sounds like she's a woman on the move," Eve said. "And very talented."

"You like it?" he asked.

"It's luxurious, but soothing at the same time. I just probably wouldn't go with a white couch. I'd be afraid of getting it dirty." She laughed. "No. I'd definitely get it dirty."

He liked the way she enjoyed the house and saw herself in it with a modification. "It's nice being with a woman who's not so—" He paused. "Overly fashion conscious."

She smiled. "Or prissy."

He smiled in return. "That word didn't occur to me."

"Bet it will now," she said.

He swallowed a chuckle. "You still haven't seen the

best part. Come on," he said and led her through the glass doors to the expansive balcony with two chaise longues, a table with an umbrella, and a view of the hippest beach in Chantaine. The music of an American R&B band rose from just beneath them.

She tilted her head quizzically. "That sounds awfully familiar. Are they a cover band for…" She glanced over the balcony. "Americans? Here in Chantaine?"

He shook his head, amused again. "We have many American visitors every year. Some Americans like it here, Eve."

"Well, of course they do," she said. "I just didn't expect to see one of my favorite R&B bands playing on one of Chantaine's beaches."

"Think about it. You play a lot of cities and concert halls. Then you get a chance to play in paradise, all expenses paid."

"How come you never see these gigs listed on the band website?" she asked.

"Privacy's also one of our charms."

"Hmm. Maybe it shouldn't be," she said.

"What do you mean?" he asked, unable to conceal a trace of indignation. "Part of Chantaine's attraction is that we're not overexposed."

"I hate to bust your ego, but before I met your sister Tina, I didn't know Chantaine existed. Granted, I'm not a world traveler, but I'm college educated and always got As in Geography. If Chantaine's economy is suffering, maybe it's time to let the cat of the bag about what a great place this is."

"It's a delicate balance," he said. "The advisers and state officials can't agree."

"Makes you wish you were the boss of everything," she said and smiled.

"Enough about business. Let's enjoy the music," he said, joining her at the balcony railing.

"And the ocean breeze," she said, lifting her chin and closing her eyes.

He skimmed his hand down the inside of her arm. "And the company. Would you like a drink?"

Her eyes flashed open, and she leaned close to him, and she whispered, "Are you sure we should raid your aunt's liquor cabinet?"

Stefan laughed, full and hard, at the ridiculous question. He hadn't laughed this hard in a long time. The notion that his aunt would be upset at his use of anything in her home was ridiculous. He led Eve inside to the bar. "I'll replace anything we use," he assured her. "What's your pleasure?"

"I'm not a big drinker," she said, looking at the rows of liquor, but stopped when she saw a bottle of bourbon. "But I could sip on a Texas Rose."

"What's that?" he asked.

She gave a mock gasp. "You mean I know something you don't?"

"What's in it?" he asked. "I'll fix it."

"You?" she asked, her eyes rounded in surprise. "I thought you had staff for everything."

"I do, but that doesn't mean I can't do most of what my staff can do," he said. "Why do you think I fired so many stable masters?"

She winced. "That's scary."

"Ingredients," he demanded and stepped behind the bar.

"I've only had it a few times," she said. "Bourbon, orange juice, cherry liquor...and champagne."

He lifted an eyebrow, but grabbed the bourbon from the second shelf. The bottle was dusty. "Prissy drink."

"Maybe," she said. "But if you drink it, too, you can always say you've had a Texas Rose."

Stefan paused as he pulled out a chilled can of orange juice and met her gaze. "I've never needed to embellish my successes."

"There's always a first," she returned and pulled her long bangs behind her ear.

Her ears were naked except for silver studs. It struck him that he would love to see her dripping with Chantaine's royal family's jewels…and nothing else. He felt himself grow hard and ground his teeth. On impulse he mixed two drinks at once, then poured the liquid into two glasses filled with ice. Walking from behind the bar, he gave Eve her glass and lifted his. "To a Texas Rose," he said, "transplanted to Chantaine."

She clicked his glass with hers and took a sip. "Not bad for a prince," she said.

Stefan resisted the urge to seduce her to lie down on one of those white couches and make wild, crazy love with her. "Let's go outside, Madamoiselle Texas Rose," he said and guided her to the balcony again.

They stood at the balcony and she sipped her drink, the wind lifting her hair from her shoulders. Stefan slid his arm around her waist. "You're homesick," he said. "What do you miss most?"

"You weren't supposed to notice," she said, giving a soft smile as she looked at him. "I was trying not to let it show."

"You didn't answer my question. What do you miss most?" he asked.

"The familiarity, my aunt, barbecue. This isn't my turf," she said.

"It will be," he said. "It won't take long. Chantaine is small compared to Texas."

"But complex and still very foreign to me," she said.

"That will change soon enough."

"If you say so," she said.

The doubt in her voice surprised him. She was usually so confident, so ready to come back at him. "What made you question your ability?"

"Today shook me a little," she confessed.

"Franz?" he said and gave a short laugh. "He's a necessary nuisance. This won't be your last run-in with him."

She made a face. "I'd like it to be. I didn't know whether I would be staying or going."

"You're too expensive to let go," he said.

"I feel so much better now," she said in a dry tone.

"You're good at what you do. You're just not accustomed to the way our press works. Just don't talk to them until you learn the ropes."

"Who's going to teach me the ropes? Franz?" she asked with dread in her voice.

"No. My assistant or me. You can always call him," he said. "You can always call me." He couldn't remember when he'd told any other woman such a thing.

The band eased into a slow, sensual tune. Stefan's hands itched to touch her in ways he knew wouldn't happen tonight. "Dance?" he asked, setting down his glass on one of the tables.

Meeting his gaze, she let him take her glass and do the same with his. Then she walked into his arms, and Stefan sighed at the sensation of her body close to his, where she belonged. He drank in the subtle spice and sweet combination of her scent. Her silky hair skimmed his jaw and her breasts brushed against his chest with each movement.

Holding her eased something inside him at the same time he felt need stretch inside him. He tried to ignore the need and focus on how good she felt. For a full moment, the only sounds were of the sultry song, their hushed breaths and in the background, ocean waves rolling into the surf.

"Have you ever had a more perfect moment than this?" she whispered, lifting her mouth just beneath his ear.

He searched his brain and came up empty. "No," he murmured, pulling her even closer.

The song finally faded away, and she lifted her head, searching his eyes. The expression of wanting he saw there made his gut twist. The connection between them was shocking in its intensity. He lowered his head and took her mouth in a kiss. She immediately responded, tasting of oranges, bourbon and something forbidden.

Although he was already aroused, he couldn't resist feeding himself on her mouth. He felt her arms climb around his neck as she kissed him with equal intensity. He slid his own hand to the small of her back, bringing her intimately against him. He wondered if she would pull away. Instead, she wriggled against him. His heart stuttered in his chest.

"You make it difficult for me to show restraint," he muttered against her mouth.

"Is that what I'm supposed to be doing? Helping you show restraint?" she asked, her voice husky, her lips already swollen. She grazed his neck with an almost kiss and another twist of need ricocheted through him, this one stronger than before.

"You need to understand that everything will change once we become lovers," he told her.

"Is this the standard warning required by the

advisers?" she asked, pulling back slightly with a sliver of wry amusement in her eyes.

"No," he said. "It's just me being straight with you."

"Aren't things already different between us?" she asked.

"Yes, but I am determined to be discreet. I don't want you or your reputation to be affected."

"Can we just make this between you and me?" she asked.

"My position makes it difficult," he said.

"I don't want the position. I want the man," she said.

Her words nearly put him over the edge, nearly made him pick her up, lay her down on the couch and take her that moment. He'd spent a lifetime being the prince instead of a man. "You really don't care about my title, do you?"

"To be perfectly honest, Stefan, I'd probably like you more without it," she drawled.

A sliver of exultation rushed through him. "I like your honesty," he said, lifting a strand of her hair. "I like you too much."

Her eyes darkened in awareness. "It's good to know I'm not the only one feeling this way."

"No fear of that," he said in a dry tone and gave in to the urge to sink his hands into her hair and pull her head toward him.

They kissed again and he linked one of his hands with hers.

Eve's heart hadn't beat regularly since she'd first laid eyes on Stefan tonight. She wasn't sure when she would breathe normally again. The world was tilted upside down, the night was spinning and heaven help her, she liked it. She liked the way his mouth moved against hers. The way his body felt against hers. The way his voice felt against her ears and skin…

She wanted to feel more of his skin. More of him. Seeking his lips, she tugged at his shirt, unfastening one button, then two… She spread her hands over his chest and sighed at the indulgent luxury of feeling his muscles beneath her fingertips. He sighed, too, and the sound was more delicious than the most decadent chocolate. The sea air and the sound of the surf only added to the ambiance.

"You have muscles," she said. "When do you *ever* get the chance to work out?"

His laugh rumbled through her. "Every morning at 4:30 a.m."

She winced, still sliding her hands over his bare chest. "That's insane."

"And what time do you get up?"

"Five-thirty," she said. "Compared to you, I'm a slacker." She kissed him again. "But maybe if I had to deal with your advisers, I'd get up at four-thirty to work off some of my frustration to keep from wringing their skinny necks."

He chuckled again. "Some of their necks are fat."

Shaking her head, she sank her face into his bare shoulder and inhaled deeply. "I like the way you smell."

"I'm not wearing cologne," he said and lifted her head. The expression in his eyes was just this side of ravenous. "Eve, you're not acting like a woman who wants me to hold back."

Fighting a flutter of nerves, she licked her suddenly dry lips. Fish or cut bait, she told herself. "Maybe my actions are doing all the real talking."

She felt him slide one of his hands all the way down

her back and he pulled her against his arousal. He made sure she knew just how thoroughly he was aroused. "Are you sure? I want you to be sure."

"Another disclaimer for the advisers?"

He narrowed his eyes. "No. For me."

She took a deep breath. "I'm sure." She smiled. "Ravish me."

He shook his head. "What an invitation," he said and pushed her dress down her shoulders. Three heartbeats later, her bra snapped loose and his mouth covered hers.

Eve knew she was venturing into new territory, but she was determined not to be shy about it. She wanted to feel everything. She wanted to feel bold and in control, but the truth was she felt vulnerable. Eve refused to give in to weakness.

Instead she focused on her senses. She traced her fingers through his crisp hair, down to his strong shoulders and chest. He slid his hands over her bare breasts and she shuddered. Her internal and external temperature rose exponentially. Eve had never been high, but she suspected this was what it might feel like. Her head was spinning, she found it difficult to breathe and a wicked euphoria raced through her veins.

Somehow, during the next kiss, her dress and panties were pooled at her feet. She scrubbed at his arms and felt remnants of his shirt. His pants-clad thigh slid between hers.

"You have on too many clothes," she said, her voice sounding husky to her own ears.

He shook his head. "Once my clothes are gone, my control will follow."

"Thank goodness," she said.

Chapter Six

Her words had the effect of gasoline on Stefan's passion. Within a moment he'd stripped off his own clothes and carried her to one of the couches and followed her down. She exulted in the weight of his body, propped on his elbows, against hers. His chest was hard and his kisses were a delicious combination of soft and passionate.

He plucked her nipples with his fingers then followed with his lips. One of his hands skimmed down over her rib cage, over her abdomen, then lower, between her legs. Everything he did made her feel more restless, more eager, more needy.

She arched toward him and he growled in approval. "Just a moment," he promised and put on protection, then pushed her legs apart.

She instinctively braced herself just before he thrust inside her. "Oh," she whispered, at the stinging, stretching sensation.

Stefan abruptly paused and searched her face. "Eve, are you—"

"Not now," she said, feeling self-conscious for the first time since he'd begun kissing her.

"Why didn't you—"

She tugged on his shoulders to draw his face closer to hers. "Can we talk about this later?" she asked and wriggled experimentally beneath him.

Stefan swore. "Stop it," he said, but brushed his lips over her jaw.

"Why? I think I'm starting to like—"

He covered her mouth with his and began to pump slowly inside her, stealing her breath. He slid his fingers between their lower bodies, stroking her at the same time. Eve felt as if she were a rubber band drawn tighter and tighter. She breathed in sharp bursts, wondering how much longer she could stand the sensation of him filling her and caressing her. A rolling surge of pleasure started in the backs of her legs and moving upward to her lower abdomen, her core, and exploded inside her, rippling throughout her entire body. Her eyes were closed, yet she saw flashes of vibrant colors.

Forcing herself to open her eyes, she looked straight into Stefan's gaze and saw the instant he climaxed. His eyes flashed with fire and he jerked, a giant spasm shooting from him into her. On top of her own pleasure, it was almost too much, physically, emotionally. She clung to him for several moments.

She finally caught her breath and whispered, "Wow."

"Yes," he said, his face pressed into her shoulder. "Wow."

He took another breath and rolled to his side, his arms

still wrapped around her. "Why didn't you tell me?" he asked.

"Tell you what?" she asked.

He lifted a dark eyebrow, but said nothing aloud. His expression did all the talking for him.

Eve sighed. "You mean that I'm not sexually experienced," she said. "Did I not satisfy you?"

He swore. "You know that's not an issue," he said. "I'm more concerned about the fact that I took your virginity."

"You didn't take it," she said. "I gave it. And trust me, if I hadn't wanted to give it, I wouldn't have." She glanced up at the swirling fans circling against the ceiling. "I've had opportunities, but it never seemed right. Or the men never seemed right. Or I just didn't want them enough. Sex isn't something I take lightly. I know there are risks. I never met any man worth the risk until you," she said and looked at him.

He met her gaze for a long moment. "Because I'm royal?"

Eve rolled her eyes. "You really are stuck on that, aren't you? You just don't get it, do you? I've never met a man who I felt was as strong as I was." She shook her head. "Oh, forget it," she muttered and started to climb off the couch.

Stefan's arm closed around her like a vise, then he turned her toward him. "Give me a break. I've never been with a woman like you."

"Is that good or bad?" she asked.

He paused a half beat. "I haven't figured it out yet—"

Hurt, she tried to roll away from him, but he stopped her. "Good Lord, you have no sense of humor."

She shot him a fulminating glare. "If I said the same to you?"

"Okay," he said. "You're good and bad for me. Good for my soul, good for my heart. Bad for my self-control. There. Does that help?"

"Does that mean you want me to go away?" she asked, her eyes dark with both questions and passion.

"Don't even think about it," he said and pulled her on top of him.

Eve's heart hammered against her chest. Every naked inch of him was impressed against every naked inch of her. She slid her fingers through his hair and lowered her mouth to his, exulting in every millimeter of the flesh of his lips. She licked them and sucked them, kissed them and started all over.

Stefan groaned. "Eve, I can't stand this," he muttered, pressing against her intimately so she knew what he meant.

"What do you want?" she whispered.

"Inside you," he said without waiting a half beat.

"What are you waiting for?" she asked.

Letting out a long groan, he put on another condom and pulled her down on his aching shaft. She moaned. He groaned again.

He guided her hips over him and Eve found herself loving this ride more than any other she'd experienced. After a few moments, however, she felt herself tighten in anticipation. A combination of neediness and want consumed her. "Stefan," she said, sensations intensifying with each passing moment. She sank down on him at the same time he thrust inside her and she felt a spasm of pleasure radiate from her core to every other place inside her. One heartbeat later, he thrust inside her again

with a loud groan of satisfaction that vibrated throughout her.

"Oh. Wow," she managed in a broken whisper.

"Oh. Yes," he said, wrapping his arms around her as
if he never intended to let her go. And a secret part of
her hoped it was true.

She secretly wished he wanted her at least half as
much as she wanted him.… And that wish could be
dangerous.

Stefan awakened with Eve wrapped around him. He
glanced around the room for a clock and finally spotted
one. 2:00 a.m. For goodness' sake, why had he fallen
asleep? And for this long?

The sensation of her silky leg twined with his kept
him pinned to the couch. Her hair splayed across her
face in waves, her eyelashes looked like a mysterious
dark fan against her cheeks. Remembering how good it
had felt to take her, to be inside her, aroused him again.
Since he needed to jet out for an early-morning meeting
in France, he couldn't give in to the urge.

"Eve," he said in a low voice. "Wake up, sweetheart."

She wiggled against him and sighed, still dead to the
world.

Her breasts brushing his chest made him clench his
jaw. It would be so easy to kiss her awake, caress her
and sink inside… He cut off the thought.

"Eve," he repeated, in a normal voice. "We
need—"

Her eyes blinked open and she stared at him. She let
out a scream and punched his face and kicked at him.
"Get away from me! Get away—"

Shocked, and his cheekbone stinging, Stefan quickly

backed away from her flailing arms and feet. "What the bloody hell? What's wrong with you?"

Sitting straight up, she blinked and shook her head. "Stefan?"

"Of course, it's me. Who did you think it was?" he demanded.

"I didn't know. I was having this dream and suddenly I woke up and a man was on top of me. It terrified me." She glanced down at herself, taking quick shallow breaths, still clearly disoriented. "Oh, my God, I'm completely naked." She grabbed a pillow and held it against her as she closed her eyes and tried to calm herself.

"Are you okay?" he asked, moving toward her warily. Bloody hell, the woman had a hard right punch.

"This is embarrassing," she said. "I just hit you, didn't I?"

"Yes."

"I'm so sorry. I'm just not used to waking up to find a man beside me," she said.

He gingerly rubbed his cheek again. "No need to prove that to me."

She cringed, rising to her feet, lifting her hand to his cheek. "Is it okay?"

"Of course it is," he said, capturing her hand and brushing aside the pain. "But we do need to leave. I'm making a three-day trip to France and I have meetings first thing in the morning."

"Oh, what time is it?" she asked, glancing around the room.

"Just after two," he said.

She looked at him in horror. "How could we have both fallen asleep like that?"

He chuckled. "One of the secrets to a good night's sleep is great sex, and I'd say that's what we had in spades."

A twinge of self-consciousness flashed across her eyes before she glanced away. "I should get dressed. What a night," she muttered, nearly tripping over an ottoman.

He caught her against him. "Wait just a moment and let me turn on a light. There's no need to be embarrassed."

"I'm not," she retorted quickly.

Releasing her, he turned on a lamp and began to dress himself.

"Okay, maybe a little. I haven't done this before," she said and scooped up her clothing. "I feel—flustered." She made a sound of frustration. "I'm never flustered."

He walked to her and put his hand under her chin, forcing her to meet his gaze. The turbulent emotion he saw in her eyes pulled hard at his gut. She was strong, but she was vulnerable. For a moment, he wondered if he should have allowed himself to take her. She wasn't as sophisticated as his other lovers had been. He also knew, however, that what had been building between them wouldn't have gone away.

"Don't be so hard on yourself. This was your first time," he said.

She growled and lifted her chin away from his hand. "Oh, good grief. It's not like I was a sixteen-year-old virgin." She stepped into her panties and pulled her dress over her head, then balled her bra into a knot. "Where's my purse?" she muttered, looking around the room.

Spotting it close to the glass doors, he collected it and gave it to her. "Here."

"Thanks," she said, snatching it from him and cramming her bra into her purse.

"I'll be back from Paris in four days. I'd like to see you," he said.

She looked up at him, shaking her bangs from her eyes. "For what?" she asked and shifted on her feet. "I mean, is this just going to be a sex thing? Am I a mistress or—"

"No," he said. "If you were my mistress, I would set you up in a private apartment and give you a monthly income. Your only purpose in life would be to be available at my beck and call."

She lifted her eyebrows and rounded her lips in an O. "Sounds like you've done this before."

"No. As a matter of fact, I haven't, but my father did several times."

She gave a slow nod.

"You and me and just you and me. As you requested," he said, wondering why his heart was hammering. He wondered if she would suddenly have buyer's remorse and back away from him. He didn't want that. Stefan couldn't remember having a relationship with a more authentic woman in his life.

"But secret," she said.

"Of course. If the press or advisers found out, it would be hell for both of us," he said.

She thought about that for a moment. "So what do you have planned for us in four nights?" she asked, her lips lifting in a slight smile.

"We could go for a ride after dark," he said.

"I'd like that," she said and took a deep breath. "I'm ready to go."

"Good," he said. He slid his hand behind her back to escort her from the room. Part of him, a big part of him, wanted to keep her with him, but he knew he couldn't.

The following day, Bridget stomped into the barn office with two cartons of Chinese food and a laptop. "I'm furious," she said. "He has no right. No right at all. Is cashew shrimp okay with you?" she said more than asked as she plopped the cartons onto Eve's desk. "Do you like Chinese?" she asked with a scowl.

Not my fave, Eve thought, but Bridget was so unhappy she decided to make do. She hadn't planned to eat any lunch at all today.

"Hey, how are you today?" Eve asked.

Bridget opened the carton of food, then lifted a hand. "I know I got a little out of hand last night. Drank a little too much—" She broke off and used chopsticks to take a bite. "But that was no excuse for Stefan using strong-arm tactics and being a party pooper."

"Hmm," Eve said, because she suspected anything else would just get Bridget more fired up.

"It's ridiculous, and I was totally embarrassed that he arranged for another ride home for you because he thought I wouldn't calm down," Bridget added and took another bite. "You and I had a very nice dinner and you weren't miserable at the club." She paused. "Were you?"

Eve squirmed in her seat. "I wasn't really miserable," she began.

Bridget's face fell. "Yes, you were. I'm sorry. I'm just so fed up with all the social appearances I have to make. I needed one night of freedom." She sighed. "I guess I went overboard."

"I'm not familiar with the security requirements...."

Bridget scowled. "They're supposed to know everywhere I go days in advance. That allows for zero spontaneity."

"Hmm," Eve said. "Do you know if there have been any threats—"

"There are always threats," Bridget said. "Lately, our citizens are very frustrated by the lack of jobs."

"That's a problem in lots of places," Eve said.

"Exactly," Bridget said. "But in general the people of Chantaine are very loving and peaceful. I have a hard time believing any of them would commit a violent act against the royal family."

Eve nodded. "But still, the palace security must protect you...."

Bridget sighed. "True. All too true. Maybe I just need a vacation."

Eve thought about what Stefan had said about letting Bridget go to Italy, but she knew she should hold her tongue. "Maybe a break is right around the corner," she said vaguely and took a bite of shrimp from the box.

"I can't bank on that. I'm the number-one girl now, and I don't like it," she confessed. "I don't want to be irresponsible, but I don't know how Valentina managed this. I think Stefan needs a wife."

Strangling over the bite she'd just taken, Eve snapped her head up. "A wife?" she echoed weakly.

"Yes, it's perfect. Stefan needs a wife who can take over the bulk of the royal duties. Then I could just be free. So, I'm starting my research today," she said, booting up her laptop. "If I put enough women in Stefan's path, surely he will want to marry one of them." She clicked on the notebook mouse and swayed the screen toward Eve.

A beautiful, sophisticated blonde appeared on the screen. "A duchess in Sweden. I think Stefan is partial to blondes. He had a passionate affair with a Swedish model a few years ago. What do you think?"

Eve took a sip of water and felt her appetite disappear like a vapor. "I have no idea," she managed and took another sip.

Bridget frowned. "But what do you think of the idea? I think it's a win-win for everyone. He's been so busy during the last two years he hasn't taken the time to have a relationship, and I have to believe a regular love life would improve his disposition."

Eve strangled over the water and set her cup on her desk. "Oh."

"Plus the advisers would be thrilled. The whole country would be thrilled. And when Stefan's new wife takes over the high-profile duties," Bridget said with a cagey smile, "I will be thrilled. So help me select a few contenders. I could invite them here for some beach time and a palace party."

"You're going to invite them all at the same time?" Eve couldn't resist asking. "Maybe you should make it a reality show."

Bridget's eyes glowed with enthusiasm. "What a fabulous idea."

"I was joking," Eve said. "I'm not sure Stefan would appreciate your manipulating his love life. How would you feel if he did the same to you?"

Bridget waved her hand. "Oh, he's done it to me a thousand times. I'm surprised he didn't try to get me engaged before I hit puberty. Stefan wants all of us to marry in a way that benefits Chantaine. When he finally gets around to getting married, I'm sure he'll choose a woman who can benefit the country in a multitude of ways."

"I realize it's not my place to ask, but what about love?" Eve asked.

Bridget shrugged. "I'm not sure love comes into it. Whoever he marries will bear a ton of duty and responsibility. High-profile appearances, bearing children, never publicly disagreeing with Stefan."

"That lets me out," Eve muttered.

"Pardon?" Bridget said.

"That lets any woman like me out of the running. If I strongly disagree, I can't hide it," she said.

Bridget giggled. "Now, that's the funniest thing I've heard in days. You and Stefan together? The advisers would fall over in one swoop. I wouldn't be surprised if an earthquake wouldn't swallow the palace whole."

"Glad I could amuse you," Eve said drily, then shook her head. "I'm glad I'm not Stefan. I would like to marry for love."

Bridget turned sober. "Hmm. The crown princes have always married for duty and often had mistresses on the side. My father did, as did his father."

"Didn't that bother your mother?" Eve asked.

"I think she was totally enamored with my father in the beginning. We don't discuss this, but she was second choice. His first love bailed on him. My mother definitely did her part in the child-bearing department. Not so much the child-rearing. My father was a playboy from the time he was a teenager until the last couple of years of his life."

"And Stefan is determined to live down that reputation," Eve mused.

Bridget nodded. "Exactly. All the more reason I should help him." She clicked her mouse and a photo of another gorgeous woman flashed up on the screen. "What do you think of her?"

"I can't help you, Bridget. I've got horses to train," she said and stood.

"But you haven't eaten the lunch I brought you," Bridget protested. "Come on, this could be enormous fun. Much more fun than working on a charity fundraiser."

"I'll help you with a charity fundraiser, but I'm not touching this."

"I'll hold you to it," she said and shoved her laptop into her pink bag. She grabbed her carton of Chinese. "We'll talk later. Ta-ta for now. If you won't help me select Stefan's future bride, then I'll just get a facial."

For the next few days, Eve brooded over everything Bridget had told her about Stefan. She wondered about his past affairs. She wondered what he wanted in a wife. She wondered why in the world he was involved with her. She was not blonde, not pedigreed, not submissive or politically correct.

It wasn't as if this was a long-term relationship, she reminded herself, even though the thought pinched. It was just something they had to do. For some inexplicable reason, they had to be with each other for this time. However short it was.

Stefan managed to leave Paris a couple hours earlier than planned. After an intense week of meetings with various diplomats and businessmen, he was looking forward to a relaxing evening with Eve. One of his long-time advisers, Tomas, however was determined to receive a detailed account of his trip. Stefan sent a text to Eve to save room for a late dinner during their ride on the beach.

"We must provide more jobs for our people. We must improve our economy," Tomas said.

"I'm working on that nonstop," Stefan said. "But you know I haven't had the cooperation I've needed."

"True," Tomas conceded, nodding his white head in response. "You're much more of a fighter than your father was. The people are afraid to believe but want to hope."

"I won't be taking a trip on the royal yacht with a bunch of playboy bunnies anytime soon," Stefan said.

Tomas nodded. "Speaking of women, though, the time has come for you to find a wife. It would benefit everyone, including you."

"That's way down the list for me, Tomas," Stefan said.

"It shouldn't be," Tomas insisted, drawing his scraggly eyebrows into a frown. "The other advisers and I have some suggestions for you to consider."

Stefan shook his head. "That's not necessary."

"Oh, but it is," Tomas said. "I'd like you to escort one of our candidates at the royal dinner next week."

Stefan sighed. "You know I'll have no time to entertain a woman, let alone talk to her."

"You have no need for concern," Tomas said. "The other advisers and I will help."

Great, Stefan thought. The candidate would be entertained by a bunch of geezers. Any woman in her right mind would run screaming. "Fine, fine," he said, glancing at his watch. "We'll discuss more at our next meeting." He stood. "Thank you very much for coming, Tomas. As always, your loyalty humbles me."

Tomas also stood. "I am proud to serve you, sir."

As soon as Tomas left, Stefan raced to his quarters, giving instructions to the kitchen as he changed clothes. As he walked out of his room, a staff member delivered a basket with food.

"Thank you," Stefan said.

"Your Highness," the staff member said. "Are you sure you wouldn't prefer another staff member to carry the basket for you?"

Stefan chuckled. "I think I can manage. Have a good evening."

"Yes, sir. You, too," the kitchen boy said.

Stefan smiled. "I'll do my best." He'd already informed security of his plans for the evening. A car pulled up next to the private exit as he stepped outside the door. Despite his long day of travel, he could have easily jogged to the stables, but riding in the car would appease security. Less than five minutes later, he arrived at the stables.

"Sir, are you sure you don't want us to bring the basket for you?" Franco asked.

"I know I seem feeble, but I can manage it," Stefan cracked.

Franco unsuccessfully muffled a chuckle. "Sir, you are anything but feeble. I ask only for your convenience."

"To be perfectly honest, Franco, I don't want you anywhere near me tonight," Stefan said. "In fact, I'm going to pretend you don't exist."

"Point taken, sir," Franco responded. "We will be invisible."

"Thank you," he said and stepped out of the car. He walked inside the stable and heard the sound of Eve's voice. He paused, listening to her coo at Gus. He heard Black stomping in his stall, almost as if he were jealous. Heaven help him, he understood. He, too, wanted

Eve cooing over him. Ridiculous, he thought and strode toward her.

She must have heard him because she turned and her eyes lit, making him feel alive inside. "Welcome back," she said. "How was France? Eat any croissants for me?"

He stepped toward her, dropped the basket and pulled her into his arms. "It's good to see you. Only one croissant. I spent half my time wondering what you would think of Paris."

"And the other half?" she asked.

"Working," he said. "Tell me you missed me."

"A little," she said.

He kissed her, and she sighed.

"Okay, a lot. How'd you score the basket of food so quickly?" she asked.

He shrugged. "I have a few connections." He glanced at Gus, already saddled and ready to go. "How's Black?"

"Ready for a ride," she said with a meaningful nod. "I didn't saddle him because I didn't want to try his patience."

"It won't take me a moment," he said.

Chapter Seven

Stefan watched Eve ride the horse with a combination of grace and sensuality that mesmerized him. He couldn't help remembering the way she'd ridden him, bringing both of them to incredible, forbidden pleasure. He wanted her again. Worse, he craved her. She'd made him feel whole and fulfilled. The sensation couldn't last, he assured himself, for Eve or him. But until it faltered, he was determined to keep her.

He allowed her to lead the way on the path to the beach even though Black protested. He clearly wanted the alpha role. Stefan would allow that on the return ride.

As soon as they hit sand, however, Gus began to run. Seconds later, Black followed, easily passing Gus. A few seconds later, Stefan saw the fire his staff had built in preparation for his evening with Eve. He reined in Black.

Hearing the slowing hoofbeats of Gus, he glanced over his shoulder and saw Eve reining in her mount. She glanced at the fire. "How did this happen?" she asked.

"I'm a magician," he said. "I wish for it and," he snapped his fingers, "it happens."

She paused a second. "You're full of bull."

He laughed. "Just sharing a legend. Myths and legends are important."

"Maybe," she said skeptically, but dismounted. "Is this when we eat?"

"Sounds like a good time to me," he said and dismounted Black. As soon as Eve slid off of her mount, he led both horses to a tree and tied them to it. "Behave," he said to Black and patted the horse.

Turning around, he looked at her as she sat on the blanket. She'd removed her black Stetson and her hair splayed over her shoulders and down her back. With the fire lighting her skin, she glanced up at him and her lips tilted in a mysterious smile, making him wonder what she was thinking.

She looked into the basket and pulled out the sandwiches the chef had prepared, along with the bottle of wine and chocolates. "Not bad, but I imagine this is a step down from Paris."

"Not at all," he said, sinking to the blanket beside her. "The company is far superior."

Her smile grew. "Oops. You're being charming. I better watch out." She unwrapped a sandwich while he poured the wine into two glasses. "Was the trip successful?"

He nodded. "Three of the consultants are committed to working on events that will include Chantaine." He gave her a glass of wine and clicked his against hers.

"Enough about my trip. What has been happening here since I left?"

"The veterinary specialist came to evaluate Black as a stud," she said.

"And?" he asked.

"In human language, he's quite virile and has the capacity to make many prize foals."

He grinned at her evaluation. "There's more value in being one of many."

"One?" she said, in exasperation. "You're not suggesting that Black should only sire one foal?"

"No, but we will be very selective about which mares will be allowed to carry on his line."

She relaxed slightly. "No problem. I'm sure we can get the best mares lining up for a stud anytime you say the word." She swirled the wine in her glass. "Speaking of stud service, your sister has decided you need a wife. She's putting together a list of prospects to…relax you."

The notion of Bridget having a clue about what kind of woman he would want was so hilarious that he roared with laughter. He quickly noticed that Eve didn't share his amusement.

"You realize how ridiculous that is, don't you?" he asked her.

"You need to get married sometime," Eve said with a shrug. "You need a wife to perform all the royal duties including continuing your family's line."

"Now you're sounding like the advisers," he muttered and took another sip of wine.

"They want you to get married, too?" she asked.

"They've wanted me to get married since I turned twenty-one. You have no idea how many times I've heard the line 'for the good of the country' when it comes to my love life," he said.

Surprise flickered across her face. "You seem to embrace all of your other duties easily enough. Why shirk this one?"

"I'm not shirking it. I just refuse to be pushed into it. I have plenty of time," he said. "If you see my name matched with a woman, rest assured it's wishful thinking."

"So there's no fiancée waiting in the wings," she said. "Because I wouldn't want to feel like I'm—poaching."

He leaned toward her and slid his hand behind her neck to bring her lips closer to his. "You're not," he said and lowered his mouth to hers.

They enjoyed a companionable meal and a walk along the edge of the ocean. He slid his hand through hers, liking the combination of calluses and smooth skin. "Are you still homesick for Texas?"

"Some," she confessed. "I miss my aunt and the familiarity of everything there. And barbecue. There's no barbecue here."

"I'm sure the chef could prepare barbecue—"

"Don't you be giving your chef any extra work because of me. He has enough to do pleasing you, your sisters and guests," she fussed.

"Our chef is accustomed to preparing dishes for all our international guests. Why should you be any different?" he asked.

"I'm not a guest," she said. "I'm staff."

He scoffed. "Maybe *I* want barbecue," he said.

She laughed and the sound created a ripple of pleasure inside him. "You're crazy."

"Maybe," he said and pulled her against him, inhaling her scent. "It's good to see you, to be with you tonight."

Her gaze met his and she nodded. "It is." She closed her eyes for a second, then opened them. "It's almost magical, the breeze, the time alone…."

His gut twisted and he was filled with a shocking longing to steal Eve away for a week or more away from everyone and everything. His schedule was packed. It was impossible. But it didn't keep him from wanting. He allowed himself another taste of her, taking her lips and kissing her.

She slipped her arms around him and he felt the thud of arousal in his blood. If he were anyone else, he would take her on the beach with the breeze kissing their skin and the sound of the surf flowing over them. But he wasn't someone else. He was the Crown Prince of Chantaine, and he refused to be the same kind of man his father had been. Hearing Black snort and paw, Stefan held Eve against him for a long moment, then released her reluctantly. "We should go. The horses are getting restless," he said.

They returned to the barn and each put away their mounts. Stefan ached with the need to bring Eve back to his suite with him, but he wanted her one way: willing. He kissed her lightly on the lips, then moved away. Any longer would have presented too much of a temptation. "I don't want you to feel like I'm giving you a booty call, so the next move is yours. You have my cell number. You can call or text me."

Eve gaped at him. "Excuse me?"

"I said, you make the next move. Thank you for a wonderful evening. I've instructed one of my security to escort you to your quarters. Good night," he said and turned away.

"We don't do that in Texas," she said, stopping him mid-stride.

He turned around. "You don't do what?" he asked.

She *almost* squirmed. "Women don't give booty calls."

Amused, he lifted an eyebrow. "You're not in Texas anymore."

She shook her head and gave a sound of frustration. "How exactly am I supposed to give a crown prince a booty call?"

Pleased that she was interested in calling him, he smiled. "You'll figure it out. Ciao, Beautiful."

"I'm not beautiful," she called after him.

"Come to my bed and you'll never say that again," he said over his shoulder and let her stew over that. He knew she would. It was small comfort considering he would be taking an ice-cold shower before he went to bed tonight.

Exasperated beyond sanity, Eve stared after him as he walked away and stuck out her tongue. *As if* she would ever give a booty call to anyone, let alone a prince. It didn't matter who it was, she just wouldn't do it. She stomped around the barn, doing a last check on the horses, then turned out all the lights except one. Still grumpy, she stared at the door where she'd last seen his smart, sensual mouth curve into a sexy smile and stuck out her tongue again.

Someone cleared their throat, scaring the wits out of her. "Who is it? Who's there?"

"It's Max Roberts, ma'am, with his Royal Highness's security," an extremely fit gray-haired man said as he stepped from the shadows. "I'm sorry if I startled you. His Highness requested that I escort you to your quarters."

"How long have you been here?" she asked suspiciously.

"Since His Royal Highness departed the building," he said.

"Oh, great," she said. "I suppose you'll tell him all about the fact that I stuck out my tongue at him."

Max's lips barely twitched. "It would bring me great joy, but I wouldn't dream of bringing you any pain."

She laughed, despite her discomfort. "A gentleman," she said. "How did I get so lucky?"

"A beautiful American," he echoed. "How did I get so lucky?" He paused a half beat. "Don't worry. I'm not hitting on you. You're just loads more interesting than most of the visitors I'm asked to escort."

"Such as?" she asked, moving toward him.

"I'm not at liberty to disclose that information."

"Discreet," she said. "You're a man after my own heart. Take me home, Max. Any insider info you can give me on His Highlyness?"

"You just said you appreciated discretion," he said as he led her out the door.

"Yes, but there's a difference between discretion and stinginess," she said, because she had to try.

"What kind of music do you like, Ms. Jackson?" he asked, clearly changing the station.

"Stingy it is," she said with a sigh.

That night, Eve tossed and turned. She threw the covers off of her, then dragged them back over her. Her dreams held images of Stefan. She ran to him, but then he disappeared. By the time she awakened before dawn, she was completely cranky. Sipping a cup of coffee after her shower, she scowled at her cell phone. Why did she have to be the one to call? She scowled again.

Through her irritable mind, an idea occurred to her. The more she thought about it, the more she liked it. Taking a deep breath, she gathered her wits and dialed Stefan's number.

"Good morning, Ms. Jackson," he said, sounding far more awake than she did. "How are you?"

"Great," she said, her heart racing. "And you?"

"I'm good. What can I do for you?"

"May I join you for breakfast?"

A silence passed, and she wondered if she had made a mistake. "Or not," she said. "If it's not convenient and—"

"I would like that very much. How soon can you join me?" he asked.

She raked her hand through her damp hair and glanced at her robe. "Twenty minutes?"

"Make it ten," he said. "And take the north entrance using the pass code of 3663. See ya," he said, mocking her Texas drawl before he disconnected the call.

Eve stared at her cell phone, then shook her head. "Nine minutes," she muttered and stripped off her towel as she headed for her bedroom. She dressed in clothes for work with her hair drying in damp waves. Clamping her hat on her head, she dashed out her apartment door and ran down the stairs to the narrow cobblestone road. She rushed, then realized she shouldn't, and deliberately slowed her gait. Entering the code, she pushed the door open and climbed the stairs to Stefan's suite.

She barely knocked on the door before he opened the door, dressed in an unbuttoned white shirt and black slacks. She suspected a tie and meetings were in his future.

"I'm impressed. You almost made it on time," he said and motioned her inside.

She removed her hat and shook her head. "It occurred to me that a gentleman should never rush a woman, and ten minutes is rushing."

"The rush was for me," he said. "I wanted as much time with you as possible. Full American breakfast."

Eve saw the table set with fine china and sterling-covered serving dishes and was stunned. "Do you do this every day?"

"Absolutely not," he said. "I have boiled eggs, a protein shake or a protein bar." He lifted one of the sterling covers. "And never ever sausage gravy and biscuits."

Eve was flattered beyond words. "Sausage gravy and biscuits?" she echoed. "I don't know what to say."

"Don't," he said. "Just eat and remember a protein bar is in your future tomorrow."

She laughed and looked down at the table. "Yes, Your Highlyness."

"That name is irritating to me," he said.

"My aunt coined it with your sister Valentina," she said and dug in to her meal. "It's a term of affection."

"Why don't I believe you?" he asked.

"Because you're a suspicious, jaded, cynical man?" she asked and took a bite of a biscuit with gravy that was almost as good as her aunt's. "This is so good. Almost as good as—"

"Your aunt Hildie's?" he asked, taking a bite of eggs and biscuit. "She gave the recipe to the chef when she visited with Valentina."

Eve laughed. "So like her. She left something out. I can taste it."

Stefan frowned. "What? She tricked my chef?"

"Not exactly tricked," Eve said. "She just didn't tell all. Think about it. You don't always tell all, do you?"

"Such as?" he asked.

"Just curious," she said. "How serious was that relationship you had with the Swedish model a few years ago?"

Stefan groaned. "Maja. Big mistake. Drama queen, and after we'd become involved, she decided she wanted to be Crown Princess of Chantaine."

"You broke her heart," she said.

"Hardly," he said. "Two days after we broke it off, she was in the papers with a French billionaire. Soon after, she got pregnant with his daughter and they got married."

"Were you heartbroken?" she asked.

"I came to my senses," he said.

The same way he would come to his senses about me, she thought and deliberately pushed it aside. "Just curious. What was so wrong about her?"

"You're very curious this morning. Are you this way every morning?" he asked.

She smiled. "I rarely have such amazing company for breakfast. You didn't answer my question."

He folded his hands together and met her gaze. "For a true marriage, I believe a man and woman must connect on several levels, physically, emotionally, intellectually. Maja and I didn't have that. My father was dying at the time. She provided a temporary diversion, but it wasn't enough to go the distance. I knew it at the start and told her exactly how I felt."

Eve smiled slowly. "In that way, you're like a Texan. We're not big on pretending."

He nodded. "What do you have planned today?" he asked, changing the subject.

"The farrier is coming. I'm working on some gait issues with one of the geldings. I'll put Black through his paces if you don't plan to ride tonight."

"That would be a good idea. What do you have planned for the evening?" he asked.

"What part of the evening?" she asked. "Dinner? Bedtime?"

"Evening," he repeated, his gaze causing all kinds of jittery sensations inside her.

She set down her fork and folded her hands in her lap. "Well, I'm a Texas lady," she said. "And we don't believe in chasing men. We don't make booty calls. I made a breakfast call," she said. "The ball is in your court."

Stefan smiled. "Rascal woman."

She met his gaze. "Who, me?"

"Okay, you've forced my hand. Meet me in my quarters at 10:00 p.m."

"That's pretty late for this working girl," she said.

"I have a working dinner with a visitor from Egypt. Would you like to join us?"

"Ten, it is," she said and put her hat on her head and stood. "Please give my compliments to your chef. Marvelous breakfast."

"I'll pass along your compliments. Maybe you can shake loose a few secrets from your aunt about her favorite recipes," he said, standing.

"Good luck with that," Eve said. "She can be a little ornery at times."

"Just like her niece," he said.

"If you're going to compare me to my aunt Hildie, you've given me a huge compliment," Eve said.

He nodded and walked toward her, tilting her hat off her head. "Interesting version of a booty call."

"It wasn't a booty call," she protested. "It was a breakfast call."

"Close enough," he said and then pressed his mouth against hers. "Best morning I've had in a long time. You can work on the booty part later."

Eve kept herself busy until dusk, which in this case was 8:00 p.m. She'd eaten a peanut butter and jelly sandwich with lots of water. She took a shower and would have normally gotten into bed and read before she fell asleep. Tonight, she dressed in a sundress but still thought about her pj's. She thought more intensely as each moment passed. Her cell rang at nine-thirty. Stefan.

"Would you join me for a cocktail on my balcony?" he asked.

She took a deep breath. That sounded so much better than a booty call.

"A Texas Rose?" he asked, and her mind turned to the romantic night they'd shared.

"I'm good with water tonight," she said.

He gave a low chuckle that rolled over her nerve endings like honey. "I have plenty of that. Max will arrive to escort you in a few moments."

"That's not necessary," she said.

"Yes, it is," he said firmly.

Just as Stefan had said, Max arrived a few minutes later and walked her to the palace door. "Enjoy your evening, Ms. Jackson."

"If I call you Max, then you can call me Eve. Thanks for the escort," she said and made her way up the stairs to Stefan's quarters. Her heart hammering in her chest, she lightly knocked on the door.

He opened it immediately and ushered her inside.

"Good evening, beautiful," he said and pulled her into his arms. "Is the dress for me?"

She felt herself flush with self-consciousness followed quickly by a prickle of irritation. "No. I was actually planning on clubbing tonight. You called right before I planned to leave," she said, tongue in cheek.

"Clubbing," he said with a frown then studied her face and laughed. "You're a bloody tease, Eve Jackson."

"Not at all," she said. "You're just too accustomed to everyone tripping over themselves to try to please you."

"Funny you don't have to try, yet you still do," he said thoughtfully, then pulled back and waved toward the balcony. "Come out. I have a little surprise for you."

Curious, she followed him outside and saw a table set with bottled water, milk and a plate of cookies. She felt a twist of nostalgia. "Oh, my aunt used to fix this as a snack for me whenever I visited her. Are they chocolate chip?" she asked, sinking into the chair he offered.

He nodded and took the chair next to her. "Since you weren't interested in a Texas Rose, I thought you might like a different taste of home."

"How did you know?" she asked and took a bite of the cookie.

"I have ways," he said.

She studied him suspiciously. "You talked to Hildie again, didn't you?"

"You know how tight my schedule has been. When have I had time to call your aunt?" he asked.

"True," she said. "But you could have gotten someone else to call her. Thank you," she said.

"I never said I did it," he said.

"Okay," she conceded, but was secretly thrilled that he would have gone to such trouble to please her.

"What was your favorite bedtime snack when you were a kid?"

"My diet was zealously monitored by a strict nanny from the time I was eight until I went away to school at age twelve."

Eve winced. "That doesn't sound like much fun."

His lips twitched. "I had sources. It wasn't a bedtime snack, but I wanted peanut M&M's and Skittles as often as I could get them. One of my uncles slipped me some on occasion. I hoarded them."

Eve laughed at the image. "Oh, my gosh, and I would have thought you'd been given everything you wanted."

He met her gaze for a heartbeat that made her lose her breath. "You would have been wrong." Glancing away, he took a drink of his water. "I can't deny I was given a life of enormous privilege, but for some reason, my family always felt fractured. We didn't feel like a family. Valentina and I were closer than the rest. I keep trying to make us more of a family, but sometimes I wonder if it's too late."

Her heart twisted and she realized what her gut had told her. She and Stefan shared more than anyone would believe possible at first, or even second, glance. She knew the pain of a family that just couldn't seem to come together. She lifted her hand and covered his. "Some people would say it's never too late."

"What about you?" he asked.

"I work at believing, but it's tough. My mother and father were a dysfunctional mess."

"Mine were, too," he said.

"But they had six children together," she said.

"The duty of progeny," he said.

"Six?" she said in disbelief. "There's duty and there's duty."

He leaned back and sighed. "My father wanted to marry someone else, but the woman dumped him. My mother was supposedly second choice. I think the first five years they gave it their best. After that, my mother tried to keep his interest by having more children. Jacques was her last desperate attempt. My father took mistresses on a regular basis and their marriage became more of a business arrangement."

"Did she love him?"

"She was a very young and innocent French countess when they married, twelve years younger than him. Nineteen years old on the day they married. I'm sure she was enamored by his position, excited to be the object of adulation from the people of Chantaine and at times, the rest of the world."

"Nineteen. Wow, that was young."

He nodded.

"How do you feel about the whole taking-a-mistress thing?" she asked.

"Why do you think I'm delaying marriage?" he returned. "I don't want the same kind of relationship when I take a wife. It may be damn hard, but I want a real family."

"I understand that. You think the odds are against you?" she asked. "I figure with my background, they're against me."

"Possibly," he said. "I've heard that expression you Americans use. The apple doesn't fall far from the tree. But I'm already a different man than my father was. A different leader with different goals. I'll do what it takes to be taken seriously so I can improve my country. I won't be marrying a *Playboy* model or beauty-contest winner. I won't choose a wife purely on the basis of her title or her beauty."

"Good for you," she said. "You and I have that in common. I won't be marrying a *Playgirl* model or a boy toy. Well," she added in a light, mocking tone, "unless he worships the ground I walk on and knows how to fix amazing baby back ribs."

"Baby back ribs?" he echoed. "I think I remember Valentina talking about ribs when she attended college in Texas."

"If she was referring to baby back ribs, she wasn't talking," Eve said. "She was moaning, saying oooohhh, ahhhh…I want more."

Stefan narrowed his eyes. "What the hell is the recipe for these ribs? Do they have some kind of aphrodisiac in their flavoring?"

She laughed. "No. They're just amazingly delicious and there are a gajillion recipes. People get into fistfights over what's the best way to fix ribs."

"Sounds primitive," he said.

"And redneck," she added. "But once you've tried to fix them, you become a redneck."

"This sounds like one of the exclusive fraternities at university that I refused to join," he said.

She shrugged. "Bet they didn't know a thing about fixing ribs."

He gave a slow smile and folded his hand around hers. "True. Learning how to cook ribs was not a priority for the students at Oxford."

"Well, that shows you how education is deteriorating even in the U.K.," she said, making a *tsk*-ing sound and shaking her head.

Stefan gave her a sharp tug and pulled her onto his

lap. "Thank God you're here to correct my deficient education," he said.

His low chuckle against her ear sent a ripple of pleasure through her body. "I live to serve," she managed, a little more breathlessly than she intended.

"Yeah, right," he said, chuckling again. Then he cupped her chin and looked deep into her eyes. "Stay with me for a while."

Eve felt herself sinking into him. She could have fought it. Well, she liked to believe that she could have fought it. But when she looked into his eyes, the word *no* was completely absent from her vocabulary.

Chapter Eight

"You're coming to dinner tonight at the palace," Bridget said in a singsong voice with a wide smile as she made her way into Eve's office at the stable the next day mid-morning. It never ceased to amaze Eve how Bridget seemed to ignore the fact that her high heels weren't a good match for the dirt floor of the stable. Bridget was currently wearing a hot-pink shirtdress, a pink hat and pink shoes. Bless her heart, the princess looked like a cartoon.

"Just curious, where have you been? Where are you going?" Eve asked.

"A visit at a home for the elderly. Yes, I know I look ridiculous, but it's cheery," she said. "Now, about dinner," she said.

Eve shook her head. "Bridget, I really appreciate the invite, but—"

"No buts," she said. "I'll be bored out of my mind

without you. Do you realize no one else within ten years of my age will be attending? Have a little pity, Eve."

"What about Phillipa?"

"The sneak got out of it, said she was working on her dissertation. Convenient excuse."

Eve groaned. "I don't have anything to wear," she said.

Bridget shrugged and smiled. "That's what shopping is for."

"I have work to do," Eve said firmly.

"As do I," Bridget said, lifting her chin. "You have the cute little black dress, but we should get you another option. Give me your measurements and I'll call one of my assistants."

Eve just stared at the woman.

Bridget wrinkled her brow. "Come along. Don't be shy. I don't have all day. Your measurements?" Bridget sighed. "Okay, just send them to my assistant, Helga. This is her number," she said, scratching the number on a piece of paper on Eve's desk. "Don't worry. She'll take your size to the grave. Our security could learn lessons from this woman. Tonight, 7:00 p.m. at the Serrisa Ballroom."

"I didn't say—"

"Too late. You didn't say no, so that means yes. You won't regret it. I'll make sure you're entertained. If you haven't called Helga with your measurements by two, then I'll make an arbitrary selection for your dress. Ciao, darling," she said and strutted away.

Eve stared after her thinking this Devereaux clan would try the patience of a saint, and heaven knew she was no saint.

* * *

Hours later, Eve dressed in a cream-colored gown and nude sandals. Helga had also sent a tiara, but that was just way over the top for Eve. She stared at herself in the mirror and felt like Cinderella going to the ball. Or like she was dressing up for Halloween. Either was uncomfortable. She picked up her cell to call Bridget. Her phone rang, surprising her so much she nearly dropped her phone.

"Hello," she said before she looked at the return number.

"No reneging," Bridget said firmly.

Eve sighed. "Bridget, this just isn't me."

"Oh, get over yourself. Pretend you're at a costume party. There will be great food, booze and me for company. Think of this as breaking out of your shell. An escort will pick you up in thirty minutes."

"I could easily walk in that time," Eve said.

"I don't want you to sweat. Sit tight," Bridget said and disconnected the call.

Exactly thirty minutes later, a different security agent appeared outside her building with a car. "Ms. Jackson, I'm Edward. I'll be driving you to the palace for the state dinner tonight."

Eve seriously considered asking him to just take her for a ride along the beach, but she reined in her discomfort. "Thank you, Edward. I'm a first-timer. Any tips?"

"Let the royals go first with everything, and you'll be safe," he said.

"Thanks," she muttered, wishing for milk and cookies. Just a few moments later, however, she walked inside the front door of the palace as opposed to the other entrances she used for her meetings with Stefan. Stepping inside the front hall, she was reminded of the first time she'd entered the palace. It was a stunningly beautiful foyer filled with sparkling crystal chandeliers, marble floors and sculptures. Tonight, the foyer was also filled with women dressed in couture gowns and men in dashing tuxedos.

Eve felt that itchy sensation of not belonging, of being a pretender.

"There you are," Bridget said and moved toward her. The princess wore a spectacular gold dress and tiara. She hooked her arm through Eve's. "Thank goodness you're here. You look fabulous," she said, then frowned. "Where's your tiara?"

"I didn't think it went with the dress," Eve said.

"It was perfect with the dress," Bridget argued.

"I'm not a princess and it made me feel like I *was* dressing for Halloween."

Bridget cackled with laughter. "Okay, you're excused. Bet you think mine is ridiculous."

"You look beautiful," Eve said. "And you can do the crown thing because you're a princess."

Eve gawked at the extravagant jewelry many of the women wore. "Do you think it's real?" she whispered to Bridget. "The diamonds that woman is wearing are the size of golf balls."

Bridget glanced at the older woman and nodded. "That's Princess Margarita from Spain, so yes, they're real. Would you like to meet her?"

"That's okay. I'm happy in the background. You go ahead and do your hostess thing," she said.

"In a moment. I want you to see the woman I'm matching with Stefan first. Come here," she said and nodded toward a tall, stunning blonde. "She's a swimsuit model from Luxembourg. What do you think?"

Eve swallowed over a sudden lump in her throat. "She's beautiful. Can she ride?"

Bridget frowned. "Ride?"

Eve shrugged. "Horseback riding is one of Stefan's passions. I would think he would want his wife to share that passion."

Bridget drew her eyebrows together. "I hadn't thought of that," she mused. "Darn, I hope she doesn't get eliminated because she's afraid of horses."

"Is she?" Eve asked, feeling a terrible, wicked relief.

"I don't know. Hmm. Now that I think of it, Stefan always rides alone. He probably wouldn't want his wife along with him anyway."

If Eve corrected Bridget, then Stefan's sister would want details, which Eve couldn't reveal. Ever. Eve clamped her mouth firmly shut.

"I should go, but I've arranged for you to sit next to me. Get a drink. Mingle. Enjoy yourself," she instructed.

Bridget left in a flourish of silk, and Eve eased her way to the side of the room to people watch. As Bridget said, most of the group appeared to be at least ten years older than she was. The foyer looked different filled with party people. She could almost imagine the same kind of party taking place a century or two ago with the people dressed in different clothes. They would have arrived by carriage instead of limo.

"You look like you're in a different world," a male voice said to her. "Is it more interesting there?"

She blinked and glanced to her side to find a thirty-something dark-haired man looking at her with amusement in his dark eyes. "I was just imagining what a party here might have looked like a hundred years ago."

"Jam-packed with mothers pushing their daughters toward the royal family," he said and took a sip of a drink in a squat glass. "These days the crown prince throws most of these parties for visiting dignitaries, investors or charities."

"And are you a frequent guest at these events?" she asked.

"I'm invited because I bring business to Chantaine. And you?"

"Oh, I'm not really supposed to be here," she said, then corrected herself. "I was invited by Princess Bridget, but I'm really just staff."

"You're an American," he said. "What do you do for the palace?"

"Are you with the press?" she asked. She hadn't forgotten what had happened the last time she talked to a stranger.

He laughed again. "Hell, no. But if you're skittish, we don't have to discuss your occupation."

"I'm not skittish," she said. "I'm the royal stable master."

The man lifted his eyebrows. "Impressive. Stefan prizes his horses."

She studied him. "Do you know him well?"

"Some," he said with a shrug. "My name is Nic Lafitte," he announced, extending his hand. "And you are?"

"Eve Jackson," she said cautiously, allowing him to take her hand. "That name is familiar," she mused, trying to place it.

"Nic?" he asked with a playful grin.

She laughed despite herself and shook her head. "No. Lafitte." She blinked. "That's the name of the famous pirate."

"I thought that was Bluebeard," he said.

"No," she said, laughing again. "Lafitte was the famous pirate in New Orleans. Unusual name. Any relation?"

He extended his hands upward in complete innocence. "Do I look like a pirate?"

Eve studied him and it was easy to imagine him with a pirate's hat, eye patch and boots. "Now that you mention it—"

"Eve, where have you been? It's time for dinner," Bridget said, then glanced at Nic and gave him a hard look. "Mr. Lafitte, what a surprise. I hope you're enjoying the event tonight."

"More than I expected, Your Highness, especially after meeting Ms. Jackson. You're looking more beautiful than ever, Princess Bridget," he said.

"Thank you," Bridget said, but clearly didn't mean it. "Please excuse both of us. We're needed in the dining room."

"I'll be happy to escort Ms. Jackson if you have other duties," he offered.

"Not at all necessary," Bridget said firmly, then grabbed Eve's wrist and rushed away.

"What was that about?" Eve asked as they headed down the hall to the ballroom. "Do you and Nic Lafitte have some sort of romantic history?"

"Absolutely not," Bridget said, with a disdain Eve had never seen her exhibit before. "I would never get involved with a Lafitte. No one in the Devereaux family would. I don't have time to go into it right now, but just trust me. There's a lot of bad blood between the two families."

"Then why in the world would you invite him to your party?"

Bridget sighed as they entered the ballroom. "Because he brings business to Chantaine. Plus he supports many of our local causes."

"Wow, real monster," Eve said, still not understanding.

Bridget lowered her voice. "His great-great-uncle killed a Devereaux, and his father seduced the woman who was originally supposed to marry my father."

Eve digested the information. "Okay, I can see how that could keep them off the Devereaux's BFF list. But if you dislike the Lafittes that much, why would you invite them?"

"We're taking the civilized approach," Bridget said. "Oh, look. Agnes and Stefan are talking. He's nodding. Now, smiling." Bridget gave a mini-applause, then frowned. "What is Countess Laticia doing with Senior Adviser Tomas?"

Eve watched, feeling her stomach sink to her knees. Both women were incredibly beautiful.

"He's matchmaking," Bridget said, indignant. "How is Agnes going to get any time with Stefan if Tomas is pushing a countess at him? Well, I'm fixing this," she muttered, and then took off.

Moments later, it appeared that Agnes would be sitting on one side of Stefan and the young countess on the other. Bridget returned with a triumphant expression on her face. "Much better now," she said. "Agnes deserves a fair fight, wouldn't you say? The games begin."

Eve wished she could be more blasé about the fact that Stefan was surrounded by two women who would do just about anything for his attention, but she felt more miserable with each course of the dinner, and it had nothing to do with the food. She was pretty sure Stefan wasn't even aware of her presence. Why should he be, when he was wedged between a model and a countess?

Bridget chatted with the rest of the table and murmured an observation about Agnes and Stefan every now and then. By the time the waiters were serving dessert, Eve thought she would scream. "I think I need a little air," she said to Bridget. "Please excuse me." She rose from the table and headed straight for the balcony doors. Stepping outside, she gulped in several breaths of fresh air. "Thank God," she whispered.

"That bad?" a male voice said from the shadows. Nic Lafitte stepped forward.

She took another breath and stepped closer to the marble rail. "It's not exactly the backyard barbecue I'm used to," she said.

"Texas," he said triumphantly. "The drawl. I knew you were American and from the South, but I couldn't quite place it. I'm right, aren't I?"

"Yes," she said, wishing she could be alone to collect herself before she thanked Bridget and left for the evening.

"Would you like me to get you a cocktail? You look upset," he said.

"I'm not," she lied. "Just out of my element. I think I'll call it a night."

"Shame," he said, then pulled out a card. "I'm in town every now and then. Give me a call."

She put up her hand. "I don't think so," she said.

"Ah, Bridget ratted on my family," he said. "I'm not all that bad. I'm even part Texan. I own a ranch there."

"So you can play cowboy when the mood strikes?" she asked. She'd heard about men like Nic, who flitted into their ranches from international destinations.

"Can't deny the appeal after spending too much time in meetings," he said. "Bet you even miss it a little."

She did, especially tonight. "I'm going to go now."

"I'll walk you inside," he said, walking with her.

"Thank you, but you don't need to do that," she said.

"I don't have anything else to do," he said, then opened the door.

It was only steps from the balcony into the ballroom. Eve stopped short when she saw Stefan standing a few yards directly in front of her.

"What timing. The prince is making his rounds. He always personally thanks everyone for attending," Nic said.

"He can skip me," she said, stepping backward.

At that moment, Stefan looked up and caught sight of her. And Nic Lafitte. His jaw hardened for a second, and Eve was hoping he would just ignore her. She didn't want to talk to him in this setting. It was surreal and disturbing to her.

Stefan clearly had other ideas as he made a quick comment to his aide and stepped toward her. Eve felt her palms grow damp.

"Ms. Jackson, I wasn't aware you were attending," Stefan said, extending his hand.

She accepted it and gave a little dip that she hoped resembled a curtsy. "Your Highness, Princess Bridget invited me."

"I haven't seen you all evening," he said.

"You've been busy taking care of your—guests," she said, forcing a smile.

He lifted an eyebrow, then turned at Nic. "Thank you for your contributions to Chantaine," he said.

"I consider it my honor and responsibility, Your

Highness. After all, my family has a history with Chantaine. A lovely event tonight, made even lovelier by the presence of Ms. Jackson."

Eve looked at Nic like he was a wack job. *Lovely.* She glanced back at Stefan and noticed that he was clenching his jaw. Interesting, she thought.

"I'm glad you enjoyed the evening. I'll be in touch later," he said to Eve and held her gaze for three seconds before he turned away.

Eve felt as if she'd been scorched and couldn't move.

"Are you sure you're just the stable master?" Nic asked.

"Of course I'm the stable master," she said, praying her face wasn't as red with heat as she thought it was. "Do I look like I could be anything else?"

Nic looked at her for a moment. "You look as if you could be a queen."

"Now I know you're full of it," she said. "I'm going to bed. Have a nice night."

"Are you sure I can't join you?"

"Not in a million years," she said.

"Princess Bridget scared you off," he said.

"It's not that," she said.

"Hmm," he said as if he knew too much.

"Find another girl. I'm sure you won't have a problem. Good night," she said and headed toward Bridget.

She found the princess standing next to Agnes, a physical example of feminine perfection. Bridget turned to her and beamed. "Eve, meet Agnes. Agnes, this is Eve. She's Stefan's new stable master, and we all adore her."

Agnes smiled, revealing perfectly white teeth that

matched every other perfect part of her. "Good evening. You like horses?"

"Yes, thank you, Agnes. Nice to meet you. Your Highness," she said to Bridget, "I'm headed home. Thank you for inviting me."

Bridget pouted. "So soon." She bussed Eve with a kiss on the cheek. "I'll see you tomorrow or the next day. Ciao, Eve."

"Ciao," Eve murmured, and then headed for the door. She picked up the hem of her dress and ran down the hall toward the foyer. Opening the front door, she stepped outside and debated pulling off her shoes.

The chauffeur pulled up to the curb. "Ms. Jackson, would you like a ride to your quarters?"

"Thank you," she said. "That would be wonderful."

The chauffeur stepped outside and helped her into the car. "Did you have a good evening?" he asked.

"Hmm," she said in a noncommittal tone. "I can't wait to get back to my room." She climbed into the car and sank her head against the seat, closing her eyes. What a mistake. She should have never gone tonight. There had been so many times when she hadn't felt as if she'd fit in, and this evening was just one more.

It seemed like only seconds passed and the chauffeur pulled to a stop. "I'll escort you to the door, ma'am," he said.

Eve pulled herself together and stepped from the vehicle. "Thank you," she said and went upstairs to her second-story apartment. Walking inside, she kicked off her shoes and sank onto the sofa. Images of Agnes, the countess and Stefan flashed through her mind like a slide show. She groaned, willing her disturbing thoughts aside. "Never again," she told herself, pushing herself to stand. Maybe a shower would wash the night from her head so she could sleep in peace.

A knock sounded on her door and she frowned. Who? At this time of night? The knock sounded again. Scurrying to the door, she stared out the peephole and saw Stefan standing impatiently.

She immediately flung open the door. "What are you doing here?"

"Good evening to you, too," he said, walking inside and closing the door behind him. "Did you enjoy your time with Lafitte?"

"Not particularly," she said "I mean, he was nice enough and he definitely has an interesting backstory."

"Eve," he said, and she noticed he was clenching his jaw.

"And he wasn't surrounded by two beautiful women vying for his attention and willing to do anything to marry him."

"I didn't invite either of those women," he said.

"Either would be perfect for *the job*," she said, crossing her arms over chest.

"I'm not marrying either of those women," he said.

"How can you be sure?"

"Because I will make the ultimate decision and I refuse to give up my relationship with you for a wife I don't love."

Eve blinked. She hadn't expected that. "This thing between us is crazy," she said. "Pure crazy."

He pulled her into his arms. "I can't disagree, but I just found you and I'm not giving you up."

His words made her heart turn over at the same time that she knew she couldn't be what he ultimately needed. "You have duties. I can't be your princess."

"Shut up," he said. "Just for tonight," he asked more than ordered. "Shut up and let me make love to you."

Eve did, and Stefan took her to the top of the world, but when she awakened, she was alone. She tried not to overthink her relationship with him, but there was a part of her that hated the fact that they had to do everything in secret. They couldn't even eat a meal together because a photog would take pictures and draw conclusions. In this case, the conclusion would be correct.

She wondered if Stefan should be choosing a wife, a woman who could meet his needs as a friend, lover and a representative of Chantaine. She worried if such a combination of a woman existed. In quiet moments, she feared that woman did and would steal Stefan's heart. But how could his heart be stolen if it didn't truly belong to her?

Shut up, she told herself. *Just for this short time, let yourself love him....*

Three mornings later, she awakened to the sight of him pacing in front of her. He had persuaded her to stay the night in his quarters.

"Repeat that," he said, then stopped dead just in front of his bed. "It's not possible," he said after several moments. "It's *not* possible."

He began to pace again, dressed in pajama bottoms and nothing else. "I always used protection."

Eve blinked. *Whoa. Protection?*

"I demand a DNA test," Stefan said and then listened for another moment. "What do you mean there's already been a DNA test? How is that possible? I want a second one, and I want it done by the best labs in existence. We'll talk later," he said and then turned off his phone, staring blankly at the wall.

Moments later, he turned and met her gaze. "I assume you heard the conversation," he said.

"I heard the words *protection* and *DNA test*," she said, pulling the sheet over her as she sat up in bed. "Kinda an explosive combination," she said with a giggle bubbling from her throat.

He glared at her in astonishment.

"Sorry," she said, but another giggle escaped. She slapped her hand over her mouth, ripped the sheet loose and got out of bed. "I really am sorry. I'm nervous. That's why I'm reacting this way. Who is the child? Who is the mother?"

"The mother is Maja, the model I dated a couple years ago. Days after we broke off our relationship, she hooked up with that French billionaire. According to the press, he was the father of her child." He paused a took a half breath. "A daughter named Stephenia. She's not quite two."

Eve's heart twisted in sympathy. "Oh, she's just a baby. Why are they calling you now?"

"Maja and her husband died in a speed-boating accident," he said. "Maja didn't leave a proper guardian in her will. She left only a confidential note that I was the baby's father. Maja's husband never put the baby in his will."

"Oh, no," Eve said, shaking her head. "That poor child. You must bring her here immediately."

Stefan stared at her in disbelief. "I don't even know if she's truly my child. I need to hear the DNA confirmation—"

"But it sounds like they've already done a DNA test," Eve said.

"One," Stefan said. "For something this important, I insist on a confirmation. Plus, I need to consider what's best for the child and the royal family. In the past, the advisers have always insisted that an illegitimate child be raised away from the palace."

Eve dropped her jaw. "You must be joking. You're going to have a toddler raised by a nanny in Timbuktu so she doesn't tarnish the Devereaux name?"

"You have no right to accuse or criticize. There's been no decision made," he said.

"This isn't about accusing or criticizing. This is about doing what's right. Figure it out yourself, Your Royal Highly *Father*ness." She dropped her sheet and went to pull on her clothes.

"Eve," he said as she buttoned her shirt.

She met his gaze and saw a world of torment in his eyes.

"I'm not prepared to be a father," he said.

"Most men aren't," she said. "The difference is you have a whole crew of advisers and you can hire a couple nannies."

"And you?"

She frowned at him in confusion. "How would this change my feelings for you?"

"I don't know. You tell me," he said.

"The only way this would change my feelings is if you neglected or abandoned your child. And I don't think you're capable of either of those."

"This will be a PR nightmare. The high-ranking officials who have lobbied against me will be cheering," he said, raking his fingers through his hair.

"Or not," she said.

"What do you mean?" he asked.

"A few pics of you with the new little princess and anyone who criticizes you will be regarded as a bully," she said. "Just a warning, though. The pics will be easy.

Being a father is going to be the tough part." Taking in the shocked expression on his face, she moved closer and touched his hand. "I think you have the right stuff," she said.

He gave a short laugh without humor. "Me?"

"Yes, you. You know the kind of father you *don't* want to be. Maybe that will point you in the direction of the father you *do* want to be."

Chapter Nine

Stefan checked his watch for the tenth time in five minutes. The plane carrying his daughter had landed, and she would arrive shortly. The plan was for Stephenia to be brought to his quarters. He glanced at the time again and paced his office.

A moment later, his phone vibrated with a text message. The limo carrying his daughter was approaching the palace. Unable to wait a moment longer, he swept out of the office and descended two flights of stairs. Nodding absently to the staff he saw along the way, he came to a stop in the lobby.

Taking a deep breath, he waited for what felt like an eternity. The front door opened and one of his security staff escorted in a very young woman holding a tiny girl with a head full of dark ringlets and her thumb securely fastened into her mouth. Her eyes were wide as she cautiously surveyed her surroundings.

"Your Highness," the guard said with a bow.

"Thank you," Stefan said and moved closer.

"This is Hilda. She has been Stephenia's caretaker for the last two months," the guard said.

"Hello, Hilda," Stefan said to the young woman.

"Thank you, Your Highness," she said, and then she jostled Stephenia. "Stephie," she whispered. "This is your daddy. Say hello."

Stephenia looked at him then buried her head in Hilda's shoulder.

"She's a little shy and tired," Hilda said, giving Stephenia another nudge. "Come on, baby. This is your daddy," she said, then moved as if she planned to place Stephenia into Stefan's arms.

Stefan froze.

Stephenia let out a blood-curdling yell of terror.

Stefan lifted his hand. "Perhaps she'd like something to eat and a nap. One of the staff can take you both to the nursery."

As the child continued to scream down the hallway, Stefan wondered what in hell he'd been thinking. This baby knew nothing of him. When she looked at him, she was frightened, and rightfully so. He didn't know what to do with a two-year-old little girl. When he'd first seen her, she'd looked so innocent, so angelic. She looked like she'd needed to be protected and he'd been determined to protect her.

When she'd opened her mouth, however, he'd wondered if she was an alien. Part of him *still* wondered. How could anything so small produce such a loud, horrendous noise?

He shook his head. Now he understood why his father and predecessors had kept their illegitimate children off-site. Hell, if all children shrieked like that, it was a wonder his parents had allowed any children to grow up in the palace. Of course, he'd had a slew of nannies to take care of him before he'd been shipped off to boarding school.

Eve had painted a lovely visual of possibilities of Stefan with his new daughter, but as her screams vibrated off the marble floors, he wondered why his daughter would be willing to let him hold her, let alone take a picture with her. At this point, Stefan suspected it would be years before that happened.

"She's a screamer," Stefan announced to Eve. "My daughter is a screamer."

Eve bit her lip to keep from laughing. Stefan was perplexed. He also clearly had little experience with toddlers. "Most toddlers scream," she said, rubbing his back in a soothing motion.

"She screamed when she thought I was going to hold her," he confessed. "It wasn't a good first meeting."

"Well, she'd just flown halfway across Europe to an unfamiliar place. Her mother is nowhere in sight. I'm sure she was tired and frightened. No one is at their best when they're frightened. You have to give it a second try. Actually, since she's your daughter, you have to give it infinite tries."

"I'm giving it another try in a few minutes. Would you join me?" he asked.

Surprised, she studied him, then nodded. "Sure. What's the plan?"

He gave her a blank look. "We'll go to the nursery."

"Okay," she said, then clapped her hands together. "This is going to go better than the first meeting. I can feel it."

Moments later they entered the nursery where Stephenia was holding a blanket and sucking her thumb as she pushed on a playboard with a spinner, a noisy flashing button and other features fascinating to a two-year-old. Hilda sat on the other side of the room, overseeing the tyke.

Both Stephenia and Hilda looked up at the same time. The nanny stood. "Your Highness."

Stephenia shot a hard glance at Stefan, then Eve, then back at Stefan.

Stalemate, Eve thought, and then moved toward the play area and sat down. She pulled off her hat and put it beside her as she picked up a book. Then she started to read a book. She read the first page, then turned it. Seconds later, Stephenia wandered closer, and Eve felt the toddler looking over her shoulder. Eve turned another page and Stephenia sat down next to her, her blanket still tossed over her shoulder, her thumb firmly in her mouth.

As Eve continued to read, Stephenia leaned against her. Eve read the rest of the book, and Stephenia sat for a moment. Then she reached for Eve's Stetson and placed it on her little head.

Eve smiled. "Are you a little cowgirl?" she asked.

Stephenia looked away shyly.

Stefan moved closer and Stephenia's eyes rounded. Glancing up at him, she stiffened. Her lower lip puckered out and her face crumpled. She began to scream and cry.

Meeting Eve's gaze, he shrugged and turned away. Eve reached for her hat and her hand slid over Stephenia's forehead. She frowned. The child was hot, too hot. "I think she might have a fever," Eve said, slipping her hand over the toddler's head again. Stephenia clutched the hat and screamed louder.

"What?" Stefan asked, turning back around.

"I hadn't noticed," Hilda said, and then wrung her hands. "With all the change and excitement…"

"I'll arrange for the royal doctor immediately. Please stay with Stephenia," he said to Eve, then left the room.

"You don't feel good, do you, sweetie?" Eve said, pulling the toddler into her lap. "Here, you can borrow the hat. What hurts, darlin'?"

Stephenia continued to moan and occasionally sob at a lower volume.

"I'm not sure I'm the best person for this job," Hilda said. "I was just an assistant until the last few weeks, and I missed her fever. I think I should resign immediately."

"Oh, no," Eve said, her stomach twisting for Stephenia. "She's been through so much change. Please give it a little time."

"But this island is so isolated and I have no friends or family here," Hilda said.

"It's a beautiful island and not as isolated as you think. Wait a little bit before you make a decision. After things get more settled, you'll have another nanny working with you."

"But ever since we arrived here, she cries with me, too," Hilda said.

"Perfectly understandable if she's sick," Eve said, stroking Stephenia's hair and trying to comfort her.

Hilda looked at the toddler doubtfully. "We'll see," she said.

The door opened and a staff member poked her head through the door. "The doctor is here to see the baby."

Within twenty screaming minutes, the doctor diagnosed Stephenia with an ear infection and administered a first dose of antibiotics. Tired out by the examination and her fit of pain and fear, Stephenia fell asleep in Hilda's arms.

Stefan and Eve returned to his quarters. They sank onto the sofa together.

"That was exhausting," Stefan said. "I can't say it was better than yesterday."

"At least you have an explanation for her behavior," she said. "I bet you'd be cranky, too, if you had an earache."

"Can't deny that," he said, raking his hand through his hair. "Is it always going to be like this? When will she ever be more calm?"

Eve patted his hand. "Calm will come and go. A toddler is like the weather, sunshine one moment and stormy the next."

"How do you know this?"

"I babysat children from infants to ten-year-olds," she said. "Didn't you?" she asked, tongue in cheek.

"I can't say I did any official babysitting, but I have five younger siblings," he said. "None of them were screamers."

"That you know of," she said. "Maybe you weren't around during the screaming stage."

"Eve, what in hell am I going to do with this child?"

"Love her," she said. "She'll eventually come around."

"When she's twenty?" he asked in a dry tone.

"Oh, no, by then you'll drop at least a hundred IQ points, or so I hear," she said.

Stefan groaned. "Good luck getting your hat back," he said.

Eve laughed, remembering the way Stephenia had clutched her Stetson with a death grip during her entire examination. "Maybe you'll get her one of her own."

"That can be arranged. How did you win her over so quickly?" he asked.

"It's not magic. You can sit on the floor and read a book, too. You're different for her. Your voice is deeper, you're taller and scary to her. You'll have a better chance of winning her over if you get down on her level."

"I can't remember a time when my mother or father sat on the floor with me," he said, stroking his chin thoughtfully.

"You said you're going to do things differently," she said.

He paused and nodded. "Perhaps," he said. "Why does this suddenly seem so much more difficult than improving Chantaine's economy?"

She lifted her hand to his cheek and smiled. "Trust me. This is going to be cake compared to adolescence."

Stefan groaned. "I can't think about that right now."

"You've met Stephenia, haven't you?" Bridget said, and then covered her mouth as she giggled inside the café where they were eating lunch. "God is just. Stefan got a screamer." She giggled again. "Serves him right. He makes all of us want to scream."

"Have you spent time with her?" Eve asked.

Bridget paused. "I've seen her," she said. "I can't deal with screaming children."

"She's a motherless baby, and she's your niece," Eve said.

Bridget pouted. "Oh, you're spoiling all my fun," she said. "I'll be a good aunty eventually. I just don't enjoy infants and toddlers for more than an hour at a time...except for Valentina's daughter. She was a dream. Stephenia is a nightmare," she said in a lowered voice, then waved her hand in a dismissive gesture. "Besides, you and I are having this lunch to discuss the children's charity event. I like the idea of a hard rock/rap party."

"And how does this include children?" Eve prompted.

Bridget frowned. "I didn't know we had to include them. I thought we were just supposed to make money for them."

Eve chuckled. "Both can be done. We could make a day of it. Sand castles at the beach during the day and a beach party at night for the adults."

Bridget thought about the idea for a moment. "I like that, but I also like the idea of auctioning children's artwork."

"That's doable. Get a good band and some appetizers...."

"Oh, it should be a four-course meal," Bridget said.

"Not at the beach. And you want to make money. If you could pull in some celebrity appearances, that would make it even more appealing."

Bridget's eyes lit up. "Stefan and his first appearance with Stephenia."

Eve bit her lip, thinking about how difficult the current situation between Stefan and his daughter was. "I'm not sure you should count on that."

Bridget sighed. "Surely we can get the screamer to stop screaming by then."

"I know you're having a tough time with Stefan right

now, but at least you have him," Eve said. "At least you have your brothers and sisters."

Bridget's smile faded. "You must miss your brother very much. Why haven't you been in touch since you both became adults?"

"I can't find him and I suspect that if I can't find him, he may not want to be found," Eve said. "My upbringing wasn't at all cushy. He had it rougher than I did." Eve took a deep breath and fought back a sudden sting of tears that caught her off guard. "I know you and Stefan are often at odds, but please don't forget how important he is to you and how important you are to him. And I don't mean you're just important because of the duties you're currently performing."

Bridget glanced down at her glass and slid her finger around the rim of it. "I know what you're saying. Even though he was horrid to Valentina, and it seemed he was upset because she'd left him with no help, the real reason he was upset was that he couldn't protect her. He would croak if anything happened to any of us." She glanced up at Eve. "I still think his temperament would improve vastly if he had a wife…or at least a lover."

Eve couldn't say a thing.

Stefan waited until his daughter's temperature returned to normal to approach her in the nursery. She still screamed when he entered. When he sat on the floor and read like Eve had, Stephenia sat on the opposite side of the room and watched him with terror on her face. It stabbed him in his heart to know that his daughter feared him so completely.

He took Eve with him late one afternoon to observe. Stephenia was far more interested in Eve than him. Eve had managed to swipe back her hat while Stephie slept one night. Stephie wanted it back.

His daughter walked toward Eve and pointed to her black Stetson. "You wanna borrow my hat?" Eve asked. "Can you say please?"

Stephie kept her thumb in her mouth and continued to point.

Eve adjusted her hat. "Gotta say please," she said. "What's up for reading tonight, Your Highlyness?"

"The Cat in the Hat," he said, then sat on the floor just as he had for the last four nights.

"Oooh, one of my favorites," Eve said, joining him on the floor and looking at the book as he read it.

A few pages later, Stephenia appeared by Eve's side and tugged at the hat. Eve shook her head. "Say please," she said to the toddler.

Stefan paused. Eve nodded. "Please continue."

Stefan did as she requested. Two pages later, Stephenia said, "Peas?"

Eve beamed and immediately transferred her hat to the toddler's head. "What a smart girl. I'm so proud of you."

Stephenia gave a shy smile as the hat covered her down past her nose. "Peas," she said again.

"Good for you," Eve praised. "You like my hat, don't you?"

Stephenia pushed the hat back slightly so she could look at Eve. "Peas."

Eve clapped again. "Good girl."

Stefan's heart swelled in his chest at the same time he sensed this wasn't going to solve his problem. "So she knows how to say peas?" he asked.

Eve frowned at him. "It's a step forward."

"True, but we don't know if she's stopped screaming,"

he said. He reached toward the child, and she squeaked. "As I said."

Eve sighed. "True. Okay. I'm going to leave the room."

"Why?" he asked, fighting a terrible sense of panic.

"Because you and Stephenia need to learn to communicate," she said.

"I've been trying to do that with no success since you arrived here," he reminded her.

"True, and I really admire you for that," she said. "After I leave the room, I want you to whisper."

He glanced at her in surprise. "Are you serious?"

"Totally," she said as she left the room.

Stephenia stared after Eve, then turned her head and glanced warily at him.

"Yeah, I'm with you," he whispered. "I wish she would have stayed, too."

Stefan began to whisper the rest of *The Cat in the Hat* and one page before the end of the book, his daughter sat down next to him and leaned her head against his side.

He almost wept.

"Your Highness, more than ever," Tomas said. "You need a wife. With the scandal you've created by fathering an illegitimate child, the best solution for this PR debacle is for you to marry. Although," Tomas said, "I'm certain several of our top contenders will decline being considered."

"Because of Stephenia?" Stefan said more than asked.

Tomas shrugged. "At the level of your potential

mates, many of them would prefer not to deal with a stepchild."

"Then I wouldn't want that woman for my wife," Stefan said in a cold voice.

The senior adviser fidgeted. "Of course, sir. My interest, all of our interest, is only for the best for Chantaine—and you."

Stefan heard the order of priority. Chantaine first. Him second…or last. He'd always accepted it before. Now he had more to consider. Now he had Stephenia. "I have no intention of taking a wife at the moment. I'm forming a relationship with a daughter whom I didn't even know existed. In my personal relationships, my priority is helping Stephenia feel safe and secure and guiding my sisters and brothers into a closer familial relationship. That was neglected by my parents and the advisers. I'm determined to repair it."

Tomas looked cranky. "You and your siblings were provided with the best education possible. How were we to know that you needed some sort of sibling bond? None of your predecessors expressed such a need. Your father had little affection for his brother."

"I'm not my father," Stefan said.

The adviser met his gaze for a long moment, then looked away. "Your father had a different policy regarding illegitimate children," he muttered.

"Explain that," Stefan said.

Tomas shook his head. "It's nothing," he said. "Just a backup plan that was never necessary, thank God."

Stefan was half tempted to ask a few more questions about the backup plan, but he had no interest in further engaging the chief adviser. "I'm glad you understand my priorities."

"Yes, Your Highness, but soon you will need to take a wife."

"First things first," Stefan said crisply. "I am, however, taking recommendations for a nanny."

Tomas blinked, then furrowed his brow. "I'll make inquiries," he said. "I am happy to serve. There have been rumors, sir, that the child is—" Tomas coughed "—a bit vocal."

Stefan chuckled. "*Vocal* isn't an adequate term. She's a screamer, but we're working with her. Funny thing. When you whisper to her, she usually gets quiet."

The adviser turned solemn. "Congratulations, sir. If you have learned the secret of quieting a female, then you have learned the secret to peace."

Stefan shook his head. "I want my daughter to feel loved and secure. I haven't learned the secret to achieving that yet."

Tomas slowly nodded. "Your father would have never voiced such a concern. You are very different from him."

"I'll take that as a compliment," Stefan said.

The following day, Stefan and Stephenia took a field trip to the barns.

"I'm not sure this is a good idea," Eve said as she met them.

Her thumb stuck firmly in her mouth and her blanket clasped in her hand, Stefan's daughter stared wide-eyed in the soft daylight. She glanced at Eve, then stared at the black Stetson Eve had retrieved for the fifth time. Stephenia pulled her thumb from her mouth and pointed at Eve's hat. "Peas."

Eve glared at Stefan as she pulled her hat from her head. "We must get her a hat."

"I gave her a white one. She prefers yours," he said, carefully placing Eve's hat onto his daughter's head. Stephenia gave a Mona Lisa smile, and he wondered just how much his little daughter knew she was manipulating the adults.

"Yeah, yeah," Eve said. "Well, you know the routine. Please tell the nanny to collect my hat tonight when Stephie falls asleep."

"Of course," he said. "Are we going to introduce her to Black?"

"No way," she said. "Are you trying to terrify her for life?"

"Black would protect her," he said.

"After he frightened her to death," she said. "Gus. Gus is our man. He's a true gentleman," she said, then walked toward the gelding's stall. "Hey, handsome," she said, and the gelding immediately came to the stall door, nodding.

"I have someone I want you to meet. Be the sweetheart you are," she whispered, then motioned for Stefan to come closer.

"Isn't he gorgeous?" she said to Stephie. "He's so soft. His hair. His ears. Look at his ears, Stephie."

Stephie stared at the horse for a long moment, then waved her hand toward him.

"You want to touch him?" Stefan asked her and gently guided her hand against his neck. "Soft?"

She lifted her hand higher, and he guided her hand gently over Gus's ears. "Oooh," she said.

He smiled at the cooing sound and met Eve's gaze. "I think she likes him."

"Yeah, I think she does," she said, then watched as Stephenia slid her hand lower to Gus's nose.

The horse flared his nostrils and snorted, startling the child.

Eve laughed. "He made a funny sound, didn't he?"

Stephenia looked uncertain for a moment, then started to giggle.

Stefan stood stock-still. This was the first time he'd heard his daughter laugh. He wondered if he would breathe normally again.

Eve stroked Gus's nose and he snorted again.

Stephenia laughed louder, a belly laugh that echoed throughout the barn.

"One more time," Eve said, stroking Gus's nose again. He snorted.

Stephenia shrieked and laughed.

Stefan looked at Eve. "Is there any way we can record Gus's snort?"

"I think we should work on it. We should definitely work on it," she said.

"Would you join us for lunch?" he asked.

Touched by his invitation, she felt her heart twist and tighten. "Are you sure you shouldn't keep this just between the two of you?"

"Very sure," he said with just a hint of desperation in his eyes.

Eve gave into her sympathy. "Okay. Thank you very much. Lead on."

They were, at first, supposed to eat at a table in Stefan's quarters. Eve suggested a blanket on the floor.

"Picnic," she said. "Afterward, you can shake off the blanket and throw it in the washing machine. No fuss. No muss." She paused a half beat. "Well, I guess you won't be washing it, but a blanket picnic will make it less stressful for everyone."

Moments later, they were served food on the blanket.

Still wearing Eve's hat, Stephenia picked up her food from a tray on the blanket. "Umm," she said as she tasted chicken, mango and avocado.

"She's not a fussy eater," Eve said. "That's a good thing."

Stefan nodded as he took a bite of his club sandwich. "I want to thank you for the advice you gave me to whisper," he said. "It works most of the time."

"You might also want to give music a try," she said. "You would have to experiment to find out what kind she likes, but I'm betting your girl likes music."

Stefan glanced at his daughter as she continued to happily stuff her mouth with food from her tray. "You think so?"

"Oh, yeah. Just hope it isn't rap," she said with a twinge of amusement in her voice.

"You're enjoying this a bit too much," he said.

"You need to remember that before I met you, I thought you were the most arrogant man in the world," she said. "You've now been humbled by a human being who weighs less than thirty pounds."

"I'm not humbled," he said. "Stephenia and I are in the process of negotiations."

She couldn't hold back a laugh. "And who is winning this negotiation?"

He shot her a glance that somehow combined extreme sexiness and amusement. "It's a series of negotiations, and I will ultimately win."

"Yeah, I'll remember that," she said. "If you and I are still talking when she's a teenager, I definitely want to hear you say those words again."

"You and I *will* be talking when she's a teenager," Stefan said. "And I *will* ultimately win."

"We'll see," she said.

He shot her a look of irritation. "You shouldn't question me when I'm certain."

"Just being honest. Do you really want me not to be?" she asked.

He paused. "No," he said. "I need to see you tonight. After eight," he said.

Chapter Ten

Stefan was in his office with the minister of…something. *Energy,* he reminded himself, which was an important minister, but Stefan was distracted by the chorus of feminine laughter filtering through the cracked window to his office. He strained to catch a glimpse out the window.

Is that Bridget? Phillipa? He couldn't quite make out the other adult female until he saw the black Stetson. Eve. The swing was soaring and he could hear Stephenia cackle with joy. He smiled. His daughter's laughter was a sound that should be bottled. He was certain it had the potential to cure diseases and solve world peace.

"Your Highness," the minister prodded. "Are you following my plan?"

Stefan slid his hand over his face and shook his head. "I apologize, Charles. I'm distracted," he said, rising to reluctantly close the window. "Would you mind emailing me your notes? Perhaps another modality might help," he said wryly.

"Not at all, sir," the minister of energy said. "I have a young one myself. Amazing how they can wear you out in an hour. My wife is my lifesaver. I don't know how you do it."

"It takes a village," Stefan muttered. "But we're coming along. Stephenia is adjusting."

"And are you, sir?" Charles Redmond asked. "Forgive me for saying so, but many are concerned for you."

Stefan wrinkled his brow. "Why? I'm healthy and responsible."

Charles paused, sliding his hand over his receding hairline. "But a wife could make things so much easier for you. Have you given consideration to getting married?"

Stefan clenched his jaw for a second, then gave the man the benefit of the doubt. "I will eventually marry, but I think it would be wrong for me to rush into such an important partnership when I've just learned that I have a daughter. First things first. I will make sure Stephenia feels secure in her new home. Does that not make sense to you?"

"When you put it that way Your Highness, it does," Charles said.

Stefan wondered how many different ways he needed to put it since he'd said the same to countless advisers and ministers during the last couple of weeks. "Thank you for your concern and confidence in me," Stefan said. "I count on it."

Charles stood straighter. "Of course, sir. I have the utmost confidence in you."

"Thank you. I will have to invite you and your wife to dinner with your children," Stefan said.

Charles looked momentarily horrified. "Oh, thank you very much sir, but my children are not mature enough for a state dinner."

"I was thinking of something more casual. Perhaps you and your wife could share some of your tips," Stefan said.

"We would be honored," Charles said, then nodded his head. "Thank you again, sir. I'll get those notes to you directly."

"Thank you, Charles," Stefan said, then stood, signaling the minister to leave. As soon as Charles left, Stefan punched the extension for the royal public relations representative.

The representative immediately answered his phone. "Yes, Your Royal Highness. How may I serve you?"

Stefan felt a prickle of irritation. He'd asked the staff to change the way they addressed him to "How can I help you?" Some, however, refused to make the change.

"I want you to send a press release informing that I am enjoying my developing relationship with my daughter, Stephenia. My personal focus is on helping Stephenia to feel safe and secure in her new environment. After I am certain she has adjusted, I will be open to finding a woman who will be a mother to Stephenia, a wife to me and a princess to Chantaine. I appreciate all the support of my country during this exciting time of change."

Dead silence followed. "You're saying you won't take a wife right now."

"I'm saying I have other priorities at the moment," Stefan said. "I want you to send the release immediately."

"But, sir, Chantaine and half the world are waiting

to hear that you have found the right woman and are ready to marry," the PR representative protested.

"They need to get off the edge of their seats," Stefan said.

"But, sir—"

"This isn't a request," Stefan said firmly.

Another silence followed.

"Yes, sir," the representative said.

"Please email the announcement to me for final approval," Stefan said. "Thank you for your responsiveness. I appreciate it very much. Good day," he said, then hung up.

Loosening his tie, he stood and walked toward the window, opening it more as he watched his sisters and Eve play with Stephenia. The richness of the moment filled him up inside. His siblings were so often at odds with each other. Could they possibly come together over his surprise daughter? Hearing another peal of laughter, he smiled and decided to join them.

As he approached the trio of women surrounding Stephenia on the swing, he wished he had a camera to save this moment forever. His daughter was laughing as his sisters and Eve took turns pushing her in the swing.

"She really is irresistible when she's not screaming," Bridget said.

"I'm sure you were quite irresistible when you were a screaming toddler," Phillipa shot back to Bridget.

"How do you know I was a screamer?" Bridget said.

"Because Nanny used to put plugs in my ears whenever you came around," Phillipa said.

"You're making that up," Bridget said.

"I am not," Phillipa protested.

"We all had a screaming stage," Eve intervened. "Some are just louder and more shrill than others. Maybe Stephenia wouldn't have such a delicious laugh if she weren't also a screamer."

"Oh, I never thought of that," Bridget said.

Stephenia let out a full laugh.

Phillipa laughed in returned. "Oh, I think I would push this swing all night for that sound."

"Is that an offer?" Stefan asked.

All three women stared at him in surprise. Stephenia was still gleefully swinging.

"I thought you were stuck in meetings," Bridget said.

"I was, but the four of you distracted me," he said, unable to keep his lips from twitching.

Phillipa frowned. "How could we possibly distract you?"

"Your window was open, wasn't it?" Eve asked.

He met her gaze and something inside him eased. "Yes, it was. I scrapped the meeting and asked for an email summary."

"Good for you," Bridget said. "If there were a bigger swing, I would offer to push you, too."

"That's okay," Stefan said, sliding a sideways glance at Eve.

"I was thinking, however, that I would love to take her on brief public outings with me. You know the people of Chantaine would love to get a peek at her, and she is gorgeous. When she's not screaming," Bridget added.

"Not yet," Stefan said without missing a beat.

"I thought I could take her to the zoo when I visit France next week. Fredericka is dying to see her," Phillipa said.

"If you dare let her go," Bridget said, clearly peeved.

"She's not going anywhere," Stefan said. "Although I can't tell you how delighted I am that you're both enjoying her. Stephenia needs to get used to her environment and current routine. I want us to become familiar to her so she feels safe. We need to protect her during this time of adjustment and I will be very grateful to you for any time you choose to spend with her," he said, then gave his daughter's swing a push.

Bridget and Phillipa stared at him as if he'd grown an extra head. Then their gazes softened.

"When you put it that way…" Bridget said. "I would love to take her on Thursday afternoons."

"Tuesdays for me," Phillipa said. "Unless you need someone to rock her to sleep occasionally. I could read her books."

Stephenia's gaze locked on Stefan. "Book," she said. "Book."

Stefan heard Eve's throaty laugh and the combination of that sound with that of his daughter's gaze made him feel as if he was standing on Mt. Kilimanjaro.

"I think Daddy's been doing a lot of reading," Eve said.

Bridget's eyes turned shiny with emotion. "Oh, Stefan, you're going to be a good father. Much better than our father was."

"I like to believe he did the best he could," Stefan said. "I also like to believe that we can all do better."

Eve met his gaze, and Stefan was scored with the instinct to take her hand and pull her closer to him. To slide his arm around her and feel her against him. It would have been the right thing to do. His duty snapped through him like a strong static shock and he restrained the urge. Barely.

"You made my day. All of you," he said, then kissed his daughter on the top of her head. He exchanged a glance with Eve that lasted longer than it should, then forced himself to turn and walk away.

Later that night after they'd made love, Eve turned to Stefan. "Let's go for a ride," she said.

"Now?" he asked, knowing it was close to midnight.

"What? Is it too late for you? Are you too old to go out this late?" she challenged.

"No," he said, sitting up in bed. "But why do you want to go now?"

She sighed. "Because I want to be with you somewhere besides your bed," she said, staring up at the ceiling. "It's hard being a secret," she said in a low voice.

"I hate it, too," he said. "Today, when I saw you with Stephenia and my sisters, I wanted to pull you into my arms so much I hurt with it."

She slid her hand over his chest, making his heart beat faster. "I understand why we need to keep our relationship secret, but—" She groaned. "Sometimes it's hard."

"It is," he agreed, pulling her against him, relishing the sensation of her breasts against his bare skin and the sight of her wavy hair hiding one of her eyes.

"We could take a quick trip to Paris," he said. "I could arrange for a private dinner, then we could take a walk at night when the photogs aren't watching."

"When are the photogs *not* watching?" she asked.

True, he thought. *Too true.* But Eve had become like oxygen to him. He needed her in order to feel whole.

The realization shook him. Stefan stared at her and felt a kick that reverberated throughout him. She was the first woman who'd ever made him feel this way. What the hell was he going to do about it?

As much as Stefan had always hated his father's playboy-with-the-yacht image, he could see the benefit of the vessel. The yacht could provide a day of needed escape from the prying eyes of the grounded photogs in Chantaine. A perfect getaway.

"Meet me in my quarters in fifteen minutes," Stefan told Eve at 5:00 a.m. from his cell phone.

"What?" she said, her voice groggy with sleep. "It's not even dawn."

"Exactly. My yacht is taking us out for the day," he said.

A pause followed. "That sounds fabulous, but I think you've forgotten that you're not dealing with a countess or a princess. You're dealing with a working girl and I have things to do today…Your Highness," she added, clearly as an afterthought.

"Surely you can reschedule or have your assistant handle your duties for the day. What if you were ill?"

"Exactly. What if I were sick?" she retorted. "I need to save my sick days for when I'm sick. I'm certain my employer wouldn't appreciate me shirking my duties for a yacht trip."

"In this case, I can tell you that your employer most certainly wants you to meet with him on his yacht."

"That almost sounds official," she said.

She sighed. "But I know it's not. I also know I would love to be with you whether we're on a yacht or in a canoe. Give me ten extra minutes," she said.

"I'll give you fifteen. A driver will pick you up."

An hour later, they were watching the sunrise from the yacht as they sailed away from the harbor.

"It's beautiful, isn't it?" she said, leaning her shower-dampened head against his shoulder.

He sifted his fingers through her hair. "Yes, you are," he said and took her mouth in a kiss.

She gave a low chuckle. "I was talking about the view."

"So was I," he said and kissed her again. He could get addicted to kissing Eve. Every time his mouth took hers, he tasted a combination of sensuality, desire, honesty and…love? Could it possibly be?

Determined not to question such a pleasurable moment, he slid his arm around her waist and drank in the sunrise with her.

"The last time I saw a sunrise this beautiful was after a foal was born. It had been a long night and it wasn't an easy delivery, but both the mom and baby survived. After that long dark night, the sunrise was glorious," she said and looked up at him. "What about you? When was the last time you saw a sunrise this beautiful?" she asked.

"Never," he said. "Never saw one with you."

She met his gaze then narrowed his eyes. "Be careful. I might start to think you really care for me. Or that you're a master seducer. Neither of those would be good."

"What if one were true?" he asked.

Her gaze turned vulnerable. "Like I said. Neither would be good." She closed her eyes for a moment as if to push away ugly doubts, then crossed her arms over herself.

In protection, he realized. Frustration slid through him. *He* wanted to protect her.

"After all this rushing around, I'm starving. Are you going to feed me?" she asked.

"Whatever you want," he said. "Including American bacon. I requested it especially for you."

"Oh, now I know you want me for your slave," she said. "Bacon."

"If that's all it takes," he said.

"I was joking," she said.

"Damn," he muttered, then waved for one of the staff.

After a substantial breakfast, Stefan taught Eve to steer the yacht. They anchored in a private, deserted cove and dove into the cool, azure water.

With her hair slicked back and water clinging to her dark eyelashes, Eve wrapped her legs around him for warmth in the water. "This is cold."

"You're used to wimpy Texas water holes," he said, sliding his hands over her silky skin.

"They're not wimpy," she protested. "But they're warmer than this."

"Our ocean is usually warm and the palace pool is always warm," he said.

"I wouldn't know," she teased. "That's off-limits for me since I'm not a Your Highlyness."

He gave her a soft pinch and she squealed. "What was that for?"

"I wonder how you would react if someone called you 'Your Highlyness'," he said.

"I have no fear of that," she said. "Because no one ever would. I'm a working girl, remember."

"Hmm," he said, his mind moving in directions he'd never thought possible. He shook his head and reined in his thoughts. "Let's go back to the deck. Your lips are turning blue."

They spent the entire day rotating between water, shade and sun. Stefan couldn't remember a day when he'd felt more free. As the sun set, he knew their time together would end soon. He had his duties, and she had hers.

They toasted with champagne and dined on fish and vegetables. He could tell Eve enjoyed the meal by the approving sounds she made.

He smiled. "Like the food?"

"Delicious," she said. "I love fish, but I'm usually so busy I just grab a sandwich."

"Then you're too busy," he said as they moved from the table to cushioned bench. "The parade is over. You can relax now."

"Black and some of the others are competing soon. I have to stay on top of them. When they perform well, you look good. I'm determined to make you look good," she said.

"And that is one of the many things I like about you, Eve Jackson," he said, lifting his hand to push a strand of her hair from her face. He couldn't quite read her expression, but he sure as hell wanted to know what was going on inside her. "Three wishes," he said. "If you could have three wishes, what would they be? And they can't include world peace or a cure for killer diseases."

"Well, darn, you took my first two. I have my dream job. I'm on the water on this incredible day with an incredible man. What else could I possibly want?" she asked. When he continued to wait for an answer, she sighed and closed her eyes for a long moment. "I'd really like to see my brother again. I'd really like to know that he's all right." She finally opened her eyes and met his gaze. "And I'd like for you to be happy."

He made a mental note of her brother, but was

surprised when she'd mentioned his happiness. "What makes you think I'm not happy?"

"Your Highlyness, you are a tortured soul," she said, gently poking her finger at his chest. "If you're not fighting the image your father left behind, then you're fighting your advisers about what you want to accomplish now and in the future. Your job is never done. Do you ever feel a sense of accomplishment?"

"I do today," he said. "I successfully kidnapped you and spent a day away from the compound."

"Do you really feel that way about the palace?" she asked. "Like it's a compound or prison? I can certainly see why you would."

"I have mixed feelings about the palace because I do a lot of work there. Although I'm protected from the press and prying eyes, it's not always easy to relax." Except with her, he thought. When Eve was close by, something inside him eased. "The sun is setting. We have a few more moments. No more talk about the compound, okay?"

She met his gaze and lifted her hands to cup his face. "Okay, Your Highlyness," she said and leaned closer to kiss him.

The next day at lunchtime, Bridget walked into Eve's office at the stable. Eve chuckled to herself. Princess Bridget was nothing if not predictable with her timing.

"Hellooooo?" Bridget called cheerily from the doorway and placed a cellophane-wrapped bag of foil candies onto her desk. "I brought chocolate this time instead of lunch since you didn't seem to enjoy the last lunch I brought."

"Good afternoon, Your Highness. How can I help you?" Eve asked.

"Oh, please drop the 'Your Highness.' You and I are friends. And I do have some juicy gossip about Stefan. I got it off the internet. Apparently Stefan went out on his yacht with a woman yesterday," she said and thrust the story and photo at Eve.

Eve's breath and heart stopped. The words blurred in front of her. The photo featured Stefan, shirtless, his head tilted back with a smile of delight on his face. Opposite him, a woman's feet and legs extended from beneath an umbrella.

"They only got a show of the woman's feet and legs up to the knees," Bridget said.

Eve curled her toes inside her boots. She cleared her throat. "Those cameras are amazing."

"Yes, they are, but it's a shame they couldn't have gotten a shot of the woman's face or even her body. All we've got now is this photograph of her feet and from the looks of it, she needs a pedicure," she said with a sniff.

Eve resolved to scrub her feet with a pumice stone and paint her toenails that evening. "It's hard to tell much detail from the photo," she said.

"True, it could just be a bad French pedicure. Either way, this is good and bad news," Bridget said.

"How is that?" Eve asked.

"It's good because Stefan is seeing a woman. It's bad because he's not seeing the woman I chose for him," Bridget said with a pout.

"Hmm," Eve said because she couldn't conjure another response.

Bridget sighed. "Well, I'll keep trying because I believe Stefan needs a wife even if he doesn't realize it. But that's not why I came to see you." She paused, staring at Eve for a moment. "You're sunburned, darling."

Eve bit her lip, thinking about all the time she'd spent on the yacht yesterday. "I've been training the horses outside a lot lately. Maybe that's it."

"You need to be more careful. Use more sunscreen. Always reapply," Bridget preached.

"Excellent advice," Eve said.

"The other reason I came is that I'm making a different appearance next week and I'd really appreciate it if you would come with me," Bridget said.

Curious, she watched Bridget almost fidget. "What kind of appearance?"

"I'm visiting disadvantaged teenage girls. I'm taking gently worn designer clothing and encouraging them to focus on bettering themselves," she said. "I hope it won't be a disaster."

"No. It's a great idea. I just wonder if it needs another element," she said.

"Such as what?" Bridget asked.

"An educational push. Are there scholarships available for these girls? Trade, academic…"

Bridget paused thoughtfully then smiled. "I like it. No, I love it. I'll talk to the educational minister right away."

"So what do you need me for?" Eve asked.

Bridget bit her lip. "Texas courage?"

Eve laughed. "You've got it."

Two nights later, Stefan invited her to dinner. Eve was torn about joining him after the internet article. She knew her relationship with Stefan needed to remain secret for both their sakes. A public outing of their affair would be devastating for the credibility of both of them.

Vacillating until the last moment, she left her apartment and sped down the stairs to the front door where Max waited for her.

"Ms. Jackson, I wasn't sure you were coming," he said.

"I wasn't sure, either," she muttered and strode toward the palace, thankful for the cleansing breeze that blew over her hot cheeks.

"Are you all right, ma'am?" he asked. "Is there something you need?"

Despite the fact that Max was trained to kill in more than fifty ways, he was a teddy bear. "I'm fine. Just a little tense tonight. Thank you."

"You're very welcome, ma'am. If you do need something, let me know," he said as they drew next to the palace door and he opened it for her.

"Thanks," she said, looking at Max. He was about the age her father would have been if he were still alive. She wondered what her life would have been like if she'd had a father like Max. "You're a good man. Good night."

She climbed the stairs to Stefan's suite, still filled with mixed feelings. She barely lifted her hand to knock and the door swung open. "Come in," Stefan said.

As soon as she stepped inside, he pulled her into his arms and whirled her around. A giddy sensation bubbled inside her. "What are you doing?" she asked breathlessly.

"It's been two long days since I've seen you. Too bloody long," he said, then took her mouth.

Her head immediately began to spin. "But the photog," she protested.

"What photog?" he asked, stopping.

"The one on the internet. Bridget showed me the article," she said.

He laughed. "Oh, that one. All they got were your feet."

"And you can be sure I scrubbed and painted my toenails right away," she said.

"I look forward to seeing them," he flirted.

"Stefan," she said, meeting his gaze. "Seriously, don't you think this was a little close? You and I agreed that we want our relationship to remain between just you and me."

He appeared to stifle a sigh. "Yes, we did. But what's the worst that could happen?"

She stared at him in disbelief. "Besides your losing credibility and being shamed because you're cavorting with staff? Or I could lose all respect for my work with horses. In fact, your entire stables could be called into question. That's all."

He raked his hand through his hair and his face lost its joy. "You're right," he said. "But I find myself straining against the secrecy. Tell me you didn't enjoy our time on the yacht," he said, sliding his hands over her shoulders.

"Of course I did, but I also don't want to cause you any pain or hardship. Your job is hard enough as it is," she said.

He slid his hands around the nape of her neck and pulled her toward him. "Are you always so sensible?"

"Not exactly," she drawled. "I got involved with you, didn't I?"

He kissed her and kissed her and they didn't have dinner until much, much later. After they dined, she rested on him, her head against his chest. Her body was still buzzing from their lovemaking.

"I've had nonstop meetings the last two days. That's why I haven't called. I think I've found another way to bring more business to Chantaine," he said. "Turns out there are jazz festival tours that draw fans from all over the globe. We just need to work on finding a discount airline to make tourist travel easier."

"I thought you didn't want to bring in too many tourists," she said.

He shrugged. "There's a balance I don't think we've reached yet. We need more employment, more opportunities for our people. I think we need to keep pushing. If necessary, we can eventually pull back."

"That sounds like a good plan," she said, but her mind bounced back to what he'd said earlier about allowing their relationship to become public. His remark had been uncharacteristically reckless. "I'm a little tired. I need to go to bed."

"I'd like you to stay here," he said.

That was the problem, she thought as her heart jumped. "I don't want to bump into your morning staff," she said with a wink and a smile. "I should go. Sweet dreams, Stefan."

The next morning, Eve's alarm awakened her way too early. She pushed the snooze button. Four times. Finally, she forced herself from bed and scrubbed the sleep from her eyes. She really was going to have to start taking a day off every week where she slept late and spent the day watching mindless TV.

Daylight seemed to be coming earlier and earlier each morning. Turning on the jets to the shower, she stripped from her nightgown, still sensitized by how Stefan had touched her and made love to her the night before.

His touch affected her in a primal way. The more she was with him, the more she wanted to be with him, the more she wanted to protect him and be protected by him. How crazy was that? It was totally irrational, she thought, as she stepped into the shower and willed the water to give her some good sense. She was no princess, no countess, no blue blood. She was a Texan hick done good by going to college, and then following her dream to make her living by working with horses. Her current job was a dream. Her affair with Stefan was insanity.

After she scrubbed herself thoroughly, she dried off and put on her terry-cloth robe. Her coffeemaker greeted her with the smell of a fresh pot. "Thank you very much," she said, then poured herself a cup. Splurging, she dumped in some cream and sweetener.

Hearing the thud of the newspaper against her door, she retrieved it, glancing at the headlines as she sipped her coffee. Unemployment. Hope for New Job Opportunities. Who Is Prince Stefan's Girlfriend?

Her heart sank to her feet, and her coffee cup shattered on the floor.

Chapter Eleven

For the next three days when Stefan texted Eve, inviting her to join him for dinner, she refused. Spotting her feet featured on the internet was one thing, but seeing a photograph of her feet on the front page of Chantaine's newspaper was a horse of a different color. Eve refused to endanger her or Stefan's reputation, and she was frankly surprised that he wasn't more upset about the publicity than he acted.

After taking Black for a ride, Eve settled the stallion in his stall with his new friend Cupcake, the hornless goat. She'd gradually introduced the two of them with complete supervision. At first Black had been curious. Then he'd ignored Cupcake. She'd just about given up on the match when she'd spied Black nuzzling the goat. Now they were best buds.

She heard a sound and glanced behind her to find Stefan carrying Stephenia in his arms. Her heart skipped over itself. "We're the search party sent to find you," Stefan said, walking toward Eve. "We've missed you."

Her chest tightened at the raw emotion she saw in his eyes. She'd missed them, too. "I just thought, after the newspaper article, it might be best if I were less visible."

"The Chantaine newspaper isn't known for their journalistic integrity," he said in a dry voice.

"I know, but I don't like being the cause of discussion and speculation about you," she said.

"There will always be speculation about me, even when there's no basis for it. I can't let that kind of speculation keep me from what's important to me," he said.

What's important to me... She hadn't intended to become so important to him and she sure hadn't intended for him and his family to become so important to her.

Stephenia pointed at Eve's hat. "Peas."

Allowing herself the distraction from her disturbing thoughts and emotions, she smiled and gave the toddler the hat. "You said the magic word."

"Speaking of magic, it looks like your idea for Black has worked well," Stefan said, glancing in the stall. "I've heard of goats settling down racehorses, but I wouldn't have thought it would work for Black."

"He was lonely," Eve said. "They're herding animals, so when they don't have anything to herd, it makes them edgy."

"Well, now that you're finished for the day, Stephenia and I would like you to join us for dinner," he said. "And we're not taking no for an answer," he added before she could form a refusal. "Right, Stephie?" he prompted, stepping closer to Eve.

The toddler lifted her arms for Eve to hold her, stealing her heart all over again. Eve took the child in her arms and drank in her sweet, clean scent. She cast a side-ways glance at Stefan. "You're playing a little dirty."

"All's fair," he began.

Panicking at the possibility of hearing the rest of that quote from his mouth, *in love and war,* she interrupted. "Yeah, yeah, yeah. What's for dinner?" she asked, changing the subject as she carried Stephenia on her hip and turned out the lights.

"It's a surprise," he said and opened the door for her. The limo waiting a few yards away sprang to life and the driver opened the door. After a short drive, the car stopped at the side entrance of the palace and Stefan carried his daughter up to his quarters with Eve walking beside him.

"I don't trust her on these stairs yet. Marble is unforgiving," he said.

Eve felt an extra warmth curl through her at his growing protectiveness toward Stephenia. "This would be a good practice activity with the nanny or you when you're feeling extra patient. The advantage to letting her do some of her own walking and climbing is that it—"

"Wears her out," he finished for her as they entered his suite. "Yes, I'm learning that. She doesn't have as much energy for screaming that way."

Eve noticed the dining table was already set. She also noticed some other changes. "Gates? No collectibles on the coffee table?" She gave a mock gasp. "You child-proofed your domain."

He shot her a darkly amused look. "I'm told it's temporary," he said as he set Stephenia down. "It will return to normal in two or three years if I'm lucky."

The toddler immediately went to a corner of the room, which held a toy box. She opened the box and began pulling out all of the toys. Eve chuckled to herself.

"You're enjoying this too bloody much, Eve," he said, sliding his hand through hers and tugging her toward him.

"Hard on your dignity to have a toddler, isn't it?" she said, and he stole a kiss before she could turn away. Stephenia was too engrossed with her toys to notice.

"I should warn you there won't be any candlelight during this dinner," he said.

"No problem," she said. "I can't wait to see how the new dad deals with the two-year-old and her food."

"For such a beautiful child, she can be a little savage," he said, clearly disconcerted. "I'll call for the staff to deliver the food."

Eve washed up and helped Stephenia do the same. By the time they returned to the dining area, the staff was serving the food. The scent of barbecued ribs filled the room.

Eve stared at Stefan in surprise as he waved her toward the table. "Are those really baby back ribs?" she asked, stunned.

"They really are. The chef extracted the recipe from your aunt. He said it required intense negotiations."

Eve chuckled. "I'm sure she swore him to secrecy," she said. "And then promised him she would come after him like a wounded animal if he didn't stick to the deal."

"You know her well," he said and held out his hands to Stephenia. "Come here little one. Time to eat."

Stephenia allowed him to place her in her high chair and surveyed her meal of carrots, Italian broccoli, apple slices and chopped up bites of meat. She picked up a carrot and shoved it into her mouth.

"She eats better when she feeds herself," he said in

a long-suffering voice. "But watching her can kill your appetite."

"I'm amazed that you're taking some meals with her," she said. "I didn't expect you would be the kind of father to—" She broke off when she realized she'd misjudged him. "I apologize for that. You don't deserve it. You barely found out you had a daughter and look how far you've already come."

"Never in a million years did I imagine that I would be a single parent with a toddler daughter. The advantage that I have is that my sisters will take part in raising her and I also have nannies. Stephenia and I won't eat all our meals together, but I plan to set aside several times during the week where she and I share meals. It's one more way for her to grow accustomed to me."

Stephenia lifted a piece of broccoli toward him.

"Thank you very much," he said and lifted the vegetable to his mouth and pretended to eat it. "Very good."

Stephenia beamed and stuffed an apple slice into her mouth.

Eve took her first bite of the ribs and moaned in pleasure. "Delicious. Wonderful. Fabulous."

Stefan shot her a sensual gaze. "Your tone of voice sounds remarkably similar to when I—"

Eve felt her face heat and shook her head "Okay. Little ears. She may not understand, but you better start practicing what you say in front of her because she will repeat it. Thank you again for the ribs."

"Do they help appease the homesickness?" he asked.

"Yes," she said. "They do and they're delicious. I'm very touched that you would go to such trouble for me."

"It wasn't that much trouble," Stefan said. "But I

would have hated to have to go through with my threat to pull the guillotine out of the dungeon if my chef couldn't get the recipe."

"Oh, you didn't," she said.

"Since the chef was successful, we'll never know, will we?"

Stephenia ate several more bites, then began to offer the rest of her food to both Eve and Stefan.

"I think this means she's done," Eve said.

"Bath time," he said and called for the nanny.

They leisurely enjoyed the rest of the meal and Eve updated Stefan on her progress with the horses. His phone beeped and he took the quick call. "Would you like to say good-night to Stephenia with me?" he asked.

"I'd love to," she said, then walked down the long hallway to the nursery. Stephenia's eyes were already drooping and her thumb was tucked firmly in her mouth.

Her gaze lit up as Stefan entered the room. "Book," she said, pointing her finger at him.

"Again?" he asked and took the child from the nanny. "Say good-night to Eve," he said.

Eve moved closer to give Stephie a kiss. Stephie surprised her by placing a wet kiss on her cheek. "Oh, what a cutie," she said. "Sweet dreams, darlin'," she said, and then backed away as Stefan sat in the rocking chair and read the book under a dim light.

His low voice was soothing and he rocked slowly as he stroked his daughter's head. Her heart twisted so tight inside her she could hardly breathe. He was being so tender with her. This moment was just for the two of them. Suddenly feeling as if she were intruding, she quietly backed out of the room.

Taking a deep breath, she closed her eyes and was stunned to feel her eyes damp with tears. She wondered why she was so emotional. Swiping her eyes, she thought back to her own childhood. Her father had never rocked her to sleep. Her father had never read a book to her. Her father had never been a *father* to her.

It all hit her at once. Seeing Stefan become a loving father so quickly showed her what kind of man he was underneath. She had already fallen in love with him, but—alarm shot through her. No, she told herself. Not the *L* word. Not with Stefan. Their relationship was impossible. He knew it. She knew it. How could this have happened?

Distressed, she turned blindly down the hallway. She needed to leave immediately. Turning the corner, she walked straight into a man. Chagrined, she patted his arm. "Oh, gosh, I'm so sorry. I wasn't looking where I was going. Are you okay?"

"I'm fine," the white-haired man said in a testy voice. "Are you staff? What are you doing on this floor?"

"I was invited to—" She stopped, realizing she didn't want to reveal more. "I was just leaving. Again I'm sorry."

"Just a moment," he said when she turned. "Do you know where Prince Stefan is? I'm trying to reach him about an urgent matter."

She felt an invisible barrier slide upward. It came out of nowhere. She wasn't sure she liked this man. "His Royal Highness is already taking care of urgent business," she said. "I'm certain he'll be available in fifteen or thirty minutes. If it's not a matter of utmost importance, then you should try to reach him again later."

He looked taken aback by her don't-mess-with-me

tone and lifted his chin. "Do you know to whom you're speaking? I am one of Prince Stefan's lead advisers, Tomas Gunter. I do not take orders from staff. Give me your name."

"My name is Eve Jackson," she said. "And I meant it when I said that Stefan is taking care of urgent business. Don't bother him."

Eve heard footsteps in the hallway coming toward them. Stefan rounded the corner, lifting his eyebrows in surprise as he approached them. "Good evening, Tomas. I'm surprised to see you here at this hour."

"Your Royal Highness, you know I wouldn't bother you if it weren't a matter of importance," the adviser said. "Your staff member here told me you were taking care of urgent business."

Stefan glanced at Eve and tossed her a questioning glance.

"Time for me to go," she said with a smile that looked more like a grimace and backed away. "Y'all don't stay up too late. Sweet dreams."

"Eve," Stefan called, not liking the look of panic she was trying to conceal.

"I'll catch you up on your stallion later," she said. "Really. G'night," she said and whirled away.

He looked after her and sighed. Something had happened to upset her. They'd been separated barely five minutes. What the hell could it have been? Stefan turned to Tomas and frowned. "What did you say to Ms. Jackson?"

"Nothing," the adviser said. "I told her I needed to talk to you, and I questioned her as to why she was on this floor. That *is* a security breach," he said defensively. "She just kept insisting that you were conducting urgent business, and that I wasn't to interrupt you. I found that impertinent, bordering on subordinate."

Stefan chuckled. "She was right. I was conducting urgent business. I was rocking my daughter to sleep."

Tomas stared at him with a blank expression on his face. "I don't know what to say, sir. I never dealt with this kind of thing from your father."

"You've just paid me a high compliment," Stefan said and walked toward his suite. He didn't appreciate Tomas interrupting his evening with Eve. He'd practically had to trick her into joining him and now she'd fled. "It's late. If you don't mind, could you reveal to me the pressing matter that brought you here tonight?"

The adviser shifted uncomfortably. "I think it's best if we speak in private."

Reluctant to let the man into his quarters, Stefan obliged the adviser. "I have another matter to address tonight. I would appreciate brevity."

"Of course, sir," the adviser said, and Stefan shut the door behind him.

Tomas locked his hands behind his back and began to pace. "Your Royal Highness, unfortunate rumors are being spread about you, and you must take action to nip them in the bud. The rumor is that you have become sexually involved with one of your staff. I don't need to tell you that this will reduce your effectiveness as Crown Prince of Chantaine. You've told me of your high aspirations to help your country, and this kind of tawdriness will do nothing to help you. In fact," he said, "it can only hurt you, the royal family and the entire country of Chantaine."

Eve spent the following day feeling emotionally tortured. She had done the stupid, stupid, stupid thing of falling in love with Stefan. From the beginning, they'd both known their relationship would be temporary, but she had not been able to turn herself away from him. In retrospect, her feelings for him had been like a runaway train and all she could do was hold on for dear life.

Now, big things were at stake, such as the future of Stefan's family legacy and his ability to help his country the way he needed to help them. Eve knew Stefan well enough that she understood his duty to his country ran deeper than his blood. He would do anything for the citizens of Chantaine, and she loved him for that devotion. She also knew that his feelings for her ran deeper than either she or he had expected. She couldn't allow him to be swayed by his feelings for her. They would pass.

Her stomach knotted at the thought. But she told herself it was the truth. There were women lined up around the world ready, willing and able to be Stefan's wife. Women far more refined and polished than she would ever be. She just didn't know how she could make him understand.

She heard the door to the barn open and stepped out of Gus's stall. She wondered if it was one of her apprentices. Eve was fortunate to have plenty of help taking care of Stefan's stables. She walked toward the barn entrance and stopped when she saw the backlit figure of the adviser she'd met last night.

"Mr. Gunter?"

"Yes, and you are Ms. Jackson, correct?" he said and sneezed into his elbow. He walked a few steps farther and sneezed again. "Excuse me. I'm allergic to horses, dogs, cats and hay."

She dipped her head. "We have a lot of hay and

horses around here. Are you looking for something in particular?"

"Yes," he said, sniffing. "I was looking for you. May we speak in private?"

Eve felt a nauseating sense of dread. She knew she didn't want to have this conversation. "Unless it concerns the horses, I'm not sure it's necessary," she said.

"It concerns the owner of the horses," the adviser said. "Please," he said. "I won't take much of your time."

The *please* got her. It usually did. "Okay. There's an office this way," she said and led the way.

She heard the adviser sneeze three times. "Would you prefer to talk somewhere else, outside of the barn where you'll be less miserable?" she asked.

"This is fine," he said. "Thank you, though, for your consideration." He closed the door behind him. "It's very rare that I would consider directly interfering in Prince Stefan's private life, but he's an exceptional man and I believe he has an exceptional future. I believe he can bring a new sense of hope and change to Chantaine. He's not content to operate the same way his father did. His Royal Highness is a workaholic. He has a passion for Chantaine. Because of that, I feel compelled to protect him from an—" He paused. "An impulsive decision that could prevent him from fulfilling what he believes is his destiny."

Eve took a breath. Mr. Gunter was only saying what she'd expected and in her heart of hearts, she agreed with him. "You're talking about the relationship Stefan and I share," she said.

"He believes he's in love with you," the adviser said bluntly.

"And you don't," she said.

Gunter sighed. "I must look at the big picture. As

lovely and caring as you are, you are still a commoner and an American," he said as if her nationality were a detriment.

Eve couldn't hold a stone face at the slur against her country. "What's wrong with being American?"

The adviser lifted his hands. "Nothing, but if Stefan chose to marry a commoner, it would be best if he married a woman from Chantaine.

"For a prince, marriage is about more than love. It's a way to seal ties with other countries, secure trade agreements."

"What you're saying is it's business," she said.

"In a way," he said.

"But what about Stefan's heart?" she asked. "Who's going to look after that? Will you? Can I count on you to make sure that he gets a woman who will love him, love Stephenia, ride horses with him, respect him, challenge him when necessary, make him laugh, make him relax, make him think?" She ran out of breath.

Gunter shot her a considering gaze. "You are more than I thought you would be," he said, then wrinkled his brow as he thought. He sneezed into his sleeve, then nodded to himself. "In the past, happiness has not been a primary consideration when choosing a wife. It didn't hurt if the woman was beautiful and intelligent, but in general, what she could bring to benefit Chantaine was considered more important. What you're saying is that Stefan's happiness should be considered. I agree and I will make it my mission to make sure that the prince achieves the best match possible and that includes a woman who will indeed love him and, as you say, make him laugh. You're an extraordinary woman, Ms. Jackson. I understand the prince's fascination with you."

She pushed her hair behind her ear. "No need for flattery. I'm going to need to leave Chantaine, aren't I?"

"I'm afraid so, ma'am," he said.

The realization slashed through her like a sharp knife, and pain twisted and thrust through her. She took a shallow breath and tried to think. Was this the right thing to do? Why did it feel wrong when her brain told her it was right? "I need to keep a commitment to Princess Bridget."

Gunter nodded. "Of course. Just try not to linger. A clean break will be easiest for all, including yourself."

"Not sure about that," she muttered.

"Thank you for meeting with me," he said, extending his hand. "I wish you every good thing in your future, and if there is anything I can do to assist you, please do call me."

With mixed feelings, she shook his hand and nodded. "I'm curious, sir. In your role as adviser, have you had to do this kind of thing often?"

"Don't quote me, but many times with Stefan's father. Never with Stefan. And never with such a high-quality individual as yourself. You made it difficult," he said and shook her hand. "Good luck, Ms. Jackson."

He turned and left, and Eve felt as if she'd cut out her heart and thrown it on the floor. Filled with confusion, she sank her head into her hands and tried to think of another way. Why did it have to be so hard for both of them? Why? she asked herself and her chest grew tight and her eyes burned with tears.

She loved Stefan. She had to do what was best for him. That meant leaving Chantaine.

That also meant she needed to get the horses in tip-top shape for the next stable master. In the meantime, she created a file of careful notes for each horse for her successor. She was determined to make the transition as seamless as possible. She reviewed the information with her assistants and spent extra time with them to ensure they understood what needed to be done for each horse.

She successfully avoided Stefan by burying herself in work at the stable, although she missed him and little Stephenia. Wednesday finally arrived and she dressed for the charity event with Princess Bridget.

Bridget picked her up in a limo. "I'm a little nervous," she said to Eve. "This is one of our disreputable neighborhoods. It's a bit dangerous," she said.

"I'm proud of you for stepping out of your comfort zone," Eve said.

Bridget widened her eyes at the compliment and lifted her chin. "Well, thank you. That's high praise coming from you."

Eve laughed. "What makes you say that?"

Bridget shrugged her shoulders. "You don't seem to be afraid of anything. I would like more of your courage."

Flattered and touched, Eve patted Bridget's hand. "You already have it. You just haven't used it very much. You would be surprised at what you can accomplish without me," Eve said.

Bridget stared at her curiously. "Whatever do you mean? That almost sounds like a goodbye and it bloody well better not be," she said. "Of course you're not leaving. You love the horses and me too much to leave," she said and laughed.

Eve couldn't find it in her to correct Bridget. Soon enough she would break the news. For now, she understood her role. Support Bridget during this appearance.

"I have some great clothes for this," she said. "I just hope it all comes together."

"Just be your encouraging self. I bet you'll be surprised at how well it goes," Eve said.

"You really believe that?" Bridget asked.

"I really do," Eve said.

Minutes later, they pulled in front of the old building that served as a community center. Eve noticed groups of young men hanging out on several corners and wondered if Chantaine had gang problems. She shook her head at the thought. Hopefully not.

Once inside, Bridget was introduced by the community center director and she delivered her speech. She also listed several scholarship opportunities and Eve helped to distribute information sheets and applications to the large group. Then the fun began. Bridget, Eve and several other volunteers helped the young women select outfits.

After two hours, it was time for Bridget and Eve to leave. Eve was pleased to see the expression of satisfaction and enthusiasm on Bridget's face.

"Can you believe how excited they were?" Bridget asked as they stepped outside the building to wait for the limo to make its way to the curb. "And not just about the clothes. They really seemed curious about the scholarship opportunities and—"

"Hey, Princess, must be nice living in the castle," a young man from a large group called as they moved closer. Too close, Eve thought. "When we have nothing."

Suddenly the group rushed them. From her peripheral vision, Eve saw Bridget freeze. Her guard was opening the limo door. Eve acted on pure instinct.

"Go!" she yelled at Bridget, giving her a hard push

toward the limo and throwing herself in front of the angry group. She felt a jab in her side. Pain rocked through her. Then, another in her chest. It took her breath. She caught the flash of the fist an instant before it hit her in the forehead. Then everything went blessedly black.

"There's been an emergency with the princess, sir," his aide, Pete, said, pulling him from a meeting with a top state official.

"Emergency?" Stefan echoed, his heart sinking. "Who? Bridget or—"

"Princess Bridget, sir," his aide said, clearly trying to keep his composure. "There was some sort of stampede at the event she and Ms. Jackson attended this afternoon."

"Eve," he said, feeling his gut clench with fear. "I need details immediately," he demanded.

"I have an incoming call from the princess," his aide said, touching the Bluetooth on his ear. "Princess Bridget wants to speak with you," he said, handing Stefan his phone.

"Stefan, she was crushed," Bridget said, sobbing. "That gang came out of nowhere and rushed us. She pushed me away and stepped in front of me and there was nothing I could do," she said, sobbing between phrases.

His blood turned to ice. "Where is she?" he asked.

"On the way to the hospital." Her voice broke. "Oh, Stefan, what if she doesn't make it? What if she—"

"You can't think that way. We don't have enough information. Eve is an incredibly strong woman." He was talking to himself more so than to Bridget, coaching himself not to think the worst.

"Oh, God, I hope so. Before we arrived, she was trying to boost my confidence. It was almost like she knew she was leaving," Bridget said, her voice full of misery.

"Leaving?" he said and shook his head. "I don't know what you're talking about, Bridget. Are you sure you are okay?"

"Yes, yes, I'm fine," she said. "But Eve isn't."

"I'm going to the hospital. I'll give you an update as soon as I hear anything," he said.

"I want to go," she said.

"You need to calm down," he said. "You're in no state to be going to the hospital. I'll call you. I promise. And Bridget," he said, "I'm very, very glad you're safe."

"I love you, Stefan."

"I love you, too," he said and disconnected the phone. Pete was waiting for instructions. "Call the driver and tell him I want to leave for the hospital immediately. I'll tell Mr. Vincent that I need to reschedule the meeting."

Although it was mere moments before Stefan walked into the hospital, it had felt like hours. His mind was racing furiously. He'd called to get an update on Eve's condition and he was told the doctors were working on her and that she was unconscious. Because of her head injuries, they were concerned about swelling.

Upon entering the hospital, he was led to a private room to wait. He called Bridget to give her his limited update and was pleased to learn that she had calmed down a bit. She wanted to come to the hospital and he told her there was no use. Even he wasn't allowed to see Eve right now.

The knowledge burned a hole inside him. He paced the room and spoke with the police about the gang that had stampeded Eve. Several members were already in custody. That brought him little comfort.

Stunned that his lungs were working and that his body was performing almost normally, he couldn't remember feeling this kind of sheer terror at losing someone before. She couldn't die. He couldn't lose her.

She was the one woman who had wanted him for himself and for no other reason. She had defended him and his interests at every opportunity. She had stolen his heart.

Until now, Stefan had chosen not to project far into the future about his relationship with Eve. His position complicated things. The only thing he'd known was that he wanted to keep her as his lover and friend. Now that wasn't enough. The realization was life-changing. The advisers could go hang for all he cared. Some part of him must have known from the first time he met Eve that she was his destiny.

Staring out the window at the sunny day, he fought an overwhelming bleakness inside him. What if he'd waited too long? What if he could have somehow prevented this? God help him, he didn't know what he would do if she didn't make it.

Chapter Twelve

"**Y**our Royal Highness," Stefan's aide said. "The doctor is here to speak with you."

"Please send him in immediately," he said.

The doctor, a middle-aged man, strode inside and the door was closed behind him. "Your Highness," he said with a quick dip of his head. "Ms. Jackson arrived with multiple lacerations, broken ribs and internal bruising. Her spleen was ruptured and had to be removed. She has also suffered a severe concussion and we're watching her for swelling. She hasn't regained consciousness since she arrived, but with the loss of blood and surgery, that's to be expected. Her condition is serious, but stable. We'll be keeping her in ICU until further evaluation."

"I must see her," Stefan said, reeling from the list of her injuries.

The doctor gave a slight grimace. "I'm not sure that's

a good idea, sir. Her face is bruised and swollen and as I told you, she's unconscious."

"I must see her," Stefan repeated, clenching his jaw.

The doctor gave a slow nod. "As you wish," he said. "Please come this way."

Stefan followed the doctor to a different floor and stepped inside the doorway of the room where Eve was surrounded by beeping machines. The sight of her in such a fragile state ripped him in half. She was so strong, so vibrant, yet now it appeared as if she were barely alive. A knot formed in the back of his throat and he forcibly swallowed it down. Her face was swollen. One of her eyes was purple.

Anger and horror built up inside him. Who could have done this to her? Why? What had she done except help his sister? In some part of his mind, he noticed that he'd clenched his fists. He deliberately released them and moved closer to her.

"May I touch her?" he asked the nurse writing on a chart just before she left the room.

"Yes. Gently," she said. "Just don't compromise her tubes or monitors."

He nodded. "Okay." Carefully, he touched the part of her arm that wasn't connected to an IV. "Eve," he said. "Hang on. I'm going to take care of you." He lifted his hand to her cheek where she wasn't swollen. "I love you. Hang on, darling. Please, hang on."

Stefan instructed his aide to update Bridget and Phillipa, and also to make sure the barns were covered. He hesitated making the call to the States to Eve's aunt because he was hoping that each passing hour would bring more hopeful news. But Eve remained unconscious. She was so still, so pale. It broke his heart to think of the pain she must have suffered when she'd stepped in front of Bridget.

He decided to stay through the night. His senior adviser, Tomas, attempted to call him repeatedly, but Stefan ignored the calls. If there were a true national emergency, then his aide would inform him. He sat in the chair next to her bed, watching her, willing her to wake up.

The next morning, she still didn't awaken. Frustration and fear battled inside him. She reminded him of a fairy-tale princess cursed to sleep.

"Is there anything else you can do?" he asked the doctor the next morning.

"We can decrease her pain medication, but we have to bear in mind that she's also recovering from emergency surgery. I know it's difficult, but sleep is giving her time to heal without being in pain. Perhaps you should go back to the palace and get some rest."

Stefan shook his head and continued his vigil next to her bed. Just after three o'clock that afternoon, he saw her stir slightly. Springing to his feet, he reached out to touch her hand. "Eve. It's Stefan. I'm here for you. We're taking care of you."

Her eyes flickered and his heart stuttered. She winced slightly and sighed, then relaxed again. "Nurse," he called just outside the room. "She moved her eyelids."

The nurse rushed inside and checked her vital signs. "Her heart rate has picked up a little. Our girl may be waking up soon," she said and smiled. "I'll check back in a while."

Still unable to relax, he paced the small room and checked on her every other minute. He took a call from Bridget and reluctantly agreed to allow her to visit later in the evening. Fifteen minutes after the nurse checked Eve's vital signs, his security guard tapped on the door.

"Pardon me, Your Highness, but one of your senior advisers wishes to see you," he said.

"Here?" Stefan asked. "He's here in the hospital?"

"He's actually waiting just outside the ICU," he said. "I can tell him you're not available, sir."

Stefan shook his head impatiently. "No, I'll give him two minutes, then be done with it," he said and strode to the hallway.

"Your Royal Highness, I've been trying to reach you all day," Tomas Gunter said.

"As you can see, we've had an emergency and Ms. Jackson has been seriously injured. What is so important that it couldn't wait until I return to the palace?" Stefan demanded.

The adviser opened his mouth, then closed it. "Sir, I believe it's best if we speak in private."

"If you can't tell me now, then it can wait," Stefan said. "Call my aide for assistance in the meantime."

Tomas shifted from one foot to the other. "Sir, as one of you senior advisers, I must tell you that your prolonged presence at the hospital is raising suspicions about your relationship with Ms. Jackson."

"And?" Stefan asked.

The adviser blinked. "Well, it isn't good for the image you've said you want to maintain to get involved with one of your staff," he said in a lowered voice.

Stefan resisted the urge to roar. "I don't give a bloody damn about my image at the moment. At the moment, the woman I love is fighting for her life. Nothing is more important. Do you understand?"

The adviser pressed his lips together. "Then you should know, sir, that Ms. Jackson had intentions of leaving Chantaine. She remained to fulfill her obligation to Princess Bridget, but she was going to leave as soon as possible."

Stefan felt as if he'd been punched. "How do you know this?"

The adviser swallowed. "I took the liberty of speaking with Ms. Jackson. I explained your goals and the importance of your reputation. She agreed that she wanted only the best for you and didn't want to be a distraction from your purpose as Crown Prince of Chantaine."

Stunned, Stefan stared at the man. "You told Eve to leave Chantaine?" he asked, trying to wrap his head around it.

"She agreed that she didn't want to compromise your future or effectiveness," the adviser insisted. "I did what I thought was best for Chantaine."

Stefan's surprise quickly turned to anger. "You overstepped your position," he said. "What gives you the right to interfere in my relationships, particularly without my foreknowledge?"

"I am your senior adviser," he said, puffing himself up and lifting his chin.

"Were," Stefan said, making an immediate decision. "You're relieved of your duties. Consider yourself dismissed."

Now Tomas looked stunned. "But, sir, I have served as an adviser since your father's reign."

"You clearly need a break," Stefan said in a crisp voice.

"You're not thinking clearly. Especially since Ms. Jackson is injured. Time will pass and you'll see that letting her return to the States is the correct path," the adviser continued.

"Not in my lifetime," he said. "You may leave."

"You'll regret this," Tomas said. "The people of Chantaine will never accept her. She has no title. She brings nothing to our people."

"How about heart, empathy and courage?" Stefan demanded, feeling his blood boil. He ached to smash his fist into the adviser's face. Glancing at his guard, he waved for him to approach.

"Please make sure Mr. Gunter is escorted to the lobby," he said, and then he returned to Eve's room.

His heart pounded with pure fury. He couldn't believe the gall of the adviser. To directly take such an action behind his back. Dismissing the man didn't seem punishment enough for what he'd done. He was tempted to strip Gunter of his previous royal commendation honors.

What must Eve have thought when she was approached by him? He wondered if she'd thought Stefan had sent him. His gut churned with the thought. He couldn't blame her for wanting to leave if she was going to have to deal with men like Gunter.

Still flaming with anger, he closed his eyes and took deep calming breaths. He suspected he would never get over his fury with the man, but for Eve's sake, he needed to get himself under control. How could he be there for her if he was ready to rip off his adviser's head?

He heard a slight rustle and turned to look at the bed. She rolled her head from one side to the other and moaned as if in pain. Rushing to the bed, he covered her hand with his. "Eve, it's Stefan. I'm here. I'm here."

She wrinkled her brow and shook her head again, fluttering her eyelashes. She blinked several times and stared at him as if she were trying to focus. "Stefan," she said in a hoarse voice. She winced again.

"What, darling? What is it?"

"Why do I feel like I've been run over by a truck?" she managed, then closed her eyes. Her face contorted in pain. "It hurts to breathe."

"That's because of your broken ribs. Rest," he said, and then punched the button for the nurse.

"My head," she said.

"Concussion," he said.

"And my gut."

"They had to remove your spleen," he said and gently touched her cheek. "Eve, I need you to know that I love you."

She grimaced again. "Oh, sweetie, that's not a good idea."

"But—"

The nurse swished into the room. "You're back, darling. The doctor will be pleased with the news. Let me check your vitals. I bet you're feeling a little rough, aren't you?"

Eve nodded and gave a pathetic sounding moan that wrenched at Stefan's gut. "She's in terrible pain," he said.

"Drugs," Eve said. "Or just shoot me."

The nurse made a *tsk*-ing sound and injected some medication directly into Eve's IV. "You poor, brave girl. This should make you feel better soon. Now rest."

Eve closed her eyes and her face gradually relaxed. Her breathing fell into a gentle rhythm.

Stefan was so relieved he sank into the chair beside the bed. "Thank God," he said.

The nurse nodded. "She's a strong woman. She's going to need to let someone else be strong for her for a while."

"She'll have that in spades," he assured the nurse.

Just as the nurse left, Bridget tiptoed into the room. "How is she?" she asked.

"Better," he said, standing to give her a hug. "She awakened for a few minutes a while ago."

Bridget's eyes lifted up. "Oh, that's wonderful. Did she talk? What did she say?"

Stefan rubbed his chin and shook his head. "She asked to be shot," he said.

Bridget bit her lip and turned to look at Eve. "Oh, my. Look at the bruises. Her eye is so swollen."

"I warned you," he said.

"I know. I just didn't realize." Bridget adjusted the sheet slightly. "It's so odd seeing her this helpless. I can't help feeling this is my fault. If I hadn't begged her to attend the event with me…"

"Then who knows what would have happened to you?" he asked, even though he understood Bridget's guilt. He had a share of his own guilt and he'd had nothing to do with the event or Eve's attendance.

"She's been such a wonderful friend to me since she arrived. Even though she's busy with your horses and doesn't party much," she said. "Being around her just made me feel—I don't know—stronger, more capable somehow. I don't know how to explain it. Please tell me her injuries will heal."

"They should," Stefan said. "They better."

Bridget glanced at him. "You're exhausted. You should go home now."

He shook his head. "I'm not ready."

She frowned. "I realize you probably feel responsible for her because you brought her to Chantaine and she has no family here, but you don't have to stay here. I can take a turn. Phillipa can, too."

"I do need to stay," he said and met Bridget's gaze. "Because I'm in love with her."

Bridget dropped her jaw and for once was speechless.

After her brief silence, she peppered him with questions, which he refused to answer. "I've told you more than anyone else knows," he said. "That's all I have to say. Right now, I'm focused on making sure Eve progresses."

Bridget studied him thoughtfully and giggled. "Well, now I understand why she wasn't at all thrilled when I was showing her photographs of the women I wanted to match up with you."

"You're not to tease her," he said sternly. "She's been through enough. What she needs right now is kindness and medication. In the meantime, give my daughter a kiss for me."

After Bridget left, Stefan stayed through the night, but he dozed off a couple of times. In the early hours, just as dawn was breaking, he opened his eyes to find Eve looking at him. Immediately rising, he went to her bedside. "How are you?"

"Floaty," she said. "If I breathe very slowly, I don't feel like screaming. My head is still—" She broke off. "Ugh."

"Can I get something for you?" he asked.

She shook her head and frowned. "Oooh, that was a mistake. No, thank you," she said in a low, hoarse voice. "How long have you been here?"

"Almost two days," he said, studying her, wanting to assure her and himself that she would be okay.

Her eyes widened. "Wow. I've been out that long?"

"You had surgery, too," he said.

"Oh. Forgot about that." She yawned and clearly

regretted it by the expression on her face. "You can go home now. I'm going to be okay."

He smiled at the way he'd given her permission. "I don't want to go home until you and I reach an agreement."

"About what?"

"About your staying in Chantaine," he said, then looked away as he tried to find the right words. "I've fallen in love with you and I need you to stay. I need and want you in my life. I realize that I'm asking a lot from a woman as independent-minded as you, but I am who I am. I have responsibilities that I can't shirk, but I don't want to live my life without you. What I'm saying is," he said, turning to face her, "I want you to—" He broke off when he saw that his heartfelt marriage proposal was falling on deaf ears. Eve had fallen back asleep.

Eve turned a corner that day and began a dramatic improvement. At least, other people considered it dramatic. She still hurt like hell every time she even thought about moving. And no one had let her near a mirror. That bothered her when she thought about it, but Bridget pooh-poohed her concerns and gently brushed her hair. Phillipa gave her reports on Stephenia. Stefan spent far too much time with her. She didn't know how she was going to tell them all that she was leaving, but she had to do it.

The day she was to be released from the hospital, Bridget arrived and applied makeup and fixed her hair. After she left, Stefan came to see her.

"You shouldn't be here," she told him. "People are going to start getting suspicious and then there will be rumors."

"No one is suspicious and there won't be rumors because we're getting married," he said.

She gaped at him. "Excuse me? Have you lost your mind? You can't marry me. I'm a commoner. I'm an American. I'm—"

"The woman I love." He wrinkled his brow. "We already discussed this. Don't you remember?"

"Remember what?" she said, searching her rusty brain. Surely she would remember this kind of conversation.

"I told you that I love you and want you by my side. I don't want to imagine my life without you. I realize being princess of Chantaine may not have been in your game plan, but I'll try to make it worth your while. I'll do my best to make you happy," he said, lifting her hand to his lips.

Her heart twisted with emotion. "Oh, Stefan, I can't. I can't do it to you. I can't do it to your future. I'll ruin you," she said and couldn't fight the tears burning her eyes.

"If what you're doing is ruining me, then do your best, sweetheart. I feel as if I'm a different man with you, and I like who that man is."

Trying to banish her hopes, she shook her head. "But you should marry someone who can help Chantaine."

"You do that," he said. "You already have."

"I mean in terms of connection or title. I really must leave Chantaine," she said.

"You need to forget that poisonous conversation you had with my senior adviser. He's been dismissed."

She gasped. "No."

"Yes. He's lucky I didn't do worse. I wanted to," he said, anger lighting his eyes. He clenched his jaw, then appeared to calm himself. "That's in the past. You and I need to concentrate on the future. You agreed to marry me, so it's settled."

She shook her head. "I did no such thing. When did we have this discussion?"

"A couple of days ago," he said nonchalantly.

She narrowed her eyes. "I was drugged. You're trying to hold me accountable for something I said when I was drugged. You're insane."

He leaned toward her, his gaze making her heart stop and stutter. "Tell the truth. Do you love me?"

She opened her mouth to protest, to lie, but the word stuck in her throat.

"Where's your courage, Eve? You face down a gang of villains for my sister, but you can't admit your feelings for me?" he challenged.

She glanced out the window, searching for strength. Her chest felt so tight she could barely stand it. "When you put it that way," she said. "I do love you. In a perfect world, I would love to be with you, but it's not a perfect world. And I don't want to mess up your destiny."

She felt his fingertips on her chin as he guided her to look at him. "You are my destiny," he said. "I know it will sometimes be difficult, but together I think we can face anything."

"I really don't see how this is going to work," she said, her eyes growing wet again. "I'm not princess material. Your people will never accept me."

"Trust me. They will," he said. "Marry me and it will be the ride of your life."

She couldn't possibly say yes. She couldn't. It would be insane, crazy… She couldn't possibly say no. "Yes," she said. "I will."

He kissed her gently and Eve clung to his hand, still not certain she'd done the right thing.

A nurse's aide arrived with a wheelchair. "Ready?" she asked.

Stefan patted beneath Eve's eyes. "You may want to check a mirror to repair—"

"Oh, the makeup," she said. "I need a mirror, please."

"Just a second," the aide said and quickly returned with a mirror.

Eve looked into it and swallowed a scream. "Oh, my God. I look like a monster."

"The swelling will go down," Stefan assured her. "You haven't seen your face before?"

"No, and I don't want to look at it again anytime soon. I need a very large pair of sunglasses," she said, setting the mirror facedown on the bedside table.

The kind aide managed to find a couple pairs of sunglasses for Eve. She chose the larger of the two and carefully placed them on her nose. The aide wheeled her down to the hospital lobby. "I hope you're ready for your fans."

"Fans?" Eve echoed and looked up at Stefan. "What fans?"

The front door opened and a large crowd applauded. Stunned, she looked at Stefan. "What is this?"

"You are Chantaine's brave heroine. My people love you," he said, helping her to stand. They walked toward the limo and were showered with rose petals.

"Viva Eve. Viva Eve," the crowd shouted.

Overwhelmed, Eve felt her eyes well with tears yet again. She bit her lip and waved, then threw a kiss.

"Just like a pro," Stefan said as they both got inside the car. "You handled your first royal appearance just like a pro."

Epilogue

Seven months later, Eve stood in an upper room of Chantaine's most historic chapel dressed in a wedding gown with a train so long it could have won a place in the Guinness World Records. She had thought it was over the top, but Bridget had insisted that the people of Chantaine wanted a grand dress for the bride of their prince. Eve was going to do her best to enjoy the affair. After all, she and Stefan had already made their own vows during a private ceremony just between the two of them. Today was a state occasion, and since she was going to be doing the princess thing, she was going to have to get used to state affairs. It was part of her role as wife to Stefan.

Even though she barely recognized herself when she glanced in the mirror, she knew Stefan was worth it all. Her hair was pulled up in front and the back of it flowed past her shoulders in waves highlighted with tiny baby's breath. The veil she wore was made of the finest Venetian lace, but crafted by local seamstresses. Her dress had also been designed by a up-and-coming local designer.

Her jewelry designer was also homegrown in Chantaine. The pearl-and-diamond drop earrings and choker had been created to complement the centuries-old tiara on her head.

"People still can't stop talking about your insistence to use only Chantaine's designers for your entire wedding. You could have had the most exquisite couture," Bridget said wistfully.

"I think our citizens did a great job. I didn't know I would be causing such a stir when I made the decision," Eve said to the small group of loving women assembled in the room with her.

Hildie, her aunt, just nodded in approval. "Practical choice. Why go to another country when you've got folks here who can do a good job?" Her aunt's face softened and she dabbed at her eyes. "Besides, she looks beautiful."

Seeing her aunt well up with emotion made Eve's heart constrict. Hildie had been there for her when no one else had been. She'd inspired her to reach beyond her situation, and Eve counted her as a huge influence on her success and confidence. Ignoring the gown, she moved to Hildie's side and hugged the woman. "Thank you for everything you've done for me. I just hope I can always make you proud."

Hildie squeezed her, then pulled back and blew her nose. "You always have."

Valentina stepped closer. "I wanted to give you this as something borrowed," she said, pressing a handkerchief into her hand. "It belonged to my great-great-great-grandmother," she said and rubbed her cheek against Eve's. "I'm so happy for you and Stefan. I can only hope that the two of you will have as much happiness as Zachary and I do."

"Thank you, Tina. The first time I met your brother, I never would have believed I would fall in love with him."

"We're all glad you did," Phillipa said. "He's a different person since you came to Chantaine."

"Thank goodness for that," Bridget muttered, then smiled. "He's happy. You're happy. The baby's happy. Now if I can finally get my year in Italy…"

Eve lifted her hands in surrender and laughed. "Not my area," she said. "You and Stefan will have to negotiate that one."

A knock sounded at the door and Bridget ran to open it a crack. Since the ugly stampede all those months ago, Bridget had become very protective of Eve. "Oh, it's you," she said excitedly. "Just a second," she said and closed the door. "Stefan's wedding gift for Eve has arrived."

"Wedding gift?" Eve said. "He already gave me a new foal."

Bridget clasped her hands together in excitement. "This gift is a little different," she said and opened the door again. A tall man stepped through the doorway and Eve felt shock waves roll through her. For the first time in almost fifteen years, she was looking at her brother Eli. She struggled with disbelief at the same time she drank in the sight of him. He was older and broader than the slight teenager she remembered. His eyes held a few character lines, but the love she saw in his eyes was the same as always.

Heedless of her gown, she raced toward him and

put her arms around his neck. "Eli, you're here. I can't believe it! I can't believe it. How did he find you?"

"Let's just say your husband-to-be is one determined son of a gun. After I left, I sent you letters, but when I didn't hear back, I figured you didn't want anything to do with me."

A knot formed in Eve's throat. "I didn't receive any letters," she said.

"That's what I figured, after Stefan tracked me down. I didn't come here to spend your wedding day talking about me, though. I came because I wanted to be here on one of the most important days of your life. I've missed a lot of other ones and I didn't want to miss this one, too."

"I'm so glad you came. So glad you're here. We will get a chance to talk, won't we?" she insisted.

"Not as much today, but I've already promised to pay another visit after you get back from your honeymoon. You're beautiful inside and out, Evie. I couldn't be more proud of you. I'm gonna head out now. I'll see you on the other side," he said with a smile and a wink.

She kissed his cheek and stared at the door after he left, her eyes burning with tears. "I'm marrying the most amazing man in the world," she said, then turned to look at the women surrounding them. Each of them was dabbing her eyes or sniffing.

Bridget was the first to recover. "Enough," she said. "Now I must touch up your makeup." Eve was fussed over and hugged, then suddenly the women left and she was alone, filled with nerves and anticipation. Sometimes she still couldn't believe all that happened, that *she* of all people was going to be a princess and do princess things. Stefan had encouraged her to adapt the role to her personality. There was going to be some give and take, such as the elaborate dress she wore today, but Eve had begun to fall in love with the people of Chantaine, so stepping outside of her comfort zone to help make the citizens happy didn't bother her as much as it once had.

A knock sounded at the door and her heart leaped. "Yes?" she said, walking toward it.

The mistress of ceremonies opened the door and nodded in approval. "You look beautiful, the most beautiful bride I've ever seen. It's time. Are you ready?"

Eve's stomach dipped. "Yes," she said, then followed the women to the foyer of the beautiful church. An orchestra swelled, signaling her to walk down the aisle. Eve took her first steps and immediately found Stefan with her gaze. She knew people would be staring at her, watching her, and her nerves could possibly overwhelm her. Looking at Stefan gave her courage.

She walked all the way down the aisle and he took her hands and greeted her with a kiss. "How is the light of my life today?" he whispered.

"Happy and excited, Your Highlyness," she said.

Stefan smiled. "After today, when you are crowned princess, I'll be saying the same thing to you. I love you, Your Highlyness-to-be."

*****

THE RELUCTANT PRINCESS

BY
RAYE MORGAN

All the characters in this book have no existence outside the imagination of
the author, and have no relation whatsoever to anyone bearing the same name
or names. They are not even distantly inspired by any individual known or
unknown to the author, and all the incidents are pure invention.

First published in Great Britain 2012
by Mills & Boon, an imprint of Harlequin (UK) Limited,
Eton House, 18-24 Paradise Road, Richmond, Surrey TW9 1SR

© Helen Conrad 2012

ISBN: 978 0 263 89400 4

23-0112

Harlequin (UK) policy is to use papers that are natural, renewable and
recyclable products and made from wood grown in sustainable forests. The
logging and manufacturing processes conform to the legal environmental
regulations of the country of origin.

Printed and bound in Spain
by Blackprint CPI, Barcelona

Dear Reader,

So what's so great about royalty, anyway? They're just people who happen to be born into a situation a little luckier than the rest of us. They're not usually any better looking than we are. They're definitely not any smarter. Or more talented. Or kinder, or better or harder working. So why do we care about them?

And we do. They fascinate us. From earliest childhood we listen to fairy-tale stories of handsome, heroic princes rescuing beautiful princesses from dark towers. We look at them and hope to see how a charmed set of people, elevated above everyday concerns, operates on a higher level than the one we inhabit.

The funny thing is, they so often disappoint us. They don't always slay the dragon, or rescue the captive hero, or protect the orphaned children from the witch. But they always seem to be running around in exotic locations, wearing stunning clothes and being treated like the celebrities they are. And all that just for being born into royalty.

So we watch with wide eyes and imagine what it would be like to live like that. They may not be any better than we are, but they certainly seem to be having more fun!

Long live fairy tales!

Raye Morgan

Raye Morgan has been a nursery school teacher, a travel agent, a clerk and a business editor, but her best job ever has been writing romances—and fostering romance in her own family at the same time. Current score: two boys married, two more to go. Raye has published over seventy romances and claims to have many more waiting in the wings. She lives in Southern California with her husband and whichever son happens to be staying at home at the moment.

This book is dedicated to Lauri and her two little princesses, Kirsten and Kate.

CHAPTER ONE

KIM GUILDER stared out the bus window into the intense eyes of the stranger in the long leather coat. He was coming down the wide, stone stairway from the hospital administration building, moving like a man with a purpose, headed straight at her.

Her heart lurched and she looked quickly at the bus driver. Would he wait? Would the man make the bus?

But no. Relief filled her as the bus began to pull away from the curb. She reached out to steady herself on the handrail as it lurched into high speed. She looked back at the stalker, feeling a strange sense of triumph. He stood very still, staring after her. There was no way he could stop the bus, no way he could catch it and climb aboard. But she shivered in a quick attack of irrational fear anyway.

She didn't know him. She didn't think she'd ever seen him before. But he knew her. The way he'd been coming down those stairs when she'd looked up and caught sight of him, the way his eyes had blazed at her, she'd known right away he was trying to catch her. And she even thought she knew why.

She glanced around at the other passengers, wondering if anyone had noticed what had just happened. No one looked up except a little girl with bouncing red curls, sucking her thumb. The child stared at Kim, but dully, without significance.

Kim took a deep breath and tried to settle her pulse rate. What was she worried about, anyway? He'd caught sight of her there in that public area and obviously he'd recognized her right away. But that had to be pure co-incidence. He couldn't possibly know where she was going or even the location of the rooms she was staying in right now. But something told her he would try.

Maybe she'd better find another place to stay, quickly. Maybe she should just race back to the rooms, grab her baby, and go.

But go where? It was coming down to that. There weren't many places left to run to.

She glanced back toward where they'd come from with a new spurt of adrenaline, suddenly wondering if he could find a way to follow the bus. No, how could he? It was almost impossible to find a taxi in this town, so unless he'd leaped up at the last minute and was cling-ing to the roof like an action hero, he had no hope.

So why wouldn't the butterflies in her stomach settle down? She looked out at the darkened streets. It was starting to snow. Half the streetlights were out, just an-other consequence of the recent war. But some optimis-tic souls had strung up Christmas lights here and there. It wasn't exactly cheerful, but it was a sign of survival.

She pulled her fake-fur coat more tightly around her and tried a couple of cleansing breaths, waiting, hoping, to feel a bit of calm return. She knew this was crazy. A man she didn't even know had picked up her world and tossed it into chaos for a moment or two. She couldn't let that sort of thing happen. She had a baby to think of.

But where had he come from so suddenly? His face,

his eyes, they looked so familiar. She didn't know who he was, but she knew two things about him: he knew exactly who she was, and he'd been sent by the Ambrian royal family, and that meant Pellea, who was now queen.

Pellea was one thing—this man was quite another. Those icy spikes of fear she'd felt were a direct response to the animosity in his eyes. He'd never met her before and he already hated her. What did that tell you about the relationship she had with the royal family?

It hadn't always been like that, at least, not with Pellea. They'd been best friends most of their lives, pampered children of the Granvilli regime which had toppled the royal family before they were born. And then Pellea fell in love with Crown Prince Monte DeAngelis and helped him invade the island, restoring the monarchy. And Kim was left behind to pick up the pieces and mend the fences—and take the brunt of the anger when the Granvillis began to lose.

Her stop was just ahead. She rose, hanging on to the metal bar and moving toward the back exit. She looked out into the dark street behind. Headlights swooped by, making her heart lurch every time, but no one seemed to linger. She stared harder into the night. She couldn't help it. She just had a feeling....

The bus slowed to a stop at the side of the slippery road. It seemed to take forever for the door to open, and when it did, she took a deep breath and headed out into the snowy night.

"Hello, Kimmee," a deep voice spoke from just behind her.

She whirled, shock rocketing through her soul. It couldn't be him. It was impossible. And yet...

There he stood, tall and dark and terrifying.

Her first instinct was to run. He saw it in her eyes and his hand clamped down on her upper arm.

"I need to talk to you."

She looked around quickly, trying to find someone who might help her, but the bus was leaving, its red taillights staring back impassively. Even more chilling, though cars rushed past anonymously, the street was empty of pedestrians. There was no one to run to. Her heart pounded.

"Let me go," she gasped at him. "I'm going to scream. The police…"

"The police are hard to find these days and you know it," he told her dryly, his eyes glittering in the light from the street lamp. "Besides, you don't need them. I'm not here to hurt you. I was sent to give you some important information. Something that could change your life."

She thought quickly. He was probably telling the truth. He wasn't the first who had been sent to try to convince her to come back to the castle. Each one seemed to have a more fantastic story meant to lure her away.

But this was a bit different. This one didn't like her.

She looked up at him, studying his face for a stealthy moment. How could he look so familiar at the same time she was so sure she'd never seen him before? Odd.

He was ridiculously handsome, with even features and a square jaw that bespoke a lack of tolerance for nonsense. His eyes were crystal blue and penetrating, framed by lush dark lashes any beauty queen would commit outlandish crimes to get for herself. Still, there was no hint of softness, not even a trace of any sort of compassion or sensitivity.

Everything about him telegraphed strength and authority, even a sense of command. And every one of those elements only made her feel more rebellious.

Still, he was bigger than she was, stronger than she was, and right now, he had hold of her arm. She figured it was useless to try to get away. Better to play along until she saw her chance.

"Okay, change my life," she said a bit sarcastically, looking at where his long fingers held her prisoner. "Tell me quickly. I've got to go."

His hold on her tightened.

"Where are you going?" he asked.

Looking up, she met his cold gaze and managed to keep from flinching. That was a plus.

There was no way she could let him know where she was staying. The rooms she'd taken were only a block away. Dede, her nine-month-old baby, was there with a babysitter she didn't completely trust. She had to get back to her right away. But letting this hostile man tag along was an impossibility. She felt trapped.

"Just tell me this important information you have for me," she said, trying to look as hard as he did while wiping snowflakes off her cheeks and shaking them from her thick blond hair. "And I'll be on my way."

The faint twist of his wide mouth almost looked like a smile, but there was no sign of that in his cold blue eyes.

"No chance," he said, then glanced up and down the dark street. Most of the shabby stores were closed, but a small café on the corner looked open.

"Let's go in there," he said, jerking his head in the direction of the coffee shop. "I'll buy you something warm to drink."

She tensed, firming her resistance. Maybe if she

showed him she was no pushover he would tell her quickly and leave her alone. Maybe.

"I don't want a drink or anything else," she told him crisply. "I don't know who you are or where you came from. If you've got information for me, why don't you send it to me in a letter?" Her chin rose and she glared at him as fiercely as she knew how.

He searched her face impatiently, looking as though he were weighing the alternatives.

"I think you know very well that Pellea sent me," he said tersely.

He was right on that one. Pellea, the queen of the new, restored Ambrian monarchy, wanted her old best friend to come home to the castle for some reason. But she didn't seem to understand that it could never be home to Kim again. Her people, the Granvillis, had been driven out. The DeAngelis royals were in charge. There was no place for her there.

Still, Pellea didn't give up, and she kept sending people to try to lure Kim back. If she'd understood how deeply Kim's feelings of pain ran, if she had a clue how she resented the way she was treated toward the end, she might not have bothered.

Kim stared at the dark man and shook her head. She didn't have a lot of choice. She could stand here and scream at the top of her lungs, but he'd been right about the police. Since the end of the war, they were hard to find. Street crime was rampant. He could knock her on the head and drag her off into an alley before anyone even noticed, and from the look in his eyes, she had no doubt he wouldn't hesitate.

On the other hand, she could go with him to the coffee shop. It was a public place. He wouldn't do anything to her there. He could tell her his information, she could tell him why she didn't care, and hopefully, that would be that.

"All right," she said reluctantly. "Let's get this over with as quickly as possible."

His wide mouth twisted with a sort of mocking amusement at her words.

"Hold on a moment," he said, letting go of her arm and turning to snap a chain and lock on an ancient, crumbling motorcycle she hadn't noticed before, fastening it to the bus bench.

So that was how he'd caught her. She sighed, rocking on her heels, tempted to make a run for it now, while she had the opening—sort of—but just curious enough to give him a chance, at least for a few minutes.

Turning back, he tucked her hand into the crook of his arm in a familiar way she found utterly offensive, and escorted her into the coffee shop as though they made a habit of meeting this way.

She pulled her hand away as soon as she was able and slipped into a booth. He slid in across from her, holding her gaze with his own icy eyes. She stared back, feeling warmth begin to creep up her neck to her cheeks.

Why were his eyes so filled with accusations?

The coffee shop wasn't much at this point, but it had obviously been a trendy meeting place before the war. The remnants of the decor were still in place, looking shabby and worn, but still hopeful. A young girl who looked like she should have been home finishing up an assignment for her biology class came to take their order. She watched them brightly, her hair pulled into braids at either side of her head, and Kim smiled at her.

"I'll have a cup of tea," she said. "Herbal."

"Black coffee," he ground out. "Bold."

The girl nodded. "Nothing to eat?" she asked hopefully. "We have a lovely apple pie. The cook just took it out of the oven."

Now that she'd mentioned it, the scent of the pie was in the air. Kim breathed it in with pleasure, then caught the dark man's gaze and saw that he was doing the same thing.

Her eyes widened.

His narrowed.

Something electric snapped between them, shocking her. She wasn't sure if it was a sign of attraction or one of pure loathing and she looked away quickly, trying hard not to react.

But her heart pulsed. Was it fear? She didn't think so. But if not that…what?

She didn't even notice that he'd ordered them a piece of pie with vanilla ice cream and two forks until it appeared on the table along with their drinks.

That was just a little too friendly, wasn't it?

She looked up and met his gaze again. He was watching to see how she would react, and she flushed, looking back down. She thought about refusing to take a bite, but she knew that would seem churlish, and it did smell so good. She hadn't eaten all day. Could he hear her stomach rumble?

She looked at the luscious piece of pie. Steam was coming off the apples. The crust looked crisp and crumbling. The ice cream was just starting to melt around it.

Maybe just one bite. Or two.

They ate in silence. He very carefully only took his share and she wondered why. It was his pie, after all. She risked another glance at his face but his cold expression didn't tell her anything.

When every bit of pie was gone, he sighed with satisfaction and murmured, "That has got to be the best apple pie I've had since…"

He didn't go on and his mouth tightened. She wondered what painful memory had stopped him. So there was more to him than pure anger. That did make him seem a little more human.

The little café was warm. She opened her coat a bit, flushing as she noticed him looking at her nurse's uniform. She wasn't really a nurse, she just played one at the hospital, since actual nurses were in such short supply these days. But the uniform seemed to give people confidence.

"Tell me something," she said, looking at him directly. "Who are you?"

He took a deep breath before he answered. "I'm Jake Marallis. Pellea is my sister."

"Your sister!" She stared at him, surprised and not sure she believed him. "That's impossible. I've known Pellea all my life. She doesn't have a brother."

"Half brother." He shrugged. "My mother was married to her father before her mother was."

She thought that over quickly. It was possible, she supposed. But she knew she'd never seen him. Had Pellea ever mentioned him? Actually, now that she thought about it, she might have. She seemed to remember something….

"You never lived in the castle?"

"No. Not in the old days."

She studied his face. Yes, she could see it now. That was what was so familiar about him. The look in his eyes was just like Pellea's, even though his eyes were blue and hers were dark. How extraordinary.

"You know she wants you to come home." He said it

softly, as though testing the waters. And he got a quick reaction.

"Home!" She winced, looking inside, probing her own response. Did it still hurt as badly as it used to? Was the feeling of betrayal healing over yet? Not a chance.

"That castle will never be home to me again."

But to her surprise, her tone came out more wistful than angry. She frowned. Maybe she *was* softening. She would have to keep an eye on that.

He leaned back, his narrow gaze penetrating without a hint of sympathy.

"What keeps you away, Kimmee?"

She grimaced. It had been a long time since anyone had called her by that childhood nickname. "It's Kim now, not Kimmee. That name is from my old life."

He shrugged. "As you wish." He raised one dark eyebrow. "The question still stands. I know I'm not the first my sister has sent to find you. Why won't you come back?"

It was none of his business, and he probably only wanted to know so that he could use the information against her, but for some reason, she found herself telling him anyway.

"Come back to what?" she said. "I've lived my whole life as part of the Granvilli era. I've never been a subject of the DeAngelis monarchy. I never backed the invasion. Ambria has been torn apart by the war between these two factions. The DeAngelis royalty now has the castle in their possession." She lifted her chin and met his gaze defiantly. "Well, bully for them. I'm with the Granvillis. And I won't turn traitor and go back to the protection of the castle just to have an easier life."

He frowned as though he were trying to understand but couldn't quite get there.

"And yet, from what I've heard, you helped Pellea hide the DeAngelis crown prince in her chambers, nurturing their relationship. How does that fit into the picture?"

She flushed. How did one go about explaining all the regrets in one's life?

"I'm a romantic at heart. What can I say?" She shrugged. "It seemed like the thing to do at the time." She shook her head, looking off into the distance, and added softly, "Who knew it would start a war?"

He didn't speak for a long moment, watching her. Finally she drew her thoughts back to the present and looked at him again. He was taking a long sip of his hot coffee. She made a face.

"I see you're planning to stay up all night tonight," she said tartly.

"Not really. Caffeine rarely bothers me."

Too cold blooded, she guessed.

"Does anything bother you?"

His eyes flashed. "Oh yes, Kim. A great deal bothers me."

She leaned toward him, curious. "Like what?"

He looked at her, seeming to see more deeply into her eyes than people usually did. She pulled back again, uncomfortable at the scrutiny, but he shook his head.

"This conversation isn't about me."

She shrugged. "I'm just trying to figure you out." She pressed her lips together, frowning at him with narrowed eyes. "Are you the enforcer? Are you supposed to get a little rough with me? Maybe even apply a few caveman tactics?"

His gaze was as frosty as ever, and completely impenetrable. His mouth twisted but he didn't deign to answer her charge. Her heart began to thump in her chest. He wasn't denying it. Just how far was he prepared to go? She hoped she wouldn't have to find out.

"Did Pellea send you as a last resort?" She leaned forward again, staring into his eyes and adding coolly, "Are you really as mean as you look?"

His eyes flickered with a flash of surprise, which he quickly quelled. "I prefer the term *professional*," he muttered crisply.

Her eyes widened. "As in professional hit man?" she whispered.

His handsome face registered a quick sense of outrage, colored by a hint of disbelief. "Oh, for God's sake…"

"No." She put up a hand as though to stop him. "I don't think I'm being ridiculous. Pellea seems to be relentless. Why shouldn't her emissary be the same?"

He felt insulted by her charge, that much was plain. "I like to think I'm a reasonable man with logic on my side," he said through gritted teeth. His gaze narrowed. "I'm hoping to avoid strong-arm tactics."

"Oh. How comforting."

He looked as though he would like to give her a good shake, but he controlled himself. "Let's get back to the point."

She could tell her eyes were sparkling at him. She was actually enjoying this in a way. He'd started out thinking he could bully her, and now she had him tied up in conversation not of his own making. Ha!

She sparkled at him some more. "Back to things that bother you. I'll bet you hate all of my favorite things."

He was beginning to look bewildered. "I don't know what you're talking about."

"Let's give it a try. How about these?" She pretended to be thinking. "Snowflakes on noses and whiskers on kittens."

A shadow flitted through his gaze and she couldn't tell if he was annoyed or amused.

"It's raindrops on roses," he said in a growl. "And why would they bother me?"

"I don't know."

She hid her amusement carefully, though she knew her eyes were a dead giveaway. He'd admitted he knew those lyrics and that just made her want to laugh out loud.

"You just seem like a bit of a Grinch. On the surface, I mean."

A look flashed on his face that surprised her. She'd hit a nerve. Or something. But he covered it up quickly enough.

"The fact is, I like whiskers on kittens as much as the next man," he said gruffly.

"Which means not a whole lot." She gave him a cynical look.

He threw out a hand as though asking for a witness to her nonsensical talk. "So now you're anti-men?"

"Not really." She shook her head. "Just mean men."

"I'm not mean." He glanced up quickly, realizing others could hear his raised voice, and he moderated his tone as he looked her in the eye, and then forced himself to relax. "Okay, so maybe I'm a little…hard. A little serious."

He appeared uncomfortable with the topic and she hid a smile. It was pretty obvious he wasn't used to letting the conversation go off on a tangent he hadn't initiated.

"Just another way of saying mean," she said, just to

needle him. "I'll bet you've never made a superfluous gesture of pure romance in your life."

"I…" He stopped himself, swearing softly and shaking his head as he looked at her with exasperation. "How the hell did we start down this road?"

She shrugged. "Just saying."

"Back to the subject. Again."

She looked innocent. "And that is?"

"You." He leaned back, pinning her with his intense gaze. "Going back to the castle. Reuniting with your family."

"My family." She grimaced. "And who might that be?"

The anger was back in his eyes, the accusations. A chill went down her spine. She knew something was coming, something she wasn't going to like.

"Are you still with Leonardo?" he asked, his voice low and menacing.

The name made her jump, and she blinked rapidly. She hadn't expected that one.

Leonardo Granvilli was the current leader of the rebel regime which had ruled the island nation of Ambria for over twenty-five years. He and his forces had only recently lost their power when the DeAngelis royal family retook most of the island, leaving the Granvilli faction a small section to the north, including the mountain city of Tantarette, where Jake had found her. Here was where the remnants of the Granvilli army and the civilian refugees had gathered, their dreams of glory ground to dust.

"Leonardo?" she asked, stalling for time. "Why would I be with Leonardo?"

His lip curled. "Because he fathered your baby."

She swallowed hard. She hadn't realized that was

common knowledge. "You don't know what you're talking about," she told him, her voice ringing with confidence even though her fingers trembled.

"I know enough."

"Do you actually know Leonardo?" she asked quickly, before he could say anything else. "I mean, have you personally talked to him?"

"Yes."

She studied his eyes. They were cold as a winter's day on the river. That thread of fear she'd thought she'd conquered was back.

"They say to know him is to love him," she said softly, just probing a bit.

His eyes flashed one unguarded spark of anger and his lip curled. "They lie."

She almost gave a nervous smile. They could certainly agree on that, but she wasn't going to tell him so.

She glanced around the café. Except for one man sipping soup by the window and an elderly couple just finishing up their meal, they were the only ones in the place.

"Aren't you afraid of being recognized? You're on the wrong side of the boundary line."

"No one knows me here. I never spent much time in Ambria before the war."

"A stranger in a strange land," she murmured.

"There's only one person I know well over here," he said, watching her eyes. "Leonardo Granvilli. He and I have a history that goes way back."

Her mouth went dry. There was something chilling in the way he'd said that. She tried to remember if Leonardo had ever mentioned Pellea having a brother, but she couldn't come up with a thing. It wasn't that she didn't believe him. It was more that she hoped he was lying so she wouldn't have to care.

She glanced down at the empty plate the pie had come on. The waitress hadn't been back to take it away. She had a twinge of nostalgia for the few moments when they had first arrived, when it almost seemed they might be able to have a normal chat. That was gone now. The sense of his leashed antagonism was palpable. He despised her. She had to get away from him.

"Listen, we're wasting time," he said bluntly. "Here's the deal. I'm taking you back. Pellea needs you and I promised her I wouldn't come back without you."

The man was direct. Painfully so. There was no warmth, no humanity to him. Except for the superficial likeness, she could see nothing of Pellea there.

She shook her head as he spoke. "No."

"You have no choice any longer. The game's up, Kimmee—or Kim, as you prefer. Everyone knows the truth now about who you really are. It's your duty to come back."

"Who I really am?" She stared at him blankly. "What are you talking about?"

His mouth twitched impatiently. "The last messenger Pellea sent must have given you a hint. You're a DeAngelis. The youngest of your generation. Last of the royal babies. Sister to Monte and all the rest."

For a moment, she thought she'd heard him wrong. Then she wondered if he were joking. Finally, as the look in his face and the tone of his voice began to sink in, she realized he really meant what he was saying.

And suddenly, she felt as though she couldn't breathe, and would probably never be able to breathe again.

This couldn't be happening. It was too bizarre. But

she knew she had heard something like this before. The last one who'd come looking for her had babbled the same words, but she hadn't paid any attention. She knew they would do anything, say anything, to get her to come back, and she hadn't bought into it. She knew who her mother was. She'd been born in the castle to Queen Elineas's favorite lady-in-waiting a week before the Granvillis overthrew the DeAngelis monarchy. Everyone knew that.

Didn't they?

But where that last messenger had been easy to dismiss, this one wasn't. He didn't seem like a man who did much kidding around.

She shook her head harder, feeling sick. "No. Someone made that up. There's no truth to it. It's ridiculous."

He gave her an incredulous look. "Are you trying to tell me you're ready to reject a place in the royal family? Are you really that reckless?"

She was trembling. Her teeth began to chatter. He was telling her what he believed to be the truth. She could see it in his eyes. But it couldn't be true. To believe what he was saying would be to smash everything she'd depended on as reality for her whole life. It was too much.

"It can't be done, Kim. Once you're royal, you're royal. It's a very exclusive club, but you can't resign from it. There's no opting out. You're stuck with it."

She put her hand over her mouth and started to slide out of the booth. "I…I'm going to be sick," she mumbled to him as she hurried toward the bathroom.

He watched her go, then shook his head and picked up his coffee mug, draining the last of it.

And that was why it took him a moment to realize

something wasn't adding up. He frowned, turned his head, and uttered a very ugly oath as he leaped to his feet.

Kim hadn't made it into the bathroom. Obviously, that had never been her destination. Instead, she'd headed out the door and was now running as fast as she could for home.

CHAPTER TWO

KIM ran down the alley and then cut in to take a short cut through a vacant lot. She hadn't lived in that area long but she had taken Dede on enough baby carriage rides through the neighborhood to know a thing or two. She was running hard, but carefully. The snow was coming down harder and there were patches of black ice. She didn't want to slip.

Her heart was thumping in her throat and the air stung her lungs. Whatever she did, she couldn't lead him back to the building where her rooms were.

Jake Marallis terrified her. The others had been easy to brush off. He had no intention of being brushed. He had the cool, clear gaze of a man who thought he knew the truth, and that was one of the scariest things in the universe. He was hard. He was unrelenting. And that was why she had to make sure he never found her again.

The things he had told her were jarring, even chilling, and definitely uncomfortable. She didn't want to believe them. She wasn't going to believe them. Why should she? And even if they were true, she didn't want to do anything about it.

"Just leave me alone," she moaned to herself as she ran. She doubled back, finding another alley that he would never see in time. She headed away from the main street, hoping to lose him in the tangle of tiny dead-end lanes.

Then she would double back, grab Dede and go.

Go where? That was a question she couldn't deal with just yet.

She planned to go in the back entrance of her building, but only once she'd made sure he wasn't right behind her. Then she would take the stairs up to her rooms, being careful not to turn on any lights that might catch his attention, and she would pay the babysitter to stay on for an hour or so more, just to make sure he didn't see her leave. Yes, that was it. If she was very cautious, it should work.

She'd been running so hard, she couldn't breathe. She had to stop, leaning against a building, to catch her breath so she could make the final race count. For the first moment, she couldn't hear anything but her own ragged breathing. But as her breath caught up, she heard something else. Someone else was running across pavement. It had to be him.

Panic flared in her chest and she took off again. Her building was just ahead. She'd barely rounded the last corner when she heard a terrible sound, stopping her in her tracks. A car was skidding, probably on an icy patch. There was a crash, metal on stone, and then someone cried out. She heard the car backing up, then racing off, metal falling from it as it went. But there was no more sound of running feet.

She stood very still, holding her breath and saying a little prayer. "Please, no, don't let it be that."

A male voice groaned in the distance and her heart sank. It looked like her prayer had not been answered. There was a very good chance that Jake had been hit by a skidding car.

What now?

She listened for another few seconds. Would another car stop? Would someone run to his rescue? But she didn't hear any more cars. The whole area had an eerie silence to it, like a ghost town, as though the snow were blanketing all evidence of human activity. There was no one there...no one to come to his aid.

She stood very still, but her mind worked frantically. Could she leave him there? Could she run on home and try to find a phone and make an anonymous call to the police? Or the hospital? Could she really do that? How long would it be before they finally came to find him?

All night, probably.

She heard something else, like metal being moved, and then a gasp, as though he were trying to get up and was in pain. She looked around at the darkened buildings. Didn't anyone hear him? Wasn't anyone going to run down to see what had happened?

By now she was almost sure it was Jake. And he was hurt. Really hurt.

And she knew, heart sinking, that she couldn't just leave him. She was scared to death of the man, but she couldn't let him lie in the street after being hit by a car. She had to go back. He was Pellea's brother. She would have to deal with the consequences later.

She waited another moment, hoping against hope that she would hear someone going to see about him. But there was no one. She was going to have to do it.

Taking a deep breath, she turned and hurried toward where the noise had been coming from.

She saw him right away. He'd pulled himself out of the street and up onto the curb, but he looked in bad shape. There was a bloody scrape across the whole left side of his face and the set of his left leg looked awkward. As she reached him, he looked up with hugely dilated eyes and didn't seem to recognize who she was.

"I...the car...."

"Hush," she said, holding back her own anxiety. "Let me take a look."

She was no medical professional but she had been working part-time as a nurse's aide at the hospital, both here and at her usual home by the shore. She'd seen more broken and wounded men from the war than she would have ever hoped to see in her lifetime, and she had some idea of what to look for.

Though his leg looked oddly askew, she was pretty sure his bones weren't broken, at least not in an obvious way. She was more worried about his groggy behavior. He still didn't seem to know her. After a quick examination, she sat back and looked at him. Now what?

One thing was certain—she couldn't just leave him here in the street. That whole running away and hiding from him scenario was by the boards.

On the other hand, he was hurt and it wouldn't be so easy for him to force her to do what he wanted now. Was it really the balanced situation she was presenting herself with? Maybe, maybe not. But she knew, as long as he could make it, she was going to take him to her apartment. What else could she do?

"Come on," she said, helping him up as he grimaced painfully, favoring the crooked leg and gasping as they began to move. "Lean on me. I'm going to take you home."

It took longer than she'd expected, but she managed to maneuver him into the elevator and take him up to her third floor set of rooms. She tried to ignore the blood he was dripping from a gash in his chin. Hopefully she would be able to get back and clean it all up later. Trying to take up as much of his weight as she could, she got him to the door of her apartment, and then inside and onto the couch.

Kristi, the babysitter, was surprised, but Kim quickly paid her off and sent her home. And then she stood and stared at the long, lean man who had dropped into the center of her life.

Dede was asleep. Jake was awake, but not really coherent. She was worried that he might have been hit harder than she'd thought at first. Reaching out, she felt his forehead. Cold and clammy. From the little she knew about such things, she didn't think that was good.

She looked down at his stark, handsome face, and her stomach did a little somersault dance. She was afraid of the man, and yet there was something so compelling about his dark, brooding looks, even with the injuries. She bit her lip and wondered if this was how some women ended up with men who were all wrong for them.

"Taking home strays," she murmured, shaking her head. "It'll come back to bite you every time."

That made her laugh a bit. If anyone was the stray here, it was her. He was a thoroughbred, through and through. Looks like that were never deceiving.

She knew very well there was no point in trying to make a call for a doctor or the hospital. The war had done its damage to modern communications on the island. The few cell phone towers they'd once had were bombed during the fighting and what land lines anyone had left rarely worked.

And even if you could get through, medical help was in short supply these days. You were lucky if you could find a physician even at the hospital where she worked.

The most competent ones had left for the winning side of the war long since, and the ones who'd stayed were haggard with overwork.

Unless she could think of some miracle, fast, she was on her own.

She did the best she could cleaning him up. Dede woke up and fussed a bit, so she alternated between her baby and the vagabond she'd brought home. Soaking a clean cloth in cool water, she wiped the blood from the scrapes across his face, then dabbed at them with hydrogen peroxide, working carefully around the gash on his chin.

He was in pain but he'd lost the grogginess that she was pretty sure must have come from shock. By the time she finished cleaning his face, he was pretty aware of what was going on.

"My leg," he muttered as she tried to cover the scrapes with gauze and bandages. "What the hell's wrong with my leg?"

"I don't know," she said. "Is that the only place that hurts? I mean really seriously?"

He looked up at her and for once, his eyes focused. He knew who she was. "Maybe we should start by mentioning areas that don't hurt," he muttered. "That wouldn't take as long."

That did it. She would have to do something. It was truly amazing how her attitude toward him could change in such a short time, but to see this large, strong and forceful man in pain and so vulnerable touched something deep inside. It made her just a little bit crazy. She had to take care of him.

"I'm going to try to get you some help," she told him. "I'm going to try to find a way to call the hospital…"

"No." His eyes were burning and he grabbed her

hand. "You can't do that. You know I'm not here legally. They'll throw me in jail."

"Oh." She hadn't thought of that. She looked at the way he was holding her hand, as though it were a lifeline. Still, that he'd told her not to contact the hospital was telling. Despite his weakened state, he still ordered her about, not asked politely.

"I…I guess I'll see if I can find some pain killers at least," she said, using her other hand to peel away his fingers and wrest herself free.

He nodded, closing his eyes and wincing. "That would be good," he whispered.

She took a deep breath and considered the options.

What would she do with this beautiful, damaged man? An expert really needed to take a look and make sure nothing extreme had happened to him. She had no idea how to check for internal bleeding or broken ribs or anything major like that. Just the thought that he might be badly hurt and not showing it made her heart begin to race again. If you didn't treat that sort of injury, bad things could happen. She felt a deep sense of urgency to do something.

There was one source of hope she could think of. She didn't know many people who lived in this building. She'd only been here a little over a month herself. But she did know one, and she'd consulted him before when her baby's problems had scared her enough to seek help. She just didn't know how useful he would be at this time of night.

The lucky part was, he'd once been a physician. The unlucky part—he was a pretty heavy-duty alcoholic. The word was, he'd lost his license to practice medicine because of that. But if you caught Dr. Harve at a good time, he could be very helpful.

Tonight, he seemed only mildly sloshed.

"Of course I'll come and take a look at your young man," he said jovially when she knocked on his door. "What are neighbors for?"

She went back to prepare Jake, pulling off his leather coat and shirt and loosening his jeans. He was conscious and he pushed her away.

"Your leg," she said urgently. "We're going to have to take off your pants one way or another."

He shook his head and she didn't know if he was being modest or if his brain was addled with the pain.

"I work at the hospital, you know," she grumbled as she grabbed a pair of strong scissors and began to cut open the denim cloth that encased the bad leg. "I've done this before."

He didn't protest again, but he groaned in a way that chilled her.

"I've got a real doctor coming," she reassured him. "He'll be here any minute. He's been a big help with my baby's problems. He's even searching for a specialist for me to take her to. You'll like him, I'm sure."

She felt like she was babbling, but it was mostly to try to keep him calm and to prepare him for what the doctor was going to have to do. There was more pain coming, she was sure.

Dr. Harve came in, cracking jokes and exuding a certain brand of warmth that probably worked with most of his patients. It was his rapid diagnosis that Jake's knee was badly wrenched and seriously dislocated, and he spent some time treating it, chatting through the whole thing. He elicited a few smothered yells of pain and a lot of writhing from Jake as he manipulated the joint, but he talked right over them all. Meanwhile, Kim closed her eyes and covered her ears and moaned softly in sympathy.

"The connective tissue will be sore for a while," he told her as he began the final wrap. "And it will be a few weeks before he will want to run any marathons. But he'll be okay soon enough."

"What about the rest of him?" she asked anxiously.

"I'd say he was lucky he was wearing that leather coat," he said, nodding toward where it lay in the corner. "Otherwise he'd be a lot more scraped up. As it is, he's got a few cracked ribs. He'll want to be careful of those, but the pain will definitely remind him of that. I can wrap his chest, but you can't do much else for ribs. You might want to watch for signs of concussion. I don't see any evidence of internal bleeding, but if you see anything strange, don't hesitate to come on over and tell me about it."

She nodded, watching him work. This was all a bit surreal. Just an hour ago she'd been running from this man, running for her life. Now she was trying hard to help him.

"What about that deep gash on his chin? It's still bleeding."

"Yes, I've been looking at that." He sighed. "You know, ordinarily I would probably give him a few stitches. But the way my hands are shaking tonight..." He held them up for her to see and didn't finish the sentence.

He didn't have to. She was amazed he was able to do as well as he had been.

He cocked an eyebrow her way. "I don't suppose you...?"

"Oh no," she said quickly. "I wouldn't trust myself."

He nodded sadly. "Don't worry. We're not going to

ruin his pretty face too badly here. I've got some good butterfly bandages that will do almost as well."

She noticed, with a slight jolt, that Jake's eyes were open and looking directly into hers. The doctor kept on talking while he worked on the bloody chin, but she and Jake seemed to be locked in a gaze neither one could tear away from. Her pulse was racing. What was he thinking? Was he trying to tell her there was going to be a pause, but no escape for her? That he knew all he needed to know about her now? That he had her trapped?

"Okay, my dear, if you would hand me my bag, I think I'll give this fellow something to help him sleep for a while so he can begin to heal."

She finally pulled her gaze away and took a deep breath, getting him his bag and trying to calm her pulse. She didn't ask where he got his drugs, she was just grateful he had some. She was sure he must have a connection with the usual black market sources. Since the war, that was the way most people got anything important. The usual supply lines were completely cut off.

She knew he wasn't supposed to call himself a doctor, but he'd been a godsend to her for the six weeks or so she'd lived here. He'd helped her with Dede's problems many times, and he'd promised to try to find a real pediatrician for her. Baby doctors seemed to have been the first things the country had run out of once the war began.

Dede started to cry in earnest and Dr. Harve laughed, looking at her. "You decided taking care of one patient wasn't enough so you added a new guy," he noted, grinning at her. "Some people are just gluttons for punishment."

The "new guy" isn't going to stay beyond the night,

she thought to herself, gearing up to be tough if she had to. *At least, I hope not.*

Dr. Harve was finishing up and he sidled closer to her and asked softly, "So who is this guy, anyway? Are you going to be okay with him here?"

She looked up in surprise. Was the latent hostility between the two of them so obvious? For just a moment, she wondered if she should tell him not to mention Jake's presence to anyone else in the building. But that would only raise new red flags. And anyway, Kristi, the babysitter, had seen him, too. It was a bit late for secrecy.

"Don't worry," she told him quickly. "He's…the brother of an old friend. I'll be fine."

He shrugged, his eyes glinting with a new, greedy light. "Well, I notice you're not calling the police to report the accident. So I figured…."

He gave her a look that made her think, for just a moment, that he might be shaking her down. But that couldn't be. The man was a doctor. Well, sort of. She looked at him more closely and he laughed, as though it had all been a joke, and went back to preparing to leave.

She got out some cash she had stashed in the closet, and gave it to him. She always paid him for his work and advice. That seemed to make him happier and he left as cheerfully as he'd come. She frowned, watching him go. What if he got in touch with the police himself? What would she do if the authorities suddenly appeared at the door?

She was harboring an illegal alien—someone connected to the highest reaches of the enemy's administration. No wonder the man was having thoughts of being paid for his silence. His whole mode of survival depended on grabbing a buck where he could.

She turned back into the apartment with a sigh. Sometimes she felt as though she lived in one of those fast-paced video games where there was danger all around and holes you could fall into and people ready to leap out at you with a mallet to the head. Where the heck was the Off switch?

She looked into the living room at her latest piece of dangerous baggage. Finally, she and Jake were going to be alone. Surely they would have to hash some of this over. She had butterflies as she came closer, looking at him tentatively, wondering how he would act. But his eyes were closed. She frowned, feeling strangely disappointed, as though she'd been ready for a fight and now it had been postponed. She went nearer.

"Jake, do you want some water? Or something else to drink?"

He didn't move. His eyelids didn't even flutter. He was out cold.

She had a lot of thinking to do, a lot of decisions to make, a bit of planning go over. But at least she had a little time now. He was in no condition to drag her off to the castle against her will. Whatever he'd planned to do couldn't be done in the next twenty-four hours. She was in a narrow safety zone.

She looked at him, so beautiful of body, so wounded and still. He had a lot of skin showing and a whole set of gorgeous golden muscles. She shivered, looking at him, and that made her realize she needed to make sure he didn't get a chill.

She went to get him a shawl and laid it gently around his shoulders, then began to tuck it in with her fingers. Her hands slipped over the hard, rounded muscles in his shoulders and she gasped at the sensation that rippled through her. Her face was getting hot.

"Ohmigosh," she moaned. "Stop it!"

Closing her eyes, she bit down hard on her lower lip, willing the delicious feelings that set off the man-woman thing to go away. She counted to ten before she opened them again. Then she turned away, not daring to look at him until her blood had stopped racing through her veins.

Leaning against the sink in her makeshift kitchen, she tried some deep breathing. She couldn't let this happen. She was not going to respond in a sensual way to this man who hated her.

And then there was the question of why he hated her. It had been a mystery to her until he'd mentioned Leonardo. The disgust in his voice, the flare in his eyes, told her the cause would probably not be a surprise after all. It seemed her relationship with Leonardo was enough to convince him she wasn't much good.

She wondered fleetingly what Leonardo could have done to him to bring on this antagonism, but that was a useless exercise to pursue. Leonardo had done something to just about everybody, one way or another. If you lived in Ambria, it was just a matter of time before Leonardo insulted your life in some way.

But she could never forget that he was Dede's father. So having him killed was out of the question. She shrugged, resigned to the vicissitudes of fate—for now.

Jake woke up with a start, not sure where he was. The baby was crying. Somebody should go to the baby.

Where was Cyrisse?

He pulled himself up, blinking hard to get the sleep out of his eyes. He was stiff, sore, miserable. Baby still crying. His leg hurt, and so did his head, but the baby was crying. He looked around, dazed. Someone had to take care of the baby.

"Cyrisse?" he said.

And then the familiar big black hole opened up inside him and he remembered. There was no baby. The baby was gone. And so was Cyrisse. He lost his balance and fell back onto the pillows, overwhelmed by the pure evil of the black hole, the hopelessness, almost ready to give in and let it swallow him.

But there was still a baby crying. He made a major effort and roused himself again, looking for where the baby was.

The light was dim. He could hardly make out the furniture in the shabby apartment. What the hell? He'd never been in this place before. How had he got here?

And he began to remember.

Kimmee.

Running.

The car.

Pain.

Was this Kimmee's baby? He pulled himself up high enough to see where the crib was. A baby was crying alright, but it was Leonardo's.

Leonardo's baby. Anger swirled in his dazed brain. In some societies it would be expected that he would take Leonardo's baby if he had the chance—as Leonardo had taken his. He'd vowed he would make that bastard pay. What was stopping him now?

Slowly, painfully, he rose to his feet, keeping his weight all on his right side. Grimacing, he began to hobble toward the crib, using various pieces of furniture along the way as a crutch. A wave of nausea came over him. He stopped, waiting for it to pass. Two more steps and he was looking down into the baby's crib.

The tot looked up at him in surprise, eyes huge in the dim light. She looked about nine months old and she wasn't crying anymore, but she made a curious noise. It sounded like a question to him, like, "Who the heck are you?"

He stared down at her. She was Leonardo's but that didn't seem to penetrate. She was a baby. Who on earth could hurt a baby? Not him. He gave her one last look and then he turned to go back.

But she started crying again.

He stood there for a moment, trying to keep his balance and at the same time, trying to make sense of this. Leonardo's baby. So what?

But it was also Kimmee's. A baby was a baby, and this one needed help. Muttering to himself, he turned back, scooped her up and brought her to his chest. And let out a quick scream of pain that almost knocked him off his feet. The baby began to slip through his hands, falling headfirst toward the floor.

"No!"

He grabbed her just in time and clung to her, holding her high enough to avoid the damaged area that was his chest, but still gasping from the pain.

The baby cried harder.

"Okay, kid," he said gruffly. "You gotta stop the crying. It's like a hammer against my head. Come on." He rocked her, wincing as he experimented until he found just how close he could go to the ribs. "Come on."

He started back toward the couch, then took a turn as he noticed the overstuffed rocking chair.

"Here we go," he told the sweet little child. "Come on, now. Let's get some sleep."

Slouching carefully into the chair, he began to rock. The baby quieted almost instantly. He tried a little humming to hurry the process along, but it hurt and he had to stop. His eyes closed. The baby slipped down to a comfortable place between his chest and his upper arm.

They both slept.

Kim was in heaven. For once, there was hot water and she was going to make the most of it. She stood in the shower and let the silvery warmth crash over her. Wonderful.

For just a moment she could forget that she'd brought her biggest current enemy into this house and let him sleep very close to her baby girl. She could forget how difficult and frustrating work at the hospital was, how worried she was about Dede, how scared Jake made her—and just exist in the wet and the warm. She even began to sing an old Cole Porter tune, just to prove how happy she was in the moment.

But suddenly, she heard something. She couldn't be certain what it was. Quickly, she turned off the water and listened hard. Nothing. She must have been imagining it. Sighing, she turned the water back on. In this building, you had to grab the good before someone came and took it away from you. She was going to shower like there was no tomorrow. And for all she knew, maybe there wasn't.

Ten minutes later she turned off the water again and slipped out of the shower, luxuriating in a large, fluffy towel. She patted down her wet hair and rubbed on some cream and sang softly to herself. For the moment, she was happy.

Slipping into her warm nightgown, she hung the towel on the hook and started out into the living room.

The first place she looked was in Dede's crib. And it was empty.

A scream began to shove its way up her throat. Panic clutched at her chest, her heart, her mind. She couldn't breathe. Turning quickly, she saw Jake in the rocking chair, Dede clutched up between his arm and his chest, and the panic left her body like air out of a spent balloon. She crumpled to the floor in front of the rocking chair and stared up at the two of them. Relief chased chagrin through her heart.

"Thank you, thank you," she prayed softly.

They looked so peaceful, both of them totally captured by sleep. Jake's face, with its gauze bandage over the chin, looked almost benign. And Dede had relaxed completely in his arms, her little face untroubled by the pain she suffered from so often.

Watching them, tears began to fill her eyes and then spill down her cheeks. She tried to wipe them away, but they just came faster.

It was the release, she told herself. The relief of knowing she had a few hours when she wasn't going to worry about how she was going to get away from Jake and avoid going back to face the DeAngelis royals, relief in knowing someone else was here to help her with Dede if she had one of her spasms. Relief in just having another adult here with her.

Most of the time it all seemed to be on her shoulders. For just a moment, she would let the burden fall away and let herself cry.

CHAPTER THREE

MORNING had come. Jake could feel the difference without even opening his eyes. Kim was murmuring to her baby and getting delightful gurgles in return.

Baby laughter was a beautiful sound. He longed for the day when hearing it wouldn't cut him to the quick any longer.

He pushed that thought away. It did no good to dwell on heartache. And he was glad to hear Kim's baby sounding happy. It seemed to him there had been a few times during the night he'd heard something different from the little girl. Or maybe he'd been dreaming.

He sighed, not so sure whether he had finally rejoined the real world and left his nightmares behind. He'd been in and out of consciousness and the hours had blended together pointlessly. For all he knew, it could be days later by the time he'd begun to regain full use of his groggy brain. Days, or maybe hours.

Now Kim was moving around the room, gathering things up. He cracked his eyes open only enough to see her standing in front of the window. Morning light was streaking in, outlining her in silhouette, showing off every curve of her lovely form beneath the lacy nightgown she wore. The power of that image stunned him like a sucker punch to the gut. The woman appealed to his senses, there was no denying that.

But only physically, he told himself quickly, closing his eyes tightly again. He despised everything she stood for.

He tried to go over what had happened in the past twelve hours, how he'd ended up here like this. His mind was fairly clear. He pretty much knew where he was and why he was here. But that didn't stop him from resenting it.

"Are you awake?" she asked him.

He opened one eye and looked at her. She was still in the damn nightgown. He closed it again.

"No," he said gruffly.

"Yes, you are." She bent over where he still half-sat, half-lay in the overstuffed rocking chair he seemed to have slept in. He felt her cool hand on his forehead and he frowned, pulling away from her touch.

"How do you feel?"

He opened his eyes again. She was too close to avoid. Her brown eyes looked sleepy but concerned. Blond hair flew around her face in disarray. She looked like a woman who had just risen from her bed, which he supposed was exactly what she was. There was no getting away from it. He was going to have to get used to watching her bounce around in a gauzy shift he could practically see through even without the backlighting.

Fate worse than death, he supposed, laughing at himself. The horror. He drew in a deep breath, suddenly feeling as though he had warm butterscotch flowing through his veins. Swallowing hard, he tried to avoid looking at her.

"I feel like I just got run over by a truck," he said, sounding grumpy. "What do I look like?"

She nodded. "That, too. It's pretty much what happened."

He nodded and gingerly touched the bandage on his chin. "Is it?" he muttered, then looked at her more sharply. "Okay, you want to tell me what exactly happened last night? How much did you see?"

"I didn't see you get hit but…"

"Whoa, slow down." He held up a hand, frowning as he went over the events of the last evening in his head. "Let's start at the beginning." He fixed her with an intense look. "We were sitting there in the café. You implied you were heading for the bathroom. Somehow you got diverted."

She nodded, dropping onto the arm of the couch nearest too him. "I saw it a little differently. We were sitting there in the café and you began to threaten me."

He looked up at her, frowning. That wasn't the way he remembered it at all. "What?"

She shrugged. "You said you were taking me back to the castle."

"That was a threat?" He made a face, wondering why women were so often so unreasonable. "I considered it a promise, not a threat."

"Then you claimed I was really a DeAngelis." Her look was full of skepticism, as though she was pretty sure he'd made it up. "I guess you thought that gave you permission to force me to go back. And I decided you were obviously a raving lunatic and I had to get out of there."

"So you ran."

"I ran."

"And I ran after you."

"But you didn't catch me." Her eyes sparkled.

"No, you're right there." He had to admit it, he'd been

off his game from the beginning and he hadn't realized she would be so hard to catch. "You were running all over the place."

"I didn't want to lead you right back here."

He looked at her, a slow sense of satisfaction taking over. "And yet, here I am."

She shrugged that away. She didn't want to concede the point. "I didn't see the accident, but from what I could hear, it sounded like a car skidded on ice and hit you."

"Hit and run?"

She nodded.

He searched her eyes, his own hooded. "Why didn't you just leave me there?"

"Please," she said, as though there had been no dilemma at all. "You're Pellea's brother."

And still, he wondered.... "So that's why you rescued me?"

"Pretty much." She gave him a look. "I can't think of any other reason."

He nodded slowly. He still didn't completely believe it. What was he supposed to think of this woman? Ever since he'd found out about her relationship with Leonardo, he's assumed she was bad news. If there really could be such a thing as a nemesis in life, that was what Leonardo was to him. The emotional side of him wanted the man dead. The more realistic side realized killing Leonardo would mean only bad things for himself. Was revenge worth destroying your life for? That was something he still had to think through.

"And you got me medical help without having me arrested," he added, grateful yet not sure how to express it without getting too friendly. "Pretty good work."

She favored him with a smile that lit up the room. "Every now and then I can be pretty terrific."

He drew back, disturbed by how pretty she could look at times. "I wouldn't go that far," he said grumpily.

"Whatever," she said lightly. "Dr. Harve seems to think you're not too badly hurt. You ought to be okay in a couple of days."

"Good." He frowned. "Hey, what kind of a doctor doesn't do stitches because his hands are shaking?"

She bit her lip. "You caught that, huh?"

"I did. What's the deal?"

She sighed. "Jake, you know it's almost impossible to find a real doctor these days. Besides the problem of you being here illegally."

"So what is he, a phony?"

"No, he's got real medical training. But he lost his license to practice at some point. I don't know what for."

He frowned. "So he's still practicing, but ineptly?"

"No. I think he did fine with you last night. But you might say he's illegal, just like you are. Only in a different realm."

"You might say that." His blue eyes were penetrating. "Or you might admit he's probably a quack. And that is something I'll never be."

She shook her head. "I just want you to be healed." She watched him closely as she added, "And then you can go back where you came from."

He looked up into her face. "Not without you. I told you that from the start."

She stared at him, all humor gone, eyes darkening. He blinked, thinking a cloud had come out to cover the sun. Had the air suddenly gone colder? She looked away and sighed, then looked back.

"If you're keeping tabs on me because you think I'll lead you to where Leonardo is, you're in for a big disappointment," she warned, just in case.

His blue eyes snapped and searched her face. "You and the leader of your country don't hang out much anymore, huh?"

She gave him a dark look, but no words in response.

"Doesn't he want to come see his baby?"

She stared at him, exasperated. He had some nerve with his nosy questions.

"See, that's what I don't get," he went on. "You've got the only baby Leonardo has ever been known to have fathered. Therefore, you've got the heir to the Granvilli empire, such as it is these days. And yet you're hiding in shabby rooms, desperately trying to locate a doctor for your child. It doesn't add up."

Did he think she had been with Leonardo to get what she could from him? That she was some sort of gold digger? Wow. If he only knew how far off the mark he really was.

"If you think anyone on this side of the island has any money, you'll have to think again. Even the Granvilli family. Losing a war makes you broke."

He nodded. He understood that. "Of course, they lost most of their holdings over the past year or so, but you never know. The South may rise again."

"Not in my lifetime." She glared at him. "And anyway, no one knows where Leonardo is."

"That's understandable," he said, his mouth twisted in something like a mocking smile. "If anyone knew where he was he'd probably be dead by now." He looked up and just caught the tail end of a grin leaving her face. "You smile at that. Now I'm completely confused." He shook his head.

"Don't be," she shot back at him. "People are complex. We all have different things that drive us. And anyway, you know darn well you would enjoy seeing him squirm yourself."

"I see," he said slowly, analyzing the situation as best he could. "You're angry that he's turned his back on you."

That would be the day. She rolled her eyes. "No, I'm angry that you keep bringing him up. I don't want to think about him. I don't want to hear his name. Please stop."

"Sure. Sorry." But he stared at her as though she was a puzzle he needed to solve.

She changed the subject. "Why did you pick up Dede last night when I was in the shower?" she asked softly.

"Is that your little girl's name?"

"Yes."

He shrugged. "She was crying. And that made me think about my own little girl."

He winced as he said it, immediately wishing he hadn't. He should have kept his thoughts to himself.

"You have a little girl?" she asked, face lightening.

He turned to look into her dark eyes and shook his head slowly. "Not anymore," he said, and then he looked away. He'd caught the beginning of her shocked look and he didn't want to see any more of it.

She touched him. Reaching out, she put her soft hand over his and leaned toward him. "I'm sorry," she whispered softly, and then she drew away again.

He looked at her. Her eyes were huge with sympathy for him. He didn't want any damn sympathy. But something in those eyes warmed him in a strange, sensual way. He had to admit, if he ever had to take sympathy from someone, hers would be the one he would want.

But that was a stupid thought. He turned away again. This was driving him crazy. He didn't want to like her. He didn't want to feel attracted. And if this kept up, he'd be tempted to do things he could only regret.

"Listen, do me a favor," he said hoarsely. "Could you go get some clothes on? Then maybe I can stop staring into corners in order to avoid looking at you."

"Oh. I'm sorry." But she laughed. He couldn't help but think an evil thread ran through that laugh. She knew the power she had over him, didn't she?

"Really, I'm not used to having a man around in the morning. I didn't think...."

Yeah, right. Women.

She put on jeans and a loose-fitting shirt and spent the next hour taking care of her baby. He didn't look over to see what she was doing. The drugs were still affecting him and he slipped in and out of sleep for what seemed like hours.

The next time he was awake, he could see that Kim was getting ready to go to work. The white nurse's uniform looked a little tight on her, as though she'd borrowed it from someone else—and maybe had washed it too often since. But the way it fit—short and snug—set off her deliciously curvy body to great advantage, at least from his perspective. Watching her move, he got a surge of a reminder that for all his injuries, he was a man and still had some male reactions after all. That almost made him smile.

"Okay," he said when she came close enough for conversation without shouting across the room. "When do we leave?"

Kim turned to stare at him. "I'm not going anywhere."

He tried to act sure of himself, but it was tough in

the state he found himself in. "Sure you are," he said as firmly as he could. "You're going back to the castle."

She stood over him, a slight, superior smile on her face, as though she couldn't believe he was even pretending he could manage any of this.

"I don't think you could follow through on that right now, even if you wanted to," she told him with a smirk.

He frowned at her and she gave him a mock frown back. "So you're Pellea's brother," she said, looking him over as though for the first time. Then she grinned. "Pellea and I grew up like sisters, you know. So that would almost make you my brother as well."

He gave her a look that told her she was so far off base, the moon was closer. "Not hardly," he said with startling emphasis. The fact that he found her sexually appealing was so obvious in the way he said it, it almost made her blush. But not quite.

"I think you're a big talker," she said. "But right now, you can't produce the follow-through." She glared at him. "I'm not going anywhere with you."

He held his own, but it wasn't easy. "I'm damaged, but not defeated. I'm ready to go, and you're going with me."

"Really? And how do you think we're going to make the trip? A magic carpet, maybe?"

"Hey, my motorcycle." His face changed as he remembered where he'd left it. "I wonder if it's still there."

"Chained to the bus bench? I doubt it."

He frowned, looking at her speculatively, but realizing right away she wasn't going to go get it for him. "It might be. No one's stolen it yet and I've had it for days."

She knew what he was thinking. "Forget it," she said.

"Besides, you only have the one cycle. We can't all go on that."

"Sure we can. It's a good old sturdy one. We could make it."

Her eyes opened wide in mock horror. She didn't believe a word of it. She knew he had to be kidding. If he was serious, he was certifiable.

"I see. You're planning to put Dede and me on the back of a motorcycle and go careening through the mountains." She glared at him. "Are you crazy?"

He sighed, realizing he was really too weak for this argument right now. His whole body was aching.

"Maybe I am," he admitted softly.

She rolled her eyes and turned away.

He flexed the muscles in his legs, wondering if he could trust them and deciding against trying. Not yet. Maybe the next time he was conscious. He closed his eyes, resigning himself to more sleep.

He woke some time later to find the doctor hovering over him, checking his eyes, then taking the gauze off the cut in his chin to make sure no infection was setting in. He talked the whole time but Jake only caught a few words here and there.

"You're probably sore all over," the doctor was saying now. "You got hit pretty hard. You're lucky you didn't break any bones."

"Tell me something I don't know," Jake muttered under his breath.

"What's that you say?"

Jake shook his head. He'd been talking to himself when you came right down to it.

"Where's Kim?" he managed to say aloud as he began to realize there didn't seem to be any sign of her.

"Kim? Oh, she had to go to work. She'll be back to-night."

Would she? A small part of his brain was signaling him with a warning. She might try to take off again. Why wouldn't she? But there really wasn't much he could do about it in his present state. The doctor was right. He had to heal fast.

"Where's the baby?" he asked.

"The babysitter took her over to her apartment," he said, and suddenly he looked shifty. "Say, what's your name anyway? In case I need to fill out any papers or anything."

Despite his condition, Jake recognized a phony cover-up when he heard one. "Jake Jonas," he lied, slurring his words and closing his eyes to forestall any more questions.

"Where are you from, Jake Jonas?"

Jake just shook his head.

The doctor hesitated, then seemed to give up. "Okay. Just take it easy. Get some sleep. The more you sleep, the quicker you'll heal."

He didn't want to sleep. He wanted to take care of the business he'd come for, but he felt the sting of an injection before he could protest, and then he was sinking into nothingness again.

He clawed his way back up and out of that dark tunnel a few hours later. The apartment was cold and quiet. Shadows seemed to be hemming him in. He stretched and tried to get up, but his muscles weren't working properly. The ache in his leg was dulled but not for-gotten.

Painfully, he began to pull himself up. He tried to stand, but he began to cough. Pain shot through his chest and his legs buckled under him. He was going down, turning just in time to make it back into the big, overstuffed chair. He sat there and caught his breath and tried to figure a better way to do this. A way that might work, for instance. But nothing came to mind. There was no one to help him, no one to talk to. It was easier just to go to sleep again.

Kim's shift was almost over and she could hardly wait to get back on that bus. Her eyes were stinging, she was so tired. Lack of sleep tended to do that to her. It had been hard to forget there was a strange man who despised her sleeping just a few feet away. And then Dede had been fussy during the night and had kept her up for hours.

If only she could figure out what was wrong with Dede, why she spent so much time wincing in pain, why her sweet little eyes looked so troubled. Everyone tried to convince her it was just colic, but her instincts told her it was more than that. It just wasn't normal.

She'd given birth to her baby just nine months before in a little seaside town called Dorcher Cliffs. It was a sweet little place, very rustic and charming, and her mother—her real mother!—had bought a local cottage there years ago and left it to Kim when she died. The war had been over for a few months at the time and the sullen men who had survived were still straggling home. It was no fun being on the losing side of a struggle. There was usually a lot of pain and hardship involved.

And one of the worst hardships, right from the beginning, had been the shortage of doctors. Kim had only seen one during all her pregnancy and Dede's birth was attended by a midwife. Luckily, there were no problems and everything went smoothly. But by the time she was six weeks old, Kim knew there was something wrong.

At first she'd bought the line everyone gave her that it was just a normal bout of colic. But she'd known colicky babies and as the months passed, she began to have to face the fact that this was something else—something worse. No one wanted to believe her, but she was Dede's mother and she could tell.

And so began the hunt for a decent pediatrician. There weren't any in Dorcher Cliffs and she couldn't find any in the neighboring towns. So she packed up and they headed for Tantarette. She'd been sure she would find someone easily in the largest city still under Granvilli control. Unfortunately, it hadn't turned out as she'd thought. Everywhere she turned, people were complaining about the lack of medical care available. It was just as bad as it had been in her little village.

Some said the doctors had all been captured by the DeAngelis royals and put in camps and not allowed to go home once the war was over. Others claimed they had mostly defected voluntarily, going for the better pay and more modern facilities the other side controlled. In any case, there were few to be found and pediatricians seemed to be in the shortest supply of all.

So she'd done the only other thing she could think of. She'd taken the first hospital job she could find, hoping it would give her access to someone who could help her. So far, she'd had very little luck. No one could tell her anything about what was wrong with her baby.

She'd taken Dede in to the hospital and begged one general practitioner, an internist, and even a nurse practitioner, to give her a quick look. But every times, she heard the same response.

"No fever? No blood? Sorry, Kim, we just plain don't

have time for normal childhood ailments right now. There are too many people damaged by the war that still need our help. Once we clear the system…"

And she couldn't give anyone any solid evidence of what was wrong. It was just her instincts as a mother that made her sure there was something. Something just wasn't quite right.

It was tough being so all alone—tough and frustrating. There'd been a time when she'd been important to the Granvilli regime—almost part of the Granvilli family itself. There'd been a time when she could have called upon her credentials to get more attention from the power structure. But that time was long gone. She'd been shunned, cast off and turned into a nonperson. Now she was alone and she had to deal with everything on her own.

"You going home?" a red-headed coworker named Ruby asked, frowning at a work schedule on the wall.

She nodded. "Just as soon as I finish with that accident victim in bed fourteen." Her gaze flickered that way. The man's injuries reminded her of Jake's, but much worse. He might lose a leg. That made her wonder if Jake knew how lucky he was to have come away from his own accident so lightly damaged.

"Oh yes, I saw him being stitched up. Pretty ugly." Ruby winced. "Reminded me a little too much of a few months ago when the war was going strong."

"The war." Kim shook her head. "Did that ever really happen? Or was it a dream?"

"I wish." Ruby sighed as she turned away. "I just go one day at a time and hope nothing like that ever happens again."

"Me too."

She looked across the room at the bed she was planning to make her last job of the day, hoping she would be able to finish and get out of the ward before someone found something more to keep her here and away from her baby. Morale was low, help almost nonexistent, and there was more work than there was time to get it done.

But in a few minutes she would leave this place and get back to her baby and...and what? Jake Marallis and his tales of phony royal bloodlines?

It made her angry just thinking about it. Why did Pellea think she would fall for this nonsense? The die had been cast long ago and things were as they were going to be. No fits of remorse from the Queen of Restored Ambria could change what had happened. Once betrayed, always wary. And that was what Kim would always be.

The others who had come looking for her had been easy to dismiss. Jake was another story. He was tough and he was ready to do things the others hadn't been prepared to do. She was scared of him and his crystal-blue eyes. They saw too much and held a grudge. She had to think of an escape plan before he got healthy again.

Walking out of the hospital and making her way to the bus stop, she pulled her coat up against the cold wind. At least it wasn't snowing tonight. But it hardly mattered. She knew what she had to do.

First priority—ditch Jake.

Second—find a doctor who could diagnose Dede.

Third—get herself and her baby back to where they belonged, the little seaside cottage they had been living in since Dede was born, far away from city noise and city cruelty.

Put that way, it seemed simple enough. Now to build up the strength and nerve to implement that plan.

Jake raised his head and listened like a swimmer surfacing for air in a pool of cold, cloudy water. He was going to wake up this time. He was determined. He'd been awake a few times before this afternoon, once to make a shaky trip to the bathroom. He'd almost passed out on the way, but he'd made it. He was getting his strength back, little by little.

There were voices in the hall. He recognized Kim's, and after a moment, decided the other was the de-licensed doctor. He could only make out bits and pieces here and there, but something in their tone told him this wasn't an idle chat.

"Look Kim, there's no guarantee…"

"Just the chance to talk to a real specialist…"

"I can't promise you…'

"…worth its weight in gold for Dede…"

"I'll give you the address when you're ready to go. I can't risk…."

"Are you sure he knows what he's doing?"

"Oh yes. He was the very best in my class at…"

"Why is he hiding?"

"He crossed someone in the Granvilli power structure. There's a price…"

"And he has to leave the country?"

"As a favor to me, he said he'd take a look. But you can't tell anyone…."

Jake frowned as they moved down the hall and the conversation got fuzzier. He didn't much like what he thought he'd heard. He couldn't be sure what exactly was going on, but he knew he didn't like it. Taking a deep breath, he forced himself not to drift back to sleep, hitching up higher in the chair.

And then he waited. It was probably only a minute or two, but it seemed forever and he began to drift off again. But he woke with a start only a short time later when Kim came in with Dede in her arms.

He heard her putting Dede down in her crib and he waited to open his eyes when she came into his field of vision. He heard her approach and he looked up.

The first thing he saw was an angel. The light was behind her and it made her golden hair glow as it flew wildly about her pretty face. Her fur coat added to the illusion, and then she threw it off and revealed her trim figure in its slightly snug nurse's uniform and wiped him out for good. He hadn't known he had this thing for nurses. Who knew?

He closed his eyes again. It was just too much. She was going to burn out his retinas.

"How are you doing?" she asked, bending over him. "I'll bet you're hungry."

He shook his head and risked a quick look at her. "Not really," he said. "But I could use a glass of water."

She got him one and he gulped it down gratefully. It not only quenched his thirst, it cooled him down, and finally he could look at her without making a joke out of himself.

"I've got some news for you," she said, dropping down to sit on the arm of the couch.

He looked up. She was close enough to touch, so he was going to have to keep his response to her reined in. He groaned and half laughed at himself. He could barely move, much less make a play for a beautiful woman. Besides, he despised her. He kept forgetting that.

"What's the news?" he asked.

"Your motorcycle is still there. Still chained to the bus bench. I just saw it."

"You're kidding. I would have thought someone would have stolen it by now."

She nodded. "You know what I think it is? It's so old, so ramshackle, it looks like a piece of urban art sitting there. I'll bet people don't think it really works."

She grinned and he found himself smiling into her eyes. He was just too weak to resist.

"And you know what else?" She produced a cardboard box. "I stopped into the café where we were last night. I figured you didn't have time to pay the bill as you dashed out after me, so I wanted to give them some money for that."

He should have known. She was the type. But that impressed him anyway.

"What a model citizen," he noted, trying to sound cynical and failing.

"Of course." She grinned again. She seemed to be in an awfully good mood. "But here's the point. They were just taking another one of their fabulous apple pies out of the oven. I stood there and watched them and I could hardly stand how beautiful it looked." Her eyes sparkled. "So I bought it." She waved it under his nose. "Can you smell that aroma? We will feast tonight!" She laughed, then sobered a bit as she added, "I invited Dr. Harve to join us for pie later. So we'll save it until then."

It was lucky that she jumped up and headed to the kitchen with her prize at that moment. That gave him time to settle down and blot out how adorable she looked when she was excited. He needed to remember who she was. Leonardo's woman. The mother of Leonardo's child. Of all the women in the world, she was exactly the wrong woman for him to start feeling this way about. He had to cut it out, fast.

He made another trip to the bathroom, feeling a bit more sure of his leg than he had before. He looked into the kitchen on his way back. She was hovering over Dede, who was fussing, and she looked as though a lot of her previous happiness had dimmed quickly.

"Something wrong?" he asked, leaning on the door jamb.

She looked up and shook her head. "No, nothing. Dede's just…" She shook her head again. "Listen, I'm fixing you some soup. It'll be ready in about half an hour."

"Thanks. I mean really, Kim. Thanks a lot."

She flashed him a quick smile but without much warmth. "Don't mention it. I'll bet you need more water."

He nodded, looking toward the sink and wondering how he was going to maneuver getting it.

"No problem. Go sit back down. I'll bring it to you."

He nodded again and did as she suggested. He had a feeling she must have been thinking over their dubious ties just as he had and she realized she was in trouble as long as he was here. She wanted him gone. He didn't blame her. But it wasn't going to happen. Not until she agreed to go with him. In the meantime, he had a serious subject he wanted to talk to her about.

He waited for her to come back out again, and she came soon enough, bringing him another glass of water, and also a pair of sports pants.

"Here," she said. "I picked these up in the hospital supply room. They're stretchy so they should go over your leg better than another pair of jeans would at this point."

He took them and nodded. "You think of everything," he noted.

She hesitated. "I felt bad just taking them," she said. "But we give them away free to patients all the time and if you weren't illegal, you would have been there, so…"

He laughed at her. "You're actually finding a way to justify it to yourself. Kim, I'm sure they've had more work out of you than they've paid for. Stop feeling guilty about everything."

She sighed. He drank down the second glass of water just like he'd done the first and she waited for the glass.

"Listen," he said as soon as he'd swallowed the last drop. "I heard you talking to the doc in the hall."

She took the glass from him but gave him a tart look. "You shouldn't listen in to conversations you're not a party to."

He almost rolled his eyes. "No kidding. Thanks for the etiquette lesson, but I've got bigger fish to fry." He grabbed her hand as she started to turn away, holding her there. "What exactly are you planning to do?"

She stared down at him resentfully. "Nothing. Nothing that is any of your business."

His fingers tightened around her wrist. "Kim…"

But she was already shaking her head. "Forget you heard anything at all. It has nothing to do with you."

She was tugging hard on his hold on her and he knew she was going to slip away any second. To keep his grip, he would have to hurt her and he wasn't going to do that.

"Wait," he said, trying to distract her. He knew the topic of the conversation with the doctor had something to do with the baby, he just wasn't sure what it was. Maybe if he understood a little more about the child, he could figure it out for himself. "Tell me what's wrong with Dede. What are you afraid of?"

Her eyes flashed, gazing into his as though trying to see just how much he'd heard. "Never mind," she said forcefully. "You wouldn't understand."

"Kim, wait," he said again. "You've got to be careful. I don't trust that so-called doctor."

She had her hand back and there was a triumphant glint in her smile. "No problem," she said coolly. "Don't worry about me. I don't trust anyone anymore." Her chin rose. "And I especially don't trust you." She turned with a toss of her head and left the room.

He grimaced, looking after her. He didn't like this. Something bad was coming their way. He could feel it.

CHAPTER FOUR

Kim spent the next half hour tending to Dede, feeding her and playing with her and trying to ignore the man in her living room. If only he hadn't appeared in their lives the day before, everything would be so much easier. Just his being here made things more difficult, and knowing what he wanted her to do made them almost impossible.

But she was riding on a bubble of excitement that she'd had since she came back from work and found Dr. Harve waiting for her down the hall with a golden gift. He'd found her a pediatrician. Finally. She was overjoyed at the news.

She only wished she'd been a bit more careful about keeping Jake from hearing any of it. She had to admit there were a few fishy-seeming details. According to the doctor, this children's physician was an old friend from medical school who had somehow become *persona non grata* with the current Granvilli regime and had to get out of town. He was hiding out at a safe house, about to flee across the border into DeAngelis territory. But Dr. Harve had spoken to him and he'd agreed to see Dede the next day. Kim was so relieved. She had to keep reminding herself that one visit to a pediatrician, even a good one, wouldn't necessarily create a miracle cure for Dede—but it was a start!

She made Jake his bowl of soup and took it out to him. He was dozing, but he didn't seem to be falling into the deep, drugged sleep anymore. That gave her pause. She knew what he wanted to do as soon as he was mobile, and she knew she had to have her child out of here before that time came. She would have to be careful judging when that was.

She cleaned up the dishes and when she came out of the kitchen, found Jake up and leaning over the baby's crib. That gave her a start but she quickly realized he was making baby-talk nonsense noises to her and she was laughing up at him. As she watched, Dede grabbed his nose and let out a yell of happiness.

He laughed, but he pulled away. "Babies are cute and all, but they have no idea of how badly they can hurt a guy with those little fingers," he mentioned wryly, rubbing his nose.

"So you're up," Kim noted, assessing his stability. "How do you feel?"

"Like I'm using someone else's legs and they don't fit very well."

She smiled. It was too bad he was so handsome. It would be easier to stay distant with a less appealing man. And the fact that he seemed to like Dede had not escaped her notice. You couldn't help but like people who liked your kids.

"Come in the kitchen," she said impulsively. "You can sit at the table and I'll make you a cup of hot chocolate."

"With marshmallows?" he asked hopefully.

She laughed. "We'll see if I can dig some up."

She made two cups, found marshmallows, and set

them on the table. Dede had started fussing so she went to get her and returned to the kitchen with her baby in her arms. Dede whipped her head around so that she could give Jake a big grin. Obviously, his appeal hit all ages similarly.

"So tell me, what exactly is wrong with her?" he said, studying her as he sipped his drink.

Kim sat down with Dede on her lap. She was never happier than when she was holding her child. The love she felt tended to overwhelm her at times. It blotted out everything , even the knowledge of who her baby's father was.

"She seems fine to you, right? Perfectly normal? Like any other nine-month-old baby?"

He nodded slowly. "She's adorable."

"Oh. Yes, she is." Kim gave her an extra hug. "But she doesn't feel normal to me. I can tell there's something wrong." Her voice got a little shaky. "And nobody believes me."

His eyes narrowed. "What do you think it is?"

She glanced at him. Did he really care or was he just making conversation?

He wasn't saying what most people said. *You're just a nervous first-time mom. You haven't had enough experience to know what she should be like. All babies cry, all babies act like they're in pain. You get used to it.*

He wasn't saying any of those things. Should she take him as seriously as he seemed to be taking her? She wasn't sure she was ready to trust him that far. Not yet.

"I don't know what it is. That's the whole point. I'm trying desperately to find a doctor who can tell me what it is."

He had a thoughtful look, like a professor noodling with an idea. "What does she do that makes you think there's something wrong?"

She looked at him in surprise. He wasn't just humoring her. He wasn't blowing her off like everyone else did. He actually listened and was reacting to what she'd said. He wanted to know the facts. She didn't really want to talk about this with him, and yet, if he was someone who actually respected her fears and wanted details, how could she refuse?

Still, she had to remember that the man despised her, bottom line. He detested her tie to Leonardo, even though he had no clear idea of how that worked at all. And he was probably going to use any information he gleaned against her in some way. And yet... He was taking her opinion seriously. She threw caution to the wind, took a deep breath, and launched into her fears.

"I just feel like something has never been right internally, from the very first. It's not just stomach aches. It's not just gas. It's not just indigestion."

She held her baby to her face, looking at her closely, and then she kissed her tenderly. Her little expression was always so pleasant, even when she was in pain. What a sweetheart her baby was. Tears filled her eyes but she blinked them away.

"Sometimes, when I feed her, she twists her body as though she's trying to get away from it. She writhes, she cries, she grimaces. Something hurts her. And in a different way than normal. I can just tell." She looked at him, sniffling. "Sometimes she cries, but more often, it's little grunting noises."

"Yes," he said, nodding as he watched the two of them together. "I've heard her do that."

Her eyes widened. "You have?"

"Sure. Last night."

She regarded him as though she'd never really seen him before. He believed her. He'd heard it, too. There was a lump in her throat and for a moment, she couldn't speak. Finally someone admitted it. There was something different about her pain.

Now if she could only convince the pediatrician. She had to be very careful not to rush things, to let him get a feel for Dede and how her rhythms worked. And right now, she had to be very careful not to let Jake know what she was planning to do tomorrow. Once she'd packed up her baby and gone to the doctor, she didn't plan on coming back here at all.

But right now, she had to change the subject. If she went on with this and he kept being so understanding, she would break down and cry right here at the table. Anything would be better than that. She couldn't show that much weakness to the enemy.

And she must make no mistake about it, he was the enemy. She couldn't forget that. Taking a deep breath, she tried to smile.

"So tell me about you," she said, her voice shaky. "How did you get here? Into the country, I mean. From what we've been hearing, the border is tight as a drum these days. They say it's almost impossible to get in or out."

He searched her eyes for a moment, as though wondering why she was changing the subject, but then he shrugged.

"I didn't find it all that hard. I walked across down near where the Brielle River meets the Ellis Canal."

She nodded, feeling more secure as Dede picked up a spoon and banged it on the table. "I know the area," she said as she took away the metal spoon and switched

Dede to a plastic one that wouldn't make such a racket. "We used to have summer picnics there."

"I waited until two on a frosty morning when the guards were dozing. No problem. I wasn't even challenged."

"Lucky you."

"I found my way to a farmhouse, slept in the barn and then bought that wreck of a motorcycle you saw me with last night. I found it in the barn and bought it from the farmer's wife in the morning. She was grateful for the cash and overlooked the trespass."

He hesitated, then went on glumly.

"Everyone over here on the Granvilli side of the island seems to be desperate for money."

She nodded. It was true. "There just isn't any. I haven't been paid at the hospital for over two weeks."

He took another sip of his drink and nodded. "That's the way it is when you lose a war," he said dispassionately. "But the motorcycle was a blessing. It let me make my way a lot faster here to Tantarette. I was lucky enough to find a tiny room in a decrepit house, rented by the day. The landlord was a bit suspicious, but I made up a story about how heroic I'd been in the war, on the Granvilli side, of course, and the man reluctantly let me have a place to sleep. I've been there for a few days now."

"Until last night."

"Until last night." He gave her a long, slow smile that looked almost reluctant. "And I spent most of my time searching for you."

Something about that smile made her pulse race a bit faster. "Until you found me on a bus."

"That was pure serendipity. But I recognized you right away."

His gaze caught hers and held. For some reason she didn't seem to be able to look away.

"Did you study pictures before you left the other side?" she asked, meaning it to be a simple question. So why did it come out sounding breathless?

"Many pictures." His voice was low and gruff. "Videos, too."

"Ah." She licked her lips and tried to stay focused. "So how did you know I would be here in the city?"

His smile was wider now. "I came from the winning side in the war. We have actual reports giving us actual information. And we still have money enough to get things done right."

"Good luck with that," she said, but she didn't sound convincingly cynical. There was a sense of his maleness sweeping over her, making her tingle. She was getting lost in his crystal-blue gaze and she couldn't let that happen.

Time to change the subject again. It took an effort, but she managed.

"And what did you actually do during the war?" she asked brightly.

Though he looked startled at her abrupt turnabout, a flash of humor showed he knew what she was doing. "I worked intelligence, mainly," he said a bit evasively. "But I fought my share of Granvilli soldiers."

"And killed a few?" she asked rather acidly.

He shrugged, eyes darkening. "Not as many as you probably imagine. But I made a few sacrifices in hopes of getting a decent regime back in charge."

"You don't think the Granvillis are decent?"

"Do you?"

She drew in a big breath, not wanting to go down that road. "Well, I spent my time in Dorcher Cliffs. Very quiet, off the beaten path. We didn't have many battles there."

"Sounds like a good place to be. Did you manage to miss most of the war?"

"Pretty much." She frowned, remembering. "We did get some unpleasant residual incidents as the war ended, though. Roving gangs, that sort of thing."

He raised an eyebrow. "What sort of gangs?"

"Mostly looting. The older men still in the village banded together to fight them off. And then, for months, we seemed to be flooded with scam artists looking to make a quick buck off the innocent village people."

He nodded. "That's typical, like vultures swooping in to see what they can glean from the weak and wounded after the fight is over."

"Exactly. They preyed on the old people, confusing them with get-rich-quick schemes, and young mothers of babies whose husbands had been killed, trying to get them to give up their babies with promises of money." She shivered, remembering one slimy example she'd had to deal with herself. "We even had fish rustlers, trying to hijack the catches of some of the older fishermen who they didn't think could defend themselves. But our little town really came together to get rid of the menace."

"Your town sounds great. Why did you leave?"

"To find medical help for Dede."

"Oh. Of course."

Suddenly, he was so tired he could hardly keep his eyes open.

"I think I'd better get back to my chair," he said, rising with difficulty. He started to leave, but he stopped and turned back.

"Listen, Kim," he said, looking less sure of himself

than usual. "I...I just want to tell you how much I appreciate all you've done for me over the last twenty-four hours. Without you, I'd probably be in a homeless shelter right about now."

"You're welcome," she said dismissively. "Now just heal and get out of here."

Her small smile softened her words, but he knew she meant them anyway.

"Okay," he said. "But you're going with me."

She stopped and stared at him, searching for chinks in his armor. "I understand that Pellea wants me back," she said softly. "But tell me this. Do you?"

"Do I what?"

"Really want me to go back to the castle. Something in your eyes tells a different story."

He met her gaze for a long moment, then shrugged. "I'm merely a messenger. I have no opinion."

Her eyes flashed. "Liar."

And his response was a grin.

And then he turned and went on into the living room and sank into his chair. All the time he expected her to say something behind him. But she didn't say a thing, and in just a few minutes, he was too far gone in sleep to hear her anyway.

CHAPTER FIVE

"How are you doing, big guy?" the so-called doctor blustered jovially as he came into the apartment an hour later. "Let's take a look at that leg."

"I'm fine," Jake said, glowering back at him. "I think I can handle this myself from here on out."

"Oh really." Dr. Harve looked a bit taken aback. "Well, I brought over some painkillers and—"

"No thanks," Jake said shortly.

He shrugged, looking puzzled. "It's your choice. But hey, the more you sleep, the faster you heal."

Yeah, he'd heard that one before.

"I'd rather leave the channels open so my body can tell me what's going on," he said. "I wouldn't want to be asleep at the switch."

"I don't know. You may regret this about one o'clock in the morning."

Jake fixed him with a cold stare. "We all have our regrets, don't we?"

Dr. Harve began to look like he wished he hadn't come over. "Uh, well…"

Kim came breezing into the room. "Hi, glad you could make it. I'm just fixing the plates. I'm sure you want ice cream, don't you?"

"Ah." Dr. Harve was on more familiar ground now. "My favorite. Apple pie à la mode."

"Why don't you just sit down and talk to Jake, and I'll bring it all out here."

"Uh." He gave a shifty glance in Jake's direction and turned to follow her into the kitchen. "Why don't I just come along and help you?"

"Well, fine." Kim cast a worried look Jake's way. In a moment they were back, bearing plates piled high with delicious confection and cool, creamy vanilla ice cream.

The doctor sat on the edge of his seat, trying hard not to look at Jake. Kim looked from one to the other of the men. For a few minutes, no one spoke but Jake ate his pie with gusto.

"Wow, that was good," he said, smiling at Kim. "Not quite as good as the one we had the other night, but good enough to give it a run for its money."

The doctor's hands were shaking, making his fork rattle against the porcelain plate. It was obvious nerves were making him even more shaky than usual.

Jake looked at him and decided to quit wasting time.

"Listen, I know what's going on," he said. "You're sending Kim to a discredited pediatrician. Someone in hiding, no less. How much is the guy paying you to send her over?"

The doctor paled and looked at Kim accusingly. "I… this is a private arrangement and you have no—"

"What did he lose his license for? The same thing you did?"

Dr. Harve jumped up and at the same time, Kim said sharply, "Jake! This is none of your business."

"Hey buddy," the doctor chimed in. "I don't know where this animosity comes from, but I don't deserve it. I'm just trying to do Kim a favor here." He glared at her. "She wasn't supposed to tell anyone."

"She didn't. I figured it out for myself."

The doctor looked flustered. "Okay. You're so big on handling everything on your own, handle how mad Kim here is going to be if my friend backs out of the arrangement."

Jake's gaze didn't waver. "That would suit me fine. As it is, if she insists on going, I want her to wait until I can go with her. If your pal is such a damn outlaw, she just might need protection. What do you think?"

The doctor was uncharacteristically at a loss for words. He sputtered for a moment, then turned on his heel and stomped out of the apartment, heading down the hall.

Kim turned on Jake, furious. "If you've wrecked this deal for me, I'll…I'll…" And then she was out the door, too, running after Dr. Harve.

Jake leaned back. "And I guess my work here is done," he murmured to himself cynically.

It didn't bother him to have the doc and Kim mad at him. But it did bother him that the man was ready to exploit a woman who was so desperately trying to find answers. He would do what he could to shield any woman from that. There was nothing special about Kim. Nothing at all.

Kim was so angry at Jake, she couldn't even look at him as she came back into the apartment. She'd caught up with Dr. Harve and pretty much mended fences with him, but she was just furious at Jake for making it necessary. Except for the fact that he was recuperating in her living room, he was nothing to her! He shouldn't even be here. She shouldn't have to know him. Where did he get off meddling with her life?

But ignoring Jake and expecting him to stay in his chair wasn't going to work anymore. As she cleaned up the dishes from the apple pie, he came into the kitchen and picked up a dish towel and began to dry the plates as she set them in the rack.

"I know you hate me right now, but, Kim, this little plan is crazy. Are you really ready to go off and take your baby to some kind of crook?"

She rinsed off her hands and turned to glare at him. "He's a doctor. He's a very fine doctor."

He shook his head in wonder. "The only evidence you have of that is that Dr. Harve told you so, and he's a crook himself."

Her mouth opened in outrage. "Why do you say that? You don't even really know him."

"I can tell." He shrugged. "I've seen his type before. Too shifty. Always looking for a way to make some easy money. He'd sell you out for a bottle of Scotch."

Her eyes flashed. "You don't know that."

She started to turn away but he stopped her with a hand on her arm.

"How much have you paid him for what he's done on me, anyway?" he asked.

She hesitated. A part of her didn't want to tell him. But she was pretty low on cash herself. What was more important, making a point in the argument, or getting her money back? Right now she wasn't sure if either were worth it.

"Enough," she said grudgingly, tugging away from his hold on her arm.

"How much?" He pulled out a wallet and began to count out bills. "Take this."

He held the money out to her. She looked at it and shook her head. "You're my guest," she said, feeling sullen. "I won't take your money."

"Oh for God's sake, Kim. You need the money. I know you do. Here." He put the money on the counter and pushed it toward her. She gave him a poisonous look, then carefully pulled two bills out that came close to what she'd given Dr. Harve. Then she pushed back the others.

"Thank you," she said primly as she turned to go check on Dede.

He watched her go, a smile just barely twisting his wide mouth. Despite everything, he got such a kick out of watching her, especially when she was upset at him. She was so darn cute.

The electricity was out. It was after midnight. Dede had been fussing and Kim had been walking her, but then the lights had flickered out and everything had gone black.

Kim put Dede down in her crib, murmured a few comforting phrases, hoping to quiet her so they wouldn't wake Jake, and then she began feeling her way through the living room to find the box of candles she kept near the front door.

"Ouch!"

She hit her bare foot on the corner of the chair where Jake was sleeping and the next thing she knew, not only did she have a foot that hurt like crazy, she was on her back on the carpeted floor with Jake on top of her.

"What the hell?" he growled, realizing this wasn't what he'd thought it was right away. "Kim, is that you?"

"Get off me, you big oaf," she cried, pushing at him as hard as she could.

"Oh. Sorry. I thought…"

But it didn't matter what he'd thought. He needed to get up off her. But she felt so good. He tried to lift himself, but he couldn't quite make it the first time. He wanted to blame it on his bad leg and generally broken-feeling body, but he knew that was just an excuse. He wanted to feel her wonderful body for another few seconds. He wanted to bury his face in her fragrant hair and cup her breast in his hand and…

"Jake!"

He rolled off her, wincing. His gesture of protective security had come at a cost to his bad leg, but he knew he would get over it. Someday. The sense of the imprint of her body against his would last longer.

"You thought I was a burglar?" she said, sarcasm dripping from her tone. "Thanks a lot, Mr. Hero." She scrambled to her feet, shaken but not hurt. "We don't have that much to steal."

He pulled himself painfully back into his chair and stared into the pitch-black darkness.

"I guess the electricity went out?" he said.

"Bingo."

She felt her way to the door and found the box. Taking out a candle, she struck a match and suddenly there was light again. Not much light, but enough to keep from more mistaken identity problems.

She looked at him in the chair and noticed the hard line around his mouth. She knew that meant he was in pain right now. She hesitated, then said, gruffly, "Sorry I woke you up that way."

He looked up at her. "Sorry I took you down that way." Suddenly, he grinned. "But I've got to say, you're the softest thing I've ever tackled. It was downright delicious."

"Hmmph," she said, turning back to her baby. But secretly, she smiled.

Dede was whimpering and Kim's smile soon faded. The poor little thing was having one of her bad spells. Kim did what she could to try to make her more comfortable, alternating rubbing her little belly and bicycling her feet.

Suddenly, she realized Jake had left his chair and was standing right beside her, looking at the baby as well. Dede was writhing, looking miserable. Kim set her lips. Maybe now he would see why she was so anxious to find a pediatrician for her little girl.

"There are some things I don't understand, Kim," he said quietly.

"Like what?"

He looked at her. "Like why you're living this way. Your opportunities are endless."

She groaned and made a face. "Not that again."

"Okay, let's just ignore the fact that the DeAngelis royals want you back at the castle. Let's pretend they don't even exist. Even without them, you have some pretty impressive connections. Dede's father is the most powerful man on this side of the divide. He's the leader of the Granvilli forces. He was the ruler of all of Ambria itself until a year ago. No one is stronger or more feared." He stared down into her eyes as though searching for answers there. "Surely he can get his own baby a decent pediatrician."

She closed her eyes and turned away. That was exactly the nightmare she faced if she couldn't get help for Dede soon. She would have to go to Leonardo.

She would rather die.

But she still had hope. No matter what Jake said, the pediatrician Dr. Harve had found for her was someone she'd heard of before, someone she was sure could help. After she saw him, if she still wasn't satisfied, she would have to begin considering finding Leonardo and making him face up to his responsibilities. But she would exhaust every other possibility first.

Did that include going back to Pellea after all that had happened between them? Could she really go back and face the woman who used to be like a sister to her—and then betrayed her? Could she really return to the people who had left her behind, forgotten all about her, used her to take the brunt of the anger when everything fell apart? That was something she still hadn't come to terms with.

She flashed a look his way. He was watching her, waiting for an answer, an answer she didn't have to give him.

Suddenly she remembered that he'd mentioned a baby of his own that morning, a baby he no longer had. Did that mean the baby had died? Or been taken from him? Hard to know. It wasn't a question you could easily ask someone. She did know instinctively that he wasn't about to tell her unless he had to.

But if he'd had a baby, had he also had a wife? He hadn't mentioned one, but babies usually came with mothers attached. She wondered what his story was. Too bad she didn't feel free enough to ask him.

Dede had gone to sleep. Picking up the candle, she started into the kitchen. Jake followed her. She knew he was still waiting.

"I told you Leonardo was out of the picture," she told him at last, putting the candle on the kitchen table and sliding down onto the front edge of a chair. "It isn't an issue."

She could see that he didn't believe her, but she

didn't care. It was true. She wished she'd never known Leonardo, and yet, how could she say that when Dede wouldn't exist without him? Her little girl was her whole world now.

Suddenly she had an epiphany. Jake had a thing about Leonardo. He wanted to find him and… Who knew what he wanted to do? But she knew he wasn't planning a friendly chat. He wanted a confrontation of some sort. The animosity he felt fairly bristled off him. That was why he'd come on this mission for Pellea. He was after Leonardo. That was what all the anger was about. Who knew, maybe he even wanted to kill him. Many people had wanted that before.

And he thought he could find the man through her? The funny thing was, she probably detested Leonardo even more than he did.

She didn't know where he was. He certainly wasn't living with her. Not now, not ever.

She looked at Jake speculatively as he sank carefully onto the chair across the table from her. Maybe it would be best to get this out in the open and let him know he was barking up the wrong tree.

"What is the deal with you and Leonardo?" she asked directly. "Why are you so fixated on him?"

Jake looked startled. "I'm not fixated on him. I hate his guts. Other than that…" He shrugged.

"You're not alone," she noted wryly, head to the side as she studied him in the candlelight. The flickering flame made interesting shadows on his skin. What was it about candlelight that seemed to create a circle of intimacy?

He grimaced. "I don't suppose I am. But that's all part of the mystery." Turning his head, he looked into her face again. "What do you find appealing about the man?"

She shook her head. "I'm not going to talk about that," she told him.

"No?" His mouth hardened. "And yet, there's something there. Something has poisoned you against your family. Is your bond with Leonardo so strong you can't even come home to see the people who love you?"

There it was. She could hear it in his voice. That was what he hated about her. Leonardo. What a joke. But she could feel his anger. He hated Leonardo and therefore he hated that she had been with him. She was tainted in his mind, ruined by having Leonardo's child. The funny thing was, she felt a little bit that way herself.

She hadn't always hated the man. By the time she was fifteen, she was working in the castle, and he'd always been there. His father, the general, had been the ruler of Ambria after the coup that had killed the DeAngelis king and queen. At some point Kim's mother, Lady Constance Day, had gone back to work in the castle and she'd gone along. For some reason it seemed to give her mother special cachet in the new regime to have been Queen Elineas DeAngelis's favorite lady-in-waiting, and it was just assumed that Kim would follow in her mother's footsteps. She'd started out as a companion to Pellea and soon became head of social services for the important ladies of the Granvilli regime. She'd been an important member of the household and everyone had seemed to respect and honor her.

Leonardo was older, but she'd found him rather droll and amusing at the time. He'd always wanted Pellea. Pellea's father, a top minister to the Granvilli government, had pushed the match, though Pellea herself resisted.

Then Pellea fell in love with Monte, crown prince of the deposed royal family scheming to make a comeback, and suddenly she was pregnant. Thinking she could never have Monte for her own, she'd agreed, reluctantly, to become engaged to Leonardo. Kim had been there to witness their bond through its many stages.

But when Monte came back to claim Pellea, it was Kim who helped hide him and smoothed the way for the couple to be with each other. Finally, she'd helped her mistress run away to join Crown Prince Monte, and she'd covered it up at the time.

Leonardo was not pleased. She shuddered, remembering.

Then came the war. The DeAngelis royals restored their monarchy and sent Leonardo and the rest of the Granvillis packing, leaving them to cling to the far side of the island with their diminished ranks.

At the time, she'd had no idea the man would end up being so important in her life. He was the most important man in her country—and the father of her child. But he was also a good part of the reason their side had failed in the war. And he'd certainly done what he could to make sure her life would never be the same again.

"I'm not with Leonardo anymore," she said carefully. "I thought I'd made that clear."

His eyebrow quirked as though he didn't believe a word of it.

"When do you see him?"

She stared at him, eyes wide. "What makes you think I ever see him?"

"He's the father of your child."

Pain cut through her like a knife. A lump rose in her

throat for some reason and she coughed, trying to get rid of it before he noticed.

"All this is none of your business," she told him, trying hard to maintain a cool exterior. "Just leave it alone. And believe me, my refusal to go back there has nothing to do with Leonardo."

She bit her lip. Actually, that was a lie. He had a lot to do with it. If it hadn't been for what Leonardo had done…

Oh well. That was not Pellea's fault. Was it?

Was that the choice she faced? If the pediatrician didn't work out tomorrow, she was going to have to choose. Leonardo, or Pellea? One or the other. The devil or the deep blue sea. Only she wished she would never have to see either one of them ever again. Either way, it would be a soul-wrenching experience.

How had everything become so insane? She blamed the war. It made people do things they would never have done otherwise. People died, people had to leave their homes, people found themselves in situations they hated—all because of the war.

"So when am I going to get this special information that is going to change my life?" she asked Jake, thinking of what he'd said when they first met.

"Right now, if you wish," he said. He'd been staring at the table and now he looked up, his blue eyes crinkling. "Ready?"

"Of course."

"All right." He leaned forward, elbows on the table, ready to reveal all to her. "You see…"

"Wait."

Suddenly, she was scared. Her heart was beating like a caged bird in her chest. What if it really did change everything? Was she ready to confront that? Maybe it would be better just to ignore this and let life move on.

"What's the matter?"

She put a hand over her chest. "I can't breathe."

He grabbed her free hand and held it tightly. "Take it easy, Kim. It's good, not bad. I think you'll realize that once you hear what I've got to tell you."

She stared at him with huge eyes but she didn't try to pull her hand away, even though she knew it was trembling in his.

He smiled at her. "Hey, breathe," he ordered.

She took a deep one and nodded. "Okay. Let's have it."

"Here goes." His fingers curled more tightly around her hand. "You know that the Granvilli clan burned the castle and killed Queen Elineas and King Grandor."

She nodded stiffly.

"The royal couple had seven children, five boys and two girls. It was assumed at first that all of them had been killed, but little by little, years later, rumors began to spread that they might still be alive. It turned out that each child had been taken by someone who worked for the royal family and raised as one of their own. Their identities had to be protected to save them from the murderous Granvillis."

She'd been listening passively up to that point, but now she tried to yank her hand out of his. He held on.

"You know they were murderous, Kim. Especially the old general. Facts are facts."

She closed her eyes for a moment, but she didn't say anything.

"You also know that a few years ago, the three old-est boys found each other and began to work on rally-

ing the Ambrians to take their country back. The war
came, and they were successful."

She nodded.

"In the meantime, two more of the boys have shown
up, so all five have been found."

"What about the girls?" she asked. "Weren't there
twin girls?"

"Yes," he said, surprised that she knew that much
about them. "No evidence of their whereabouts has ever
been found."

"Oh." Her eyes looked very sad for a moment. "How
old would they be?"

"I'm not sure. In their late twenties, I'd say."

She nodded, her eyes haunted. She was thinking of
how she would feel if Dede were taken from her and she
couldn't find her again for twenty-five years. It broke
her heart to think of such a thing.

"But now it turns out there was a third girl."

She turned her gaze to him, fear flashing in the
depths of her eyes.

He shook his head, wishing he knew how to convince
her this wasn't the end of the world. "Queen Elineas
had a baby girl born just before the Granvillis struck.
No one ever knew, as they kept it secret, fearing what
was about to happen to them and their monarchy."

Kim's face was set now. She stared at the wall, no
hint of what she was thinking. But something about the
tilt of her head reminded him of a painting he'd seen of
Anne Boleyn, waiting for the executioner.

"Kim, that beautiful little girl was claimed by one
of the queen's favorite maids as her own. She took her
home with her when the fighting began. She raised her.
And Kim…that little girl was you."

"No," she whispered, still staring at the wall and

slowly shaking her head. "My mother was Lady Constance. She was older when she had me. That's why she didn't tell anyone until it was all over. It was quite a surprise to her that all went so well. But she always told me that having me was the biggest joy of her life." Turning slowly, she stared at him, her eyes dark in the candlelight. "She would have told me the truth," she said softly. "She would have told me before she died."

He shrugged. What could he say to her about that? Anything he thought of sounded like a made-up excuse and he didn't want her to think he was conning her. He was telling her truth and he wasn't going to set up doubts by adding salesmanship.

"I don't believe it," she said firmly, then gazed at him in defiance. "Someone is just tricking you. This is all crazy. I don't want to be a DeAngelis. I don't want to be a stupid princess of the realm. I want to be who I am." Tears welled in her eyes and her voice broke. "I want to be left alone."

She rose clumsily, almost overturning her chair, and went to the sink, turning on the hot water as high as she could and scrubbing the sink with a brush.

"Kim." He rose and stood close to her, wishing he knew what to say. Tentatively, he reached out and touched her hair. "Why don't you give it some time. Why don't you…"

She turned to face him, her eyes shooting daggers through the tears. "Why do you expect me to accept all this from you? You hate me."

He was taken aback. "Hate you? Why would I hate you?"

"Admit it. I can see it in your eyes. Every time you mention Leonardo."

"Hey." He took her by the shoulders, looking down into her face. "I'll admit to hating *him*. But you…"

"You despise me because I slept with him." Her chin rose in a teary challenge. "Don't you?"

He hesitated. He wasn't even sure that was true any longer. But his hesitation made her more sure of it.

"See? You can't deny it."

"Yes, I do deny it," he protested. "I may have felt that way at first."

"Yes, you made it very plain. I'm not much good." She turned away, her shoulders shaking and her voice breaking. "Me and my…my…Granvilli baby."

A sob broke through her misery and he couldn't take it any longer.

"Kim." He pulled her into his arms and up against his chest, gasping as she hit the ribs, but not about to stop her for it. "Kim, don't. You have nothing to cry about. Really."

He looked down and she looked up, her face wet and beautiful, and he bent down and kissed her. He hadn't planned that. If he'd thought things through, he never would have done it. But the moment came and he kissed her.

"Oh!"

She was surprised, but she didn't pull away. He was big and he was male and he smelled so good. His kiss was perfect, gentle and comforting rather than aggressive. There was no demand in his touch, no urgency, but the sensuality was an extra thrill, a sweet and sexy charge of electricity that couldn't be ignored.

It had been so long since she'd felt the protective arms of a man around her. She couldn't help but let herself sink into it. It was so extraordinary, so wonderful.

"Even better than a hot shower," she whispered to

herself as he began to draw back. Her eyes were still closed. She was savoring the moment.

"What?" he said, frowning at her and wondering what he was getting himself into at the same time. He shouldn't have kissed her. But he couldn't really say he regretted it. She tasted as good as she looked—sort of sweet and tangy, like a lusciously ripe citrus fruit. It was a taste he was pretty sure would linger with him.

"You feel good," she told him, blinking rapidly and backing away. "But I still don't want to be a princess. And I still think you hold Leonardo against me. And Dede."

He shook his head, taking her seriously. It was true that the thought of her being with Leonardo made him cringe inside. The man was such scum, he couldn't understand why any woman would let him anywhere within touching distance. Still, that didn't mean the baby was to blame.

"No one can ever fault the baby," he said reasonably. "They have no say in the matter."

She looked up at him, her eyes dry now, but filled with a rueful sense of irony. "And you think *I* did?"

His head jerked in her direction. "What do you mean by that?"

She turned her head away. "Nothing. Nothing at all."

"Kim…" There was something there, but he lost it when she turned back and touched his cheek with the palm of her hand, making his heart jump in his chest.

"Take care, Jake. Be good to your sister. She needs a champion like you to guard her. Things are likely to get a lot rougher before we heal this rift."

He grabbed her hand and wouldn't let her withdraw it. "What are you talking about?" he asked her. "You sound like you're saying goodbye."

"Do I?" She shook her head and gave him a sad smile. Her gaze ranged restlessly over his handsome face. "I'm just so tired, I don't know what I'm saying. I'm going to bed."

She pulled on her hand and he let it go reluctantly.

"When is your appointment tomorrow?" he asked before she had a chance to leave the room.

She looked back at him. Her eyes were hooded. "In the afternoon. Two o'clock."

His mouth hardened. "Where is it?"

She shrugged. "I don't even know yet. Dr. Harve said he'd tell me just as I left, so as not to risk anyone else knowing."

He grunted, annoyed. "Me, he meant."

Her sad smile was back. "Maybe."

He looked at her assessingly. "Are you going into work in the morning?"

"No. I'm staying here. I took the day off."

He nodded. "All right, then." He watched as she started out of the kitchen, into the gloom, and he went to the doorway and called her back one last time.

"Kim, don't go to the man," he said, the urgency of his feelings clear in his voice. "It's no good and you know it."

She shook her head, but before she could speak, he went two steps closer and took both her hands in his, gazing at her earnestly.

"There's a simple solution to all this, of course. And you know what it is."

"No." She shook her head so hard her hair whipped across her face.

He held her hands tightly. "Go back with me to the castle and you'll have access to all the medical help and the best facilities you could ask for." He almost wanted to beg her. "It's a short trip across the island, Kim. I can take you there in one day."

She gave him another sample of her sad smile and slipped her hands out of his, then headed for her bedroom.

"We'll talk more in the morning," he said hopefully.

She nodded, looking back at him, and this time she made it to her room.

She'd lied about the time of her appointment. It was ten in the morning. She planned to get out of here with her baby, go to the appointment, and not come back to the apartment. That would mean finding another place to stay for a week or so. By then, hopefully, Jake would give up and go back to the castle without her.

Could she get away with it? Why not? If the pediatrician turned out to be as good as they said he was, it was worth a try. Only time would tell how this would all shake out.

One thing was sure—she wasn't going to be a DeAngelis princess. And she wasn't going back to be Pellea's pet again. Not ever.

CHAPTER SIX

THE morning sun scattered her fears and doubts like blossoms in a strong spring breeze. What had she been thinking last night? She'd let a combination of the electricity failing, being awake after midnight, the crush of all her troubles, and finally, Jake's influence, put her in a very bad place—a place where she didn't have to be. So when he'd come at her with this crazy story about her being royal, and tried to convince her it was serious, she'd been very low on defensive power and couldn't resist the emotions he'd conjured up for her.

This whole fantasy that the royals were trying to foist on her was complete nonsense. She'd heard bits and pieces of it before and had dismissed it out of hand. She knew who her mother was, she knew who had raised her and loved her and made her into the person she was today. For them to try to tear apart her reality and destroy the feelings she had for the only person in this world who ever truly loved her, just to force her to come back to their side, was despicable as far as she was concerned. She wasn't going to let them.

As for Jake—she couldn't believe he could actually be in on it, not fully. She was pretty sure he thought he was telling her the truth. He just couldn't be that good a liar. Much as they were at dagger's point with each other on a lot of things, she would like to think he at least had the integrity not to fall in with that sort of scheme. Somehow, they had convinced him.

But none of this mattered anymore. After today, she hoped never to see Jake again. And then, hopefully, the messengers from the castle would stop.

They'd been coming for the past six months, one after another. The first had been a young footman named Billy she'd known in the old days. He'd come to her cottage in Dorcher Cliffs with a simple message. Pellea wanted her best friend back and was ready to coax her. What would it take to get her to return?

That one had been easy to laugh off. She'd always liked Billy. That was surely why they had chosen him. So she'd fed him a nice dinner and gave him too much wine so that he'd told her everything—how Pellea and the rest of them were always plotting and trying to arrange matters. As if they didn't have anything better to do. Once she'd found out everything she wanted to know, she'd sent him packing.

The next came a month later, a nice young girl name Posey who had a flair for the dramatic. Kim had known her mother when she worked in the castle kitchen in the past. Posey pretended to know dangerous secrets and hinted around about dark spells and magic potions and foundlings who had to be returned to their proper places. Kim couldn't make heads nor tails of what she said, but when she announced that saying any more would endanger them both and might send Kim to the royal dungeon, she'd had enough and sent her packing as well.

And they were only the first two. Others came over the border to find her. None was very effectual. They begged, they pleaded, they claimed that Pellea was moping about for want of her best friend. Kim didn't believe a word of it and she stopped even being polite about it.

But Jake was the first to find her since she came to the city. He was also the one with most stature and rank, making her wonder why Pellea would send such an important person. But then he began trying to peddle a story of misplaced birth mothers even more seriously than the others. Hah. She didn't believe a word of that, either.

She was picking up clutter in the living room when Jake opened his eyes. He looked at her. She looked at him. The memory of what had happened the night before grew between them and before she knew it, they were both laughing.

"You know that it all didn't mean a thing, don't you?" she insisted right away. "You realize it was all part of the usual night terrors you get when the shadows are too thick and the time is too late."

He growled at her. "Are you saying that kissing me reminds you of your most ugly nightmares?" he asked softly.

"No, of course not." She laughed again, shaking her head. What was she saying, anyway? She wasn't sure. Luckily, Dede was crying and she had an excuse to turn away from him.

Dede wasn't doing very well this morning. Her little lower lip was pouted out and Kim could see the pain in her. Still, her pretty little eyes tried to smile. She was the sweetest of babies. Kim's heart broke, watching how hard she tried to remain cheerful, and something fierce grew inside her. She would do anything for this baby. No one was going to stop her from taking her to the pediatrician. Nobody.

"Have you been listening to the news?" Jake asked a

bit later, after Dede had been calmed and fed and was cooing happily in her crib.

There was no television in this skimpily furnished apartment, but Jake had found an old radio and listened to it now and then.

"No," she said, surprised by his tone. "What's going on?"

"It looks like the Granvilli government—or what's left of it, is about to fall apart. They say the only thing that could save it would be for Leonardo to show up and rally the factions to work together again. But nobody seems to know where he is." Staring at her, he raised one dark eyebrow.

She blinked. "Don't look at me. I've told you over and over again that he has nothing to do with my current life."

He nodded, noting the careful way she'd put that. On one level, he believed her. Why? Just basically because she was the sort of woman who tended to tell the truth. But there was so much more going on than simple relationships could encompass. There were international ties and incidents and remnants of war and power struggles. As someone had said once, their lives didn't matter a hill of beans compared to the major forces gathering and preparing to vie for power, wealth and influence. The big boys were at their games, and the regular people had better get out of the way if they could. They were the ones who tended to get hurt when the last card was played.

"You do realize that this isn't going to last," he told her calmly. "They might pull the government together one more time, Leonardo might even show up and rekindle some spirit, but it's all just in one big holding pattern. Everybody's waiting for the end."

"I'm not," she said stoutly, casually folding some baby clothes to put into the bag she was going to take with her and hoping he wouldn't think a thing of it. "For me, the end came long ago. I'm busy dealing with the fallout."

He frowned, not sure what she could mean by that. But he let it go. He was tired of arguing. What would be, would be.

"The whole of society is falling apart," he told her rather dolefully. "You can't find a decent doctor. The police are nowhere to be seen. Electricity is unreliable, cell phone service is out. I wonder how Wifi is doing. The country is regressing to conditions of a hundred years ago."

She kicked a baby blanket out of her path, annoyed with him for going on this way. Deep in her heart, she knew it was probably true. But what good did it do thinking about it now? There was nothing she could do about it. Besides, her goals were more short-term at the moment.

"The DeAngelis royals are eventually going to come in and take over this side of the island, too," he said flatly, following her progress through the room with his crystal-blue gaze. "You know it. And what are you going to do then?"

"I'll deal with that when it happens." She threw him a quick glare. "Maybe I'll just go further into the mountains. There are people up there who have lived away from the rest of Ambrian society for decades, you know."

"Okay. I see. You'll join the mountain people." He grinned, obviously amused. "Hey, that sounds like fun. Maybe I'll come with you."

She resisted the temptation to grin back at him. He would be fun if she would only let him be. She knew that. But she also knew that it didn't pay to get too friendly with people. You began to rely on them, and then they always let you down. And sometimes, they did worse than that.

She glanced at the clock. The minutes ticked by. In another hour, she would be arriving at the pediatrician's location. She only hoped and prayed that he would be able to help Dede.

She'd packed away her baby's things and a bottle in case she needed it. She was pretty much ready to go. The only thing that was worrying her now was whether or not Jake would go back to sleep before the time came for her to grab Dede and go.

To her chagrin, she'd actually played around with the idea of trying to drug him. She certainly had enough medicine still hanging around from what Dr. Harve had given him that first day. But when it came right down to it, she couldn't do it. It just wasn't right. If he didn't go to sleep, she would tell him she was taking Dede to the park and she would slip out anyway.

And then—a miracle. She looked over at him, and Jake was asleep in the big, deep chair. Her heart jumped and she went quickly to her notebook, tore a paper out and wrote him a quick message. Then she gathered together as many of Dede's things as she could possibly carry and gave one last glance at Jake. It gave her a pang to see him sleeping there, oblivious to what she was doing. He was so handsome. She looked at his full, beautiful lips and smiled as she remembered the kiss. She paused a second longer, itching to reach out and brush back the dark hair that had fallen over his forehead. But she couldn't risk waking him.

It was time to go.

* * *

Jake woke up almost an hour later. He stretched, yawned and glanced around. There was no one in sight. Suddenly, the eerie quiet of the apartment was ominous. It didn't sound as though someone had left the apartment and would be back soon. It sounded as though someone had left and was never, ever coming back. How he could tell the difference, he wasn't sure. But he knew it.

Rising from the chair, he hobbled to the bathroom, then did a quick tour of the room. Kim had taken the big bag she used to carry Dede's things in. That didn't necessarily mean anything. She took it everywhere. But something didn't feel right.

And then he saw the note. He went quickly to the table and dropped into a chair before he picked it up.

Dear Jake,
I think it's only fair if I let you know, I'm taking Dede to the pediatrician. We're going earlier than I told you. Sorry that I felt I had to lie to you. I won't be coming back. You won't be able to find me again, so you might as well go back and give Pellea my regrets. Once again, I must refuse her generous offer.
　　Goodbye, Jake. Take care.

Crumpling the paper in his fist, he growled his anger. Rising slowly, he tested his leg. It was still painful, but that was just too bad. He wasn't going to let it hold him back. Not this time.

Then he hesitated. He couldn't go anywhere with his jeans pants cut almost to the crotch. His gaze fell on the pants Kim had snagged for him at the hospital. Quickly, he tugged off his jeans and put on the stretchy pants. They weren't stylish, but they would do the job. He grabbed his coat and slammed out of the apartment, heading for Dr. Harve's place.

He found it at the second door he tried. Dr. Harve opened the door and immediately looked as though he regretted it.

"Oh. Hello. I was just…"

Jake didn't wait for niceties. He used his forearm as a bar at the doctor's throat and pushed him back against the wall.

"Give me the address," he demanded coldly.

The doctor sputtered, choking. "I…I don't know what you're talking about."

He jammed his arm at the throat harder, in no mood for mercy. "You know she's in danger. Give it to me."

The doctor turned bright red, choking and gasping for air. "No, no, I gave her the name of a friend of mine. He's a fine doctor, really…." He was now almost turning blue.

Jake relented long enough to let him get a breath. "Good men can turn bad when they get desperate," he pointed out harshly. "And from what you've said about this guy, he's desperate."

"Oh no." He grabbed at his bruised neck, his voice sounding as if it was coming from the bottom of a food mill. "Not Henry."

"Give me the address. Now."

His eyes flared and he tried to pull away, looking frightened. "I can't give it to you, I promised."

Jake's hand grabbed his throat and he picked him up by it, smashing him against the wall behind him.

"Give me the address, you bastard," he snarled. "You just sent Kim and her baby into a trap and you probably suspect it yourself."

"No, no! You've got it all wrong."

He pushed him back harder. "Give it to me now or I'll break your damn neck."

Dr. Harve made a strangling sound, flailing like a rag doll, but Jake could make out parts of a word that sounded like acquiescence. He let him drop, but stood close enough to threaten him, and Dr. Harve reached into his jacket and produced a crumpled paper.

"Here," he said, his voice sounding ruined. "Now get out of here. I've got a gun, you know."

"Really?" Jake took the address and put it into his pocket, then looked down at the man with contempt. "I wouldn't bring it out if I were you. I'd probably just use it to kill you."

And without another word, he was gone.

He had no idea where the address was. His leg ached, but he didn't care. He was driven by time, and he was afraid it might already be too late.

The street outside was empty, and when he got to the main street, a block away, it wasn't busy. Still, there were a few pedestrians who looked like they might know a thing or two. He only had to ask three before he found someone who could tell him where the address would lead him. It was only about a mile away.

"Not a good part of town, however," the man who was helping him warned. "You'd better watch your back in that neighborhood."

"Don't worry," Jake said through gritted teeth. "I'm ready for that."

To his amazement the motorbike was still chained to the bus bench, just as Kim had said it was. He'd have thought someone would have sawed off the chain by now. Maybe that was the advantage of having a bike so old and disreputable that no one else wanted it. He found the key in his coat pocket, and in minutes he was on his way. He had no idea how long ago Kim had left the apartment, but he was pretty sure she either had to walk, carrying Dede, or take the bus. Either way, he was just hoping there was a chance to catch up since he had the advantage with the bike.

Until it ran out of gas.

At first he just stared at it, unable to believe the timing. He had to restrain himself from giving it a kick. But there was no other option than wheeling it along the road until he found somewhere with gas for sale. And he knew from experience that wouldn't be easy.

He kept up a steady chain of swear words under his breath as he walked, angry at himself, angry at fate, angry at Kim, angry at the whole medical profession. And at the same time, he pushed himself to walk as fast as he could on his bum leg. The pain was stabbing now, every time he took a step. It was just this side of impossible to stand, but he felt the urgency of time passing drumming at his back and he had to hurry. He had to get there before…

He tried to tell himself that he didn't know for certain that the man was a crook and a kidnapper. But he was pretty sure that was the case. If Kim lost Dede just because he ran out of gas, he wasn't sure he would be able to live with himself.

Another thing bothered him. He was regretting that he'd left Dr. Harve in one piece. What if he found a way to call his friend and warn him? That would not be good. He had to go faster. If only the stupid bike hadn't crapped out on him.

And then—a miracle! A gas station that actually had some gas. He wheeled his bike up to the pump and filled the tank. New life—for him and his motorcycle.

Another moment and they were off through the winding streets.

"Hold on, Kim," he muttered into the wind. "Just hold on a few minutes longer."

It took much too long to find the address. He went up and down streets, asking everyone he could find. But as his original helper had said, it was a bad neighborhood. People weren't very forthcoming in a place that smelled like too many people used the sides of buildings as a lavatory.

He retraced his steps, knowing it had to be there somewhere but unable to pin it down, and panic started to claw at his gut.

"I'm coming, Kim," he muttered, almost in despair. "If I could just find the damn…"

And suddenly, there it was, the street sign hidden behind a large parked truck. He turned and found the building right away, stashing the bike and taking the crumbling stairs two at a time, biting back the cry of pain that tried to come up his throat. He found the number and he didn't bother to knock, thrusting the door open and staring into Kim's wide eyes.

"You're still here," he panted out, struggling for breath. "Thank God."

She was furious, her face strained, her eyes huge with anger.

"What are you doing here?" she demanded. "How dare you interfere with my life this way? How did you find me, anyway? Did you hurt the doctor?"

But he didn't answer any of that. Looking around, he realized she didn't have her baby.

"Where's Dede?" he demanded hoarsely.

"Jake, you can't…"

He grabbed her by the shoulders. "Where the hell is Dede?" he yelled.

She looked at him blankly. "The doctor took her into the examining room, just to weigh her, while I fill out these papers. They should be back any second."

Something about Jake's tone and the look in his face was finally communicating the seriousness of the situation to her. She still didn't believe anything was wrong. But if Jake was this worked up, maybe she ought to check.

Jake couldn't wait for her to decide what was important and what wasn't. He pushed past her into the area she'd called the examining room. It was empty. He flew to the window and just caught sight of someone disappearing down the outside fire escape.

Kim was screaming behind him but he couldn't stop. He tore out of the doorway and down the metal stairs, jumping the last portion. He'd never run so hard before in his life. His entire being, every part of him, was focused and determined. He was going to get Dede back.

And then he fell, tripping over a cement boundary in a parking lot and coming down hard. He cried out in pain, but a part of his consciousness wouldn't accept it. He had no time for pain. Leaping back to his feet, he ran again, more determined than ever.

He saw a long black car ahead, a driver waiting, and he knew that was the destination. He could see the snatcher, judge their relative distances from the car, and he knew he would never catch him in time. He had to think fast. Another few seconds and it would be too late. Dede would be gone forever.

They would never find any police who would help them in time. The snatcher would have her out of the country before they even found someone who would take a report.

He knew he would never catch the snatcher by following behind. He had to take a chance. Instead of running down the sidewalk behind him, he took a short cut, leaping on the back of a parked car, and from there, onto one that was moving.

The people inside began to yell and the driver looked for a place to pull over, but he got a good start and when he leaped from the stopping car onto another that was moving in the right direction, he got another boost.

He was gaining, but not enough. He could see the so-called pediatrician about to jump into the long black car. Everything in him made a surge. He almost thought he could fly, if he just willed it. And this time he took a wild, insane short cut across three cars, and from there he dove, tackling the snatcher around the legs just before he stepped into the car.

He felt bones crunch and heard the yell of injury from the snatcher, but his focus was all on Dede, and he saw the man let her go as he fell. She was wrapped in a blanket, but she landed hard on the cement. Jake aimed for her, leaving the man behind as he sailed across the space between them and grabbed her. She was crying, hiccupping in hysterics, and he held her close, then turned to see the snatcher disappear into the car and the car take off like a bat out of hell.

He suddenly realized that he hadn't been breathing enough. His chest felt as though it had caved in. He gasped for air and the pain from his cracked ribs was excruciating. But he held Dede, cooing sweet comfort into her tiny baby ear, and thanking every spirit and god he could think of for the victory.

Suddenly, Kim was there. She didn't say a word, just

opened her arms for her baby, and he handed her over. There was a bump growing on Dede's forehead and a bloody scrape right beside it, but she stopped crying once her mother was holding her.

And Jake collapsed in a heap on the sidewalk.

"Crazy insane. Both of us were crazy insane. Me, for trying to convince myself it would be okay to go to that awful man. And you for saving Dede the way you did."

She shook her head, staring at him in wonder again as she had been for the past half hour.

"You flew. I saw you. You were in the air, flying, as though just the force of your will could make it happen." She threw up her hands, shaking her head. "It was like in a movie. If I hadn't seen it myself, I wouldn't believe it."

Jake didn't say anything. His head was back and his eyes were closed. They were in a small coffee shop, sitting in a corner booth, drinking iced tea and trying to recover from what had just happened.

"By all rights, I should have broken my neck," he said, pretty much in awe of it all himself. "Or at least my leg. My bad leg. The one I can hardly walk on. But somehow, it all worked."

"Adrenaline," Kim said, nodding. "That is what it had to be."

"Maybe. Or just a little magic." He straightened and looked at her, then looked down at a sleeping Dede in her arms. A feeling of overwhelming happiness washed over him and he frowned, forcing it back.

Okay, so he saved this woman and her baby. He was lucky. And no, it didn't make up for not saving his own wife and his own baby that awful day. Nothing could make up for that.

But it was still good. So good. He took a deep breath and then he sighed. Okay. He was going to allow himself a little happiness. Hey, he deserved it. Didn't he?

"How did you know?" she asked him, dropping a kiss on Dede's downy head. "How did you know he would turn out to be a crook?"

"I didn't know for sure. But the signs were all bad." He shook his head. "This is what it's often like when you lose a war. It brings the best out in some people, but too many lose sight of their humanity and resort to any means to survive." He glanced at her sideways. "And those roving bands of child snatchers you said appeared in Dorcher Cliffs a few months ago have shown up all over the island. It's just that on the Granvilli side, law and order is breaking down. You see it everywhere."

She nodded. She knew it was true.

"You know there are plenty of people on the continent who want babies and can't have them for one reason or another. A lot of them will pay plenty for a child they can adopt. And many don't care where they came from."

She sighed. "I know that. It's just hard to believe when it comes this close to you." She shook her head. "To think of Dede in that man's control." Her voice broke and she looked down at her child. The lump was going down and she'd cleaned up the scrape with water in the bathroom. But it could have been so much worse. She shuddered.

Jake was thinking about the same thing, just thankful that he'd taken out after her when he did. If he'd slept another half hour…

He glanced up at Kim. She was looking thoughtful and his antennae went up.

"What now?" he said softly. "What's the plan?"

She looked at him, her dark eyes candid. "I want to go home," she said.

"To the castle?"

"No!" She glared at him. "That's not home. Dorcher Cliffs is home. I have a cottage there. I was raised in it until…until I went to the castle."

He nodded slowly. "Great," he said. "Let's go."

She started to laugh. "I don't remember inviting you to come along," she noted.

"That's where you're wrong. There was the distinct element of invitation in your voice. I heard it loud and clear."

"Really?"

"Yes, really." He reached out and grabbed her hand in his. His eyes were dark and serious as he gazed into hers. "Do you think I'm going to let you go anywhere by yourself after what happened today?"

She was shaking her head, but she was still laughing.

But he wasn't amused. "You've got to stop running from me," he said. "I'm not the enemy, Kim."

"Okay." She sobered. "I won't run away from you. But…"

"I know." He nodded. "You don't want me to think you've given in. I understand. That doesn't mean I'm going to quit working on it." He flashed her a quick smile. "But I don't expect you to cave in. Not yet."

She sighed. She knew she was supposed to be guarding herself against him, but after what he'd done now, how could she hold him off the way she had before? Impossible. She leaned toward him.

"We're partners now, right? I need to go where I can think about things. I'm going to decide what's best for me to do. But I've got to get some stability, some peace and quiet. I need to go to the cottage."

"I agree. I think it would be good for you—and for Dede."

"Yes. We can stay there. We can talk things over and…we'll see." She gave him a warning look. "But I want your word that you won't pressure me. You're not going to try to grab me and throw me over your shoulder and drag me to the castle, are you?"

"Mixed metaphor, kind of," he noted. "I can't drag you if you're on my shoulder."

She punched his arm. "You know what I mean. Are you?"

"I swear to you I won't do that."

The waitress brought the sandwiches they'd ordered. Jake ate his ravenously, but Kim couldn't eat. She was still in shock, at least emotionally, over what had happened.

What if Jake hadn't arrived when he did? What might have happened? It made her hold her baby closer and whisper a little prayer of gratitude.

She glanced around the shabby little café. Someone had strung multicolored lights around the edge of the counter and there was a small Santa Claus by the cash register. At least someone had remembered what the season was. She shivered and looked down at Dede. She wanted an old-fashioned Christmas for her, with snow and Yule logs and horses pulling sleighs.

The trouble was, you didn't get those where they were going. For that, they would have to stay up here in the mountains. She'd never had a Christmas like that herself. So where did she get the sense that it was the ideal? She sighed. Somehow she would make her baby's Christmas special. She would find a way.

"Do you want to go back to your apartment before we head out?" Jake asked her.

She smiled. She thought it was interesting how completely he was invested in this trip already. "No," she said. "I didn't leave much behind and I'm fully paid up for the month." She stopped, suddenly anxious. "What did you do to Dr. Harve?" she asked as she realized he must have done something to get the address of where she was going. "Do you think we should go back and check on him?"

Jake barely met her gaze before his skittered off again. "No," he said shortly. "I'm sure he's okay."

"Uh-huh." She shook her head, but she really didn't want to know the details. "And how about you? Are you okay? You put that body through a lot today. Maybe you should have a day of rest before trying to travel."

"Don't be ridiculous," he scoffed. "I'm ready to go when you are. We can be in Dorcher Cliffs by dinner time."

"Really?" She wrinkled her nose. "How are we planning to do this?"

He looked astonished that she didn't understand that already. "On the motorcycle of course."

"Oh?" Her eyebrows rose. "That sounds exciting. Do we each get our own motorcycle?"

He frowned as though he thought she was being silly on purpose. "No. You'll be riding behind me, holding on for dear life."

She was beginning to realize he really meant it and her eyes got very wide. "On that crummy little thing?" she said, looking out to where he'd locked it to a lamppost.

"Sure. It can handle the load. I'll be careful."

She opened her mouth, but nothing came out. She was speechless.

"It's a fine little machine," he said quickly, reassuring her. "It'll get us there, don't worry."

She stared at him, trying to picture what they would look like flying down the highway. "But…but how will I carry Dede and hold on at the same time?"

"No problem. We'll tie you on. And put Dede in that sling carrier you have and strap her to you. It'll be fine."

"Tie me on?"

"Sure. It's the only way that will work. No one will pay any attention to us. We'll be instantly incognito."

She let out a sigh that was more exasperation than anything else. "Because only fools would ride that way?"

He grinned as though he thought she finally got it. "Something like that."

"Wonderful." Her sarcasm was showing, just a little bit.

He frowned, realizing she really wasn't with the program just yet. "Do you have a better idea?"

She shrugged, wishing she could think of something, fast. "We could take the bus. That's how we got here about six weeks ago. The bus is pretty incognito, too."

His scowl showed her what he thought of that idea. "Not incognito enough. We need to fly under the radar."

She shook her head, at a loss. "Why?"

He hesitated, realizing that was a pretty good question. "Because I'm illegal and you're a runaway princess. Don't you think those are a couple of pretty good reasons?"

Shaking her head, she gave in. Despite all he'd been through, he was the one with more energy, more spunk left. She just felt wrung out and lifeless. She needed to get where she could relax again, something she hadn't done in weeks.

And so she gave him the answer he was waiting for. "All right. I'm ready. What do I do?"

CHAPTER SEVEN

THE snow began as they were leaving the city.

"Don't worry," Kim told Jake. "It never snows in Dorcher Cliffs, or anywhere down near the shore. We'll be out of this soon."

Famous last words.

The bike was steady, but not very fast. As they chugged along, it began to snow even harder. Jake was right about one thing—they were incognito—hidden by the driving snow. There wasn't anyone else on the road to see them, anyway. Most people wisely stayed indoors.

Kim wasn't sure she would make it. Every mile seemed more and more excruciating. The wind whipped her face, snow matted in her hair, her ears were frozen. She had to hold Dede so tightly, she kept wondering if she was about to smother her in all the cloth and binding. What on earth had she let herself in for? This was pure misery. They had to go back.

She let Jake know how she felt when they came to a pause at a crossroads. At first he tried words of encouragement.

"Just think of pioneer women in the American West," he told her cheerfully. "Crossing the snow-covered Sierras in little rickety wagons."

"At least they had some protection from the elements," she noted rather sharply.

"Not a whole lot. Besides, this is only going to last for a few hours, not days or weeks like their journey did."

It was obvious he was having the time of his life. He seemed to thrive in the freezing cold wind. Snowflakes stuck to his eyelashes, making him look even more rakish than usual, and his eyes were shining with adventure. But once he'd looked back into her face, he seemed to realize her complaint was no passing fancy.

He pulled over as they came up to a small shed ahead, pulling out of the weather as much as he could and turning to look at her again.

"If you're really this miserable, we'd better do something about it," he said soberly.

She looked up at him in surprise. Something about his willingness to see her side of things made her feel much better.

"We could find a farmhouse," he suggested. "There have to be a few near here. And maybe they would let us in for a bit. Once the snow lets up, we could go on, or turn back, whichever seems best at the time."

She studied his serious face, wondering how she could ever have thought he looked like a man filled with hate. He seemed to be ready to accommodate her in any way she needed.

"No, you know what?" she said, shocking even herself. "I can do this. I'm just letting myself sink into whining a bit. I'm over it now." After all, the main thing was to get home so she could think things through and decide what she was going to do about finding a doctor for Dede.

He frowned, searching her eyes. "Are you sure?"

"As long as Dede's okay, I can do this."

He glanced down at the baby and smiled. "Okay. Let me know if it gets to be too much." He looked at her speculatively. "We might find an inn, you know. If we do, we'll stop."

She shook her head. "The only inn I know of along this road gets a little wild at night. Let's just push on through. We wouldn't want to stop there."

Wrong again. The one thing she didn't anticipate was that Dede would be so hungry after the crazy day she'd had that she would let fussing turn into outright crying. That was unusual for her. So was the wrestling match she was trying to have with the sling and everything else that got in her way. Then Kim remembered that she'd only fed her once since lunch. In time, the struggle was just too much and Kim had to ask Jake to stop again.

"We're going to have to pull over," she called out to Jake.

"Look," he said. "The inn is just ahead. Why don't we go in there and get warm for a bit before we go on?"

Despite her reservations about the place, the prospect of getting warm sounded like heaven.

"We'll just go in and get a little cup of soup to warm us up and we'll be on our way again," Jake suggested. "Meanwhile you can get that little fussbudget fed."

Once inside, Kim's spirits started to rise. Waves of warmth enveloped them, and then the happy sounds of patrons singing songs and engaging in some good-natured teasing that included a lot of laughter. It seemed a crowded, cheerful scene. A lot of the men looked like they'd only been out of the army for a short time, and some still wore their uniforms—Granvilli green was everywhere.

Once inside the pub, they found a table in the far corner and Jake left them to go to the bar and order a couple of cups of chowder. He was back with the soup moments later, sliding into his seat, turning his face away from the crowd and pulling up his hood over his head.

"Wouldn't you know it?" he said to her. "The one place I see someone I know from the other side and it has to be here and now."

"What?" she asked, alarmed.

His face was grim. "There's someone here who knows me."

She drew in a sharp breath. "Where?"

"See that bunch by the fireplace? The tall fellow with the purple scarf?"

She looked where he'd directed her. A group of three or four men were gathered in front of the fire, each holding a drink. They seemed to be having a great time together. She picked out the one Jake was talking about and noted he seemed to have a roving eye as he kept track of every buxom waitress who passed him.

"Who is he?" she asked him.

"Hiram Bounce. He was actually one of my lieutenants at the beginning of the war." His face darkened. "He got caught sleeping with another officer's wife and he defected before his court martial. I thought he'd gone to the continent, but it seems he ended up here in Granvilli territory."

She nodded. He seemed the type. "He hasn't seen you, has he?"

"I don't think so."

"What do you think he'll do if he does?"

Jake shrugged. "Act like he's glad to see me and turn me in behind my back."

She sighed. "Then we'd better make sure he doesn't see you."

He turned and looked out, being careful to stay under his hood as much as he could. "That is getting harder and harder to imagine," he noted. "He and his group are edging closer and closer to the pathway in front of the door.. That's going to make getting out of here a problem."

She chewed on her lip for a moment, thinking it over. Luckily, there were enough people milling around in the room to give them cover for the time being. But Jake was right. There was no way he was going to be able to walk past the man to the doorway and not be noticed.

"What are we going to do?"

He shook his head, eyes troubled. "We can't stay here in this booth all night."

She nodded. "Maybe we could leave through the kitchen?" she suggested, but once they took a look at that route, they knew it wouldn't work. The way the waiters came barreling in and out through the swinging doors left no room for sneaking.

They ate their soup and it was wonderful, warming them from the inside while the heat of the fire warmed them on the outside. She fed Dede, which put her back to sleep. And then they watched Hiram and his friends laugh and joke and down more alcohol and wondered what to do.

Finally, Kim made a decision.

"Okay. How do I look?" She turned her face toward him and lifted her chin for examination.

"How do you look?" He gazed at her, puzzled. "Beautiful, as always. Why?"

"No, I'm serious. How do I look? My hair is all wet

and the snow has washed off all my makeup. So how bad is it?"

He shook his head, bemused by her words. "Kim, hasn't anyone ever told you that you have a luminous quality that shines right through all that?"

She smiled at him. "You're being very sweet, but not very helpful. I need to know if men are going to find me attractive."

He almost laughed aloud at that one. "In a word, yes."

"Okay." She began to gather things together. "You take Dede and just skulk around the outskirts of the crowd, going that way." She pointed it out. "Just lie low until I create enough of a distraction so that you can slip out through the door without anyone paying any attention to you."

He frowned. "Wait a minute. What exactly do you have in mind?"

"I'm going to make a brave attempt to be captivating enough to draw the men's attention. Wish me luck. In my bedraggled condition, I'm going to need it."

He frowned, looking stubborn. "I don't know. I don't like you putting yourself in jeopardy like that."

She gave him a look of pure exasperation. "Oh come on! I can do this. You don't think I can do anything, do you?"

He looked shocked at such a suggestion. "Of course I do. I know how talented you are. I just don't think you ought to waste those talents."

"Come on." She gave him a bright smile. "Let's do it."

Jake was still reluctant. He turned and glanced at the men over his shoulder.

"They've all had a few by now. What happens if they

don't let you go?" He turned back and looked at her. "What if they get a little too friendly, too fast?"

He had a point. The war had made everyone just a little bit harder, a little coarser, and a lot more difficult to deal with. But she put on a good front.

"I grew up in the castle. I know how to handle myself around a group of rowdy men."

He watched her for a moment and then a slow smile began to grow. "I imagine you do," he admitted at last, his gaze traveling so slowly over her face, it was almost caressing her cheek.

She smiled back. He'd done something to save her baby today. Now she hoped she could do something to help him.

Still, her heart was beating like a drum as she sidled up to the revelers. She'd talked big to Jake, but she wasn't sure just how rusty she might be at this sort of thing. She waited until Jake seemed to be at just the right angle across the room, holding Dede and getting ready to charge out the door, and then she made her move.

"Hey guys," she said, flouncing in the midst of the three and flashing her smile all around. "Is this a private party or can anybody join?"

Hiram was the only one she really focused on and he appeared startled, then immensely pleased.

"We've got special openings for girls as pretty as you, sweetheart," he said, leaning toward her. "What's on your mind?"

She gave him a flirtatious look. "My friend and I were just wondering how late you guys were going to be hanging around. We have an obligation we have to take care of, but if you're still going to be here in an hour or so, we thought we might come back and see what sort of celebration we can work our way up to."

All three men were practically drooling with anticipation by now.

"Any time, baby."

"Hey, if there's not a party when you get back, we'll make one happen for you."

But it was Hiram who noted something missing. "Where's your friend?" he asked, looking in the direction she'd come from and not seeing anyone interesting.

"She's...uh..." Kim craned her neck in the direction she wanted the men to look. "Well, she's back there somewhere. We were sitting at that booth."

From the corner of her eye she could see Jake beginning to sidle toward the doorway.

"Which booth?" Hiram began to frown, as though suspicious, and she felt her heartbeat stutter.

"That one," she said, pointing.

But Hiram was turning back. "I don't see her," he said, and his position was turned enough to see the doorway, just what she didn't want.

Jake was almost there. She had to do something fast.

"Well, come on," she said, reaching out quickly to take his arm and turn him away from the door. "Let's go look. She's got to be back here somewhere."

So now she had him by the arm and he was looking down at her as though he couldn't believe his luck.

"Hey, never mind. What do we need with her when we've got you?"

She knew her answering smile was a little shaky, but she gave it all she could. Jake had to be out the door by now. She risked a quick look over her shoulder.

Nope, he was still there. A woman with a large puff of red hair had stopped him, wanting to see the baby.

Kim whipped her head back around and went back to pretending to be fascinated by Hiram, but all she could think about was Jake, and silently, she was urging him to hurry.

All three men were saying things to her but she had gone beyond hearing them, so she just smiled and nodded and prayed Jake was gone by now. She held out as long as she could, then finally let herself steal another look.

Relief flooded her. He was gone.

"Hey, you know what?" she told her new friends. "I think my girlfriend has gone out and is waiting for me outside. I'm going to have to go. But we'll be back. You can count on that."

She flashed them each a quick smile and started for the door, hurrying, hoping.

But she wasn't going to get away so easily. Hiram was right by her side, slipping an arm around her shoulders and giving her a slimy smile that seemed to mean he was claiming her as his own.

"Hey, I'll go out with you," he said, hugging her closer than she liked as they left the room and went into the foyer. "I want to meet this friend. Is she as pretty as you?"

Her heart was in her throat. Now that her mission was accomplished, how was she going to shake this guy?

"Prettier," she said automatically, then glanced up at him and felt a shudder coming on. "But she's not for now, honey."

Pulling away from him, she pushed him back into the room.

"You just wait here. We'll be back."

Turning, she opened the door and the blast of cold air coming in from outside almost set her back on her heels. But even worse, Hiram was back again by her side, worse than a bad penny.

"I'm not going to risk losing you, now that I've found you," he said, and there was a steely glint in his eye as though he were warning her he didn't like all this kidding around. "Where is this friend of yours? In one of these cars?"

Kim looked out through the parking lot and her pulse raced. There was no sign of Jake. Where was he?

"Uh, I don't see her," she said, stalling for time and wondering a bit desperately how she was going to get Hiram to go back into the inn.

The door flew open again, and there were the other two men, each calling out to Hiram and Kim. Hiram turned back to yell a response at them and in that moment, they seemed to come together, each yelling something, like a scrum of young men pretending to be unruly puppies.

And at that moment, Jake came shooting out from behind a car and stopped the bike right where Kim was standing. He had Dede strapped to his chest and his hood down and there was no way anyone was going to recognize him. She jumped aboard, grabbing on to him, and off they went. Looking back, she could see that the men were just beginning to understand that she'd left them and seemed too befuddled to know what to do next. She held on to Jake more tightly and began to laugh.

But Jake wasn't laughing. "That was a little too close for comfort," he grumped.

Kim laughed again, exhilarated.

"It was a good thing they were stumbling all over each other or they might have noticed me waiting for you," he said. "As it is, I don't think they have a clue."

"You're right. I'm sure they thought my 'friend' was a surprisingly large, burly sort of girl piloting a motorcycle."

He looked back. "At least they don't seem to be following us. Probably couldn't find their car keys. We're lucky."

"You don't think we could have beat them on this trusty steed?"

"Not if any of them had anything that ran."

She laughed again, face into the cold wind. "That was fun. Let's find another inn and do it again."

Jake hunched over the handlebars and shuddered.

They drove on for another hour. The snow was letting up, but darkness was falling. Suddenly, Jake pulled off the road behind a small stand of trees and got off the bike, walking back toward the road and staring ahead.

"What is it?" Kim asked.

"I can't tell for sure, but it looks to me like that might be a roadblock up ahead." He pointed toward an area where there seemed to be a group of cars circling a set of floodlights.

"Why would there be a roadblock?" she asked, frowning.

He shrugged. "Who knows? Sometimes local militias get frisky and decide to take the law into their own hands. You never know." He turned and looked into the gathering gloom. "I think we'll head out into the open country for a while. You game?"

He looked at her. She looked up at him.

She had Dede again as they'd stopped and changed partners a while ago. But something about this trip was pulling the two of them closer together and forming a bond between them that she never would have expected.

"Sure," she said, feeling a little breathless from what she thought she saw in his eyes. "I'm ready for anything."

He smiled at her and reached out to touch her cheek. But only for a second, and then he was swinging back onto the bike, dousing the light, and they were off, leaving the road behind. But the tingle where he'd touched her was harder to lose.

"Hold on tight," he called back as they hit a rutted meadow.

The bike began to bounce like a bronco. She held on tight. Now, not only was it miserably cold and the going rough, her bottom was being punished like it had never been before. She felt as though a giant had taken her up and shaken her, then thrown her down in a way that made her bounce. For just a few minutes, she had some doubts about the survival of certain body parts.

But it didn't last much longer. He found a smoother path near a river, and then, finally, they were back on the road.

Jake stopped and looked back up the way they would have come. The lights of the blockade were just barely visible. They started off again, but he waited another couple of miles before he turned on his lights and it was a little spooky dashing through the darkness.

The wind had died down, and the snow was just light-as-a-feather flakes now, but it covered the countryside and coated every tree.

"Hey, remember what you said about it not snowing down at the lower levels?" he called back to her.

"Who, me?"

"Yes, you. You ready to revise that opinion?"

"Yes."

"Okay, just checking."

She sighed. "I've never seen it like this before. Isn't it beautiful?"

It was like a fairyland and eerily silent. The only sound was the bike as it putted along. A magic night, a magic journey. She sighed, wondering how she could so easily go from fearing him to being annoyed with him to being grateful—and now this. What was this exactly? She didn't know and she didn't want to think about it too hard. It was what it was, and it was obviously temporary. So it hardly mattered, did it? Whatever.

And then, finally, they reached the cliffs that Dorcher Cliffs was named for. The whole town spread out below them in lights, like a diamond necklace thrown carelessly upon an open beach. Many houses had lights strung, and some of the boats in the harbor were strung with lights, too. The entire town seemed to be aching to celebrate something.

Kim felt happy just looking down at her little town. She was home. They began to make their way down the winding road toward the cottage and she leaned forward and said, "You know what's coming up? Tomorrow is Christmas Eve."

"No kidding. I haven't been paying attention, I'm afraid."

"I know. You've been a little busy trying not to get killed lately."

"Exactly."

"I don't think you'll be in danger in Dorcher Cliffs," she said serenely. "So you can relax and enjoy the holiday."

She began to hum "White Christmas" against his neck.

He shook his head as she started to laugh. Suddenly she realized she'd been laughing a lot in the last few hours. She didn't laugh much these days. In fact, she thought she'd probably laughed more today with Jake than she had in all the months since the war began put together. It really seemed to be true that attitude was everything.

When they had started out from the city, she'd thought there was no way she could do this. But just being with Jake and listening to his silly jokes and feeling his concern and seeing how he looked at life as an adventure had changed everything. She had to remember that.

The cottage was small, just two bedrooms and a living room/kitchen combination, but there was a nice little yard with a covered patio that gave it a garden quality. The atmosphere was cozy. If you stopped and listened for a moment, you could hear the waves on the rocks, not far away.

This was where Kim had spent her early childhood, before her mother had been lured back to working and living in the castle despite the fact that it was under the Granvilli regime. Kim had gone with her and received early training in castle work, besides being accepted as the personal companion to Pellea.

Her mother had died before she turned eighteen, leaving her the cottage that they had used mainly for holidays in those last few years. Despite the fact that she didn't know many of her neighbors very well, she thought of Dorcher Cliffs as home and always had. Her mother's sister, Grace Day, had a small house down by the shore, but she'd lived in Paris for years and seldom visited.

Even after she'd been banished from the castle shortly after the war had begun and had fled here to have her baby, she'd kept to herself. Leonardo had never tried to find her here. She was pretty sure he'd gone on to other concerns. The good citizens of Dorcher Cliffs seemed to respect her need for privacy. They might leave a basket of freshly baked buns or a sack of home-grown fruit occasionally, but a smile and a few words of thanks seemed to suffice. They kept their distance but she never had a sense of animosity from them. All in all, it was a comfortable place to live.

As they drove in, she was surprised to see her aunt's house, with its old-fashioned Captain's walk around the roof peak, lit up as though someone was living there. Maybe her aunt was home for a visit. She would have to check that out.

The cottage smelled a little musty, as though no one had been in it since she'd left. She pointed out the fire-place to Jake and he quickly began to build a fire in the grate.

"That should take the chill out of the night," he said as he rocked back on his heels in satisfaction, looking at the results of his handiwork.

Kim smiled. It was so nice to have someone else there to help with things that had to be done. She re-alized, suddenly, how tired she was of being responsi-ble for everything. She changed poor Dede who'd been in the same diaper for hours, giving her a quick bath in warm water in the sink. She loved the water, bab-bling and cooing and splashing with her fat little hands, laughing as the bubbles rose. And then her little face registered a twinge of stabbing pain.

Kim could hardly stand it. She'd gone off to the city for six weeks to find relief for Dede and now she was back and not one step closer to finding help. As a mother, she was a class-A failure. She had to do something and do it now.

"What's it going to be, girl?" she asked herself softly. "What's it going to be?"

She picked her baby up and held her close, singing an old song that came readily to mind, and trying to use her love to heal her baby, even if only for the moment. That wasn't enough, but it was all she had tonight.

Carrying Dede out into the living room, she was still humming as Jake looked up and gave her a crooked smile.

"You know what, go take a shower," he said, reaching out for Dede. "That'll make you feel better. I'll take care of this little girl."

"Really?"

"Of course." The way he held her showed he knew what he was doing. "I've got a little bit of experience with this sort of thing, you know."

She remembered he'd had a baby of his own once. She smiled and did as he suggested. The shower restored her spirits. It was always a boost to feel clean and fresh.

She came out into the living room and found Jake in a rocking chair again, only this time it was a slender, rickety model her mother had used. Dede seemed to be sound asleep and Jake's head was back, but his eyes were open, if barely, and he gave her a slight smile as she got closer, though he didn't say a word.

She went on into the kitchen, opened the freezer and pulled out two sacks of frozen soup, popping them into the microwave. It was late and there was no time to fix a complete dinner, but a good soup was always welcome on a cold, snowy night. She hesitated, wondering if Jake would like some toasted bread with his soup, and was just about to go out and ask him, when she stopped herself.

No, doing that would be getting a little too friendly and accommodating. He would start to think she was trying to butter him up—either that, or falling for him. She had to keep her dignity and her distance. The trip through the snow had been one thing, but now that they had made it to their destination, better not to get too close.

Interestingly enough, Jake's thoughts were running along the same lines. He'd been sitting in the rocking chair holding this extremely loveable baby, enveloped in a cloud of baby happiness, and feeling nothing but peace and goodwill toward everyone—and it had to stop. This was not what he'd come here for. What did this have to do with the healing powers of vengeance?

It was Kim's fault. Something about her appealed to his senses—all of them—like no other woman he'd ever known. When he looked at her, he wanted her, wanted her in a deep, primal way that would make him take steps he knew he shouldn't take. And if that wasn't bad enough, he wanted her for more dangerous things as well. He liked talking to her. He liked the way her eyes lit up when she thought of something new. He wanted to touch her hair, her face. He liked looking at her, at the way laughter seemed to bubble up from inside her. Just catching sight of her made him feel warmer when it was cold. And when he looked at her, the urge to do something to make her happier began to fill the empty void he'd carried inside him for so long now. And that wasn't good. She wasn't the one to fill it.

But the worst thing was, he was feeling all these traitorous emotions and urges around the woman who had been with Leonardo and had his baby—the last person on earth he could ever let himself love.

Love? Where had that word come from? His subconscious was dredging up old terms just because they seemed to fit his situation. But his subconscious was wrong. Love was not a word that would be relevant to him—never again.

No, this was just simple lust and hunger for human contact. That was all. And even that was too much. He held the baby as though she were the most precious thing in the world, and he knew, at this moment, she was. She couldn't help who her father was, so it had no bearing.

But Kim could help it. And he couldn't forget that.

"I like your cottage," he told her as she served up the soup at the dining room table. "It feels like a place one could call home."

"And I do." She took Dede from him and put her sleeping baby down in her little crib, then stood looking down at her.

Jake came up beside her, looking down as well. He was so close, his arm touched her shoulder. Why did that make her heart jump? She bit her lip, willing it to stop, but he'd turned his face toward her and she could feel his breath ruffling her hair. If she didn't watch out, her knees were going to buckle.

She looked up at him and he looked down at her and she felt like swooning. If he kissed her again, it would be different this time, and he had that look in his eyes. And no matter what she was telling herself, she knew she wanted it even more than he did.

She had to think fast—think of something that would stop this in its tracks.

"Jake," she began, her voice shaky, "tell me about your baby."

She felt his body stiffen. This was not a good question. But looking at his face, she decided she needed to know. It was time for him to talk about it, time for her to know the truth. And maybe it was time he let out some of his feelings. Who knew? She didn't get the sense that he had a lot of people he could talk to. If he needed someone, for now, let her be the one.

He was looking down at Dede again and it was soon apparent the sensual mood that had been developing between them had been blown to smithereens by her question.

"Not now," he said dismissively, though without turning away. He was too tired, suddenly, to argue, and yet too wound up to sleep.

And she seemed to feel the same way. But staying here, standing too close, letting emotions build, was out of the question.

"I'm going take my soup and sit on the couch and watch the fire until it burns out," she said. "It's that kind of night."

"I'll go with you," he said, but the tone of his voice warned her he might have more in mind than sipping soup.

Still, neither one of them spoke while they enjoyed their meal, letting the warm, nutritious comfort food do its work along with the fire. And even then, they sat for a few minutes and just soaked it in.

"Hey," Kim said at last, looking at him sideways. "I need to thank you. You saved Dede today, and you got us home, even though it took quite an effort. I owe you one."

He shook his head, staring into the fire. "Babies

are the most vulnerable ones in wartime. They can get caught in the crossfire so easily."

"Yes."

He turned and looked at her. "I've got to know, Kim. You've got to explain something to me."

A shiver went down her spine.

"What do you want to know?"

He turned back and stared into the fire for another minute. "I want to know why you think you belong with the Granvillis," he said softly. "I want to know why you have such animosity toward the royals."

Well, there it was. How was she going to explain this to him?

"Hey, there was just a war in this country, remember that? People had to make choices, pick sides."

His dark blue eyes looked haunted. "And what made you pick the side you went with, Kim?"

How could she explain her emotions at the time? She still didn't completely understand them herself. When Pellea had fallen for Monte, she'd helped her all she could. She hadn't thought twice. But later...

"A lot of people, even some in the castle, decided to back the invasion by the old DeAngelis royal family. I guess they had nostalgia for the old days or something. Or they wanted to return to the monarchy."

"But not you."

"No." She shook her head. "I grew up with the Granvillis, lived in the castle when the Granvillis were in charge, worked for them most of my adult life, and I stayed loyal." She said the words with fierce conviction, as though the harder she made her defense, the more valid it was. But glancing into his eyes, she had a feeling he wasn't buying it.

"Is that what you call it?" He said it softly, but his bitter streak was showing.

She gave him a resentful look, but she didn't say anything.

"Bad choice," he added.

That certainly put her back up. "You dare say that sitting right here in the heart of Granvilli territory?" She leaned back, watching at him with a sense of distance, as though she was trying to find a way to keep him at arm's length. "You shouldn't say things like that. You might be overheard, you know. Someone might turn you in."

His gaze was hard and pointed. "Someone like you?"

She turned away. Of course she wasn't going to turn him in and he knew it.

"Don't kid yourself, Kim. The Granvillis have had their day. They're done. Monte allowing them to stay on this side of the island while things are sorted out was a pity play. It's over."

Deep in her heart, she knew he was right. But there were reasons she couldn't accept it. At least not in front of him.

"Where was your loyalty to Pellea?" he went on. "You were best friends for years. Where did that friendship go?"

She closed her eyes, keeping her temper in check as much as she possibly could. She might ask where Pellea's loyalty had been, but he wouldn't understand. He hadn't been around when the world of Ambria had fallen apart and everyone had been forced to make their choices. What did he know of that? There was no point in even bringing it up.

"And now that we know you are the last royal baby," he went on in a matter-of-fact tone that she supposed was meant to help her start to accept it. "I think it's time you made some adjustments to your thinking." He turned in his seat so that he could see her more clearly. "Once you relax, you can start looking at the benefits of being a DeAngelis royal and maybe you'll even begin to be happy about it."

She'd taken all she could and she turned on him with a vengeance.

"I'm supposed to be happy about this?" she demanded sharply. "If this fairy tale you're trying to spin is true, do you realize what that does to my life? If you're right, you've just taken my world and ripped it apart. You've shown me that everything I believed to be true was lies. That the whole foundation of my life is a sham. That nothing is real. It's all an illusion. I'm a fading ghost lost in a funhouse of mirrors and cackling clowns."

He looked mystified at her reaction. "Kim, don't do this to yourself. This should be so easy."

"Easy? Easy?" She glared at him, her eyes shimmering with tears. "If all this nonsense is true, how am I supposed to go on living? It would mean that I've lost my mother. She was the woman who raised me. She was the one I loved. The only one who loved me." Angrily, she brushed her tears away.

"I never gave two figs for the DeAngelis king and queen. I never knew them, but what I knew of them was laughable. I mocked them time and again. And now you tell me they were my parents? How shall I make amends? Shall I jump off a bridge or s-s-omething?"

There was a lump in her throat and a sob tore into her last word.

"Kim," he began, reaching for her.

"Don't touch me," she snarled through clenched

teeth. Her fists were clenched and her eyes were a bit wild. "I'll…I'll scream or something."

"No, you won't," he said calmly. "Come here."

CHAPTER EIGHT

JAKE took Kim by the shoulders and pulled her closer. Despite all her fierce talk, she didn't do a thing to stop him. He held her face and kissed away her tears and murmured soft, comforting words that seemed to weave a magic spell around her. She closed her eyes and gave herself up to the feeling. When his lips touched hers, she kissed him back hungrily, begging for more.

She knew this was wrong and that she would regret it, but she couldn't stop herself. It had been so long since she'd felt the strong, protective arms of a man around her. She'd been so alone for so long. His mouth was hot and she accepted him eagerly, reaching up to dig her fingers into his hair and pull him ever closer. His hands flattened on her back and she arched toward him, aching for him to touch her breasts.

But he pulled his mouth away from hers, whispering something soft again, soothing her.

"Hush, Kim, take it easy," he said. "Don't let yourself get crazy. You're so tired…"

Pulling back, she stared at him, realizing he had just rejected her. She knew he felt the sensual tug between them as strongly as she did. So why would he do this?

Oh, of course. She knew exactly why.

"What is it?" she asked him evenly. "Did you just

remember I've been with Leonardo? Does that make me impossible to tolerate?"

His face registered shock and then a sort of stunned horror. That only made things worse. People always reacted like that once you'd put your finger on their secret.

"Kim." He grabbed her shoulders again, looking like he wanted to shake her. Then he calmed down, blinking rapidly. "Oh, Kim," he said, shaking his head. "This is really hard for you, much harder than I would ever have imagined."

Her return stare was a challenge. "So make it easier," she suggested.

He took a deep breath, then reached out to brush the tangled hair back off her forehead. "Okay," he said. "This is the best I can do. I'm going to batter you with facts."

She shrugged, unimpressed. "Batter away," she said coolly.

"Here goes. The reason I believe all this stuff you call nonsense and fairy tales, is because there is scientific evidence behind it all. Now I know that a lot of scientific material is subject to interpretation, and different scientists come back from the same facts with different opinions, but this stuff is DNA. It's like two plus two equals four. You can't argue with it."

"Whose DNA are we talking about?" she asked, frowning.

He didn't let her question sidetrack his narrative. "This research has been going on ever since the DeAngelis family took back the castle. Archivists have been doing surveys and sending out samples and all sorts of scientific things. The results have come back from all over the world, from everyone they could find who was even tentatively related to the DeAngelis royals. And then, more samples were taken from hair, from skin, from anything they could get. The rumors of a last baby had always been there, but no one had any proof, so they used DNA from anyone who was around in those days, and anyone affiliated with the castle since."

She was waiting anxiously now. This was like a mystery. She wanted to find out who the real killer was.

Or rather, the real last royal baby.

"And?"

"The results are in. It's official. They've found evidence that you belong in the DeAngelis family."

"What are you really saying?"

"I thought I was being quite clear. You're a DeAngelis, a princess of the realm. Now that there is a realm again."

She tossed her head back and forth, still anguished by this theory. "Sorry, but that just can't be right. Who else did they test?"

"Everyone. You are the only one who matched."

She thought fast. "Maybe they had a bad sample?"

"They had your hair from a brush in your room. They had your clothes. They had a sample of your blood from when you donated for the war effort. They had…"

"Okay, okay." She put her hands over her ears. She didn't want to hear any more.

"The other messengers that came. Didn't they try to explain it to you?"

"They told me gobbledygook and fairy tales that made no sense. I couldn't make heads nor tails of it."

He shook his head. "This is it, the straight scoop. You are the last of the DeAngelis family. You were born three days before the castle was burned by the Granvillis, twenty-five plus years ago."

"I know that part," she reminded him. "It's common knowledge. My mother was Lady Constance Day, lady-in-waiting to the queen. She hid her pregnancy as long as she could."

He took her face in his hands and smiled at her sadly. "No. Your mother was Queen Elineas. Lady Constance pretended you were hers so that the Granvillis wouldn't kill you."

She shook her head. It felt like she was doing it in slow motion, like she was watching herself from far away, and she saw her head move, and her hair spray out, but too slowly. It wasn't real.

"No," she said, and it sounded as though she were in an echo chamber. "No, that's ridiculous."

"It's true. Your DNA checks out." Reaching out he took her hand in his. He could see how this was affecting her. Somehow he had thought, despite everything, that this might make things easier for her. That she might cling to these facts in a changing, shifting world where the sand underneath your feet tended to leak away when you weren't paying attention. "Kim, it's true. It's science. You can't fight it."

"No." She was still shaking her head. "No. I don't want to be a part of the royal family. I was raised as a servant, taking care of a certain class, but free as a bird. My mother was a servant to the queen. I was a servant to the independent ladies of the citizens' regime. That was my place. Royalty wasn't even an issue. We didn't have any royals. We didn't want any. We hated the DeAngelis pretenders with their snooty ways. We were free, we were proud. We didn't need all that nonsense."

"That was then," he said simply. "Things have changed."

She stared at him. "They would never accept me

anyway," she whispered to him. "They didn't treat me like family when the chips were down. Why should I trust them now?"

He stared at her, aware there was something here he didn't understand. She'd been through things he couldn't even imagine. He didn't know what had happened, but he could see the shadows of the pain and anguish in her eyes.

"They hate me," she whispered, more to herself than to him.

"What are you talking about? They always accepted you. They love you."

"No." She knew things he didn't. Deep inside, she felt hollow and alone. "Not when the chips were down, they didn't. Leonardo…" But she wasn't going to talk about that.

He took her shoulders in his hands again and stared down into her face. "What about Leonardo?"

"Nothing." She shook her head. "Nothing."

He searched her eyes, but she wasn't going to give him any more. Still, he wanted to give her something. He had to help her get through this and come out the other side. And so he made her a promise.

"Listen to me, Kim. I want you to come with me to the castle. I know it will be for the best, for you and for Dede. But I'm not going to force you. The only way I'm going to get you there is if I can persuade you to come willingly."

He cringed inside. What was he doing here? His ace in the hole was always his physical prowess, the strong-arm stuff. His powers of verbal persuasion had never been strong. He had no gift of the silver tongue. And here he was, playing at the big table and putting all his money on the persuasion card. Wow. What an idiot he was.

But it was too late to turn back now.

"I swear to you, the only way I'm going to take you back is once I've persuaded you," he went on. "When you come with me, it will be of your own free will."

She stared at him. This was new. He hadn't felt this way before.

Could she believe him?

Maybe. Maybe not. She would have to take a leap of faith.

"Sleep on it," he suggested. "Let's go to bed."

It really was late. Their lack of sleep was finally catching up with them. Kim directed Jake to a bed he could use.

"You can sleep in my bedroom," she told him, pointing it out. "Right in there. I'll sleep on the little bed in Dede's room. I want to stay with her anyway."

He hesitated, looking down at her, then swallowed hard and turned away. It was better to start learning to avoid kissing her. No good could come of it anyway.

"Good night," he said over his shoulder.

He went into the room and started to unbutton his shirt, kicking off his shoes and reaching for the covers to pull them back. And there, on the newly uncovered pillow, lay a note. He took it up and held it to the light, but somehow, he already thought he knew who it would be from.

Kimmee my darling, it said in a large, masculine scrawl. *I have to see you. It's been too long. But I have to be careful. Watch for me on the holy day. L.*

He felt cold and then he felt hot fury and then he felt lied to. So she had no contact with him? Then what the hell was this? The thought of her with Leonardo almost doubled him over with pain. And then he was mad at himself for caring. He swore a blue streak, kicked a rug, and stormed out into the living room again.

"Kim," he said loudly. "I've got to talk to you."

She came out, dressed like an angel in that damn white nightgown again. He tightened his jaw and hardened himself.

"What is it?" she asked, suddenly anxious. "What happened?"

He handed her the note. She looked at it blankly, then began to read it. All the color drained from her face.

"Oh no," she moaned, looking around as though she expected him to jump out of the shadows. "He's coming. He's coming here!" She looked into Jake's face, her own eyes frantic. "We have to go. We have to get out of here. You don't know what he's like. I can't be here."

"He's not only coming," Jake said calmly, "he's been here."

She nodded, looking stricken. "I thought he didn't know about this place. I never thought he would come here. I…" She looked around as though for someplace to hide.

He watched her for a moment, and then he took her into his arms and held her close. He was convinced. She hadn't lied to him. And she didn't want to see Leonardo.

And yet, oddly enough, he did. This was playing right into his hands. The timing couldn't be better. If everything worked out the way it should, he would get his chance to make the man pay for what he'd done. Poor old Leonardo. He wouldn't know what hit him.

"Kim," he said, stroking her hair and holding her loosely, but still being careful of his ribs. "Calm down. I'm here. I won't let him do anything to you." He pulled back enough to see her face. "Has he hurt you in the past?" he asked, wondering at her reaction.

She looked at him, eyes wide, but she didn't answer. "I think we should go," she whispered. "He can't see Dede. What if he starts to want custody? He has all the power." She took Jake by his shirt and tugged. "Don't you see? We have to go."

"Doesn't he know about Dede?"

She hesitated, then shook her head. "I think he knows she exists, but he's never seen her, so she's just an abstract to him right now. But once he sees her in the flesh and realizes she's his...." Her face started to crumple, but she held it off. Still, her breathing was jagged.

"He said he was coming on the holy day. I assume he means Christmas."

She nodded. "I'm sure he thought he was being cryptic. As if a five-year-old couldn't figure out what he means."

"So we have over twenty-four hours," he said. "We need rest. And we need to plan." And he was going to have to find a way to explain to her that they needed to stay—because he needed to have it out with Leonardo.

She was shaking her head. "No. We need to go."

But as she looked up into his face, she realized that he wasn't really there standing with her any longer. Instead, he was back in some past time, viewing something horrible. For just a moment, she wondered what exactly it was that he was in danger of unleashing.

"You asked me earlier about my baby," he said. "About my family. Maybe it's time I told you." He glanced at her, then away again. "My baby and my wife were both killed in a market bombing over a year ago," he said flatly.

"Oh. Oh Jake, I'm so sorry. This damn war." She

saw the desolate look in his eyes and her heart broke for him.

He shook his head. It wasn't just the war. It wasn't a random act of violence. That marketplace was deliberately selected for punishment, and the man who meted it out was the man Kim had selected to father her child, Leonardo Granvilli. The ruler of the exiled realm.

"I've never told anyone the whole story. Not even Pellea." He looked down and touched her cheek. "But I'm going to tell it to you."

"Why? Why me?"

"I think you'll understand that by the end."

She nodded reluctantly, not sure why he put it this way, as though once she'd heard his story, she would assume some responsibility for it. She wasn't sure she wanted that job.

"Okay."

"I'm going to start way back at the beginning. You know that I grew up away from Pellea and my father, away from the castle, and mostly, away from Ambria. But I went to schools where other Ambrians went." He smiled faintly. "In my own way, I've always been a patriot."

She led him to the couch again and they sat down, closer together this time.

"I never met Pellea until we found each other in Hungary where she'd gone to find medical care for our father. I heard she was there and I went to see them both. It was amazing how suddenly that old family tie reasserted itself with a vengeance. Pellea and I looked in each other's eyes and we felt the connection immediately. It was like looking in the mirror. I knew who she was and she knew who I was. Instant rapport."

Kim frowned and looked away. She'd felt that way

with Pellea at one time. How could she warn him to beware? It wouldn't last.

Or maybe it would for him. After all, he was a real brother, not a pretend sister like she'd been.

"I got closer to my father," he was saying. "I met Monte. I met the whole crew and we all got along famously."

"They're all very charming," she said with a pang of memory.

"Yes. I liked them a lot."

Of course. She'd liked them, too.

"So you decided to throw your lot in with the new rebels," she said, a trace of her sarcasm showing. "You got yourself involved in the invasion of Ambria."

"Yes. I signed on to their cause. I thought what had happened to the royal family when the Granvillis took over and burned the castle and killed the king and queen was outrageous and deserved punishment. I was all for the invasion."

"And yet, your father…"

"I can't be held accountable for what my father did," he interjected sharply. "I can only offer my own opinions."

She nodded. She accepted that. "Bad things happen in wars," she said, sounding like an automaton.

"Oh yes, they do indeed. But we invaded Ambria and we got the castle back. It all happened so fast, even we were surprised at how immediate our success was. We came in from the sea and we drove them back and they went."

Kim looked down and realized her fingers were trembling. He remembered this as a time of triumph. She remembered the panic, the mad rush to find transportation away from the castle, the way everyone turned on everyone else. She'd been accused of spying for the DeAngelis royals, of all things. There was actually talk of jail time while charges were developed. Instead— Leonardo stepped in. And that was even worse.

At first, she'd thought he really wanted to help her. What a fool she'd been.

"And at that time," Jake was going on, "we thought, well, if it's this easy, maybe there doesn't have to be any more killing. Maybe we can do this through talk and negotiation. Maybe it could all be over."

Kim's smile was jaded. She wasn't that naive. She'd seen too much. "Not in this lifetime."

"Maybe not." He shook his head. "At any rate, it just so happened that I knew Leonardo."

"Really?" Yes, he'd mentioned that before. "Where did you meet him?"

"We were at Eton together, but only for one term. We were rivals in everything from sprinting to debating." He laughed shortly. "We hated each other even then."

"I can imagine." By now she had curled into a ball of instant misery, but he didn't seem to notice.

"But having the advantage of this connection, I tried to contact him. I wanted to help the DeAngelis royals. From my perspective, I find them a fine set of people who want the best for this country."

"By 'this country', I assume you mean a united Ambria."

"Of course."

She sniffed and he gave her a look.

"I sent him messages. He had his man respond, but he didn't answer himself. Still, I thought we'd developed a line of communication. I offered to meet him in a coffee house on the square in Tristan, just off the Novio marketplace. A fairly neutral area."

She nodded. She knew that place. And she was afraid she also knew what was coming next.

"I told him where I would be sitting and that I would be open to setting a foundation for the beginning of negotiations. I tried to give him a broad opening and a sense that there would be a place for him in the new Ambria if he wanted to lay down arms and join us."

She rolled her eyes. "I can just imagine his response to that."

"He agreed to meet."

She shrugged. Even that was surprising, from what she knew of the man. "But did he actually show up?"

"No." He was silent for a long moment, and when he spoke again, his voice was hard and steely. "And here's the really stupid part. I let my wife and baby come along with me."

She sat up, staring at him with her mouth open. "What?"

"Not into the coffee house," he explained quickly. "But to the marketplace. Cyrisse had a good friend who ran one of the high-end shops and she went to visit her while I waited for Leonardo."

"So you treated this like a day at the mall?" she said, aghast. He couldn't be this naive. Here she'd thought he was so tough and worldly wise.

"You had security guards, didn't you?" she asked, shocked at such casual disregard for human safety.

The Granvillis were not known for their compassion. In fact, they were pretty much known for murder and mayhem. And she was sure Jake quickly found that out.

"Of course. And so did my wife." His groan was more angry than sad. "A lot of good that did."

Kim began to get a hint of what was coming and her blood ran cold.

"Oh no," she whispered.

"Yes. I was so stupid. So inexperienced in dealing with evil. I really thought there was a chance we could get together and begin work on restoring Ambria to what it deserved to be. I thought Leonardo would be willing at least to listen."

"But no."

"No."

They were silent for a long moment, each thinking sad thoughts.

"A little girl?"

"Yes."

"How old was she when...?"

"Six weeks."

"Oh my God. So young."

He couldn't speak for a moment, and when he did, his voice broke often. "So young, so new, so bright, so full of promises...gone in an instant."

She waited a moment before she spoke again. "What exactly happened?"

"They bombed the marketplace. I'm sure they meant to get me, but they were off a bit. They got my life instead and destroyed it in front of my eyes. I suppose, in their view, that was just as good."

She nodded, knowing that the people who set the bomb didn't care. They just wanted mayhem. They wanted blood. They didn't know much about sitting in a coffee house and having a nice polite discussion about power and who was going to get it. All they knew were weapons and killing.

"And you blame Leonardo."

His was voice was like ground glass. "I want him dead."

She nodded. If he only knew how close his sentiments were to her own.

They sat silently for a few minutes, mulling over what he'd just told her.

Then he seemed to have himself together again and he turned and looked at her.

"So now you tell me," he said, studying her pretty face. "How is it that you ended up with Leonardo? How did you manage to screw up your life to that extent?"

She looked at him and weighed how much she wanted to tell him. "Okay, here's how it was," she started off. "It was right before the invasion began that…that… Well, there was a lot going on in the castle at the time. Leonardo's father was dying, leaving him in charge, and he had to fight off a lot of other factions who wanted the control and the power that looked up for grabs to them. But Leonardo stuck to his guns and he won out over all the others."

"In the meantime, Pellea was gone. She'd left with her father to search for medical help for him in Europe. At least that was the reason she gave when she got permission to leave. But she didn't come back and soon we heard that she was with Crown Prince Monte." She winced, remembering that time. "Leonardo went crazy. He'd pretty much forgotten about her while he was in his power struggle, but now that it was over, he wanted her back. He knew he was about to be invaded by Monte's forces. He couldn't stand to think the woman who was supposed to have married him was now with his enemy."

Jake snorted. "What a loser."

She shrugged. "He was insanely jealous at the time, and when he couldn't have Pellea, he decided…" Did she really want to tell him about this? Oh, why not? He would learn it all eventually. "He decided I would do in her place, at least until he could get his hands on her again."

Shock echoed through Jake's crystal-blue gaze. "What are you saying, Kim? Did he force you...?"

Her dark eyes were haunted with regrets and memories. "I'm not going to talk about that. Not ever. I'll just tell you that it was a very difficult situation. And it lasted too long. I wanted desperately to get out of it. I sent letters to anyone I could think of. And when the DeAngelis forces invaded, and so quickly won back the castle, I sent messages to Pellea directly, asking her to intervene and get Leonardo to let me go."

"But?"

She steeled herself. This was one time she wasn't going to allow her voice to break. No emotion. Just the facts. "No one ever came. No one rescued me. No one cared."

She didn't want to think about the details, the days she spent pacing the room where he had her locked away, how desperately she looked through the messages they allowed her to receive, how she prayed and prayed that someone would come. And the nights... Best not to think about them.

"Did she ever get the messages?"

She gave him a look. "I sent them with a very trusted envoy. I'm sure she got them. She just didn't answer. I guess at that point, she was just too busy becoming queen."

He frowned. This was something he hadn't heard about. He was going to have to look into the truth of this. He knew how much his sister loved Kim. He couldn't imagine that she would have ignored a cry for help from her.

"So you stayed with Leonardo for an extended period of time."

"It seemed like forever."

"Did you…love him?"

"Love him?" She looked almost physically sick. "Love had nothing to do with it."

Jake felt a little sick himself. "What did he do to you?" he asked, his voice harsh.

She avoided his gaze. "I told you that was something I'm not going to talk about."

He nodded.

"I spent a lot of time hoping someone would pay some attention. And then suddenly, the DeAngelis family was back and they were in charge of the castle and everybody on their side was celebrating. They were in all the papers, all the magazines. They were tooting horns and singing songs, and they never seemed to remember that I had ever existed."

She took a deep breath. "I felt more than betrayed. I felt erased. Like everything I'd ever done was gone, forgotten, no longer important. Everyone I'd ever loved had just turned their back on me and didn't care. That I was only important when I was useful."

He looked at her, expecting to see tears, but her voice was hard as diamonds and her eyes were dry and filled with anger. He wanted to do something to make her feel better, but what could he possibly do? Maybe get her to look at this in a broader perspective, see it in the larger scheme of things.

"But Kim, don't you see?" he tried. "That's the way it always is in life. People are basically self-centered and see the world through a selfish lens. They often don't think about others until their own needs have been fulfilled."

She gave him a scathing look. "You can say that all you want, and I know it's often true, but that doesn't make it any better. It still hurts."

He stared at her, at a loss for words. He wanted to grab her and kiss her pain away, but he knew that wasn't going to work. It might make him feel a whole lot better, but it probably wouldn't do much for her.

"Go back to the castle," he said shortly. "Talk to Pellea. I'm sure you two can work things out. I know how much she cares for you. There has to be some reason."

"Forget it."

He looked at her, a bit exasperated. "You may not be able to forgive those who have hurt you, but your baby shouldn't have to pay for that."

"Oh no," she said quickly. "You're absolutely right."

She looked at him, realizing they had left his own heartbreak behind to talk about hers. And really, his was so much worse.

Gazing at him, she was suddenly filled with a warmth she didn't expect. Here he was trying to make her feel better. And what had she done for him? She'd criticized his handling of the meeting that had resulted in his beloved family dying. Nice person she was.

"Jake," she said, getting his attention. "Stay still."

Leaning toward him, she kissed his warm mouth. His lips parted in surprise and she took advantage of him, flicking her tongue inside and teasing him. She heard a growl, deep in his throat, and then he was kissing her back, wrapping her in his arms and leaning her back onto the couch. She began to laugh, and he kissed her harder. He tasted like red wine and he felt like a gladiator, all muscle and hardness. Except for his mouth. And for a moment, she couldn't get enough of it.

But they both knew the dangers they were courting, and they drew back easily, laughing in each other's eyes and pulling away. It was late. They needed sleep.

But Kim was glad she'd provoked a little romance for the evening. And now she had a kiss to build a dream on.

CHAPTER NINE

DEDE woke up early, and that meant that Kim woke up early as well. Kim got up to feed her and play with her, so she had time to think over what had happened the night before. Despite all the stories and experiences they had related to each other, all the emotional turmoil, it all meant little when you got to the bottom line.

And the bottom line was Dede. She needed to see a real doctor, and that was all that mattered. Kim was resigned. She was going to the castle. Getting the menacing note from Leonardo had put the seal of certainty on it. There was nothing else to do, and no other way left to do it. She would have to face Pellea and all her old friends—the ones who had turned their backs on her.

But she wouldn't play their game. She was going to tell them that even if the DNA said she was a DeAngelis, that didn't make her a princess. She didn't want to be one. They could put her on the lists and put her picture on the wall and announce her name at balls—but she wouldn't appear in person. No participation awards for Princess Kimmee. She had other things to do with her life.

Still, she had to admit, the things Jake had said were eating away at her tough-girl stand. Maybe there were explanations for what had happened. Maybe she shouldn't have been so quick to decide she'd been left behind because no one cared about her. Maybe her resentment had been simmered in too thick a sauce of self-pity. Just a little.

She wasn't really as frightened anymore at the prospect of seeing Leonardo as she had been the night before. Just the thought that he'd been inside her little cottage gave her the creeps, but there was nothing for it but to move on. What was done was done. Time to pick up the pieces and find a new way.

Oh, who was she trying to kid? She was still terrified that the man would try to take Dede from her. And that was a big part of the reason she'd decided to go to the castle.

She looked around. She loved her cottage but she was afraid it might be a long time before she would be able to come back to it.

She had Dede in her highchair and was feeding her creamed peaches when she heard the front door open. She jumped up, her heart in her throat, sure it was Leonardo arriving early. What was she going to do?

"Hey, anybody here?"

It was Jake's voice she heard, and she let the air out of her lungs with a rush, half laughing, half annoyed, but completely filled with relief as she turned to greet him.

"I thought you were still asleep," she said, her hand over her heart.

"I got up early, so I went out in the snow." His smile was full of mischief. "I've got a surprise for you."

"What have you got?" she cried.

He reached back out the door and brought in a little cone-shaped tree with a wooden base already hammered on.

"I figured, as this is Dede's first Christmas, she needed a little Christmas tree. So I went up to the woods and cut her one."

It was perfect, a small conifer shaped exactly like what was needed. He set it in on the table and reached into the pockets of his coat, pulling out items he obviously planned for decorations.

"We have here some red berries I found in bushes growing along the side of the road," he said. "And some little pine cones that look almost golden. In the right light. And a garland of holly-like vine that was growing down by the stream."

"Perfect," she said, her eyes shining. "I'll get some yarn to make hangers for them."

"And I have one more thing," he said, reaching back into his pocket. "Just for Dede." He pulled out a little mechanical Santa Claus, all dressed in red with a big white beard. "Look Dede. What do you think of this?"

The baby laughed and clapped her hands with delight. Jake made the little Santa dance for her, bringing on peals of laughter.

"Where did you get that?" Kim asked him, loving the way he made her baby laugh.

He gave her a sheepish look. "To tell you the truth, I stole it," he admitted.

Her jaw fell. "What?"

"Well, there aren't too many stores open at this time of the morning."

"But to steal it! Where? What did you do?"

"It was in a yard over near the church."

"Right in front of the church you stole something!"

He was laughing at her and he reached out and

touched her golden hair. "Will you listen? It was in a yard, half buried, as though kids had been playing with it yesterday and forgot it when the snow started. So I picked it up and brought it home for Dede to see."

"Jake!"

"I'm taking it back," he said defensively.

She had her hands on her hips. "When?"

He shrugged. "When Dede is tired of it."

She was exasperated with him, but still, she started to laugh. "Next thing you know, one of the town elders will be banging on the door, wanting your head on a spike. You can't do these things in small towns. Someone is bound to have seen you."

"Don't worry. They'll never connect it with you. I made a lot of maneuvers on my way back here."

"Wonderful. I'll bet you looked guilty as all heck from the lookout area on the town hall bell tower."

He gaped at her. "Why would anybody be up there at this time of the morning?"

"Trust me. Someone saw you. They always do."

She began to work on hanging the home-grown ornaments and he watched her, enjoying her ready smile and the way her eyes flashed with humor at the slightest provocation. Was it just the proximity that was making him like her this much? Was it just the heightened excitement of the journey they were on?

Memories of Cyrisse, his wife, flickered into his thoughts, and he frowned, wondering if this was a betrayal of her and all she'd meant to him. They had known each other for years and been good friends, then, briefly, lovers. When Cyrisse told him she was pregnant he'd been surprised, but willing to take on the responsibility of a family. It seemed to be the right time for it, he'd argued with himself, and though the two of them had never been particularly passionate partners, love would probably grow out of shared responsibilities and experience. When she was killed, he'd mourned her, but it had been the baby, little Jessica, whose loss had created the hole in his heart.

All things being equal, he knew he could fall hard for Kim. She engaged his senses like no other woman he'd ever known. She filled his head and his heart in ways he had never imagined. How easy it would be to pull her into his life—if only she didn't have ties to Leonardo.

And despite everything she said, despite the way she really did seem to fear him, those ties still existed. It would take more than the short time he'd known her to analyze how deep emotions ran between them. Had she ever loved the man? That would be hard to believe, but people did strange things at times.

"I think we should go soon," she was saying as she hung the last spray of red berries on the little tree.

"Go where?" He looked up, coming out of his reverie.

"To the castle." She was biting her lip, looking worried.

"Are you sure?"

"Yes. Things have changed."

"And you want to go now?"

"Yes. As soon as possible."

He looked out the window, grimacing. How was this for irony? She was finally ready to go to the castle just when he had a chance to come face-to-face with Leonardo. A part of him wanted to rebel, to tell her the trip to the castle could wait until after....

After what? After he had a chance to deal with the

man? Right here in front of his child and that child's mother? That wasn't going to work.

Didn't they say vengeance was a dish best served cold? This one was going to be icy. But it would be served. It was just a matter of time.

"How about going right after lunch?" he suggested. "Then we'll reach the border about nightfall. That's a good time to get across without being seen."

"Sounds good. I'll start getting things ready."

She spent a half hour cleaning the kitchen, then pulled out the ingredients for cookies—big, meaty peanut butter cookies with chocolate chunks—for the trip. Soon the kitchen was filled with delicious cookie-baking smells.

Jake went to take the little Santa back to its yard without too much prodding and Kim was taking the last batch of cookies out of the oven when the doorbell rang. Kim froze, sure this had to be bad luck. Either that nosy village elder had come calling, or Leonardo was early. Her heart pounding, she looked out the window—and to her surprise, found her mother's elderly sister from Paris at the door.

"Aunt Grace!" She hurried to let her in. "It's wonderful to see you. Please come in."

It had been years since she'd seen her aunt, who spent most of her time living with her new husband in Paris. She looked lovely, her skin smooth, her coloring rosy, her ensemble chic and stylish. This was the way Grace had always been. Kim's own mother had tended more toward hair in a tangle and a dress that didn't quite fit, but her sister was interested in finer things.

"You look amazing," Kim said, shaking her head at her beautiful aunt.

"That's because I live in Paris," Grace said with a

lovely laugh. "We do pay more attention to appearances there."

"Well, you've certainly learned to be a Parisian then, haven't you?"

"In my way."

"How long are you staying?"

"We just came for the holiday. Jacques—my new husband. He's so young, you know, and I wanted to show him where I used to live when I was his age."

"I see," said Kim, somewhat taken aback. "Well, if you're around at the end of the week, maybe we can get together. I'm afraid I must make a trip to…well, away, for a few days."

"Ah, what a shame. Well, I'll stop by again before we leave to see if you've come back. I'm hoping we can connect and do something together."

"I hope so, too."

As her aunt turned to go, Kim thought of a question she could ask her.

"Aunt Grace, maybe you can help me with something. There have been rumors swirling lately, rumors about my background."

"Oh dear."

"Because of my connection with the castle."

"Of course."

"And…well, I'd like to know the truth."

Grace laughed. "Be careful, my dear. As you grow older, you may find that the truth is something best hidden from public view."

"Oh no," Kim said, reacting reflexively with a saying she'd always heard. "The truth will set you free."

"They lied to you, my dear. The truth will often make you cry." She patted her shoulder. "But ask away. I'll see what I can do to clear up any false rumors."

Kim took a deep breath and decided she might as well come straight out with it. "Was your sister, Constance, really my mother?" she asked in a rush.

Grace blinked, surprised at the question. "You see, this is just the kind of thing one really doesn't want to get into."

"I just need to know. They…they're saying someone else was my mother and…and…"

"I can't tell you for sure. I wasn't living with Constance at the time. But I did visit her about a month before you were born and she didn't seem pregnant to me."

"Oh."

"Now, she may have been very clever at hiding it. Who knows? But when she came back home with you in her arms, we were quite surprised."

"I see."

"And as you know, Constance was not the sort of woman to have an affair. In fact, she was pretty vocal about women who did so." Grace made a face. "Even when that woman was her own sister."

"Oh, Aunt Grace!"

Kim reached out to comfort her, but Grace laughed. "We all make our own choices in life, darling. And we learn to bear the consequences. I've lived a wonderful life. But so did Constance. And she never said a word about who your father might be."

Kim nodded. Grace's information filled in a few gaps, but only marginally. "I think you've given me my answer," she said anyway.

"Have I, dear? I hope it doesn't make you cry," Grace said, turning toward the door.

"No, don't worry about that. I've cried enough for one lifetime."

Grace turned back as though she'd forgotten to say something. She hesitated, then reached out and patted Kim's cheek. "I hope you know that Constance loved you as deeply and truly as any mother ever would," she told her earnestly.

"Yes. Yes, I do know that." Kim kissed the older woman and smiled, eyes misting with tears. "But thank you for reminding me. I loved her, too."

Once Jake got back from returning the Santa, they both seemed to feel a sudden urgency to get going.

"I've agreed to go with you to the castle," Kim told him. "Just don't give me any of that malarkey about being royal."

"I won't say a word," he said. "The motorcycle isn't great for conversation anyway."

She made a face at him and frowned. "I don't suppose we could borrow a car from someone."

"We'd have to abandon it in a ditch when we get to the border."

She sighed. "I guess borrowing is out."

It felt strange piling on top of the rickety bike again. Most of the sense of adventure she'd had by the end of the ride the day before seemed to have evaporated. It didn't help that Dede was fussing and Jake had a hard time getting the bike started. But once they were back on the road, it wasn't so bad. It wasn't snowing but the air was crisp and cold. They cruised along the coast, enjoying the scenery, then turned inland, heading for the best border crossing, aiming at an arrival near dusk.

"Why is it that you can't find a policeman anywhere in this country but the checkpoint is full of soldiers?" she asked in exasperation.

"They're trying to keep people from deserting a sinking ship," he said. "Plus, from what I've heard, the soldiers haven't been paid and this is their way of making a living. They shake down travelers."

"Lovely."

"Granvilli honor in action," he said, trying to keep from sounding too bitter.

"It's Christmas Eve," she had reminded Jake before they left. "Let's hope some of them are distracted by that in itself."

"You expect the Granvilli border guards to be off singing Christmas carols?" he asked with a grin.

"You never know," she said defensively. "They might be putting on a pageant."

"Maybe we could be the wise men," he said, mocking her gently.

"Right. I'm sure they'd like that."

But it did feel momentous, traveling across the country like this, planning to illegally cross a border. Her heart was pounding harder than usual, especially when she remembered she would probably be meeting with Pellea in just a few hours.

Night was falling when Jake pulled over to the side of the road. "Look up ahead," he told her. "See the lights? That's the checkpoint. We're going to ditch the bike and walk in, but we won't be far from the lights. Unfortunately, we have to go in really close, close enough that they might see us. But it's the best place to cross, so we'll have to risk it."

She got off the bike and put Dede down while she helped him hide the bike in a gully, covering it with leaves. Then they gathered their things and Jake took the baby and they started walking, staying in the thickest brush they could find.

"Come this way," Jake whispered, leading her into a

stand of pines, then doubling back through lower shrubbery. He began to walk more slowly, more carefully, and she followed suit. She could see the lights coming nearer and nearer, but the first time she heard a man's voice, sounding just a few feet away, she jumped and had to bite down hard to avoid a small scream of surprise.

Jake motioned for her to come through and then hunker down where he was.

"This is closer than I expected," he whispered. "If they tried hard, they could see us. The brush cover is pretty thin."

She nodded, not daring to say anything aloud. She could hardly believe how near they were. She could see faces plainly and hear snatches of what was said. She was afraid to even breathe.

"I think we'll be okay as long as Dede doesn't cry," Jake whispered.

She looked down at her baby. Wide eyes met hers.

"Oh boy," she breathed. This would be touch and go. When Dede was awake, noise was her business.

"Look."

A black sedan with tinted windows was approaching the border guards and they went into readiness. The driver slowed the car to a stop and said something out the window. The border guard seemed to disagree, shaking his head as he looked at the credentials he'd been handed.

They held their breaths, knowing this might be the perfect time to make a run for it, but hesitating.

And then the back window of the car opened and a tall man leaned out, barked an order and got immediate respect from the guard.

Kim gasped and grabbed Jake's arm. "Leonardo!"

But he already knew that. He stared at the man. Everything in him went cold and his gorge rose. Leonardo. He pushed Kim's hand away and tensed, adrenaline flowing. If he called out, would Leonardo meet him halfway? Would he take the challenge? Would he know why it had come to him? No matter. The man needed to pay. He dropped his backpack and took a step toward the checkpoint.

Kim stared at him for a split second and then she realized what he was doing. "No!" she whispered, throwing herself in his way, physically holding him back. "No, you can't."

They stared at each other. She saw the look in his eyes and it scared her. He wanted revenge and he was like a machine programmed to get it.

"No!" she whispered again, shaking her head.

They looked back at the car. The window was rolling up and the car was beginning to move. The guard stood back, saluted and let them through. In a moment the car was gone, most likely on its way to Dorcher Cliffs.

Kim drew air into her lungs. It felt as if she'd been holding her breath for a long, long time. Jake was swearing and shaking his head. She looked at him and shook her head, as well.

"Are you crazy?" she whispered at him. "Come on. We have to get over that border."

Jake nodded. He knew she was right. But he was shaking with anger, with hatred. If ever a man deserved a good killing…

Was he going to get it? Not today. But soon.

A quarter of a mile later, and they were solidly in DeAngelis territory. Jake took out his cell phone. It worked! Quickly he called the castle and ordered a car to come out and get them.

"Hey," he said, smiling happily at Kim. "We're home."

The castle rose above the darkness and the mist like a legendary, magical place where fairy tales and stories of King Arthur were born. A lump rose in Kim's throat. She hadn't expected to feel this way, but there it was. The place she'd once called home. She still loved it.

Memories surged all around her—good and bad. Tears welled in her eyes and she couldn't seem to get rid of them.

The car dropped them at the side entrance and they were waved in by guards. The corridors looked so familiar, though the people working there were complete strangers on the whole. Kim stayed close to Jake. Funny—she was the one who had lived here for so long, but he was the insider now.

He led her to an elevator, and then to a familiar large wooden door.

"Pellea thought you might like to use the chambers she lived in all those years you and she were like sisters. And if you decide to stay, they can be renovated to suit your needs."

Pellea's courtyard! She'd always loved the place. It was a garden retreat built right into this side of the castle. There was a small lush forest open to the sky, along with a greenhouse garden filled with flowers. The surrounding rooms—a huge closet filled with clothes and a small sitting room, a neighboring compact office stacked to the ceiling with books, a sumptuously decorated bedroom—each room opened around the courtyard with the same French doors, making the living space a mixture of indoors and outdoors in an enchanting maze of exciting colors and provocative scents. It was a space fit for a princess. Walking into it was like walking into an enchanted place.

Was it a bribe?

"Where are you staying?" she asked Jake, holding on to his arm as though it were keeping her afloat.

"I have a suite on the other side of the wing." He looked down at her and at the way her fingers were digging into his arm. "But I'll stay with you as long as you need me."

"Need you?" She blinked and looked up at him, not sure what he meant.

He covered her hand with his. "I can see how tense you are. You're scared to death."

"No, I'm not." But the shivers that kept coming up in waves through her body gave lie to her claim.

"You've got a lot to worry about," he told her. "I know that. If you want, I'll go with you to face Pellea."

"Will you? Really?" She was embarrassed. She wasn't usually such a coward. But the way she felt about Pellea went right to the core of her being, and this fight with her had been tearing her apart. The thought of having Jake there to steady her, to act as her backup, to lean on, if need be, brought her such a sense of relief, she knew she had to have him with her.

A young woman, evidently assigned to be a nanny for Kim, stood waiting and ready to help, but Kim didn't want to hand Dede over to anyone until she was secure and sure of just what was going to happen.

"Thanks," she said with a quick smile. "Maybe a little later."

"Anytime, miss. Just ring and I'll come quickly."

"Thank you."

It made her a little nervous to have someone ready to wait on her. That was her job!

"You go ahead and get settled in," Jake told her. "I'll go see if Pellea is ready to see you."

"That's right. She is the queen, isn't she? She probably has to see all kinds of people all the time."

"Yes, she does. But I know she'll make time for you whenever you're ready."

She nodded and took a deep breath. "I'm ready. Just let me wash up and..."

"And I'll be back to escort you over in a few minutes," he said. He used his bent index finger to lift her chin and smile into her face.

"Everybody loves you here," he reminded her. "No need to stress."

She nodded like someone who wasn't convinced, but she watched him go and turned back to her baby. The one solid feature of her life. Dede was all that mattered. It was for Dede that she was here.

Taking a deep breath, she got on with it.

Pellea was excited when she saw her brother come into her reception room. She excused herself from the local energy minister who was conferring with her, and came to Jake and took his hands as he kissed both her cheeks.

"Well?" she asked. "Is she here?"

"She's here." He frowned. "She's in a bit of a fragile state, though. Be gentle. Be kind."

Pellea looked insulted. "Am I ever anything else?" Then her gaze sharpened. "Why do you care so much?" she probed, pretty sure she already knew the answer to her question.

He hesitated and she laughed, her eyes sparkling with delight.

"Never mind. What I want to know is, has she told you why she wouldn't come back to us?"

He nodded, considering just what to say. "She feels betrayed."

Pellea frowned. "In what way?"

"She felt abandoned and forgotten. She reached out and no one responded."

Pellea shook her head thoughtfully. "We were trying to get in touch with her the whole time."

"You'd better find a way to prove it to her. She's pretty bitter."

"Oh, I hate to think of how hurt she must have been." Pellea was distressed. "But don't worry. I think I've got some evidence that will convince her."

His frown was dark and brooding. "I hope it's good."

"And you?" she asked. "How are you getting along with her?"

He looked surprised. "Fine. And none of your business."

She laughed. "Oh. Good."

"Now about the baby," he said earnestly.

"Yes. I've heard Kimmee is very worried about her, but isn't sure what is wrong."

"Exactly. She's been searching for a decent pediatrician for months with no luck."

Pellea nodded. "I've already sent for the best we have. It's a bit of a struggle, being the holidays and all, but I think I've got four who have promised to show up by tomorrow afternoon. If they can't figure out what's wrong, we'll send to the continent."

"Great. That will be a big relief to her."

"And to you."

"But I need to warn you. I'm going to have to go back over to the other side."

"Why?"

"I know where he is."

"Who? Leonardo?"

"Yes."

She gripped his arm. "Jake, let the guard take care of it. There's no reason for you to risk your life."

He covered her hand with his own. "Pellea, there's every reason for me to do it. I have to do it. I'll go before dawn, the day after Christmas."

"At least take a few of the guard with you."

He shook his head. "I'll make better time on my own." Leaning forward, he kissed her again. "Don't worry. I'll be careful. I'll be safe. And I'll be back."

CHAPTER TEN

JAKE returned in a few minutes with Dede in his arms and Kim in tow.

"Here she is."

Pellea came forward, her heart beaming from her dark eyes. "Kimmee! Oh my darling Kimmee! I feel like I've waited forever for this."

Kim was looking a bit stiff, but Pellea ignored that and threw her arms around her. "I'm so glad to see you."

"I'm…I'm glad to see you, too."

After a few seconds of hesitation, Kim hugged her back, but gingerly. Pellea pulled back to smile into her face.

"I know you have some resentments and I think we should air them fully right away. We can figure out what caused the misunderstandings and come to grips with them."

She hugged her friend again, then stepped back and looked serious.

"But first I need to tell you a few things. We spent a lot of time away from you, I know. We were on the continent, preparing for the invasion, and that took up all our time. And then there was the wedding." She looked into Kim's eyes, shaking her head with regret. "I wanted you in my wedding."

Kim blinked, wishing she didn't still have these feelings of doubt. "But you didn't send for me."

"Kim, I sent a request. In fact, we sent many requests. And every time, the Granvilli government refused. They said you couldn't be spared. And by then, most of the people I could trust seemed to have disappeared. I couldn't find anybody to use to get a message to you. We had to go ahead with the wedding without you. I had to have one of Monte's newfound cousins stand in for you. Look." She pulled out a beautiful wedding announcement card, printed on fine linen paper and decorated with elaborate calligraphy and showed it to her. There on the face of it she saw "Mandy Kraktus, standing in as Maid of Honor for Kim Guilder."

Kimmee stared at the card. She couldn't deny what it meant. Her eyes were shining when she looked up at Pellea again.

"Leonardo went insane when he heard you had married Monte," she told her.

Pellea shuddered. "So I've heard."

"And then you invaded and everything went crazy."

"Yes. People start to feel like it's every man for himself and then you don't know what they'll do." She hesitated, then looked at her friend sideways. "They say that you went into hiding with Leonardo."

Kim's short laugh was bitter. "That's one way to put it, I suppose."

Pellea's eyes flashed and she reached out to take Kim's hands in hers. "He took you to the chateau, didn't he?"

Kim nodded. "Yes."

"And kept you there for…"

Her hands tightened on Pellea's. "Pellea, believe me,

I didn't go willingly. But I'm not going to talk about what happened there."

"Oh, Kimmee…"

"What he did to me was mostly out of anger, rage, frustration at how he was losing his country. All things being equal, I would have loved to see him punished. But that can never be. Leonardo is my baby's father. And that is that. If I have my way, she'll never know even a fraction of what happened. It could only hurt her and scar her life. And I won't allow that." She took a deep breath, her gaze steely. "In fact, this is the last time I will ever speak of it. From now on, it's a lost chapter in my life."

Pellea had tears in her eyes and she hugged her friend tightly. "Oh, Kimmee. I'm so, so sorry. But I completely understand you on this and I promise to comply."

"Thank you." Kim looked over her shoulder at where Jake held Dede. He was looking at her with a strange light in his eyes and she blinked, trying to get a fix on it. Suddenly she realized what it was. Sympathy. Compassion. Understanding. And most of all, love.

Her heart jumped. Was she imagining it? No, there was something in his gaze that seemed to put a protective shield around her. He wanted to keep her safe. She could almost see his determination. She smiled, but he didn't smile back. Still, the connection between them was strong and real. A certain joy filled her and tears began to threaten again.

She turned back to Pellea as her friend reached out to touch her cheek lovingly. "How did you get away?" she asked.

"He got tired of me at last and let me go. He'd found someone else and lost interest in making my life a misery. And I left quickly and never looked back."

Pellea nodded, her eyes full of tragedy, but a smile fixed on her face. "Of course."

Kim closed her eyes as though putting all that behind her, then opened them again and looked more accusingly.

"And I want you to know that I sent you letter after letter telling you what was going on. Why didn't you answer? I would have given anything just for one answer, just to know someone understood."

"Kimmee, I didn't get any of those letters. I had no idea what you were going through until we got back here, and even then it took some time. We'd been back for weeks before one of the maids came to tell me she'd found a stack of letters in a cabinet in the library—letters to me that she thought I should take a look at. Come with me. I'll show you."

Kim followed her a few doors down the hall to the residential library. Pellea threw open the cabinet to reveal the letters. Only one had even been opened.

"I wanted to leave them this way so you would see that I never got them."

"Oh." Kim sank into a chair, tears rimming her eyes. "Pellea. And all that time I thought…" She shook her head. "I feel I've wronged you terribly."

"No, darling. We're the ones. We were on the edge of invasion and things were so confused and chaotic. What little communication we managed didn't get through to where you were. We should have known, we should have tried harder."

"Hush." Kim rose and hugged her best friend. "It's over." Then her face changed. "But beyond that, all this talk of DNA and my being a princess—tell me it doesn't mean a thing."

Pellea's beautiful eyes were wide with innocence. "But it's all true. That's what's so amazing."

Kim stared at her. Somehow it didn't seem so ridiculous when Pellea took it seriously.

"But never mind that now. We can talk about it later. What's important right now is that you understand how much we all love you." She kissed her cheek and smiled into her eyes. "And even more important, where's that little girl of yours? I want to meet her."

Jake was holding her and he stepped forward.

"What a duckling you are!" Pellea cooed, pinching her cheeks gently.

Pellea had heard all about Dede's problems. Jake had filled her in.

"We've got four pediatricians coming to see her tomorrow," she told Kim. "We'll see what they come up with. Surely at least one of them will know something."

Kim choked up. She couldn't even get out the words to say how grateful she was. Meanwhile Pellea showered Dede with love and admiration, and Jake gave Kim a look that said, "See?"

Kim did see. A bubble of happiness was growing in her chest, but she wasn't sure if she dared let it keep on going and fill every corner. She had to keep it contained, a little bit to the side, a little bit safe. She still wasn't sure she believed all this niceness and love. She had to keep herself just a little bit protected.

A little later, when she told Jake how she felt, he chided her.

"Kimmee, would you stop looking a gift horse in the mouth? Of course they love you even more now that they have found out you're their sister for real. It's only human. You can't fault them for that."

"Yes, but..."

"Why do you keep looking for the worm in the apple? I say, bite the apple and don't look."

She smiled. "Okay, Jake. You seem to have all the answers." She stretched her arms out above her head, feeling suddenly safe and luxurious, all at once. They were in the courtyard garden that was a part of her new chambers, and for the first time in months, she had a feeling things might work out after all. "We'll do it your way."

Dede was asleep. They were sitting on the huge sectional couch that filled one corner of her room. It was late. Jake would be leaving soon for his own rooms. And Kim realized, suddenly, that she didn't want him to go.

"Thanks," she said to him, almost shyly.

He raised an eyebrow. "For what?"

"For making me come back here."

He reached out and brushed hair back off her cheek, then let his fingers cup her ear. She looked at him, at his crystal-blue eyes, at his dark, slightly wavy hair, at the scrape on his face that was almost healed, at the full, sexy shape of his lips, and she knew what it was like to melt a little.

He moved toward her and she lifted her face. He kissed her lips softly, once, twice, and then one more time. She closed her eyes and yearned toward him, but he pulled back and the next thing she knew, he was lying on the couch with his head in her lap.

"How did this happen?" she asked him with a smile, threading her fingers through his thick hair.

"I don't know," he said. "Sometimes you've just got to do what comes naturally."

"Oh no, you don't," she said, teasing him. "I prefer a little civilization."

"Phony," he murmured at her.

She sighed and leaned back, enjoying the feel of him so close, enjoying the night. Was she in love? Was life calming down to the point where she could let herself be? She did love a lot of things about him. She loved that he was such a tough guy, and yet he was never harsh with her. She knew he wanted her. She wanted him. And yet she also knew he would take it easy, wait until she was ready. It all seemed so right.

And yet…

There was one ugly obstacle to everything and it was huge. Leonardo. She knew how he felt about the man. She felt the same way. But she also knew he couldn't get past it. There were feelings in him that he couldn't seem to get beyond. And that might mean they would never be able to get together the way they both might want to.

They talked softly for another half hour, and then it was time for him to leave. They lingered at the big wooden gate. His good-night kiss went on and on, until they were both out of breath and clinging together as though they couldn't bear to be apart. And when he finally left, Kim missed him before he even disappeared from sight.

Christmas was a lovely day with celebrations in the chapel and a feast in the main hall. There was a dance and plays performed and an old-fashioned jousting tournament. But through it all, Kim was anticipating the afternoon when the pediatricians were due to arrive. And though she enjoyed the festivities and soaked up Jake's growing signs of affection like a kitten in the sun, her focus was Dede.

At one point, Pellea took her into the library again to show her the documentation on the DNA evidence.

"There's no getting around it, Kim. It's all here in black and white."

"I don't get it. I never had a moment's doubt that Lady Constance was my mother."

"Then she did her job well." Pellea took her hand. "It was all done for your benefit, you know. They were all so afraid the Granvillis would kill you if they knew."

"Okay, tell me how you know that. How do you know what they were thinking at the time?"

She shrugged. "We have Queen Elineas' diary. She wrote it all down in her own hand."

"You mean…?"

"This was found a few months ago when tearing down a wall near what was the burned-out area from the original invasion. A worker found the diary in a small hiding place. You'll have to read it."

What a treasure! "I plan to."

"The queen tells of how she kept her pregnancy a secret, then enlisted Lady Constance to help her hide you. She was so afraid all her other children would be killed. She wanted one to carry on the name. And she thought that one might be you."

"Poor lady," Kim murmured. She wished she could feel closer, emotionally, to the old queen who might possibly be her real mother. But a lifetime of propaganda was hard to dispel so quickly.

"Indeed. Read the diary. I think you'll start to appreciate being a part of this family." She gave her an impish grin. "I know I have."

And she left, on to other duties, just being a queen. And Kim stayed and did some reading.

But finally she was in the examination room with

Dede while four physicians in white coats nodded gravely over her child and began to confer. Jake had come with her. She held his hand tightly and thought about how much his support was beginning to mean to her.

There were tests, tests and more tests for Dede. They needed to check internal organs and for that she had to be sedated. Kim didn't like it, but she gave permission. Then she had to leave her baby, which was very hard, and Jake took her away to have lunch in her courtyard. Pellea stopped by for a quick visit, and so did a couple of other friends from the old days. But her heart was with her child. It was late in the afternoon when they let her see her baby again.

And then, the verdict.

"Your baby has a low-grade infection and has had it for some time. It was perceptive of you to realize it was different from the normal baby complaints. It would have been better to start treatment long since, but all we can deal with is what we have before us. Ordinarily, we would check her into the hospital for a ten-day period of controlled antibiotics. But since you have such appropriate facilities in your living compound, we should be able to attend to her right here in the castle. With constant professional oversight, of course."

Kim's head was spinning.

"Don't worry," the pediatrician told her kindly. "This is eminently treatable. Left alone, it could prove debilitating in time. But you've brought her in and we're going to get to work on it. She'll be fine in no time at all."

Relief flooded her body and she hugged Jake as the doctor left the room.

She had to leave Dede in recovery for now. She and

Jake took a walk around the viewing level and talked softly, first about Dede, then about Kim's reaction to Pellea, and finally, about Jake's plans.

"I'm so glad you've been here to help me through all this," she told him. "I can't thank you enough."

He was silent for a moment, then he said, "Then I'd better warn you. I'm going away for a few days."

She turned in horror. "What? Why?"

"I have something I have to do and I…"

Her blood ran cold. "You're going to find Leonardo, aren't you?"

He took a deep breath. "Yes."

This was what she'd been dreading, even though she hadn't let herself focus fully on it. This was how the past could reach out and ruin things in the future. It wasn't fair. It made her want to scream.

"Jake, I hope you understand," she said carefully. "If you kill Dede's father, we can never be together."

The truth of that statement seemed to resonate in the cold air. And the central situation was starkly clear. Kim wanted Jake. She'd never known a man who seemed so right, so real for her.

And he wanted her. He'd only known her for a few days and she already filled his head and his senses. Things were possible here. They already had the beginnings of a real romance. With a little luck, they had the foundations of a real relationship.

But if he did this…

He knew that. Hatred of Leonardo consumed him, and not in a good way. He didn't like feeling this way. He wanted it over. There had been a time when he'd thought he couldn't love Kim because of it. And Dede, too. But now he knew that nothing about Leonardo had anything to do with either one of them. Leonardo had happened to them, the way he had happened to Jake and his family. All the rest was dust in the wind.

But he did have to take care of things. He couldn't leave it hanging. He had to go.

"Please, Jake," she whispered, tears welling in her eyes. "Please don't go."

"I have to go, Kim. It's a strange thing. Almost like destiny. I have to do this. Otherwise I'll never be able to live with myself."

"Jake…"

"Kim, he had my family killed. He has to pay for that. And what he did to you…how can you want me to let that go? He has to face up to what he did. And I have to make sure he never does that to anyone else."

She turned away. Either Leonardo would kill him, or he would kill Leonardo. She couldn't win. Either way, she was doomed. She drew in a shaky breath.

"When will you go?"

"Tonight. When it feels right. I want to cross the border before the first light."

She nodded, feeling strangely lightheaded. "Goodbye. Please be safe."

"Don't worry about me, Kim. I'll be back."

She hoped so with all her heart and soul. But if he came back as Leonardo's killer, everything would be over.

He saw the devastation in her eyes and he pulled her up and kissed her, hard, as though his heat and passion should convince her. And she kissed him back, just as hard, as though her love could persuade him. But they both failed. Sadly, she went back to her rooms alone.

It was almost dawn. Dede was fast asleep, exhausted by all the probing and testing and medication. Kim had slept earlier but now she was awake, and she knew she wasn't going to go back to sleep. Her mind was racing, trying to find a way out of what she was sure would be disaster. She knew Jake was already on his way back into Granvilli territory. There was nothing she could do. So why was the entire issue still roiling through her mind?

She was trying to keep busy, but it wasn't working. Two nurses had been assigned to watch over Dede for the night. They were both very nice and it was wonderful to have people who knew what they were doing care for her baby. But Kim couldn't help but feel a bit superfluous. If anything happened, she would be the one standing back and trying not to scream.

She wandered through the courtyard, from the rose garden to the mini forest, stopping to sit near the waterfall, then trying to see if she could find the secret passage Pellea and Monte had escaped through.

She heard one of the nurses get a call on her phone, but she hardly paid any attention until she heard the words, "Is he still alive?"

She looked up. The second nurse had come out into the courtyard and was watching the first take the call. They exchanged significant glances and the first nurse asked more questions.

Frowning, Kim made her way to where the two nurses were standing. "What's going on?" she asked.

"Oh, miss!" The first nurse turned to her excitedly. "They say…the word is…Leonardo Granvilli is dead."

Kim clutched her arm, filled with dread. "How? Where?"

"Near the border. They say it must have happened right around midnight. My friend says she heard he was seen in Dorcher Cliffs on Christmas day. They think he was trying to come in from that direction, but his body was found near the last roadblock. Multiple gun-shot wounds. Some say it's him, some say not." She shrugged. "We can only hope."

For just a moment, Kim couldn't breathe. Had there been enough time for Jake to get to the border? Yes. Plenty of time.

"Oh," she said, then clamped her hand over her mouth. "Oh! Oh!"

The nurse laughed. "Yes, it's wonderful. Isn't it? I mean, it's never nice to wish someone ill, but that man was pure evil and he ruined a lot of lives. Now we can go back to being one Ambria again. I'll get to go visit my sister in Tantarette."

Kim could hardly stand upright. She was weaving and she knew it. Time to get control.

"Will you be here for my baby?" she asked, stumbling over her words. "I mean, I have to go. Please, please, I don't want my baby left alone."

"Oh course, miss. We'll both be here. That's our job."

"Oh." Kim ran and shrugged into a huge furry jacket she found in the closet. "I'll be back as soon as I can. But not real soon."

"Take your time, miss."

Time. The term rattled in her brain. Where did she think she was going? What did she think she was going to do?

She didn't know. She only knew she had to try to find Jake. There would be soldiers looking for Leonardo's killer. She had to warn him. Someone had already done what he was going out to do.

At least, she hoped that was it. What if…what if the killer *was* Jake? What if he'd made a lucky move and found Leonardo just at the right time and…

No, she couldn't think about that. If he'd killed

Dede's father, life would be impossible in so many ways. But if he was just out there, not knowing the new danger he was facing….the soldiers looking for anyone who might have had anything to do with the killing…anyone who might have had a motive…. She had to try, at least. She had to find a way to warn him. For the moment, his safety was everything to her.

She made a futile attempt to use her new mobile to find him, but she knew in advance there was no coverage where he was going. If she was going to do this, it had to be the old-fashioned way.

She raced down the long stairway to the basement motor-pool bay. She'd spent most of her life in this castle and she knew how things worked. The lot would be filled with cars to choose from. There would be no one attending at this time of the morning. And she knew where the keys were kept. She would have her choice of fast cars.

She reached the basement and turned slowly, looking at all the shiny vehicles. What had Jake chosen for his dangerous journey back across the border? Something that could outrun the authorities or something inconspicuous that would let him slip past the guards unnoticed? Something he could easily ditch at the crossing so that he could go over on foot? Who knew? And how was she going to know it was him if she met his car on the road?

She swayed, suddenly overcome with hopelessness. This was a fool's errand, wasn't it? Finding him would be nearly impossible. What was she going to do? Tears of fear and frustration filled her eyes and she leaned against an ancient Bentley and sobbed. What in the world was she going to do?

A strangely familiar sound interrupted her tears, and

she lifted her head and listened. There was a sputtering, a feeble roar, and suddenly Jake came cruising into the parking garage, riding the decrepit motorcycle that had brought them out of Granvilli territory just days before.

Jake! Relief surged in her veins. He was alive, at least. But with all these wonderful cars to choose from, why would he have gone off on that old thing? And what had he done?

She ran to him and he quickly parked the bike, surprised to see her.

"Oh, Jake!"

He took her into his arms and held her close. "What is it?" he asked. "What's happened?"

She turned her tear-stained face up to him. "Oh Jake, I was so afraid that you…"

"Hush." He put his finger to her lips to stop her. "Before you say anything more, I have something to tell you."

"To tell me?" She blinked, dread back again. Had he done it? Was he the one?

"Yes. I want you to listen before you say anything at all. I want you to understand what I've done and why I've done it."

"Oh, no," she wailed, sure she knew exactly what he meant.

"Just listen." He dropped a soft kiss on her lips. "I left tonight, determined to find Leonardo and kill him. I felt I had to do it. I wanted to do it. Justice demanded I do it. The honor of my family demanded I do it. And I was ready."

"Oh Jake," she moaned softly, shaking her head in sorrow.

"I'd heard the intelligence that pinpointed his location. I knew where he was and where he was headed.

Everything was working out just right. So I felt pretty good as I rode along. I even chose our motorcycle as a sort of spiritual nod toward destiny. You understand?"

She nodded mournfully.

"But how did you get it?"

"Some of the local boys who scout around the border looking for useable items found it and brought it in. When I saw it, I couldn't resist."

"Oh, Jake."

"But the motorcycle isn't very fast, and as I made my way, I had a lot of time to think." He smiled down at her and raked his fingers through her hair, holding her head like a precious orb. "I'm not a killer, Kim. If I kill Leonardo, a part of me will be satisfied. But another part will open like an infected wound, a wound that won't have a way to heal. I'll lose you, I'll lose Dede, and what will I gain?"

He kissed her lips again, softly, sweetly, and she returned the kiss with a hunger that grew out of love.

"I finally had to come face-to-face with the truth," he went on. "I'd rather respect myself for decency than for vengeance. I'll work with any entity that aims to bring that foul man to justice, but I won't kill him with my own hands." He smiled down into her eyes. "I have to be a man you could love. Not a monster."

"Oh Jake," she sighed, melting against him. "I'm so glad. I'm so, so glad."

He kissed her as though it was his last chance, and she arched into his body with her own, wanting to feel him everywhere. A sound at the entry stopped them cold. Morning was coming. People would begin arriving.

"Let's go to my room," he murmured near her ear.

She nodded. "I've got something to tell you," she said, happiness sparkling in her eyes. "Come on."

They dodged early morning maids and footmen through the corridors, giggling and chuckling as they snuck past sleepy workers. They ended up at last in his dark outer room and he led her straight for the bedroom. She couldn't see a thing.

"Jake? Are you there?"

As her eyes grew more accustomed to the dark, he pulled her down onto the huge bed with white sheets and pillows and an enormous canopy.

His arms came around her and he was kissing her again, holding her tightly, breathing in her scent.

"Wait," she muttered, half laughing, half tempted to spend the rest of her life in his arms. "I have to tell you this. Guess what?" She could hardly talk as she was raining kisses all over him. He'd shrugged out of his jacket and his shirt was open and his wonderful chest was uncovered and vulnerable to all the attention she wanted to give it.

"Save the guessing games for later," he murmured, using his tongue to explore her ear.

"No, I'm serious. Listen. Everything's changed."

He took hold of her shoulders, holding her back a bit and protecting his ribs. "What's changed?" he asked groggily.

"Everything. You don't have to worry about bringing Leonardo to justice."

"What are you talking about?"

"Jake, they found his body. Either someone's already killed him or he's killed himself. So you don't have to."

He went very still. "Are you serious?"

"Yes. The news came in about an hour ago."

Jake shook his head as though trying to shake some reality into it. "He's gone?"

"Yes, that's what they are saying. I only hope it's true."

"Where? How?"

Quickly she ran over all the facts she knew. He heaved a huge sigh and she realized a part of him was disappointed.

She groaned. Men really were different, weren't they? She didn't care about revenge. She didn't care about anything much other than her adorable baby—and Jake.

Morning light was beginning to come through the window, enough so that he could see her beautiful face. He framed it with his hands, loving her. This was where his destiny lay. This was where he would build his life from now on. His heart filled with pure, sweet happiness and he smiled down at her.

"Dede?" he asked, suddenly remembering that she was still in jeopardy.

She nodded. "She seems to be fine. Or healing, at least. They all say so."

He nodded back, satisfied, and then he pulled her close again. "In the meantime, what are you doing in this huge furry jacket thing? I can hardly find the real you down under all this stuff."

She grinned. "You don't like it?"

"No. Not a bit."

"Then it goes." She pulled it off and tossed it aside. He laughed. "Good. Now about that shirt…"

"It stays." She sighed, leaning close to kiss him again.

"Okay," he muttered. "As long as you stay, too."

He soaked in the look of her in the morning haze and managed to get her under the covers and curled up against him. She closed her eyes. She knew she couldn't get any closer to heaven without making the transition to angel—and that was a long way off.

"Jake?" she whispered.

"What?" he answered sleepily.

"I think I love you."

"Good. Let me know when you're positive."

"Jake?"

"What?"

"You're supposed to at least give me a hint."

"Oh. You mean, you want to know if I love you?"

"Exactly."

He tugged her closer and kissed her neck. "You'll do."

"Jake!"

He chuckled, deep in his throat. "I surrender, Kim. I love you, too. And I'm more sure than you are. So I win."

"Oh no, my darling Jake," she said, laughing as she cuddled in closer. "I win. I win it all."

* * * * *

A sneaky peek at next month...

Cherish™

ROMANCE TO MELT THE HEART EVERY TIME

My wish list for next month's titles...

In stores from 20th January 2012:

❏ Back in the Soldier's Arms – Soraya Lane

& Here Comes the Groom – Karina Bliss

❏ A Match for the Doctor – Marie Ferrarella

& What the Single Dad Wants... – Marie Ferrarella

❏ The Chief Ranger – Rebecca Winters

In stores from 3rd February 2012:

❏ Invitation to the Prince's Palace – Jennie Adams

& The Prince's Second Chance – Brenda Harlen

❏ Miss Prim and the Billionaire – Lucy Gordon

Available at WHSmith, Tesco, Asda, Eason, Amazon and Apple

Just can't wait?

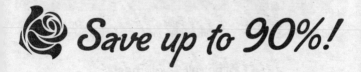

Have Your Say

You've just finished your book.
So what did you think?

We'd love to hear your thoughts on our
'Have your say' online panel
www.millsandboon.co.uk/haveyoursay

- 🌹 Easy to use
- 🌹 Short questionnaire
- 🌹 Chance to win Mills & Boon® goodies